Heart of the Human

Book 1 in The Eternal Souls series

C K Scott

C K Scott

Contents

Content Warning

This book is written and intended for mature readers 18+. This book contains sexually explicit acts and graphic violence. If any of the below are triggering to you please prioritise your mental health, and consider if this book is suitable for you

Attempted Sexual Assault

Body Shaming

Bombing resulting in Graphic Deaths

Death of a Child (past-witnessed during flashback)

Death of a Spouse (past)

Graphic Violence and Death

Kidnapping

Murder in Self-Defence

Non-Consensual Acts (mentioned in passing no details)

Psychological torture

PTSD like Flashbacks

Separation from Children

Sexually Explicit Acts

Sexual Harassment

Starvation due to War

Talk of War

Themes of Mental Health

This book is for every reader who grew tired of teenage main characters, with miscommunication tropes, making frustratingly bad decisions.
Instead, this story focuses on found family, persisting against the odds and adapting to the everchanging world we find ourselves in, themes that are real for all of us.
There are topics in this book that may hit close to home, particularly regarding mental health, so I remind you to look after your wellbeing.
Go get that drink of water, have a snack and curl up with your favourite blanket.
Because it's time to go on an adventure.

***

To my husband, thank you for supporting this book every step of the way.
You set the standard for partners every single day.
I love you.

C K SCOTT

Prologue

Kohlvar

The portal had not permitted humans to enter Balidran for over 60 years. Inanimate objects, vegetation and the occasional stray cat? Sure.

But humans? Not in decades.

So why, after all this time, was there a human woman lying at the foot of the portal? A woman dressed in strange clothing, ash and blood coating her skin.

Had she been sent here intentionally? Or was this an accident?

She looked like she'd been through hell. What has been happening in the human world all this time? Perhaps they were going through as much hardship as this world.

Regardless, Kohlvar felt the small flicker of hope that she would be their salvation, not their damnation.

Chapter One

Josephine

Sunshine streamed through the cracks in the battered blinds, waking Josephine before her alarm. She squinted, perturbed, but aware she would've been awake soon regardless.

She smiled down at the young child snuggled into her chest. Danielle, her dark curls fanning out and off the edge of the bed. Isabelle cuddled into her back, her arms wrapped tightly around Josephine's waist.

Josephine looked back at Isabelle and smiled contently. Waking up with her daughters was her favourite moment of the day. Knowing they were safe, loved and together made every struggle worth it.

She laid with them until her phone buzzed, signalling the start of another monotonous day. She planted kisses on both girl's foreheads, watching their peaceful slumber. Josephine crawled out of bed, allowing her girls to roll towards each other and giggle in greeting, as the twins had done every morning since they were infants. She watched over them as she looped a long chain around her neck, a small golden band and a set of dog tags settling between her breasts.

Josephine left them to their chattering as she started on breakfast. The mulberry tree had been remarkably fruitful this season, providing them with fresh fruit and jam for toast. Coffee was too expensive to purchase, but the invasive mint plants terrorising her garden provided plenty of leaves for tea. Eggs were a rarity; this dozen she'd purchased from her neighbour. But the girls needed them more than her, so she only fried two.

Josephine laid out the simple spread and called to her children. She smiled as Susan walked out from the downstairs bedroom, already dressed for the day.

"Morning Auntie, how are you this morning?" Josephine slid a cup of tea and some toast towards her, noticing she was wearing scrubs this morning.

Susan worked at the hospital as a nurse. She'd left the profession after a particularly bad few years of illness and death, but the failing economy and shortage of jobs had forced her back into it. Every shift seemed to take more from her, but she insisted on contributing, and realistically, they needed the money.

"Oh, the usual, like I've been run over by a truck. The shift was only until midnight, but I must be getting old. I want to be in bed most nights by eight o'clock."

Josephine hid a smirk. Objectively, Susan was getting old, pushing mid-sixties. But she never liked to admit it; who did? Josephine wasn't getting any younger either. Having two children certainly reminded her that she was over thirty on a daily basis.

The girls came racing downstairs and threw themselves at Susan. She pretended to be gruff and make a fuss at their affection, but really, she adored the girls almost as much as Josephine did.

"Go on, eat your breakfast. You'll be late for school!" She scolded half-heartedly.

The girls rapidly devoured their breakfast, in a way that made Josephine wince. She slid her toast onto the girls' plates, leaning back to sip her mint tea.

She knew the twins would be fed at school, although it would be minimal. Government lunch rations were now being handed out, to prevent children from going hungry. At least while they were in school. What happened at home was up to their family.

Isabelle noticed the extra toast on her plate. "But Mum-" she started.

"Just eat it darling, I'll have something at work," Josephine reassured, hoping it wasn't a lie.

Hunger quickly won the girls over, and the toast disappeared immediately. Josephine drained the last of her tea, gave Aunt Susan a quick kiss on the cheek, and walked out the door with her daughters.

"I'll see you at three!" Susan called out to the twins.

The trio walked down to the school, the girls skipping and jumping around happily. Josephine occasionally cast her eyes skyward, but the skies were clear. Both of foul weather and of planes.

As they reached the huge security fence surrounding the school, Josephine knelt and gave both of her daughters a firm hug.

"I'll be home in time for dinner, we're having lasagne tonight! I love you," she reminded them as she kissed their foreheads again.

The girls squealed with excitement. "Love you too, Mum!" They yelled, before running off into the school, hands tightly joined.

At least they still found joy in being children, despite the world they live in.

Josephine smiled as she continued down to the bus stop. She didn't like to take the bus with the girls; too many unsavory characters on board causing problems. But it was essential for her job, so she climbed aboard as school students leapt off and darted into the secure grounds behind her.

Josephine rode the bus in silence, ignoring the unpleasant odour of a few individuals or the raucous behaviour of a drunk man in the back. She rested her head against the window, enjoying the winter sunshine despite its lack of warmth.

A few stops later, a young redheaded woman boarded, relief flooding her face when she saw Josephine. Josephine shuffled to make room for her.

"Morning Sienna, how are you?"

"I'm good, just not in the mood to be harassed today." She shuffled closer to Josephine, away from the predatory looks of a few male passengers.

Josephine smiled sadly at her. Sienna was the most beautiful woman she'd ever seen, causing her to draw the wrong kind of attention everywhere she went.

"Let's hope Robert has fallen off a cliff then." Josephine retorted snidely.

Sienna laughed before quieting herself, rolling her eyes at her blatant disregard for their boss.

Robert was the office creep, who frequently used the fact they had limited job options to make every woman uncomfortable.

"You should sit with me, sweetheart," the belligerent drunk called out from the back of the bus. He'd sprawled out on the rear seat, a brown paper bag dangling from his hand. His attempt at smiling was horrifying, flashing more stained gums than teeth.

"Ugh," Josephine scoffed. Sienna stiffened, refusing to turn to the cat-caller. She busied herself smoothing out her coat over her lap.

Josephine took a casual glance around before sliding her hand under Sienna's coat, gently caressing the top of her thigh. Sienna kept her gaze forward, but a small smile appeared as their hands met.

Josephine squeezed Sienna's hand one last time as the bus pulled into their stop.

***

They joined the mass of men and women walking towards tall office buildings. As they turned the corner around a large building, Josephine swore under her breath.

Between them and their destination, a crowd of protesters stood, waving posters and chanting.

"Again?" Sienna sighed.

"Don't they realise that we've got to pay the bills too? We're not working for the government because we love it." Josephine scowled at the crowd as she linked her arm with Sienna's.

They held their heads high as they moved through the protesting crowd, ignoring the jeers and insults hurled at them. An ear piercing shriek froze them in place, Josephine flinching as a glass bottle exploded against the brick wall beside them. She felt Sienna try to bolt, but she held her arm firmly, willing her to stay calm.

"If you run, they will chase," Josephine warned in a hushed tone, nodding to the security guard standing warily at the entrance. He nodded back, opening a side door and ushering them through. She breathed a deep sigh of relief as the door locked closed behind them.

Josephine paused beside the elevators, turning to see Sienna's wide panicked eyes. "Hey, you're okay. We're safe now."

The redhead pulled her arm out of Josephine's grip. "They could've killed us! If that bottle had hit us in the head, one of us could've died." Tears welled in her soft brown eyes. "I hate this world."

Josephine embraced her in a hug, rubbing her back while listening to her breathing calm. "Yes, the world sucks. Has for a while unfortunately. But this will pass, we just have to survive it for now."

Sienna scoffed angrily, "You're only eight years older than me, don't give me the 'I'm older than you and know better' speech."

Josephine chuckled, rolling her eyes at the young woman's petulance. "Come on, I'll make you a coffee. Coffee fixes everything."

***

The morning passed in quiet normalcy, with administrative tasks and emails to read. It was almost comforting for this one thing to be the same after so much had changed with the war. There were always endless emails to read.

With the lingering protestors, lunch was held inside today. Josephine caught Sienna's gaze across the office when she rose, noting several other staff members following her lead. She busied herself making a coffee and raiding the lone vending machine, with its "healthy" food options, before sitting at the largest communal table in the shared kitchen.

Josephine sipped her barely palatable instant coffee while waiting for the others. They had to be more discreet in the office, as certain managers had taken offence to their lunching together. Heaven forbid women support each other during a time of war.

Sienna soon sat beside her, pushing half a sandwich towards her. Josephine pushed back one of the cheese and cracker slices from the vending machine, chancing a wink before eating the food. She could see Sienna's blush out of the corner of her eye; she was so easy to rile up.

"Jo! I didn't catch you last week, are your daughters well?" Margaret enquired as she sat down with her tomato soup and toast, her grey curls framing her face elegantly.

"They brought home another virus, so naturally I came down with it too. Susan of course was immune to it." One perk of having worked in a hospital most of her life was that Susan had fantastic immunity.

"Oh dear, well I'm glad you're all recovered. I know it's winter but I'm surprised at how many illnesses you've caught."

"It's all from school. I thought we'd dealt with this stage in day care, but apparently this is round two."

"It has been a particularly vicious season for it." Annika commented, her straight black hair pulled into a low ponytail as usual. "Dad's been struggling to meet the demand for his cough medicine." She continued while opening her Tupperware container, allowing the aromatic scent of pho to escape.

"Damn Annika, that smells amazing," Josephine admitted as her stomach grumbled. She reached for an apple, kindly supplied by work, knowing it would not fill her for long.

Annika smiled. "One of the few perks of still living with my parents. Mum is restless in retirement, so she cooks to remind her of home."

"You'll find no judgement here; Susan is basically my mother and lives with us. I wish she cooked like your mother," Josephine joked, cringing at the memory of Susan's burnt toast after her nightshift a few weeks ago.

Before long the table was fully occupied by women from various departments. They chatted over their meals, trading stories and updates about each other's lives. This was a regular occurrence every Wednesday, making it the highlight of Josephine's week. Aside from seeing Sienna of course.

Whilst the ladies had originally gathered to socialise, soon trading became a staple of their weekly lunches. It had started out innocently enough, lending each other books to read, exchanging clothing. But as the war worsened, it had become a haven when rations weren't enough.

Annika's mother grew a variety of edible and medicinal plants, Margaret kept chickens and ducks that produced beautiful eggs whilst Sienna repaired clothing and household items. Josephine and Susan worked together to provide vital medicine when it wasn't available, in addition to basic supplies like bandages and antiseptic creams.

Simple items that were once easily accessible, were now becoming increasingly difficult to acquire.

Josephine locked eyes with Margaret as she pulled out a copy of *Little Women*, sliding it across the table. Really, it contained epilepsy medicine for her son, but she promised to enjoy reading it as she slid it into her bag. Sienna was locked in conversation with a young woman about her jacket and the alterations she wanted, when Annika let out a loud cough.

Josephine locked eyes with Margaret and shook her head, watching as the woman lowered the carton of eggs back to her bag.

"Well, this looks fun, is there room for one more?" Josephine forced herself to remain neutral as Robert looked over Sienna and the blonde woman, the youngest women at the table.

"I was just about to go." Annika offered, rising from her seat beside Margaret. Robert didn't take the hint, continuing to loiter beside Sienna. He had once possessed the build of a rugby player, with his broad shoulders and muscular build. However, his fondness for fermented beverages hadn't been kind to his mid-section, his thinning hair really highlighting that he was past his prime.

"What exactly were you two discussing?" He bent down, hovering far too close to Sienna.

Sienna was still looking at the jacket. "We were discussing how to fix this jacket," she uttered in the barest whisper.

"Sorry, I didn't quite hear that," Robert leaned even closer, cupping his ear mockingly. Sienna's hands began to tremble.

Josephine abruptly stood, allowing her chair to push back with an alarming shriek. The women jumped, while Robert turned his attention to her. His face descended into a scowl as he straightened to his full height again.

"She said, they were discussing how to repair the jacket." Josephine repeated, loudly. "Whether to hand stitch the hole in the pocket, or to repair it on a sewing machine. The loose button, of course, would be repaired by hand, but the pocket could be done either way. What's your opinion, Robert?"

She used her uncommon height to its full advantage, holding his glare and refusing to allow him to intimidate her. Josephine could feel the other occupants of the shared kitchen looking, but she only watched him.

"I would not know how to repair clothes, obviously," Robert sneered, angry red blotches forming under his greying beard.

Josephine raised her brows coyly, "I see. Well, you can inform upper management that we were simply discussing *womanly things* then."

His glare turned to the remaining occupants of the table. "What of your birds Margaret? Any eggs to share with the rest of us?"

Margaret rolled her eyes. "You don't need it Robert, you look like you eat well enough. Bugger off and leave the girls alone."

His eyes reduced to furious slits, "You can't speak to me that way!"

"I outrank you while Celina is away. You'd do well to remember that." Margaret rose from the table, signalling to the women that lunch was over.

Josephine watched him until the others had moved away, his anger radiating off him in waves.

"I'll catch you yet, *Jo*," he hissed, voice lowered for the two of them.

She plastered an insincere smile across her face. "I'm quite sure I have no idea what you're talking about, *Robert*."

Josephine did not move until he had stormed out of the kitchen, her face dropping into a scowl. Sienna cleared her throat, nodding towards the bathrooms.

Once inside, Sienna whirled towards her. "Are you crazy? Why were you antagonising Robert? He could have you fired, Jo, *fired*. Then how would you feed and shelter your girls, or send them to private school?"

Josephine quickly checked the empty cubicles, before turning back to the angry redhead. "Sienna," she breathed, "I can't stand to watch him harass you. I know how much it distresses you." She reached up to stroke her face, but Sienna pushed it away.

"Don't, we're at work. It's not safe." Her warm brown eyes seemed conflicted, but Josephine respected her decision and lowered her hand.

"I promised to keep you safe, and I meant it." Josephine said quietly.

Sienna shook her head. "Not above your daughters, they come first. Don't you dare risk your wellbeing for mine. They need you, Jo."

She couldn't argue with her logic, as much as she wished she could. "Hug?" she asked, knowing they could play it off as a comforting hug between women if anyone walked in.

Sienna glanced towards the door before barrelling into Josephine's chest. The botanical scent of her hair washed over Josephine, as she tucked the redhead under her chin.

"We have to get back to work," Sienna murmured as she pulled away, too soon. "I'll see you after work." She seemed to force a smile, before leaving the restroom.

Josephine looked into the mirror, sighing at her tired complexion. The grey hairs were starting to appear in her long brown hair, her complexion was pale, with slight shadows under her eyes. Her shirt fit awkwardly, not knowing how to accommodate her ever-changing body. Between a twin pregnancy, multiple hormonal issues and the occasional food shortage, her figure and weight were constantly in flux. Large deflated breasts, a soft stomach that swelled when she ate too much dairy and knees that popped when she crouched. She'd long stopped caring about the numbers on the scales, as long as she was healthy, but it felt like life was really taking its toll on her.

She washed her hands slowly, looking at this version of herself with concern, before returning to her desk.

***

An alarm sounded, breaking through the mid-afternoon slump. Josephine frowned and looked around. Was there a drill planned for today? Her anxiety spiked, heart pounding in her chest. The skies had been clear today, surely there wasn't an actual threat?

Three slow whoops echoed before a robotic voice sounded, "Please exit the building."

Josephine threw her belongings together and quickly walked across the office to Sienna's desk. To her alarm, she found the redheaded woman backed against her desk by none other than Robert. Rage filled her vision, her hands balling into fists around her bag.

"Robert!" Josephine's voice sliced through the air. "What the fuck are you doing? There's an evacuation, we need to go now."

Robert turned his sneer to Josephine, eyes raking over her trembling hands. "You can't speak to me like that, I'm your superior."

Josephine briskly walked over to Sienna, grabbed her wrist and pulled her away from him, maintaining her furious glare for him. She quickly glanced at Sienna; her brown eyes filled with unshed tears that bolstered Josephine's rage.

"It's bad enough you harass every woman in the office, but endangering her life? That's fucking low, even for you," Josephine shot back at Robert as she grabbed Sienna's bag and turned for the exit.

"Fuck you, Jo, you always think you're so much better than everyone else!"

Was he *seriously* trying to argue with her now? Every cell of her body was screaming to get out, this was not the time for this discussion.

"I'm certainly better than the office pest," Josephine muttered as she dragged Sienna to the fire exit.

Suddenly she felt a large hand rip the bags away from her. She turned to find an enraged Robert barrelling towards her, slamming her into a wall.

Fumes of alcohol assaulted her senses. *Shit, he's drunk.*

"Josie!" Sienna screamed, her nails scratching at Robert's arm, trying to pull him off her. With alarming ease, he shoved her away, causing her to crumple to the floor.

"What is it, are you two in love? Is that why she's not interested? You're always so quick to jump to her defence," he snarled, spit flying from his face.

"Sienna! Get out!" Josephine tried to swing her knee up into his groin, but he had her pinned against the cold concrete wall. The only thing she could do was smash her forehead forward, striking his nose with a satisfying crunch.

He recoiled with a scream as blood sprayed from his face. One hand flew to his nose, the other slamming into Josephine's stomach as she tried to flee.

All the air rushed out of her as she flew back into the wall. The concrete was unforgiving, she could feel her brain slamming against the back of her skull.

Her knees buckled, but she stayed on her feet. Clumsily she ducked under Robert's outstretched grasp and fled towards the exit. She clutched Sienna's hand as the siren changed from slow echoing whoops to a single blaring alarm.

Bombs.

They slammed into the emergency exit and barrelled down the stairs. She could barely hear Robert's shouts over the terrifying alarm. They merged into the rush of people in the stairs, mercifully separating them from Sienna's boss.

They tore around corner after corner; curse the office for being so many floors up. As Josephine turned onto the second floor, she let out a scream and came to a halt.

Death.

Death was leaning against the wall, lazily looking over the oncoming crowd.

No!

"What are you doing? Don't stop, go!" Sienna yelled as they both were shoved by panicking staff.

Please don't take me today.

Josephine stumbled past Death, ignoring the pounding in her skull, the assault on her ears as screams and sirens merged into a singular blaring cacophony. One more flight of stairs and they'd be out of the building. Just one more.

The bomb struck halfway down the last flight. The sound was deafening, drowning out terrified screams as the building shook. Josephine clung to the hand rail, her feet slipping down the stairs. She lost Sienna's hand in the chaos, and as she reached out to find it, the ceiling came crashing down.

*****

Time felt like it was moving in slow motion as Josephine blearily opened her eyes. Dust filled her sight, blood and smoke clogged her nose. She felt a heavy weight on her legs and something sharp digging into her back. She looked up to where she last saw Sienna, as she'd dragged her down the stairs.

Sunlight penetrated through a hole that had not been there before, an oddly calm blue sky visible beyond the grey walls. It pained her eyes briefly, until they adjusted to see ribbons of red flowing over the stairs.

Sienna.

Her body lay twisted, arms outstretched, with her hair strewn out behind her. But it was not her hair that flowed in ribbons down the stairs.

It was her blood.

No, please God no.

Josephine felt what little air there was vanish as she desperately tried to free herself. She shrieked as the pain in her calf intensified, the heavy chunk of ceiling pinning her impossible to move.

She let out a sob, sharp pain radiating through her ribs. Josephine desperately reached up, just wanting to hold Sienna's hand one last time. If she could just move a little, she might be able to touch her.

But Sienna was out of reach.

Never would Josephine hold her in her arms again. Never would she wake to the sunrise gleaming off her beautiful hair. Never would she see her at peace again.

The sobs turned into tearful screams as Josephine panicked, kicking at the fallen concrete to no avail. Her breaths were shorter, more painful now. Had she broken a rib? Perhaps she'd punctured a lung, and soon Death would be coming for her too.

No, she couldn't die today. Not when her daughters still needed her.

Josephine pushed the thought of impending death from her mind, steeling herself. She needed to calm down, slow her breathing and get out.

With agonisingly slow movements, she wriggled, inching further out from underneath the slab pinning her to the staircase. The pain in her calf was excruciating, but she couldn't bear to be trapped for a moment longer than necessary.

After what felt like an eternity, Josephine freed herself. Her leg was a broken mangled mess of blood, gravel and bone, but she averted her eyes. She refused to turn to Sienna, for the sight of her would only distract her further. Her singular thought was to find an escape.

But where was the exit? All she saw was concrete, crumbling into the lower staircases. Sound flooded in, as the ringing in her ears subsided. She heard the screams and cries of those trapped below, begging for someone to help them.

Josephine looked up where the sunshine shone through; but it was too high. No one would survive jumping from there. All they could do was wait.

Someone will come. Someone will save us.

She shuffled up to Sienna's hand, resting her head in it. She did not wish to see her vacant eyes, her broken body. She only wished to remember the beautiful soul that had been taken by Death too soon.

Josephine prayed to whatever gods there were, who she'd long stopped believing in, that her daughters were safe. That they would survive this cursed war and live to see a better world. That they would never be separated, never have to survive without the other.

She was still thinking of her daughters when the second bomb hit, turning everything in her vision to white.

Chapter Two

Kohlvar

Kohlvar slumped in the tiny chair, having hit his head on the ceiling beam for the second time today. If it weren't for his fondness of the old man sitting across from him, he'd refuse out of principle to enter buildings that could not accommodate his profound size.

He accepted the warm mug of spiced tea offered to him, grateful for the hot beverage on this chilly morning.

"So, how goes the mission?" Valtherion asked, settling comfortably across from him. An orange cat immediately jumped up into his lap, demanding affection. The man smiled warmly at the fluffy creature, brushing his spine with long strokes of his hand.

"About as well as expected," Kohlvar mumbled, immediately draining his mug dry. "Nearly everyone proficient with magic has already been found and recruited. And those who have not been found, don't want to be."

The floor beneath his feet vibrated, rattling his mug. Kohlvar shot Valtherion a questioning look.

The old man sighed, scratching his ebony cheek. "The portal has been most unstable lately. As if I don't already have enough to do, keeping the forest in check."

Kohlvar noticed that his age was catching up with his appearance. His short-cropped hair and beard were more grey than black now, and he looked exhausted to the bone. Portal work was said to be taxing, but Kohlvar had never seen him run this ragged.

Another rumble hit, causing the plates on the table to clink together. "Has anything come through?" Kohlvar asked.

"No, not in months. I used to get the most interesting items, before they had to be destroyed of course. But now there is nothing. I fear one day we may lose the portal forever." His black eyes turned hollow as he gazed past Kohlvar, lost in memories of the past.

"Would that be such a bad thing?" Kohlvar remembered the stories of travelling humans, arriving in different places from a world called 'Earth'. They varied from curious scholars to downright problematic individuals. They had changed this world, some believed in ways that were not for the better.

He sighed. "Since we stopped having humans arrive, everything has deteriorated. Fertility rates are down, the climate is unpredictable, crops are struggling and disease has affected every species."

"The humans didn't control those events though."

"No, but I fear their disappearance is a symptom of a greater problem. A problem we have failed to address." Valtherion met Kohlvar's gaze again, a heavy sadness weighing on his face.

Kohlvar heard the explosion before he felt it. An earthquake hit them, sending both men flying off their chairs. The cat screeched and leapt away, as earthenware rattled and smashed to the floor. Kohlvar threw himself over the old man as the house creaked, fearing it would come down on them. He felt the sharp sting of an object hitting his scalp, before hot blood ran down his neck.

The blast did not linger. Kohlvar scrambled to his feet, hauling Valtherion up with him. He raced outside, narrowly missing the doorframe, as he searched for the source.

"The portal!" the old man gasped, pointing into the thicket of trees behind his house.

They quickly made their way to what had once been dense forest. The trees had disintegrated into splinters, flattened further out from the centre. A smouldering orange light flickered, hovering in the air. Kohlvar squinted, noticing the flapping movement of a thin translucent veil. It was ripped open, showing a glimpse of smoke and grey rubble beyond.

Valtherion yelled, racing towards it with his hands raised. Kohlvar shot twin streams of water from his hands, which sizzled and steamed upon contact with the burning rift. The old man quickly worked to seal the portal, his hands emitting a bright white light as the veil slowly knitted closed.

Kohlvar's gaze dropped to the ground as he heaved a gasping breath. There, lying at the foot of the portal, a woman was sprawled face down. He quickly approached, noticing the unusual clothing she wore, the brightly coloured bangles around her wrist.

The woman suddenly moved, shoving herself off the ground as if to stand. Terrified hazel green eyes locked on Kohlvar, before she whimpered and collapsed. He stumbled forward and caught her, scanning for injuries.

"Are you hurt?" A thick rope of brown hair flopped over his arm as her head rolled back.

"I think I'm dead." A soft, distinctly female voice reached him. He scanned her, noting ash and specks of blood marring her attire. Aside from her bloodied leg, he could not see any life-threatening wounds.

"You don't seem dead to me, love," he murmured. Her eyes fluttered closed, her breathing quick and uneven.

Kohlvar brushed back hair that had come loose from her braid, looking over her face for significant bruising or bleeding. He froze as he reached her ears. They were round, with small golden studs in her lobes.

This was a human woman.

Humans had not come through the portal for over 60 years. Why was one coming through now?

And, more importantly, who was this strange woman? Why was she the only one? Was she sent for a reason?

Kohlvar looked to Valtherion, who wore an expression of shock that mirrored his own.

Chapter Three

Josephine

Was this the afterlife?

Brightness obscured her vision, but she could feel cool damp grass against her cheek, a soft whistling breeze stirring through trees. It felt eerily quiet, surely the afterlife would at least have birdsong?

Her vision slowly reappeared, revealing a mottled green ground covered in brown sticks. How odd.

Two figures raced towards her, causing panic to rise from her stomach into her throat. She shoved herself up from the ground, finding two ice blue eyes staring at her, before the excruciating pain of her calf had her crumpling.

"Are you hurt?" The large man had caught her, not that it had spared her any pain.

"I think I'm dead." Josephine whispered as her eyes moved from his to the brilliant blue sky.

If he replied, she didn't hear it, for her body finally succumbed to the overwhelming agony of her injuries, sending her back into darkness.

****

Ash and the metallic tang of blood soured Josephine's mouth and nose. Pain shot from her calf, ribs and head, flaring on every inhale. Everything ached, like she'd been caught in a storm, battered by large hailstones.

All she wanted was to succumb to sweet blissful sleep.

But surely, if she was in pain, she was alive?

Josephine cracked her eyes open to pitch blackness. Panic rose in her chest until her eyesight adjusted, showing the dim flicker of burning coals. She was in a bed, with a blanket over her body, a small creature purring against her calf. She frowned, they didn't own any pets. Perhaps the girls had brought in another stray cat.

Relieved, but also bewildered, she slipped back into a fitful sleep.

******

Josephine woke to early sunshine warming her face. She squinted as she struggled to adjust to the harsh brightness. She tried to move out of the stream of light, but pain rushed through her. A strangled scream wrenched from her as she clutched at her ribs. She was vaguely aware of movement to her right; a dark being approaching her. The figure held a small cup to her lips, a sickly-sweet liquid filling her mouth. Josephine swallowed it, wincing at her hoarse throat. The liquid was smooth and viscous, coating her dry throat and soothing her pain.

She drifted, half-asleep, half-awake, vaguely aware of people coming and going. She didn't hear much, where was she? Were there others from the bombing who had survived?

Her thoughts circled back to Sienna, whom she was certain had died. Unless somehow that had been a dream, but she doubted it. Besides, no one could survive losing that much blood.

At least her death had seemed quick. Not that Josephine would forgive Death for taking Sienna too soon. But she was relieved her co-worker, and dear friend, had not suffered long.

When the befuddlement had passed, Josephine estimated it was nearing dusk. The pain in her body had reduced to ebbing, so long as she didn't move.

She noticed a figure sitting at the foot of her bed. They seemed tall, too tall for the wooden chair they sat in. They were hunched over, staring at the floor.

"Hello?" Josephine's voice was incredibly quiet, as if she hadn't spoken in years. She painfully cleared her throat and tried again.

The figure slowly raised their head to meet Josephine's gaze.

"You're alive." A deep, distinctly male voice flowed over her.

Josephine tried to glance down at her body, still not brave enough to consider the state of it under the blanket.

"Apparently. Where am I? Who are you?" She didn't recognise this place; it looked like a holiday cabin. Why wasn't she in the hospital? If she was being treated at home, why wasn't she in *her* home?

The man didn't answer, instead he rose slowly from his chair.

Holy shit.

This man was enormous. He had to be over two metres tall, the top of his hair brushing the ceiling. His torso was incredibly broad, thick muscles covering his body. His skin was a strange complexion in this light, almost greyish, with dark wavy hair framing his face.

She must still be affected by the painkillers. That was the only logical explanation, as she gawked at the giant towering over her. Josephine briefly wondered if she should be afraid of him.

The man moved towards her, looking over her body. "How do you feel?"

"Like a building fell on top of me," Josephine responded wryly.

He frowned, "Do you need more pain medicine?"

"I don't think it will help," She closed her eyes remorsefully. "How many died? My daughters, Susan, do they know where I am?" Josephine tried to shift herself up the bed, but pain caused her to hiss.

"Please, rest, you shouldn't move. It could affect your healing."

Josephine panted and persisted despite his words. "Actually, it's better if you move. Staying still for weeks on end isn't good…for…you…" Her vision spun, causing the man to split into three shadowy figures. "Woah." Nausea slammed into her, and before she knew it, she was gagging.

She found a bowl in front of her, swiftly provided by the tall man, and she retched into it. Only bile came up.

"Ugh," Josephine groaned, her entire body on fire with pain from the exertion.

"Here," a cloth was pushed into her field of view. She wiped her mouth and nose, realising she was surprisingly clean after the explosion.

"Sorry," she mumbled.

"Don't apologise, it's normal. You almost died."

Josephine closed her eyes and took slow breaths, as deeply as she was able without severe pain. "How bad are my injuries?"

"You'll recover. It'll just take a few weeks."

"What? A few weeks? Don't you mean a few months?" She fought the dizziness to look up, noticing his pale blue eyes locked on her.

He didn't respond.

"My leg was crushed. I probably broke ribs. That takes…months to heal from… Where am I?" she repeated, more firmly than the first time.

"Saltus."

"What?"

"You're in Saltus, in the forests of Balidran."

Josephine was too stunned to speak.

The strange man went on, "I was hoping to explain this when you were healed, but you have been quite insistent." His tone implied this was not the first time they'd had this conversation. "You should lay down."

Josephine remained sitting and found his eyes again. They seemed so calm, and reassuring, yet all she could feel was panic. With her last scrap of control, she uttered one word.

"Explain."

The man nodded, reaching to retrieve his tiny chair. He sat and leaned forward with a heavy sigh. "You are not in the human world anymore. Something tore open the portal between your world and ours. We heard the explosion, then found you barely conscious. Your injuries were quite severe, we weren't sure if you'd survive."

Josephine frowned, "There was a bomb in my world, maybe more. I remember... two explosions, I think. It destroyed the building I was in."

The man nodded grimly, "That would make sense, you were covered in ash when we found you. Are there often explosions in your world?"

"We're at war, but I'm not sure if the bomb was from that. There was a protest before the explosion... It's all a bit foggy," Josephine winced as the sharp pain throbbing through her head.

"Allow me to try and fill in some gaps then," the man radiated confidence, in a way that made her feel surprisingly reassured.

"It's been almost a week since you arrived, and the worst of your injuries have been healed. Your leg was badly crushed, you had broken ribs and punctured a lung. In addition to those injuries, you had a bad concussion and pretty significant hearing loss."

Josephine started to interrupt, but the man held a calloused hand up.

"Please, let me explain. I'll answer all your questions at the end."

She paused, then nodded resolutely.

"Your world would not have been able to save you, we used magic to heal your critical injuries. However, too much movement could cause the bones to break again, or your lung to tear, or your brain to bleed." At that he looked pointedly at her pillows and waited patiently while she painfully shifted back to a reclined position.

Josephine grimaced as her body spasmed from the movement. Was he honestly trying to tell her that magic was real? This still felt like a strange dream.

Josephine looked around, confirming that they were in a tiny log cabin, and not a medical facility. "Why me? Why not heal everyone else?" she asked, thinking of Sienna and the countless others who must have died or suffered injuries.

The man frowned at her, "You were the only person at the portal."

"What? But there were others, with me in the building."

His face shifted into a solemn expression. "I'm sorry, but I do not know what has happened to them. You were the only person that was sent through the portal."

Grief weighed on her, as she tried not to think about her coworkers. "So, when can I go home?"

The man winced, "Unfortunately, you cannot."

Dread sunk through her stomach. "Why not? You said I came through a portal, just send me back!"

"It doesn't work like that. That portal has always been one way, we used to have humans crossing into our world regularly. But they could never make it back."

"Why not?" She asked, more firmly this time.

"Well, they died, rather violently, upon trying to go through the portals. Anything we tried to send through was incinerated."

Horror spread across Josephine's face. "No," she gasped, ignoring the harsh pain in her chest. "What the fuck is wrong with this world?"

An unexpected chuckle burst from the man. "Oh, there's plenty wrong with this place. But regarding the portals, I don't know, they've been like that for a long time."

Crestfallen, she closed her eyes. "Look, I'm not accepting that I can't go home, that's simply not an option. But, what am I supposed to do now?"

He shifted on his chair, studying her thoughtfully. "Well, it's been a long time since humans came through, but I'm sure there would be some human descendants in the villages down south we could house you with."

"And do what?"

He shrugged, "Work in the fields, as a barmaid, a cook? Depends on your skills."

There was a note in his voice that implied this was not the only option. "No, that won't get me home. What's the alternative?"

He shifted uncomfortably on the tiny chair, a concerning squeak coming from it. "Or you'll come with me and be assessed for magic wielding."

Josephine frowned, deflated. "But...I don't have magic."

He smiled flatly, "Magic isn't something you 'have'. It is the living, breathing essence of this world. It is a creature you must learn to connect with in order to use. Our world runs on magic, but the number of magic wielders is dwindling along with our population."

This information was overwhelming in her current state, but Josephine tried to persist, despite the absurdity of it all.

"So essentially, you brought me back from the brink of death, and now I'll either have to become a farmer or work for you as a magic user?" The sentence sounded utterly ridiculous.

"Yes."

"No," she shot back, anger rising in her throat.

"Look, I understand this must be a big shock-"

"I have *children*, you can't just expect me to abandon them!" She fixed her furious glare on him, willing him to feel intimidated by her fury. Instead, he just looked sad.

"I'm sorry, I was not aware of that. But there is no way for you to return home."

She closed her eyes as tears threatened to fall. This could not be happening. "Just kill me then."

"Excuse me?"

"I do not wish to forge a new life without my children. I would rather die and hope I get to watch them from the afterlife."

An unfamiliar voice joined their conversation. "With all due respect, I did not spend the last week healing your wounds and managing your pain just to kill you."

Josephine turned her attention to the figure standing by the fire. She had not noticed him, for his skin was the darkest shade of brown she'd ever seen. His clothing was similarly dark, allowing him to blend in with the shadows.

"Besides, if you can wield magic, perhaps you will find a way home."

Intrigue sparked within her, her eyes flicking between the two men.

"Don't give her false hope Val, it's never been achieved before," the man by her side grumbled.

"Humans haven't come through the portals for sixty years, who knows why she's here now. Maybe she has a purpose in this world."

"I don't want a purpose here. I just want to be with my children." A whimper escaped her, as her chest shook painfully. She bit down on her tongue, trying to suppress the sobs that threatened to overwhelm her.

She felt a large hand encompass hers. "Look, this is a lot to take in. You still need to heal; nothing needs to be decided tonight. You should rest."

Josephine looked up, noticing the rest of his face with more detail. He had a strong jaw, with a distinct scar curving around his jawbone. Large nose, slightly crooked, with jutting brows and cheekbones. He was a strange mishmash of elegant and harsh features. His hair was just long enough to reach his collar, tucked behind his pointed ears.

Josephine frowned at him, "Why are your ears so long?"

The man startled, clearly not expecting the question. "Excuse me?"

"Your ears… they're too long at the top. Why?" Was she delusional? Who asks a man they've just met what is wrong with their appearance? Any sense of manners had clearly left her.

"Oh," he murmured softly. "They're different from yours, but most people here have ears like this."

"Oh, okay," it only felt like half an answer. "What's your name?"

"My name is Kohlvar. And that grumpy old bastard over there is Valtherion."

Valtherion grumbled from the corner, "Please, call me Val."

She half smiled, "I like grumpy old bastards, they've got good hearts."

A gruff disgruntlement echoed from across the room, confirming her theory. Kohlvar's lips quirked briefly, his hand squeezing hers lightly.

"I'm Josephine," she whispered, feeling exhaustion overwhelming her again.

"Josephine. We will talk again soon, I promise." He squeezed her hand gently. "You should sleep, you still have plenty of healing to do, Josephine."

With the soft repetition of her name, Josephine settled back into the bed, and before she knew it, she was deeply asleep.

Chapter Four

Kohlvar

He didn't have time for this.

He needed to return to Balidran and ensure his recruits had arrived safely. He needed to ensure they were trained and prepared for the challenges ahead.

He didn't have time to look after a lost human woman.

However, even though he could palm the responsibility of her off to Valtherion, a deep instinct told him not to. He'd felt foolish offering to recruit her, for she had not demonstrated any magical capability. But something about her was different, surely, she must be important if she was sent from the human world.

Kohlvar sighed deeply, resting his chin onto his hand, as he observed the sleeping woman. Her dark hair fanned out behind her, her face pale with shadows under her eyes. She had curled into a ball, clutching her pillow to her chest.

She was a mother without her children. The thought struck Kohlvar more painfully than he'd expected.

There were many children in this world displaced from their parents, himself included. Yet, somehow, he'd never considered the impact it would have on those parents. Perhaps because so often the parents were deceased, or they had abandoned their unusual children.

To see this human woman distraught over being separated from her daughters...It made him wonder about his own parents.

Kohlvar sighed and pushed the nagging thoughts from his mind. He really didn't have time to dwell on this.

"Are you really going to take her with you?" Valtherion's voice had lost the gruff amusement he'd shown while Josephine was awake. "She'll be in grave danger if you do."

"Do you really think she's going to be safe anywhere in this world? If anyone finds out where she's from, she'll be hunted, for all the wrong reasons," Kohlvar shot back defensively.

Valtherion raised his hands. "Easy, Kohlvar, I was just asking. If that's your decision, then I will prepare her for the journey. Just know that I can find a place for her too. You already carry a heavy burden."

He rubbed a hand across his eyes, the exhaustion of the past few weeks hitting him. "What's one more person to care for? She'll be protected with me."

"She would be safe here Kohl, she could stay and help me tend to the forest. Then no one would have to know about her, and you know I could use the help." It was a rare moment for Valtherion to admit his age was beginning to affect him. Portal weavers weren't known for living this long, due to the hazards of their work, but it was clear the magic required to restrain the portal was taking its toll.

"Doesn't it feel like fate to you?" Kohlvar met the old man's dark gaze. "I visit you once a year, and on the day I arrive, the first human in decades comes through the portal. Surely that is a sign from the divine that she is here to help?"

Valtherion looked at the sleeping woman thoughtfully. "Or that she will be our destruction. You cannot know the intentions of the Eternal Souls."

Kohlvar sighed, "I am trying to not give up hope Val, but it is getting more difficult with every year that passes. Despite everything I do, it's just getting worse."

"Then you are beginning to understand why many of us have lost hope, Kohl." Valtherion shuffled over to the purring cat curled up in his chair, giving him a scratch before leaving Kohlvar to his thoughts.

Kohlvar leaned back in his chair, gladly soaking up the radiant warmth from the hearth. He'd spent many nights sleeping on the ground, so he truly did not mind that Josephine was in the bed intended for him. It was the warmth of a fire he missed. Being exposed to the freezing elements brought back many memories he'd rather forget, and the next winter was expected to be a challenging one.

He looked down at his hands, noticing the new and old scars highlighted by the flickering flames. He was so *tired*, in a way that sleep had failed to restore. Maybe exhaustion would kill him in the end, and he could finally rest when he was dead.

Kohlvar shook his head, willing those thoughts away. He could not give up, not now. His gaze fixed back on Josephine, her relaxed posture indicating she had slipped into a deep sleep.

Valtherion had a valid point, she probably would be safer here with him. But Kohlvar couldn't give up that last shred of hope that they could fix this broken world.

Chapter Five

Josephine

Josephine woke up in her bed, sun streaming in between the blinds. She looked around, seeing the familiar room, her clothes hanging in her wardrobe, her books stacked beside it. She heard the incessant tick of her ceiling fan and smelt her perfume. She was home.

She sat up, inspecting her limbs for injuries. There were none, like the bombing had never happened.

Had it all been a terrible dream?

Josephine suddenly realised her daughters were not with her. She leapt out of bed, racing for the door. It swung open, the smell of bacon and coffee reaching her nose. She rushed downstairs to find the kitchen empty of people, only a cup of coffee and a hot breakfast waiting for her.

She frowned at the setting. Why was there only one serving? Where did the bacon and coffee come from? They hadn't been able to buy those ingredients in months.

"Isabelle? Danielle? Susan?" She called, spinning around the kitchen. Panic began to set in as silence loomed. Josephine started for the front door when a voice interrupted her.

"They are not here."

The soft lilting voice sent shivers down her spine. Josephine had never heard her speak before, but she knew, without seeing, exactly who was there.

She turned to see Death drifting through the kitchen, towards her. Her long black hair floated ethereally, contrasting harshly with her white skin. She was shrouded in heavy black fabric, yet moved with an unburdened grace as she leaned on her kitchen counter.

"Where are my daughters?" Josephine growled.

Deaths' soft grey eyes gave her a pitying look. Sometimes her appearance was comforting, like when Josephine had first seen her as a child. Other times it was cruel, with skeletal features peeking through the black shroud. Today she was neither. She just looked like a normal woman, tired, with the weight of the world on her shoulders.

It was a feeling Josephine could relate to.

"They are safe for now," there was no threat in her voice. "But I'm afraid that will not continue to be the case for much longer," she said dismissively.

"What? Why not?" Panic constricted Josephine's chest, her heart beating violently.

"This cursed war...It tires me. So much death, and so much to come. I can feel it," the woman rested her head in her hands.

Josephine inhaled shakily, trying to steady her racing mind. "So, the bomb...that really happened, didn't it? I saw you, in the stairwell. Why am I alive? Why am I in another world? How are we even talking?" The questions tumbled out of her, one after the other.

Death held up a hand, like a weary mother fielding incessant questions from her children. "All will be explained. I just need you to know that you must stay in that world for everyone's sake."

"But my daughters-"

"Will die if you don't," she interjected sharply. "These bombs are only the beginning; this world isn't safe for them anymore. If they do not die in a

bombing, they will die of starvation, or infection, or worse. This damned world is cursed."

Hot tears ran down Josephine's face. "How will keeping me from them save them?" Her voice cracked.

"If you can succeed in that world, you can build a life there for them. And I think you may be the key to healing both worlds."

"But how will-"

Death held up her hand again. "Please, I am tired. So very tired," her eyes fluttered as she breathed in a long breath. "I will watch over them and try to protect them."

Josephine had to ask one more question. "Why? Why help us?"

Death opened her eyes, looking her up and down thoughtfully before responding. "I admire anyone who escapes death, let alone someone who has managed it three times. Besides, despite what your world thinks of the Gods or death, we never enjoy taking children. I would prefer not to see your girls perish."

They stared at each other in a thoughtful silence. Eventually, Death broke it.

"Drink, they don't have coffee in the other world."

"I think you need it more than I." Josephine half-smiled as she noticed the purple bags under Death's eyes.

A wry chuckle escaped the woman, as a second mug of coffee appeared in her hands. They drank their coffee together, as Josephine looked around her home, the life she had built the last 7 years.

She would miss it, but not nearly as much as her children, and Susan, in this period of absence. A temporary absence, she reminded herself.

"I must go," Death rose from the bench. "Rest well, Josephine. We will talk again soon."

***

Josephine woke with the bitter taste of coffee on her tongue. She looked around, noting the pale early morning sun and deserted room. With a sigh, she stared up at the ceiling.

Three times she'd escaped death. The first, when she was a child, in the car accident that had killed her brother. The second, when she gave birth to the twins. And now the third, when she survived a bombing.

Surely there was a reason she had escaped death so many times? She'd thought it was for her children's sake, but perhaps there was a greater purpose at play. Or perhaps she was just incredibly unlucky to have faced death so many times.

Chapter Six

Kohlvar

The human woke, radiating a mixture of grief and calm acceptance. She'd clearly been through unimaginable trauma over the last week; therefore her grief did not surprise Kohlvar. She was still hurting too, radiating both physical and emotional pain. However, he was pleased by how quickly she'd come to accept this plan. She seemed to be a resilient woman, which would be a requirement for her to survive in Balidran.

Kohlvar and Valtherion both spent time educating Josephine about the Continent. They'd begun by explaining that the Continent was divided into Realms, named for the predominant species living there. She'd taken the news that elves, dwarves and other mythical creatures were real surprisingly well.

Josephine had fallen through the portal into Saltus, the Elven Realm of forests. The Realm boasted beautiful vegetation year round, neighbouring with the Caerulen Realm of the Sirens. The largest city was Balidran, home to the elven military base and major trade routes. Kohlvar had explained that he had been recruiting individuals for magical training to address the shortage of suitable magic wielders and was due to return to commence their orientation.

While Kohlvar had been preparing for the return trip, Valtherion had insisted on taking Josephine with him to monitor the forest. He presumed Val was teaching her about the portals, the vegetation and creatures of concern. Regardless, he was glad that Josephine was rebuilding her strength; the daily walks would ensure she could manage the journey to Balidran.

"We leave tomorrow." Kohlvar declared over their evening meal together.

Valtherion and Josephine both looked at him in surprise. "So soon?" Disappointment radiated from Val. Kohlvar couldn't help but feel apologetic.

"Yes, we are running out of time. It's been a good visit, old friend." Kohlvar smiled warmly at him.

Valtherion scowled fiercely. "Who are you calling old? You're not that young anymore."

Kohlvar could see Josephine holding back laughter, focusing on the orange cat in her lap. He was surprised Valtherion hadn't become jealous that Ginger had taken such a strong liking to her.

Kohlvar kept his face neutral, "Forgive me Val, I only mean to say, I am sorry to be leaving. It's been good to see you, as always."

"How do you two know each other?" Josephine asked as she stroked the purring cat.

Val came alive again at the question. "Well, I used to be a portal wielder for the old King, and Kohlvar was only a wee baby recruit when we met."

"A wee baby?" Kohlvar scoffed. He could not remember a time he was considered small.

Valtherion continued, ignoring him. "He was recruited as a soldier, training which most of our population completes regardless of magical or hierarchical status. The general who recruited him did so hoping to utilise his strength and size. However, once they realised he could wield magic, well there was only one path for him."

Kohlvar avoided Josephine's curious stare, stabbing his potato with a little more force than necessary.

"He was quickly promoted to an officer, where his physical strength and magical prowess made him an ideal choice for certain missions. Sometimes I was there, more often I wasn't. But we eventually became friends." He adopted a thoughtful expression, his fingernails scratching his grey stubble absentmindedly.

"I imagine you can't tell me what these missions involved?" Josephine smiled coyly at Valtherion, earning a chuckle from the old man.

Kohlvar felt surprisingly disgruntled by their playful banter, even though he could sense that the teasing was entirely platonic. "It was mostly peace keeping and negotiating with the other Realms."

Valtherion scoffed into his mug of tea. "You make it sound boring, Kohlvar. We had to get out of a few tricky diplomatic situations. Remember that time-"

"Val, we really shouldn't talk about it."

"Gah! You're no fun tonight! Fine, I was getting tired anyway." Valtherion finished his tea, rising to face Josephine. "I will say farewell in the morning, but I wanted to tell you how much I've appreciated your company these past few weeks. I'm glad you did not die, I would appreciate it if you kept it that way."

Kohlvar was surprised by the warmth that radiated off Josephine. She beamed, setting Ginger down on the floor, before pulling Valtherion in for a firm hug. Kohlvar shifted awkwardly, feeling like he was intruding on their moment.

"Don't go causing too much trouble," Valtherion murmured over her head.

Josephine huffed as she pulled away. "Same to you, old man," she nudged him affectionately with her elbow.

"You too, Kohlvar." Valtherion turned his stern gaze on him, their height difference minimising the severity of his expression. "Stay alive."

Kohlvar gave him as genuine a smile as he could muster. "I'll do my best, Val." He watched as the old man shuffled away into his bedroom, Ginger silently slipping in before the door closed.

Kohlvar turned to Josephine, sensing her warm aura fading to worry and sadness. "Are you alright?"

Josephine gave him a watery smile that didn't meet her eyes. "As much as I can be."

For all his abilities to sense emotions, Kohlvar had yet to master the art of soothing others verbally. "You can still decide to stay here. It would be safer."

Josephine's eyes were locked on Valtherion's closed door. "Will he be okay by himself?"

"I believe so, he has been alone for many years."

"Then there's no reason for me to stay. Besides, I need to get back to my daughters." Josephine fixed her determined gaze on him. He was struck by the strength of her conviction, the thin tendril of hope wafting out from her heart.

Kohlvar didn't feel like reminding her of the impossibility of her goal, for it would only dampen her spirits. So, he simply nodded at her and bid her goodnight.

Chapter Seven

Josephine

Balidran was exactly what Josephine imagined an elven city to look like. Houses and buildings made out of natural materials, roads of dirt and cobblestones, nature present every few hundred metres. The further they walked, the grander the dwellings became, with intricate architecture and various coloured metals woven through the walls. Kohlvar mentioned that the metalwork came from the dwarves, who mined beneath the great mountains for precious ores.

Josephine was struggling too much with the uphill walk and her aching body to voice any questions about the city. She noticed many strange glances their way, however Kohlvar seemed to draw most of that attention. He was ridiculously tall, with jet black curls and tan skin that tinged blue, or grey, depending on the light. Never had Josephine felt completely dwarfed by another person, yet Kohlvar was easily twice her size. His thick build made him significantly larger than most of the slight, elven people wandering around.

They finished the ascent to the fortress in silence, exertion affecting both of them. Just before they approached the gates, Kohlvar made a sweeping gesture behind them, and Josephine turned to take in the view.

The city sprawled below in the valley between several green hills, with the elven fortress located at the highest point. Clear blue skies with fluffy white clouds lazily floated, a chilly breeze cooling the sweat beaded on Josephine's skin. It was surprisingly mild weather for their proximity to the giant snowcapped mountains beyond the fortress.

"Huh," she breathed, welcoming the brief respite. "Not a bad view."

Kohlvar scoffed beside her. "Not a bad view?"

Josephine shrugged. "My world has many beautiful places; you'll have to show me more than this to impress me."

She threw him a teasing grin, pleased to see him warmly smiling back at her.

"I'm glad you're finding this amusing?" His tone and subtle frown implied he was confused by her response.

"Consider it a cultural trait," she quipped as she continued the final trek to the wrought iron gates. "Even in a disaster, my people will find a way to joke about it."

"Hm, you might just survive us yet, Josephine." Kohlvar drew to a stop as the gates loomed over them. "Any last questions before we go in?"

Josephine looked thoughtfully at him. "If I'm missing home, can I come and talk to you about it?"

"Oh. Yes, of course." His blue eyes crinkled at the edges as he looked down at her.

"Thank you, Kohl."

***

"You must be starving," Kohlvar looked her up and down, as if her hunger were visible.

"Food would be nice," she admitted reluctantly, ignoring the grumble of her stomach at the thought of food. She wondered what food would even be like in this world. Would it be similar to human food? Could she even eat it? What if it were magical?

As if reading her mind, Kohlvar murmured, "There's food here for you, we have quite a variety of soldiers to feed."

Hesitantly, Josephine asked what felt like a silly question. "Is the food...enchanted?"

Thankfully Kohlvar didn't laugh or show any sign of amusement at her question. "Not typically, we only enchant food or drinks for festivals or special events. Occasionally, we have drinks made from fermented fruit, but surely your world has that too?"

Josephine nodded in affirmation.

"Excellent. Each intake has at least a couple incidents of new acolytes overindulging. It's one of the more tedious parts of being in leadership, having to wrangle intoxicated acolytes."

He strode forward and pushed open the carved wooden doors leading into the dining hall. The large room was filled with sunlight, streaming in through floor-to-ceiling stained glass windows. Golden timber lined the floor and walls, with dozens of tables and benches of various heights lined in neat rows. An open kitchen with multiple bays for food was stationed on the far right, with a raised podium to their left. The seating area was almost empty, only a handful of people enjoying a mid-afternoon meal. Kohlvar immediately walked over and into the kitchen, past the designated waiting area.

"Hirwen! How are you?" Kohlvar embraced a short elven woman with brown leathery skin and speckled grey hair tied up into a bun. She gave a toothy grin as she struggled to look up at Kohlvar's face. She was particularly short, even by human standards, with legs bowed outward and a twisted arm held close to her side.

"Kohlvar! My dear, you are too skinny. What have they been feeding you? No, no, this won't do, sit. Sit! I'll bring food." She pushed Kohlvar, albeit ineffectively, towards the long table within the kitchen.

Hirwen turned towards Josephine, a cautious look on her face. "Friend?"

"Acolyte, her name is Josephine, she'll be starting with the next intake."

Hirwen curiously studied Josephine. She shifted awkwardly under her surprisingly sharp gaze. "She is human? Why?"

Josephine wasn't sure how to answer that.

Evidently Kohlvar wasn't sure either. "She hasn't eaten since breakfast; I'm sure Josephine would be appreciative of any food you have to spare."

The inquisitive look slipped from Hirwen's face at the mention that Josephine was hungry. She ushered her to sit next to Kohlvar, refusing her offers to help. Hirwen quickly set about preparing food, rapidly throwing food into pots and chopping fresh fruit. For a physically impaired woman, Hirwen moved with impressive speed around the kitchen.

Soon a small feast was laid before Josephine and Kohlvar. The first platter contained handfuls of dark berries, large black grapes, slices of green apple and a soft white cheese, alongside a leafy green salad. Then came a steaming mound of long pasta with fresh herbs, garlic and chili oil, flaky white fish and warm brown bread. Finally, a pitcher of honeyed tea with floating citrus slices was placed between them.

Kohlvar smiled warmly at Hirwen, leaning closer to kiss her on the cheek before piling food onto his plate. Josephine sat in shock, her eyes roaming over the bountiful food.

"You don't like it?" The hurt tone jolted Josephine out of her stunned silence.

"No-no, this is so much, it's not that, I just...I..." She struggled for words to explain her feelings.

"The Human Realm is starving, Hirwen." Kohlvar's tone was surprisingly gentle.

Hirwen scowled, "Did you not feed her? Could you not find food on the road?"

Kohlvar half laughed. "Of course I fed her, though the food we had was quite basic. This is a feast by comparison."

Hirwen scoffed, "Gah, this is nothing, eat! You will be well fed here, I promise you." She patted Josephine's shell-shocked shoulder.

She nodded, tentatively picking up a grape and biting it in half. It burst with sweet juice, causing her to close her eyes at the decadence of it. It reminded her of home, of her home-grown mulberries, and of the hot summers and freezing winters they endured. Sadness washed over her, as she fought to keep the tears at bay.

You're being ridiculous Josephine; you're crying over a bloody grape! Pull it together.

Josephine took a deep breath, finally looking up to see Kohlvar's gaze on her. She quickly looked away, distracting herself by composing a plate. She noticed Hirwen pouring the pitcher into 3 glasses, 2 tall and one small, before shuffling away with her beverage to continue chopping vegetables.

The tea tasted magical; Josephine had frequently made tea at home; however, the generous amount of honey dissolved into this brew left her mouth and throat coated with the sweet nectar. Slowly, she finished two plates of delicious food until she was completely full, while Kohlvar devoured a shocking amount of food. He must've been under-eating this past week, especially considering the energy he would've burned on their multi-day walk to arrive here.

Josephine tried to stack the dishes and move them to the sink, but Hirwen scoffed and fiercely shooed her away. She heard a stifled chuckle from Kohlvar, who bent down to give Hirwen another kiss on the cheek as he thanked her. She beamed as she carried away the plates, looking like she might topple over with the stack.

"How do you know Hirwen?" Josephine asked as Kohlvar led her to her assigned dormitory.

He hesitated before answering, his lips pulling taut. "I met her when I was young, when she was working as a dishwasher in an inn. Sometimes the patrons were...unkind to her. I stopped them from bothering her, she fed me. When I joined the military, she came with me."

"Were they unkind because of her disability?"

He nodded. "Hirwen was born that way; we don't know why. She's an elf, but they aren't particularly forgiving of faults. She struggles with sickness and weak bones, but that doesn't stop her."

"How old is she?"

He chuckled. "It's considered rude to ask that, but I don't know. She's older than I am."

That didn't really narrow it down, as Josephine couldn't get a read on Kohlvar's age either.

"I'm 31, before you ask." He gave a small, knowing smile.

Josephine nodded her thanks. "But...you're not just an elf, right?" At over 2 metres tall, with deltoid muscles larger than her face, Kohlvar did not resemble the other elves she'd met so far.

His half-smile vanished. "No."

She cringed. "Sorry, that was rude to ask, wasn't it?"

He sighed. "I should explain the political tensions here. As you know, this is the elven army. But not all of its members are elves. Most have some elven heritage, but not all. There are a few dragonoids, dwarf hybrids and members of the sea Realms, as they are very useful for specific roles. But our king is quite...preferential towards elves, particularly those with substantial elven heritage."

"Hang on, did you say *dragonoids*? As in *dragons*?"

Kohlvar nodded. "No one has seen a true dragon in almost a century though."

"Why not? What killed them?"

"We don't know. They just seemed to vanish about a hundred years ago."

Josephine frowned. "Then how... you know. How did they make dragonoids?"

To her surprise, a deep pink spread across Kohlvar's cheeks and neck. "Oh, um, I'm not sure about the logistics."

She snorted derisively, "The logistics, sure. That's one word for it." After a moment, Josephine voiced the question that had been niggling at the back of her mind. "Am I the only human here?"

"Yes, you will be the only full human enlisted in the elven military. There are some members with human heritage, but it's been a long time since humans appeared in these lands.

Josephine wanted to ask why, but Kohlvar had come to a stop in front of a wooden door with a circular symbol carved into the top.

"This is the women's dormitory; you will find a pack with basic items for you on the bed. There's a bathroom at the far end. Tomorrow, come down for breakfast and we'll sort out your uniform and anything else you need." Kohlvar met her gaze for a moment, assessing, before turning away.

"Kohlvar?"

"Yes, Josephine?" He turned back to face her.

"Thank you," she gave a small smile. "For the food and for showing me around."

Kohlvar seemed taken aback. "Oh, sure." He looked as if he was going to say more, before he nodded once and walked away.

Josephine stepped inside the dormitory, where a dozen beds lined the walls. She sat on the nearest one, numbly staring at the pack and night clothes laid out for her. She was finally alone, having been constantly in Valtherion or Kohlvar's presence this past week.

It was almost strange, the pull she felt towards Kohlvar. She should have been intimidated by his imposing presence, however being near him brought her a strange sense of calm, the likes of which she hadn't felt since before her husband's passing. The days they spent traveling to Balidran, made her feel a closeness to him she wasn't sure how to handle. The nights they spent talking around their fires, the feel of his clothes brushing her bare skin. His presence had been her grounding force since she arrived in this strange new world. Now that he wasn't there, she could finally feel the full extent of her homesickness.

As tears threatened to overwhelm her, Josephine made her way to the bathroom. She took a long shower and cried until she couldn't cry anymore.

Chapter Eight

Josephine

Josephine woke early, as the sun began to peak over the horizon. Anxiety had her heart racing before she'd fully woken. Her sudden cessation of anti-depressant medication wasn't doing her any favours. She'd experienced these symptoms previously, when shortages meant she could not access the medication. But there was no way to access the medicine here, and no alternative that she was aware of to help ease her transition.

It didn't help that today was her orientation into a foreign military, with strange people, many of whom had likely already decided they didn't like her. Perhaps that was just her anxiety talking, though any drastically unusual situation was enough to make one stressed.

Sighing, Josephine tried to shake the intrusive thoughts from her mind. She quietly rolled out of bed and tiptoed to the bathroom, scanning the unfamiliar faces scattered across the beds. They all looked so young, did these people age like humans? Or were their appearances deceptive?

Either way, they seemed like children to her.

The thought inevitably brought her back to her own daughters, who occupied her every waking and dreaming moment. Were they asleep, as they should be this early, or was there a time difference between this world and theirs?

Josephine splashed ice cold water onto her face, inhaling sharply as it trickled down her neck. She smoothed back her frizzy curls, knowing they'd be a mess shortly anyway. She inhaled deeply, feeling the bite of frigid air searing her lungs. She held her breath, focusing on the discomfort as she slowed her heartbeat. When she exhaled, she noticed her foggy breath on the bathroom mirror.

Josephine sighed, thinking of the many times her daughters had written on the mirror, when steam from the shower obscured it. They loved to leave "secret" messages to each other, as if they were the only ones who could decipher them.

Josephine moved closer to the mirror, impulsively raising a hand to write a secret message of her own. It would vanish long before any of the other acolytes woke up, and she knew it would never reach her daughters. It didn't hurt to pretend though.

I love you,

I miss you,

I'll see you soon.

Lots of love,

Mum.

She added a smiley face and a heart for good measure, as they were her daughters' favourite images to draw in the mirror.

Josephine stared at her handiwork for a long moment before she bitterly erased the message, deciding on an early breakfast over attempting to sleep a moment longer.

***

Josephine didn't expect that the most difficult part of her day would be clothing. She'd simply held the offered clothing up to her body, several centimetres of her hips and thighs visible on either side, and looked at the clerk. He'd sighed, seeming irritated, before writing "custom" next to her name.

How typical that clothing failing to fit her plus-sized body would be an issue in this world too.

At least she'd been measured up for appropriate clothing, but that would take time to have made. She did notice a few other unusually sized individuals coming and going from the tailors, though she still felt a tinge of embarrassment. It hadn't helped when the seamstress gawked at the measurements from her stomach, hips and thighs.

She pushed it down, reminding herself that her body had been through a lot, and it was the only one she had. Last thing she needed to be worried about were elvish beauty standards.

In addition to the embarrassing uniform failure, she'd had to answer a barrage of questions about her past, which were difficult to answer in a way that made her seem normal. She'd been examined head to toe by the physician, who had scowled at her and said she would need a lot of work. When she'd started to get defensive, asking what he meant, he'd only said scars were outside of his responsibility for initiates. She looked down at her stretch mark ridden stomach and thighs, along with a surprising amount of scars. She'd told him she didn't want them removed and he'd looked at her even more suspiciously.

How Kohlvar thought she was going to fit in and avoid raising suspicion, she had no idea. At least they all knew she was human, and hopefully knew little enough of the Human Realm to attribute any oddities to her "background".

"Why are you still in your travelling clothes?" Kohlvar asked as he speared a cube of beef with his fork.

"They didn't have anything remotely close to fitting me." Josephine responded wryly as she pushed her lunch around her plate.

He frowned, chewing thoughtfully. "I'll ask Torva if you can borrow her old clothes. You'd be similar heights, she's quite broad and muscular."

Josephine scooped up a piece of succulent chicken. "It's okay, it's not a big deal."

He sighed. "It's frustrating, I would've thought they had better options by now."

"I take it you needed custom made clothing too?"

He chuckled. "Oh, definitely. It did not help that once I started training, I became even larger, immediately outgrowing my uniform."

Josephine smiled at the thought. "So, you're a regular customer for them."

"Much to their chagrin, yes. I get a lot of repairs done too." His eyes rose above her head, a warm smile gracing his lips. "Torva!"

"Kohlvar," the deep acknowledgment reverberated through Josephine's spine. She turned to see an impressively tall female, with close cropped hair and chocolate brown eyes. She was dressed in tan leathers, a padded vest clinging to her broad torso.

"Torva, this is Josephine. Josephine, meet Torva, my second in charge."

Josephine swung her legs over the wooden bench, standing to offer a hand out to her. Upon closer inspection, she noticed the subtle swells of breasts underneath the padded vest, her pants clinging to her broad hips. Her androgynous appearance was striking, the contrast between her strength and femininity appealing to Josephine.

"Lovely to meet you," rolled off her tongue as Torva stared at the outstretched hand. She warily took the offered hand, gripping it firmly. Why did it feel like Josephine had done the wrong thing?

"Where are you from, Josephine?" Torva's tone was suspicious, as she eyed her appearance closely.

"The Human Realm, down south."

"I know where the Human Realm is. You're far from home."

Josephine averted her eyes, emotion unexpectedly rising in her chest. "Yes, I am," she murmured.

Torva released her hand. "I'd suggest you find something other than those clothes to wear, they won't be suitable for your training."

"Actually Torva, I was hoping you could help with that." Kohlvar chimed in, rising from his seat to embrace her. "Do you have any spare clothes she could borrow while her uniform is being made?"

Torva assessed Josephine, making her shrink under the scrutiny. "I may have something. I can't promise they will fit well though. We are quite different builds." She said it neutrally, without unkindness, but Josephine's already bruised ego ached.

"That will do, thank you, Torva. Have you eaten?"

"I have, I was just looking for you to give an update."

"Good, let's take a walk then. Josephine, I will see you outside shortly." Kohlvar gave her a reassuring smile before leaving with Torva.

Josephine returned to staring at her food, her mind an endless cacophony of worries and worst-case scenarios.

Chapter Nine

Kohlvar

"How were your negotiations with the dwarven border towns?" Kohlvar rumbled, as he and Torva walked out to the courtyard.

She sighed, her damp hair flicking over her eyes. She pushed it away with annoyance. "Tense. They're not happy, though I can't blame them. It's not like the Elven King is known for his kindness."

Kohlvar nodded grimly. "There's only a dozen recruits this time, which I'm sure the King will also be displeased with."

Torva hummed thoughtfully, "I'm not surprised, it's getting more difficult every year to find young people with magical skills. Speaking of," she turned to face him, her brows furrowed. "Why the human? Are you trying to provoke the King?"

Her tone was half-teasing, half-questioning. Kohlvar sighed, "There's something unusual about her. I could be wrong, but it's not like we don't have room for her."

"Still, he's not going to like it."

"No, I suspect he won't." Kohlvar conceded.

Torva leaned against the sandstone bench, staring down the hill towards the village. "He'll be here for their final assessment, so I hope you're right. It doesn't bode well for any of us if she's talentless."

Guilt reared its ugly head as Kohlvar followed her gaze. He watched as fellow soldiers jogged around the fortress, disturbing a small flock of birds searching for seeds.

"How's Valtherion?"

Kohlvar looked at her curiously. "Since when do you care how he's going?"

She rolled her eyes. "Just because we don't agree on much-"

"You mean *anything*."

Torva shot him a glare, irritation radiating from her. "Doesn't mean I can't ask how the old man is doing."

Kohlvar assessed her warily, surprised by her sudden interest. "He's...he's tired. He's exhausted looking after the forest, the nearby villagers and keeping the portal stable."

She frowned. "Is the portal causing more trouble than usual?"

Kohlvar almost winced, quickly schooling his expression into one of nonchalance. "Not really, I think he's just getting older. At least he's taken in a cat for company. I worry about him, all alone in the woods."

Torva patted his shoulder reassuringly. "He'll be fine Kohl, he's dealt with worse things than being alone."

Kohlvar nodded slowly, his eyes roaming to the large lake and surrounding forest. He felt the familiar tug in his chest, pulling him towards the water. He pushed it down, focusing on the young uncertain faces filtering into the courtyard.

"Let's do this," Torva grumbled, following the path down to the lake.

Chapter Ten

Josephine

Josephine stood in the open field next to the lake, anxiously tapping her fingers on her thighs. She tried to focus on the lush green trees surrounding them, the smooth ripples of water across the expansive sapphire lake. She continued her deep inhales of the fresh fragrant air, admiring the warming sensation of the sun on her face. This sun was gentle in comparison to the sun back home. Even in winter, the Australian sun and ultraviolet radiation could burn you to a crisp. At least sunburn was one thing she didn't need to worry about here.

She scanned the people assembling. Most were elves, with slender builds, long hair tied back, emphasising their pointed ears. They grouped together, looking around the crowd with minimal interest, talking amongst themselves. There seemed to be a hierarchy amongst them, with elves falling into a known place within the group. They looked young, clean shaven, generally well presented.

One male amongst them appeared dishevelled and scruffy, his unbound dirty blonde hair moving in different directions. His shirt was crumpled, like it'd been picked up from the floor, and his boots were barely laced. The elf next to him looked over his appearance with horror; conversely, he was immaculate. His boots shining, shirt neatly tucked into his belt, his hair gelled into a shorter cropped style. He began admonishing the male with an exasperated tone, similar to an older brother responsible for his younger sibling.

The blonde male gave a nonchalant shrug, his eyes scanning the crowd. He noticed Josephine's gaze, cracked a smile and gave a scandalous wink.

Josephine felt her brows rising in surprise, before she huffed a laugh. He was a child, but his cheekiness smacked her out of her anxious spiral. She rolled her eyes with a smile, watching him laugh and wink at a few more acolytes eyeing him.

What a shameless flirt, good for him, Josephine thought with amusement. She noticed a few more people had joined the group around her, which was notably lacking elves.

A young woman with long black hair, deep brown eyes and pale skin moved up beside her. There was something otherworldly about her, despite her appearance passing as human or elven. She kept her hair covering most of her face, shying away from curious gazes. Josephine looked her over quickly, not wishing to make her uncomfortable, but feeling drawn to her.

The next few acolytes caused murmurs to break out amongst both crowds. A trio of humanoid figures approached; each with varying degrees of scales spread out across their skin. The first male only had a few blue scaly patches, visible on the back of his arms and across his cheekbones. The female was vibrant, golden scales shimmering over her arms and chest, matching her golden blonde hair.

However, the last male drew the most attention. Some elves started pointing, rapidly speaking in increasing volume, which was impossible for the trio to ignore. The blue-scaled male shot a fierce glare at them, reducing their volume to a whisper. Yet they continued speaking, in awe of his appearance.

The young male was almost entirely covered in ruby red scales, his face more serpentine than human. Ridges formed around his eye sockets and over his skull, covering where his hair should've been. His hands, or rather, *claws*, extended into great talons, likely capable of eviscerating anyone who got too close. The creature stared pointedly at the ground, trailing along behind the other two.

"Damn, that's one hell of a dragonoid." A soft voice muttered behind Josephine, causing her to jump and turn around. Initially she saw no one, until she looked down. There, at barely 4 feet tall, was a tiny blonde child. At least, she looked like a child. Blonde ringlets framed her petite face, with piercing blue eyes meeting her hazel ones.

Josephine looked at her in horror. "Are you meant to be here? How old are you?" She blurted out before she could stop herself.

The small female's eyes narrowed with alarming ferocity, before she tilted her head to the side. "How old do you want me to be?" Her voice had changed to a high-pitched sweet melody, her eyelashes fluttering seductively.

Josephine recoiled, disgusted. Clearly this was no child, but her response was alarming, nonetheless.

Unsure how to respond, she opted for banter, hoping it would be received well. "Sorry sweetheart, you're not my type. But seriously, are you old enough to be here?"

The creature scoffed, losing her innocent childlike facade. She turned her brilliant blue eyes back to the dragonoids.

Josephine turned back to see Kohlvar approaching, his giant frame easily visible from afar. With him were two elves, a broad tall woman and- wait was it *flying?*

Josephine gaped at the diminutive creature, fluttering frantically to keep up with the group's swift pace. He looked like a cherub angel, but old, with white hair and translucent wings that caught the sunlight. He wore a simple grey smock and carried a scroll that was as wide as he was tall. He seemed to struggle to keep his balance, seeming relieved when he reached the centre of the field and landed.

"Welcome acolytes, future magic-wielders of the Elven Realm. I am Professor Fissius, Head Scholar of the Elven libraries. I will be overseeing your education on the history of magic and of Balidran. Here we have Galathir," Fissius indicated the older male elf with silver-streaked hair. "Alfion," he indicated the younger elf with a warm complexion. "Finally, we have Kohlvar and Torva. They will each contribute to your training, though given the wonderful size of this year's recruits, we will be dividing the responsibility between Galathir and Kohlvar."

Josephine raised her brows at that. There couldn't have been more than a dozen young people in the field. Was he being sarcastic?

"Galathir and Alfion will be taking those of you who were recruited from within the elven army, and those who possess similar magical potential to themselves. Kohlvar and Torva will be taking the outliers, those with unusual or unknown potential." His beady eyes scanned across the group, focusing on the non-elven acolytes.

How subtle, Josephine mused silently. Fissius started reading out names, with acolytes moving towards their respective leaders.

"Persephone, you will join Kohlvar's team."

The diminutive blonde girl shuffled past her, eerily silent in her movement. As Persephone stepped free of the cluster she'd been hidden in, a cry broke out from the elven students.

"YOU!" A male voice shouted angrily. The girl froze, turning towards the noise.

One of the elves had broken free from the cluster, charging towards her. His face contorted with unbridled rage; fists clenched by his side.

"Ah, fuck." Persephone grumbled, squaring off to the young man.

"You're the reason my father is dead, you-"

"Am I? Why's that?" She cocked her head, ringlets flailing.

The man stopped short. "Why?" He shouted incredulously. "Because you lured him to a lake and killed him, you cursed siren!"

The girl sighed, as if the accusation bored her. "No, I didn't lure him. I was simply visiting my friends, and your father followed me. Why do you think he did that, Benji?"

The young man spluttered, his dark hair falling free of his braid. "I don't care why he did it, I only care that YOU KILLED HIM!" He moved forward again with purpose, raising a fist to strike.

Josephine stiffened, moving to try and defend the girl. She bore a deep hatred for men who threatened to harm women, or anyone smaller than themselves.

"No, I don't think so," Persephone murmured as she raised a hand. The man froze, as if held back by invisible hands. "Your father followed me, because he saw a little girl all alone-"

"You're no child!" The elf spat, hatred burning in his eyes.

"No, but that's what he saw that night." She spat back with equal tenacity, anger radiating from her entire being. "He saw a defenseless child and followed them, because he was a *fucking pervert*."

"No, that's bullshit! Those accusations were false-"

"They were not, but regardless, he followed me and tried to hurt *me*. I don't need any more proof than that." Persephone snarled, her voice dangerously low.

"Even if what you say is true, which it isn't, it didn't give you the right to kill him!"

"Oh, I didn't kill him." Persephone smirked. "The lake did. I just...helped it." She batted her eyelashes again, feigning innocence.

"You *bitch*-" Benji finally swung forward, stumbling with the sudden momentum and landing on his hands and knees. He quickly jumped to his feet, charging towards her, only to be caught by Kohlvar and lifted off his feet.

"ENOUGH!" He bellowed, looking pointedly at Persephone before turning to the male. "Persephone was already arrested over this-"

"She wasn't punished! It's not good enough." The elf protested, flailing in Kohlvar's unrelenting grip.

"There was *insufficient evidence* to prove she did it, Benji. He had been drinking and died by drowning."

"She just admitted to it! She should've been killed, drowned in the same lake she murdered him in." He directed his words directly at Persephone, still fighting the giant's hold. Persephone hissed back at him; fine needle-like teeth barely visible under her lips.

Kohlvar sighed, "You're going to have to tolerate her training here-"

"I will not, she killed-"

"I WASN'T ASKING." His voice boomed so loudly Josephine's eardrums buzzed.

Silence fell, or perhaps they'd all been rendered temporarily deaf.

Kohlvar was glaring furiously at Benji, his icy blue eyes deadly. "I appreciate you lost your father, but we both know he wasn't a good person. You can either fall into line, or go home. This is the only time I will offer you a choice."

Hurt crossed the young man's face, as he looked between Persephone and Kohlvar, weighing his options. Eventually, his shoulders slumped, staring at the ground with defeat.

Kohlvar set him back on the ground, before turning to Persephone. He simply shook his head, before returning to the leaders. Persephone moved to stand behind him, her chin held high.

Professor Fissius shot a disapproving scowl her way before continuing down the list.

"Josephine," he finally called. "You are assigned to Kohlvar."

No real surprise there, although the tension in her shoulders relaxed. She felt safer with Kohlvar, rather than an unknown elf.

She gave the scholar a nod, throwing a nervous smile to Kohlvar as she joined his ranks. His face was impassive, which did little to ease her anxiety as the whispers began.

"Gosh look at her ears, she couldn't even be a quarter elf!" A female elf exclaimed.

"Maybe she's a dwarf?"

"Pfft, she's six feet tall! Although she is rather round." The woman sneered.

"Maybe a giant fucked a dwarf, could you imagine that? How would that even work?"

Josephine ignored the remarks, though she noticed Kohlvar's hands forming fists.

"Don't be stupid; giants *eat* dwarves."

"Well maybe her mother ate her father *after* getting it on."

As Kohlvar's agitation visibly grew, Josephine sighed and turned around. "Spiders do that."

Every single face turned to her.

"Excuse me?" The elven woman scowled, her green eyes narrowing to slits.

"I said, spiders do that. Some species, after mating, the female will capture the male in her webs to eat and ensure she has enough nutrition to produce healthy offspring. I thought everyone knew that," she added flippantly.

Now even Kohlvar was looking at her in bewilderment. Silence persisted, causing Josephine to rapidly tap her fingers behind her back. She would not back down, or appear weak, to these ignorant assholes.

A howl of laughter broke the silence. The blonde shaggy-haired elf stumbled out of the unselected crowd, clutching his stomach. He continued to chuckle as he walked towards Josephine, a huge smile spread across his face.

"You'll have to forgive that lot; they never could pass up an opportunity for gossip. Best to ignore them." He winked, pointing two finger guns to the scholar. "I'm joining this lot."

The scholar huffed. "Excuse me, that is not how-"

"Please, you're going to have most of this lot refusing to work with them, just put me with them." The blonde elf turned around and walked backwards. "Eryn, you with me?"

The impeccably dressed elf stepped out from the crowd with a loud sigh, "Seriously? Fine." He trudged over, avoiding eye contact with the seething scholar and the gaping crowd.

Josephine threw the pair a grateful smile as the tension dissipated. She stepped back into the misfit group, remaining close to Kohlvar.

Soon the division of the crowd became quite obvious. Those who appeared to be elves were assigned to Galathir, and all of them had prior military experience.

The rest were assigned to Kohlvar. The golden and blue dragonoids had approached, engaged in a brief conversation with Kohlvar, then nodded their farewell to the young dragonoid. He had remained completely silent since. The young woman with a curtain of dark hair, Seralie, had barely uttered a squeak, her stiff posture giving away her nerves. Persephone looked irritated, rolling her curls around her long fingers. Josephine noticed a slight shimmering on the back of her hands but looked away when the young woman glared at her.

Finally, the two elves, Kaelith and Eryndal, carried on an animated conversation with only their facial expressions. They had to be related, that level of affection and exasperation came from a close sibling bond. Josephine smiled at it, unsure why she felt relieved to have them with her.

The professor rolled up his scroll with a huff before turning and fluttering away without farewell. Josephine raised her eyebrows, but no one else seemed surprised. Kohlvar and the older elf, Galathir, briefly spoke before shaking hands. She watched as Kohlvar turned to face them, Torva standing strongly by his side.

"Everybody listen up!" Torva bellowed, her short hair adding to her harsh masculine features. She was a similar height to Josephine, but built with a significantly larger bone structure, giving her an imposing figure. Perhaps she was part giant?

Kohlvar scanned his gaze over each meeting of his misfit crew. "Given the unfortunate start today," he looked pointedly at Persephone, "I shall remind you all that fighting is forbidden amongst elven acolytes, or any elven military. There are enough adversaries outside our borders; we do not need to make more within this compound."

He paused to allow his words to sink in before continuing.

"Soon we will test your capability with magic and try to gauge your potential abilities. Before that though, we will show you the areas of magical significance. If you feel yourself drawn to any particular area, please tell Torva or myself. Take a moment to introduce yourselves, before we walk down to the lake."

Josephine turned expectantly, waiting for the elven boys to start the conversation. When they didn't, still engrossed in their secret communications, she approached the blonde girl.

"Persephone, right?" She held out a hand, ignoring the instinct to bend down to her height.

She flicked away a speck of dirt under her nail. "That's me," she responded glumly, ignoring the outstretched hand.

"Seralie?" She shifted her hand towards the dark-haired girl.

Deep brown eyes met hers, striking a wound in her heart at the similarity to her own daughters. The fear in her eyes stirred her motherly instincts, so she reached out and looped her arm through the young woman's.

"I'm Josephine, but everyone calls me Jo or Josie, any variation is fine. We'll have to get to know each other more." She offered a comforting smile, relieved to feel the young woman's stiff posture relax slightly.

She turned to the dragonoid, offering a friendly smile, however he looked straight through her. The elven boys had turned their attention to him, failing to draw any communication out of him. Could he even talk? Did dragons talk like humans in this world? She was still bewildered by the fact dragons existed.

"I'm Kaelith, Kae for short. This is Eryn, my cousin. He's the smartest guy I know." Kaelith's frantic energy radiated off him as he bounced back and forth on the balls of his feet.

"Oh, I'm not that smart. But I do like to read. Did you know that there are several types of sirens? Lake Sirens can only survive in fresh water, which is why they're found in lake and river systems. But Ocean Sirens can survive in both, so they can be found in rivers and lakes, but usually they're closer to the ocean. The sirens in this lake are said to be friendly." He beamed at them, clearly pleased with his recital.

Josephine heard a scoff from Persephone. "You know nothing of sirens, they're anything but friendly." Her eyes turned towards the lake, an indecipherable expression spreading across her delicate features.

"You're Persephone, right? You're a badass, that was so cool how you stopped Benji. Did you really kill his dad? I mean I know he was an arsehole, always hitting people, including his wife, but wow, that's wicked." Kaelith rambled as he danced over to her.

She turned to meet his eager expression with one of disgust. "What the hell is wrong with you?"

"What? I think it's impressive. Plus, you're tiny, how did you manage it?" He seemed genuinely curious, as if the morbidity of his question was lost on him.

She turned away, pointedly facing her back to him.

"Ugh, fine, keep your secrets, Pixie." Kaelith turned away from her, clearly working hard to keep a smile off his face.

"What did you just call me?" Her voice was quiet, but her eyes were furious.

"Pixie. Pix-ie. You know, like a pixie." He enunciated each syllable with a mischievous grin sliding across his face, imitating a little fluttering creature with his hands.

Persephone's scowl deepened, her nostrils flaring, pupils dilating in blind fury. "Don't call me that." She snapped furiously.

"Or what?" He stood in front of her, teasingly allowing his nose close enough to almost brush hers.

"Call me Pixie again and I'll hurt you so badly, you'll wish you had never been born."

"You promise?" He whispered, his hands firmly clasped behind his back, like he was fighting to keep them restrained.

Persephone flinched back from him, shock registering across her face. A resounding slap echoed loud enough that Josephine winced, leaving Kaelith stunned with a bright red handprint across his cheek.

"You're a fucking freak." Persephone hissed as she backed away from him, her tiny fists clenched by her sides.

Kaelith simply chuckled, brushing his fingers across the angry welt. "You're just too easy to wind up, *Pixie*."

Persephone inhaled sharply at her unwanted nickname, fists shaking as Kohlvar barked at them.

"Persephone! What are you doing?" He took in the red mark on Kaelith's cheek with a scowl.

Persephone whirled towards Kohlvar instead. "Why do you *always* assume that I'm doing something wrong? It's not always my fault!" She screamed, jets of water rising up from the ground, swirling rapidly around her.

Kohlvar stopped his approach. 'Perse-"

"Sir, it's my fault." Kaelith stood tall to face him, moving to Persephone's side, ignoring the water soaking him. "I was teasing her, calling her Pixie, and intentionally annoying her. The fault lies with me."

Josephine watched as Persephone's spiraling water tower splashed back to the earth, her stunned expression on Kaelith.

Kohlvar sighed. "Right, in that case, I see Persy has already delivered an appropriate punishment for annoying her, and I would appreciate it if you found your entertainment elsewhere."

"I will, sir. At least, during class." Kaelith said with a straight face.

Eryndal let out a groan, smacking a hand to his face. Persephone's glare narrowed on Kaelith again as he gave her a wink before falling back to stand beside his cousin.

"Persephone, I'm sorry I presumed fault incorrectly. That said," Kohlvar hesitated, "you need to work on controlling your emotions. We don't need any magical incidents, from anyone." He scanned the team seriously. "We're already on fragile ground here, don't break it."

"At least not on the first day," Eryndal muttered, smacking Kaelith on the arm when he chuckled.

Kohlvar sighed, casting his eyes skyward for a brief moment. "Right, time for the tour."

Chapter Eleven

Josephine

The next hour was spent walking around the grounds surrounding the elven military fortress. Josephine learned this was not the true Elven palace, rather a secondary residence for them when they conducted military business. Their real home was a secret location higher in the mountains, away from the public eye.

According to Torva, there were several sources of power, which contributed to the decision to build the major city and military base here, despite the inconvenient hills. The lake, the forests, a specific patch in an otherwise boring paddock all supposedly contained a vein of magical power, moving throughout the ground beneath their feet.

Josephine felt absolutely nothing special about any of them.

***

Josephine just felt confused. Why was she here? This wasn't exactly what she'd envisioned when she'd agreed to join Kohlvar. But, she supposed she would have to trust the process, for it was too late to turn back now.

"Is anyone else *famished*?" Kaelith yelled, as they hiked back up the steep hill to the barracks.

No one responded, Josephine suspected because they were too busy trying to breathe. She was completely preoccupied with her gasping breaths at the steep incline, mentally pushing herself to the top of the hill.

"Come on, Eryn, aren't you positively *ravenous* after today?"

The dark-haired elf sighed. "Sorry guys, Kaelith found one of my textbooks and decided to memorise every possible word to say he's hungry."

"Well, your dad said I couldn't complain about being hungry anymore! I had to improvise." Kaelith cast out a cheeky grin, mischief dancing in his eyes.

"They have plenty of food here," Josephine offered between her panting breaths. "What's your favourite?"

Kaelith nearly bounced up the hill in glee. "Ooh, I love potatoes, bread, cheese, and the stew Eryn's mum makes, it's the best. Any kind of roasted meat or vegetable. As long as they don't taste like green, you know?"

Josephine smiled, "I do know. Do you prefer sweet or savoury?"

"Both! Always both."

"And you Eryn?" Josephine gestured, making a point of including others in the conversation.

He shrugged. "I guess I like both."

"I like sweets," Seralie whispered, her round eyes flicking between them cautiously.

"Ugh, no, I can't stand sweet things." Persephone argued. "But I guess that's to be expected."

Josephine gave her a curious glance. "Why?"

Her face morphed into an incredulous expression. "Because I'm part siren, obviously."

"Why is that obvious?" She looked at the young woman, surprised to find genuine confusion across her face.

She scrunched her nose up. "You don't know anything, do you?"

Josephine fought to keep from rolling her eyes. "I'm not from here, remember? I bet there's plenty you don't know about the Human Realm."

"I've read about the Human Realm. Is it true that you guys don't use magic?" Eryndal tilted his head towards her, also struggling with the last section of the hill.

"Yes. We don't have magic, as far as I'm aware."

"Then, why are you here?" Persephone raised a brow at her.

Josephine shrugged. "To see if that's still the case, I suppose."

They walked in a comfortable silence, catching their breath in the courtyard. Josephine took a moment to gaze back down the hill, watching the setting sun casting pastel colours over the lake. The mirrored reflection created a beautiful scene, the kind one would eagerly capture with a photo, or a painting. Homesickness resonated in Josephine's chest again, reminding her of days past with her daughters playing in the yard until the sun set.

She was jolted from her reverie by Kaelith's animated question.

"Do you think they'll have sticky buns? Come on, I don't want to miss out!"

She chuckled, following them into the fortress.

Chapter Twelve

Josephine

Unsurprisingly, sleep didn't come easily for Josephine. She tossed and turned, her mind racing between memories of her daughters and bombs raining down on her. She felt trapped, like her heart was being ripped out of her chest, as she saw Sienna lying on those lifeless concrete stairs, before she woke in a cold dark field, surrounded by ominous dark shapes.

This dream was always the same, haunting her nearly every night. She knew it was normal after a traumatic incident to have these flashbacks, but she would really appreciate it if they'd just stop. She didn't need the daily torture of reliving one of the worst moments of her life.

Eventually, her dreams settled to a calm one. She and Susan sat on the veranda, sipping tea and nibbling crackers, while the girls chased each other around the backyard. They ran around the veggie patch, squealing and shouting happily. The sky was slowly dimming, streaks of orange and pink starting to dance across the sky.

Josephine called across the nightly reminder, "Girls, it's time to come in, it's getting dark!"

"Not yet mum!" Danielle yelled.

"Five more minutes, please!" Isabelle pleaded.

They did this song and dance every night, but she was rarely truly annoyed by it. She'd give anything to feel frustrated at her daughters defying bedtime again.

"Are they behaving for you?" she turned to Susan, noticing her tired, haunted expression.

She scoffed. "For the most part, yes. They gave me hell when I forgot about our Friday movie night. You should've heard the screaming." She trailed off, rubbing her thin hands. They were redder than usual, eczema spreading across her knuckles. She must be working more shifts at the hospital.

Josephine sighed. "I'm sorry I'm not here, Susan. I'm trying to come back, I really am."

"I know dear. We'll be okay." Susan gave a comforting smile. Josephine knew this conversation was only a figment of her imagination, all the things she wanted to hear, but it helped. Susan was one of the most capable people she knew. The girls would be alright, and she would make her way back to them.

"Mum!" One of the twins called. Josephine turned, expecting a 'look at me' request. Instead, she saw the twins barrelling towards her, their game abandoned.

"What's wrong?" Alarm shot through her, causing her to rise from her chair.

"Mum, wake up. Wake up now!" They both screamed, fear written across their faces. Just as her daughters were about to reach her, the dream vanished into darkness.

Josephine's eyes shot open as she sat upright, throwing the blanket off her bed. Where were they? Were they sick? Were they hurt?

She suddenly realised that she was not in her bedroom at home with her daughters. Instead, she sat next to a dark tall figure leaning over the bed next to her, with a large knife in his hand.

Her maternal instincts took over. She leapt for him, clamping one hand around his wrist, twisting it backwards until her shoulder met his elbow, forcing it to hyper-extend. She heard him yell in pain, knife clattering to the ground, before he twisted and shoved her away. Josephine hit the side of her bed, wincing as her ribs collided with the wooden frame.

"This doesn't involve you!" an enraged male voice hissed. Josephine looked up to see him turning back to the bed, just as a blur of blonde curls flew towards him.

Persephone.

Josephine gritted her teeth as she pushed herself to her feet, squinting to understand the scene before her. Persephone had leapt at the man, causing a strange tussle where she was clinging to him like a backpack. He screamed, and Josephine felt something hot splash across her face.

"Get off me you siren bitch!" he screamed as he reached over his head, grabbing her hair and neck, before flinging her over his head. Josephine screamed as Persephone smashed down onto her bed, the frame fracturing from the force. She lay still, head limply hanging off the side.

"She fucking bit me," the man cursed as he scanned the floor.

Josephine realised he was searching for his fallen knife, just as she'd spotted it. She kicked it under Persephone's bed, causing the man to swear vehemently. She raised her arms but could not fully block his furious assault, taking multiple punches to her head and torso.

"Leave her alone!" Seralie screamed, as she flung a book at the intruder, running forward to kick his legs.

The man backhanded her with minimal effort, sending her tumbling to the floor. Josephine took the opportunity to swing her leg up towards his groin, but she hit his thigh instead. He snarled angrily, punching her cheek hard enough she staggered backwards. His hands stretched around her throat, squeezing tightly.

"This didn't have to involve you, but if you want to defend that bitch, it's your death sentence." His voice hitched, his pupils wide and dark as he looked down to her throat, the pressure from his hold increasing.

Panic struck her as she desperately clawed at the hands crushing down on her windpipe. She kicked out again, trying to land a blow, but coming up empty. Something hot and viscous splashed over her hands and face, as Seralie screamed for help. Her vision started to blur as tears flooded her eyes, her rapid heartbeat screaming in her ears as burning agony flooded through her chest.

Suddenly his grip loosened as the full force of his body slammed into her. Josephine collapsed underneath his weight, gasping for air as her lungs struggled to draw it in. She frantically shoved at the man, reminding her painfully of being trapped in a bombed stairwell. A sob escaped her as the memory threatened to overwhelm her, fighting to stay in this moment and survive.

Finally, Josephine scrambled free of him, clutching her aching throat. She tried to get back on her feet, but the sudden influx of air left her dizzy, dropping to her knees and crawling away instead.

Thin arms wrapped around her, gently enough that she didn't immediately panic.

"Are you okay?" Seralie's trembling voice washed over her, cutting through the fog of smoke and burning buildings taking over her sight.

"Are they dead?" Josephine could barely keep herself from slipping into unconsciousness, the effort to turn and look at the two still bodies behind her felt too great.

"I don't know," Seralie whispered, sniffling quietly.

A loud bang causes both of them to jump as the door to their dormitory slammed open. Through the black swarming spots in her vision, Josephine saw Torva, closely followed by Kohlvar and Galathir. They barged into the room, prompting a few shrieks from the far end of the dormitory.

Torva jogged towards them, but Josephine raised a shaking hand and pointed towards the mangled bed. "Persy," she croaked. Torva stumbled at the sight of two crumbled bodies. "Kohlvar!" She barked, rushing to Persephone.

"What the fuck happened?" He growled, looking around the dormitory for answers. His gaze landed on the man lying still between the beds. He knelt, turning the man over, head hanging low. "Is she dead?" His words were so quiet Josephine almost didn't catch them.

"No, she's alive. But she needs the healers, *now*." Torva shifted Persephone's body, her head was resting on the bed, instead of dangling off at a painful angle.

"I'll take her," Kohlvar wiped his hand, which was stained a dark colour, over the man's shirt. He scooped Persephone effortlessly into his arms and sprinted out of the room.

Relief flooded through Josephine. Persephone was alive, and if the magic of this world could save her from a bombing, surely it would save her too.

Exhaustion started to overwhelm her, the urge to close her eyes so tempting.

"Oh no, you need to stay awake." A male voice echoed by Josephine's ear, a hand shaking her shoulder firmly. "What happened?"

"I don't know, I just woke up to Jo and Persy fighting this man. I tried to help, but... there wasn't much I could do." Seralie's voice quivered, her slim hands gripping Josephine tightly.

"Torva, this one needs the infirmary too. Would you prefer I take her, or check on the rest of the women?" Galathir's voice was surprisingly soft.

Warm hands touched her neck, causing Josephine to flinch. "You take her, and Seralie too. I'll manage the rest."

"Jo? Jo, I need you to open your eyes for me." Another arm wrapped around her waist, and soon she was hoisted onto her feet. "Can you walk?"

Josephine grumbled as she nodded, sharp pain cutting through her mental fog as her ribs expanded fully. She slowly stepped forward; her eyes locked on her feet as they shuffled out of the dormitory.

***

The bright lights of the infirmary came into view, with an alarming amount of noise echoing from the rooms. Most of the staff are gathered around a single bed, with a worried looking Kohlvar standing at the end. Several voices overlapped, in an unfamiliar language.

Josephine allowed herself to be guided to a nearby bed, but she could not lay herself down. She sat and watched, intent on gaining an insight about Persephone's condition. She felt Seralie brushing a wet cloth over her face and hands, yet she could not tear her gaze away from the chaotic scene before her.

It looked like they were doing next to nothing. They were using barely any medical equipment, no monitoring, no medications or IV. Had they given up? Fear rose in her chest, and Josephine clutched at the underside of the bed.

"What's wrong, are you in pain?" Galathir's voice cut through her focus.

"Why aren't they doing anything?" The words slurred, thanks to her swollen mouth, a fresh split stinging on her lower lip.

"They are," Seralie promised, dabbing at her lip. "They're trying to stabilise her, then they can take their time healing her properly. You just can't see what they're doing."

Josephine turned to the young woman. "Can you?" she whispered.

She startled, looking past her. "No, of course not. I'm not a healer. But I can understand what they're saying."

Josephine turned back to the scene unfolding, just as Galathir walked towards her with a cup.

"Here, for the swelling and pain."

She gave the tiniest of head shakes. He sighed. "Persephone will be fine. You need to drink this before your swelling gets worse. It's more effective if taken before an injury completely swells."

"He's right," Seralie murmured, squeezing her arm reassuringly.

Josephine reluctantly took the cup. When she pressed it to her lips, she fumbled, feeling like she'd just had a dental procedure with swollen numb lips. She messily drank it down and allowed Seralie to clean her up after.

As the medicine took effect, and the adrenaline started to wear off, Josephine felt the gentle pull of sleep. But she insisted on seeing Persephone through to stabilisation, so she rested her head on Seralie's shoulder, watching as the healers worked together.

Eventually, after a period of time that could have been minutes or hours, the healers quieted. Josephine straightened, nudging Seralie for an explanation.

"I think...I think she's stable." Seralie croaked. "They'll keep her asleep and heal her over the next couple of days."

Relief overwhelmed her. "Thank goodness," Josephine's eyes shifted to Kohlvar, who still clutched the foot of the bed with a white knuckled grip, however his face looked marginally less tense.

Soon the healers were administering their attention to Josephine, soothing the bruised muscles of her neck and offering various potions. She was too exhausted to do anything but follow their instructions dutifully, and soon, the allure of sleep was too strong to resist.

Chapter Thirteen

Kohlvar

"It was Benji, Kohlvar."

A troubled sigh escaped him, as he leaned over Persephone's bedside, watching her thin body rise and fall with every breath.

"I suspected it was. Does Galathir know?"

Torva moved into his line of sight, standing opposite him. "Yes."

Kohlvar met her gaze, waiting for an elaboration. "Just tell me how bad it is, Tor."

Her lips thinned into a tight grimace. "He's angry, but I think it's more at himself than you. Benji did try to attack Persephone on their first day."

"But?"

Torva sighed. "You know the King does not take kindly to the death of elves, especially not within his ranks."

Kohlvar nodded, expecting as much. "The first year we manage to convince the King to recruit hybrids for magical training, and one of them kills an elven recruit a few days in. Yeah, it's bad." He sunk his head into his hands.

"Doesn't help that Persy's killed a few elves previously," Torva added wryly. "But if the King kills Persy, the sirens will seek revenge. They're already furious she's here."

"You know she had no other choice." Kohlvar leveled a firm stare at Torva. Torva nodded, looking down at the unconscious girl.

"Poor kid."

"She's 19."

Torva scoffed, "She's a child, Kohl."

"Not by the King's laws she isn't," Kohlvar murmured sadly. "And she was never able to be a child."

Torva rested a hand tentatively on his shoulder. "She may be immune to the King ordering her death, but the rest of them don't have that immunity."

"Kaelith and Eryndal are elves."

"They're elves who accepted the hybrids willingly. Everyone's at risk if we don't pull this off Kohl."

"I know, Torva, I don't need the reminder." He regretted the admonishment as soon as it left his mouth.

"Of course not," she snapped irritably, pulling her hand away briskly. "I just hope you have a plan to keep us all from being dead in a few months." She stormed away, her heavy boots echoing through the infirmary.

Kohlvar groaned, his neck popping as he straightened. He scanned the room habitually, confirming Seralie had not moved from the bed opposite them. The healers came and went, congregating in an adjacent room lit with candles. The moon had risen high, brightening the infirmary through the tall arched windows behind Persephone and Josephine.

It was going to be a long night.

He returned to Persephone's side, gently cradling her tiny hand in his. Her mouth was still covered in blood from ripping out Benji's throat, blonde curls stained red and pink. He wanted to clean her, but too much disturbance could affect the trance. Even holding her hand came with a small risk, but he wanted her to know she wasn't alone.

"Is she going to be okay?"

Kohlvar jumped, startled by the raspy voice behind him. He turned, finding Josephine's hazy eyes on him. "You're awake. How do you feel?" He rose from one bedside to face the next.

"Marginally better than the time a bomb dropped on me. How's Persy?" She tried to smile, though it came out pained.

A pang of guilt sunk in Kohlvar's chest at her discomfort. "She's going to recover, but only because of you. I cannot thank you enough for saving her life. None of us should be threatened in our own beds."

Kohlvar reached out a hand towards the bruises on her neck. She pulled back, flinching. He froze, waiting until she relaxed to brush back her hair and examine the bruises. A hot burning anger rose in his chest at the purple marks across her throat. He felt his teeth grinding as he tried to hide his fury from her.

"The healers will be able to mend your neck in the morning. Are you hurt elsewhere?" Kohlvar scanned down her body, assessing for further injuries.

Josephine winced as she brushed her hand over her ribs. "Just bruised, I think."

"How did you know she was being attacked?" His hand trailed through the section of hair that had fallen loose from her braid, fingers brushing absentmindedly over the dark strands.

"I didn't. I was having a dream about my daughters, they told me to wake up. I had forgotten where I was, but I knew that a man standing over the bed next to mine wasn't right, especially as he had a knife." Her eyes squeezed shut momentarily, brow furrowed as if the memory brought her pain.

A string of guttural curses in Dwarvish escaped Kohlvar, before he cut them off. "Perhaps I should've dealt with him on the first day. I was hoping to avoid bloodshed, but I guess revenge was too powerful a motivator for him. She likely would be dead if you hadn't interfered."

Quietly, Josephine murmured, "I'm just glad I woke up in time."

"I think this means I owe you a favour." Kohlvar gave her a small smile, trying to shift her emotions out of the miserable spiral he could feel her sinking into.

She smiled thoughtfully, "I'll settle for you keeping me alive. Seems like this world is more dangerous than you suggested." She said it lightly, but the words felt worse than a slap. Guilt wracked Kohlvar again, as he looked between the women in his life he'd failed recently. As he started to apologise, she spoke again.

"Is she your family?" Josephine croaked out.

Kohlvar looked at her in surprise. "I don't have any family," he responded gruffly.

"I very much doubt that," she whispered, her dark eyes capturing his. "You might not share blood, but you care for her like she's your family."

Kohlvar looked back down at the tiny prone form. "Then it's a good thing I will never have children." He whispered darkly, avoiding her gaze. "I would not make a good father, when I cannot keep my own students safe."

Josephine sighed, her fingers brushing the back of his hand, which was still touching her hair. "Could you have prevented this?"

Kohlvar looked at Persephone thoughtfully. "Not without harming Benji."

"Then stop blaming yourself."

Kohlvar looked at her in surprise. "Excuse me?"

"I'm tired Kohl...I just don't think...you should..."

Kohlvar watched as exhaustion rapidly won, her eyes closed with the occasional snore escaping her. His lips twitched in amusement, did she always talk until she passed out?

He straightened her blanket, wrapping it around her arms until she was cocooned. It was criminally cold in the infirmary during the winter. Her mental turmoil had quietened with sleep, but it was still there, hiding in her subconscious. He could feel every emotion from Josephine despite his mental shields. He knew humans were emotionally volatile, but he'd never been in such constant proximity to one before. It was a challenge he did not need right now.

Kohlvar brushed her long brown hair away from her face, lingering near her rounded ears. He leaned over her, gently pressing his fingers into her temple and scalp, as he projected a sense of calm and serenity.

She resisted his suggestion, unsurprising given the adrenaline still lingering in her body, but he was able to settle her nerves enough to soothe her into a deep healing sleep. He took a heavy breath, slightly dizzy from the exertion, his nose brushing her forehead. He jolted away, not realising how close he'd gotten. He straightened, breathing quickly in shock. Josephine was becoming the kind of person that he could drown in, if he wasn't careful.

Kohlvar gave her one last assessing look, trying to reassure himself that she was safe, before he turned back to Persephone. He checked on the young woman, confirming that he could not sense any distressing emotions from her in her heavily sedated state. He patted her hand one more time, before settling back down on a hard wooden chair for a long night.

Chapter Fourteen

Josephine

Persephone was still in a healing trance when Josephine woke the next morning. Kohlvar was asleep on an upright chair, his hand resting on Persephone's. Despite his protests, it was clear to Josephine that this young woman was important to him. She just hoped that she would recover, that they hadn't been too late to save her.

She pushed herself up to a seated position, feeling surprisingly well rested given the events of the previous night. The potion given to her by Galathir had helped reduce the worst of the swelling, and the healers were quick to mend her most severe injuries. She would certainly feel tender for a few days, but Josephine was mostly relieved to still be alive.

Seralie had escaped with bruises, only needing minor attention before they were both swiftly guided out of the infirmary. The idea of going down to breakfast and pretending everything was normal felt strange, but it seemed like they didn't have much of a choice.

Josephine looped an arm through Seralie's, giving her a resigned smile as they walked in silence.

***

They'd missed the rush of morning showers and breakfast, but Hirwen took one look at them and piled two plates exceptionally high with a great variety of protein, carbohydrates and fruit. Josephine almost hugged her, but she shooed them out as quickly as she'd whipped up the food.

Josephine stared at the eggs, her stomach growling loudly, as she thought of the last breakfast she'd shared with her daughters. Here there seemed to be an abundance of food, a concept that felt sadly foreign to her.

"Goodness, she's given us so much." Seralie murmured as she nibbled on a slice of pear.

"She'll expect us to finish it too." Josephine savoured the scrambled eggs, mopping them up with heavily buttered toast. She closed her eyes after each bite, enjoying the pleasant chew of the dark bread, the melted butter coating her tongue.

"What happens if I don't?" Seralie's panicked voice jolted Josephine out of her reverie.

"Just eat as much as you can," Josephine smiled reassuringly. "I'm sure she'll understand."

Seralie looked uneasy, eagerly spooning her honeyed porridge with a contented hum.

The dining hall doors swung open, banging loud enough to make both of them jump. Josephine immediately jumped to her feet, scanning the room for danger. Her fists were clenched around her cutlery, body tensed in anticipation of an attack.

"There you two are! We heard about last night, you're alive!" Kaelith looked particularly disheveled, his blonde hair hanging in his eyes. He batted it away as he quickly strode towards them, Eryndal following close behind. The red dragonoid lingered at the door, watching them with his yellow eyes.

Kaelith frowned at her defensive position. "Are you alright? Where's Persy? Or Benji? We haven't heard from either of them yet."

"Benji?" Josephine and Seralie asked in unison.

"One of the recruits in our dorm, he wasn't there this morning." Kaelith explained, looking between the two of them with concern.

"The girls said someone attacked you?" Eryndal looked at them apprehensively, his eyes lingering on Josephine's bruised arms.

"Yes, a man broke in and tried to kill Persephone," Josephine awkwardly sat back down, her heart still racing from the sudden noise.

"And?" Kaelith asked eagerly, hopping from side to side.

Josephine frowned at him. "This wasn't an exciting incident, we almost died."

"Sorry, he's been like that since he was a kid, he can't stop moving when he's nervous or excited or any strong emotion really." Eryndal gave an apologetic smile.

"Ah, I see." Josephine frowned into her plate before answering. "I'm not too sure on exactly what happened, I hit my head at a point, it's all a bit fuzzy."

"Do you know who attacked you?"

The woman both shook their heads. "It sounded like a man," Seralie offered.

"And Persephone?" Eryndal pressed, worry creasing his brow.

"She's still in the infirmary, she was badly hurt," Josephine confirmed.

The cousins turned to look at each other. "Well maybe Benji is there too, maybe he fell and hurt himself." Kaelith offered, tapping his foot rapidly.

"No," Seralie corrected. "We were the only patients. Kohlvar stayed with us, Galathir brought Jo and I to the infirmary, and of course there were the healers, but no other patients."

"Nobody tried to harm you three, did they?" Josephine asked, her tone more worried and maternal than she'd intended.

Kaelith scoffed. "No, no one is usually ever attacked, it doesn't make any sense."

"That's because you're not a hybrid, Kaelith." Eryndal added glumly. "Do you think that's why Persephone was targeted?"

Josephine frowned, trying to remember the few words their attacker had said. "He said it didn't involve us. I think he was just after Persephone."

Eryndal froze, his warm brown eyes widening in horror. "Oh no."

Josephine threw him a questioning look, just as a loud growl reached their ears. The dragonoid appeared tense, lips curled over his canines as he *growled.*

"Uh, you okay friend?" Kaelith hopped over to him, before he was shoved backwards, landing on his backside with a squeak.

"Hey!" Eryndal yelled, as their fellow elven recruits pushed past the dragonoid and barged into the dining hall.

"Where is she?" An enraged female elf stepped towards Eryndal with fists clenched, as he helped his cousin to his feet.

"Who?"

"That siren bitch you traitors call friend, Eryn! How the hell could you join them? After everything the sirens have done to us, and you agree to train beside one?"

"Done to *us*?" Eryndal straightened his spectacles nervously. "Has it escaped your notice that the elves have restricted the siren's waterways and trade for the last 60 years? That they were never informed of this change, only learning of it when they appeared in border towns, ordered to be executed on sight. It seems a little ridiculous to call this issue one sided, Freyda."

Freyda scowled at him, her pale brows forming a furious V. "They have lured countless men and women to their deaths, including the one you call friend!"

"Well, I'm not sure she's our friend yet, she's a bit prickly, hard to get to know." Kaelith nervously fired off.

"Shut up Kaelith, you never stop talking and you really should," she snarled coldly, and Josephine watched as the words landed their mark. Kaelith's head drooped, his foot tapping intensifying as his hands buried into his pockets.

The dragonoid growled at the elves again, in what Josephine sensed was a warning.

Freyda tossed her blonde hair back, turning to face him. "I don't speak *beast*, so you can either talk to me in the common tongue or not at all, you *freak*."

"Hey!" Josephine found herself rising, hands slammed onto the table. "Leave them alone, they had nothing to do with this."

"Oh, but you did," Freyda snarled, moving towards her and Seralie. "You stopped Benji from killing Persephone, as was his right."

"He had no right!" Eryndal yelled as Kaelith gasped, "He did WHAT?"

Realisation hit Josephine. That's why the elven women had not interfered; they knew it was going to happen. "You fucking coward." Josephine fixed the woman with a glare, hoping she could see every emotion coursing through her body.

She gave a sinister smile. "Your friend won't survive the next week, Benji will just try again."

Josephine shook her head. "No, he won't."

Freyda laughed, looking back at her teammates, who chuckled and scoffed. "Oh, and why is that?"

"Because he's dead." The memory struck her rapidly, his hot blood pouring over her, his sudden collapse into complete silence and Kohlvar checking his prone body. He wasn't in the infirmary, and she doubted he would've survived losing that much blood.

The smile slipped from her face. "What? No, he was injured...wasn't he?" She whispered, deathly quiet.

Josephine stepped towards her, glaring down at her pale green eyes. "I said, he's fucking *dead*."

Josephine wasn't sure who threw the first punch, Freyda or Kaelith perhaps, but in the space of a breath they were in an outright brawl. Rage coursed through Josephine, as her vision flashed between Benji strangling her, blood spilling over her, while that same fear and indignation fueled her punches. She found herself kneeling over Freyda, driving her fist into her face over and over.

"ENOUGH!" An amplified male voice bellowed, causing many shouts of pain as his words ricocheted through their ear drums. "What in the *Souls* do you think you are doing? You are soldiers of the Elven Army. This is not how the King's men and women behave."

Josephine looked up, her fist soaked in blood, as Galathir screamed at them from the doorway. Towering behind him were Kohlvar and Torva, who both looked absolutely furious.

She released Freyda, leaving her clutching her broken face, to scan the aftermath of the fight. Kaelith's eyes were alight with adrenaline, grinning wickedly as blood oozed from his gums. Eryndal stood beside him, looking shocked but unharmed. The dragonoid stood protectively in front of Seralie, who had hidden under the banquet table, peeking out from the wooden bench. Long talons extended from his hands, but thankfully they were free of blood. Josephine did not think the elves would have survived an evisceration from the dragonoid. The cadets with Freyda all sported a variety of rising bruises and minor wounds, looking unlikely to be hiding lethal injuries.

Josephine looked down at Freyda, her nose pouring blood, her cheekbones swelling from the brutal assault she'd given. Nausea rose in her stomach as she met her pale green eyes, seeing the fear and hatred reflected in them. She rose, stumbling back from Freyda's prone form. She tried to breathe but her body screamed that she was still in danger, still about to be killed. She looked to Seralie, the fear in her soft brown eyes fueling her panic further.

Josephine felt her breaths coming quickly, verging on hyperventilation. Her eyes locked with Hirwen, who stood scowling from the kitchen. When their eyes met, her expression softened slightly, looking over her frantic actions with what felt like sympathy.

Her steady gaze focused her racing mind just enough that she could try to slow her breathing. She couldn't have a panic attack, not here, in front of these people. How had this all gotten out of control so quickly?

A hand on her shoulder had her whirling around, swinging her fist again. It grazed Kohlvar's chest as he dodged, catching her wrist and pulling her close. He placed a hand on her chest, his fingers looping over her collarbone. Calm rushed into her like a tidal wave, her heartbeat dropping so rapidly she felt dizzy.

"You need to calm down." His voice was abrasive, admonishing her. But his eyes said something else entirely. "I could hear your heart racing from across the damn room," he murmured. "Now breathe."

Josephine drew in a deep breath, relaxing at the sensation of the warm air flooding her lungs. "Oh," she gasped. "Th-thanks."

He released her, turning abruptly towards Kaelith and Eryndal. Torva had coaxed Seralie out from under the table, who was staring at the dragonoid. He was staring back, both sharing a look of mutual shock. Galathir was directing his students to leave, shooting a furious look at Josephine as he examined Freyda's face, before sending the elven woman to the healers.

Alarm jolted through Josephine. She darted forward to Torva, grabbing her forearm. Torva scowled at her, pulling her arm away pointedly.

"He's sending her to the infirmary." Words vomited out of her mouth in a panicked rush. She saw Kohlvar turn and frown at her.

"What?" Torva grunted.

Josephine pointedly breathed in before she spoke again. "Galathir is sending Freyda to the infirmary, where Persephone is lying unconscious."

Torva looked across to Galathir and the blonde woman walking away. She turned to Kohlvar, speaking rapidly in a harsh language, drawing confused looks from the entire group. Kohlvar fired back just as rapidly, the sound almost grating on Josephine's ears, before Torva turned back to her.

"Persephone is guarded, and patients cannot use their magic in the infirmary. She'll be fine."

Josephine scoffed. "That Benji guy didn't use magic to try and kill her last night, what's stopping Freyda from stealing a scalpel and cutting her throat?"

Seralie gasped in horror at her words, Torva's scowl deepened into menace. "Not that it's your concern, Josephine, but there are protection wards on the infirmary, on most healing centres, preventing the harm of patients and healers. If she tried, she would find those injuries inflicted on herself."

Josephine gave her a surprised look, ignoring the anger still written across her face. "Oh, that makes sense. Good to know."

Torva's scowl turned into a frown. "Are you saying there are no protection wards at infirmaries in the human villages?"

"Ah, well, no. The healers are often hurt by distressed patients. It's kind of a huge problem to be honest." She cut herself off before the nervous ramblings revealed too much, catching Kohlvar's eye briefly as he assessed Eryndal. "We should clean up."

Torva's brows rose. "Excuse me?"

Josephine looked at the blood and food splattered across the dining hall. "It's not fair for Hirwen to have to clean this up."

"Whilst I'm sure Hirwen would appreciate the sentiment," Kohlvar turned towards them, finished assessing the men, "she's quite particular about cleaning, cooking and, well everything really. It's best to leave it to her."

Guilt still nagged Josephine, so she threw an apologetic smile to Hirwen, who was crossly staring at them from the kitchen.

"Right, go wash your faces, then I want all of you outside in the court-yard immediately." Kohlvar sighed, shaking his head as he turned to leave, with Torva following in quiet conversation.

Josephine felt Seralie's hand gently tuck around her elbow, tugging her to the washroom. As soon as the door closed, she whirled and grabbed her. "Jo! He heard me!"

"What?"

"Draka, he heard me when I called for help."

"Who's Draka? The dragonoid, is that his name?"

"Yes, one of the elves tried to grab me and I froze, I was screaming to the animals for help. You know how I talk to the birds in the morning and Persy always thinks it weird? Well, they talk back, it's a witch thing, I think. And Draka heard me!"

Josephine reeled from the information overload. "Okay? Is that normal?"

"No!"

"Oh."

Seralie was panting, releasing Josephine to pace back and forth. "I've never heard of people communicating this way, maybe it's because of his dragon heritage? So little is known about them, let alone the dragonoids, I'll have to see if I find anything in the library."

Josephine nodded along with her. "That sounds like a good idea. We shouldn't keep Kohl waiting though."

"Oh! Yes, you're right." Sera turned away to wash her hands and face, allowing Josephine to catch her reflection in the mirror. Her left cheekbone was beginning to swell and darken; she must've taken a punch from Freyda. She hadn't even felt it. Spots of blood stuck to her chin and neck, whereas a thick layer of dark red covered the back of her fist. She shivered, taking care to clean herself thoroughly.

That was twice in less than one day she'd been wearing someone else's blood.

Chapter Fifteen

Kohlvar

"What are you going to do?" Torva grumbled, the guttural language of the dwarves rolling naturally off her tongue. "They can't keep their shit together for five damn minutes."

"We didn't start this, Benji did."

"No, but we'll sure as hell get the blame for it. Especially given he's dead, and Persephone's not."

Kohlvar groaned, pacing the small courtyard in easy quick strikes. "He pardoned her, for fucks sake. Why would he condone this if he went to the effort of pardoning her. If he wanted her dead, he would've executed her."

"Because she's an incredibly powerful young woman, both in her siren abilities and her elemental manipulation. Of course he wants her in his army." Torva replied flatly.

"She won't be alive long enough to discover her full powers at this rate." Kohlvar paused, giving Torva a thoughtful look.

"Right...let's not give up on them just yet, Kohl," Torva frowned at him, looking concerned.

He shook his head. "She can't survive unless we teach them to fight."

The tall dwarf scoffed. "There are several problems with that idea-"

"Do you have a better one?" His voice was low, irritation sneaking into his otherwise calm voice.

Torva ignored him. "One, what are you going to teach them in a day that is going to keep them alive? Two, Persephone can already defend herself, and she's still vulnerable. Three-"

"You're still going?"

She levelled a glare at him. "Three, Galathir is going to lose his mind if he finds out about this. Let alone *the King*."

"They're his soldiers, they're meant to be physically capable."

"You know as well as I do that they will see it as the hybrids training against the elves." She gave him a thin smile, resignation etched across her face.

Kohlvar let out a frustrated string of curses, resuming his pacing. "So, what's your idea?"

Torva turned towards the grand doorway, watching as the boys sheepishly approached. She reached out to Kohlvar, a small glass orb nestled into the palm of her hand.

"Train them, discretely."

Chapter Sixteen

Josephine

Josephine looked around her team gathered in the courtyard, an assortment of bruises starting to change from pink to purple on her teammates. The tension was palpable, with even Kaelith rendered silent, with his swollen cheek squishing his eye closed and his gums weeping blood.

She noticed Kohlvar and Torva in quiet conversation in the corner of the courtyard, so she forced herself to stand straighter. She should speak for the others; it wasn't their fault. If any of them should face punishment, it should be the acolytes who attacked them.

Just as she drew breath to defend them, Kohlvar broke the silence.

"It has become apparent that you all need a lesson in self-discipline. Follow me." Kohlvar turned towards the lake, his tone leaving no room for arguments. Josephine reluctantly followed, with Torva bringing up the back of the group.

Her anxiety spiked, along with her heart rate, and the urge to speak overwhelmed her. Josephine jogged to catch up to Kohlvar, his stomping footfall reverberating through the grassy fields.

"Kohlvar-"

"No," he warned, not even turning to look at her.

Josephine reached for his arm, gripping it firmly. "Please, it wasn't their fault-"

He whirled with alarming speed, batting her hand away. "I said *no*."

Josephine flinched back from him, clutching her hand to her chest. A mixture of anger and hurt flushed through her, as she stared into his furious gaze. Where was the Kohlvar who expressed concern for her wellbeing? Who thanked her for saving Persephone's life?

"Understood." She responded coldly, allowing Kohlvar to continue past her.

They reached the lake in silence, huddling together to face their two scowling leaders. Kohlvar's eyes moved to each of them, before he slipped an opaque sphere from his pocket and set it on the ground. He rested a hand upon it, his brow furrowing as a blue light emanated from his palm.

Josephine frowned, noticing her classmates wearing similar expressions. They all gasped as a wave of magic moved past them, enclosing them in a shimmering dome that refracted the bright morning sunlight.

"Right," Kohlvar began as he rose to his feet. "I'm supposed to be scolding and punishing you for fighting with your fellow acolytes. However, I'm not an idiot," his gaze flicked to Josephine, "and I'm well aware of what started the fight." His gaze moved around again, resting on Draka, the only one to meet his gaze with cold indifference.

"Instead, we will be going over basic self-defence techniques. The first line of defence should be de-escalation, if possible. However, I want you to be prepared physically should the need arise again."

Relief flooded through Josephine. He knows, of course he knows. He must have faced the same prejudice when he was a student. Still, why did he act like an ass about it in the courtyard?

"This dome is insulated for sound and will camouflage us. Anyone up there," he pointed up towards the barracks, "will see what they expect to see. Any questions before we begin?"

Eryndal raises a tentative hand, "Why do we need the dome at all?"

"Because every one of you is already a threat to the King's non-magical soldiers." Torva answered. "If they saw you training physically, as well as magically, they may feel threatened and try to eliminate you."

Startled expressions appeared across the group, hands tightening into fists and eyes going wide. Kohlvar sighed. "Thanks for that Tor." He ran a hand across his face. "Aside from the lynching, she's right. I do not want you to get in the habit of physically fighting. But you must know by now that being part of this team makes you a target."

Eryndal shot an accusatory glare at Kaelith, who grimaced back sheepishly.

Torva stepped forward, adopting a calm yet defensive stance, feet spread widely with her hands clasped in front. "Let's get you familiar with the basics, go for the weak spots: neck, knees, eyes, stomach, all are good targets."

"Can't forget a good kick to the groin." Josephine grumbled, earning a horrified glance from Eryndal. Torva nodded in reluctant acknowledgement.

"That works too, though kicking a leg up can destabilise your position and make it easier to throw you off balance. I want you to copy my actions to get yourselves familiar with the positions, should you need to defend yourself again."

She taught them to stand securely, rotating their hips with their hand movements, and how to correctly form a fist that wouldn't break your thumb. Soon, Kohlvar joined her to display defensive and offensive actions, which they mimicked in pairs. It felt a little ridiculous, given no one was actually trying to harm their partner, but the repetition of the movements felt reassuring.

"Great." Torva declared after half an hour of training. "Now you will try it out on us."

Everyone froze, with several fearful gazes looking to Kohlvar.

"We aren't going to hurt you." Kohlvar reassured. "We just want you to be able to practice without worrying about hurting your opponent."

"But..." Seralie started, before looking away. Kohlvar looked at her expectantly until she continued. "What if we do, hurt you?"

Draka grumbled, his yellow eyes narrowed. Kohlvar shot him a questioning look, before focusing on Seralie again. "You won't, and even if you manage to, we can take it."

The young woman didn't look reassured, but nodded nonetheless.

Kohlvar beckoned to her. "Step forward and tie your hair up. It's a hazard like that."

Seralie froze, looking hesitantly to Josephine. She frowned at her, unsure why she was concerned. She pulled out a spare hair ribbon, offering it to her.

The young woman winced before pulling back her hair to reveal her face.

She had an oval face, with round eyes and small lips. But most strikingly, were the tiny silver marks extending from her hairline over the outer quarter of her face. They were so faint they were near invisible, with the sunlight glinting off them strangely. Her lip trembled as she took two steps forward, stepping to the edge of the circle of engagement.

Kohlvar frowned, scanning her exposed face briefly, before slowly stepping forward, reaching out an arm as if to grab Seralie. She darted away, skirting the perimeter.

"Good, avoiding conflict is the goal here, nice evasion." He acknowledged.

Kaelith chuckled, and Josephine jabbed his shoulder with an elbow. "Don't be rude."

"Ugh, okay *mum*," he scoffed, before Torva pointed at him. He rolled his eyes and shuffled towards her.

A pang of sadness struck Josephine at his words. She returned her focus to Seralie and Kohlvar, trying to ignore the heavy weight on her chest.

Seralie kept circling away from Kohlvar, who was barely trying to catch her. Yet her breathing had become laboured, her eyes widened in fear.

Josephine frowned, looking at Torva, who was engaged in hand to hand with Kaelith. She hadn't seemed to notice the duo or her look of concern.

Kohlvar suddenly took two large steps, closing the gap between them, and reached down with both hands to grab her shoulders.

Seralie screamed.

Every head turned towards her piercing shriek of fear, as Kohlvar quickly backed away, hands raised. "Seralie? Were you just trying to distract-"

"Get off me, leave me alone, leave me alone!" Seralie screamed, her hands shielding her face as she stumbled backwards.

Shit.

Josephine started towards her, watching as Seralie collided with Kaelith.

"Woah, Sera-" Kaelith placed a hand on her arm, trying to steady her.

"Don't touch me!" Seralie screamed as she spun around, swinging her leg up into Kaelith's groin.

He let out a startled grunt as he crumbled to the ground, covering his groin protectively. Seralie backed away, hyperventilating in rapid squeaks.

"Seralie!" Josephine called out, approaching her with wide open arms. "It's okay, you're safe, I'm here. Listen to my voice. I'm here, and you are safe."

Seralie whipped towards her with dizzying speed, looking between her and Kaelith. "Oh no, what did I do?" Tear-filled eyes met hers. "I'm so sorry," she gasped, before spinning on her heel and bolting.

Josephine looked to Kaelith, Torva, then Kohlvar, all of whom looked entirely baffled. "I'll go get her."

Kohlvar reached out a hand. "Will she hurt you?"

"I doubt it. I suspect I'm not the same gender as whoever caused her to react like *that,*" Josephine gave him a pointed look.

He flinched, then nodded his consent. Josephine broke into a jog, following Seralie around the lake as she fled.

Chapter Seventeen

Josephine

Josephine quickly lost sight of Seralie as she bolted into the forest. She followed the sound of the girl's cries as she stumbled through dense vegetation, vines snapping at her ankles.

Birds chirped loudly overhead, as if protesting the intrusion. She continued, slowing as Seralie's cries grew louder. She stepped into a small clearing, barely a couple metres wide, where the young woman was curled into a ball, sobbing.

More interestingly though, were the assortment of animals gathered around her. Birds rested on low lying branches, chirping as they tilted their heads towards her. Small squirrel-like creatures gathered around her head, dropping seeds and nuts. A bulbous lizard the size of her forearm nuzzled under her legs, its large blue tongue flicking out sporadically.

Josephine stopped, marvelling at the sight before her. She knew Seralie liked to go out in the morning and connect with nature, but she hadn't realised they communicated back to her. Were they under her command? Or was this the result of a relationship built with the many creatures of the Elven forest?

"Sera?" Josephine called out softly. "Can I give you a hug?"

Her cries paused briefly, as she hiccupped loudly. "I'm okay."

"Oh honey, you are far from okay, you don't need to pretend you're fine. Do you want to talk about it?"

Seralie's eyes were glassy, her face blotchy and wet. "Is Kaelith alright? I didn't mean to hurt him!" A fresh wave of sobbing shook her slim frame.

"He'll be fine. I suspect it's not the first time he's been kicked in the nether regions."

"Why?"

Josephine shrugged. "Because he has a tendency to wind people up. I'd be surprised if Persephone hasn't at least tried to do it intentionally, let alone anyone else he's annoyed in the past."

That got a small laugh out of Seralie, before she quieted again. "Persy is much braver than I am."

Josephine nodded. "She's certainly a brave young lady, but that doesn't mean you aren't as well."

Seralie laughed bitterly. "I'm really not brave or strong. I'm just a freak running away from danger."

Josephine stepped into the clearing, conscious of the many curious eyes turned towards her. "Sometimes running from danger is the smart thing to do," she admitted, cautiously taking another step. "Will your animals try to hurt me if I get too close?"

Seralie looked around in confusion, before closing her eyes briefly. "No, you can come over. They know you're a friend."

Josephine slowly walked towards her, sitting by her back and gently patting her shoulder.

"I was never supposed to come here." Seralie whispered.

"That makes two of us. What happened?"

"A man broke into our house and tried to steal my mum. He didn't know I was there. He said he didn't want to hurt me, but he really needed the money." Her shoulders shook silently.

Josephine looked down at the frail young woman in horror. "Why was he trying to kidnap your mother?"

"Because she's a witch. She has magic and other Realms need those who can use magic." A sniffle escaped her. "It's all my fault."

"No, honey, it's not your fault," Josephine squeezed her shoulder gently.

"It is. We used to live in a village, we were protected there. She was a healer, everyone loved her. But when my magic came in…I couldn't control it." Her voice was barely a whisper. "We had to move to keep me hidden, and it might have been my magic they sensed when they found us. They just thought it was from my mum."

Josephine sighed, contemplating how best to respond. "Oh Sera, that is a heavy burden to bear. But I need you to know, she didn't regret that sacrifice."

Another squeaky sob escaped her. "How could you possibly know that?"

"Because, I am a mother too. And I know as a mother, we will do *anything* to protect our little ones. Surely, you've seen it with nature too?"

Seralie turned towards her, her puffy eyes meeting Josephine's. "You're a mum? What are you doing here? Where are your children?"

Josephine gave a tight smile. "We got separated; they're with my Aunt. This is what I have to do to get back to them."

"Why?"

"It's a long story. Besides, the point is that I know your mother would not want you to be blaming yourself for what happened."

The young woman's chin quivered as tears rolled down her cheeks. Broken-hearted sobs shook her, as Josephine pulled her tightly into her arms, rocking her gently as she let everything out.

Chapter Eighteen

Josephine

"She's okay," Josephine called out as she returned to the lake, finding Kohlvar alone.

Kohlvar ran a hand through his hair, his gaze surprisingly anxious. "You're sure?"

She nodded. "Yeah, you just reminded her of why she had to come here. We talked, she'll be alright."

He sighed. "Do I want to know? Is it like Persy's past?"

"No, a man broke into their home looking for her mother. He panicked and tried to stop her waking up her mother. You're lucky she didn't bite you. She said she took a good chunk out of him."

Kohlvar scoffed with laughter, before holding a hand over his mouth. "That's not funny. Good she's got some fight in her though. I wasn't sure she had any."

Josephine nodded. "So, are the others at lunch? I could eat."

"You haven't trained with me yet."

Josephine rolled her eyes, "Look, I'm hungry, I'm exhausted, and I have taken a self-defence class before. It seems I remembered some of it in the last 24 hours," she mused bitterly. "I'm good, let's eat."

Kohlvar raised his brows, looking at her with amusement. "No, I need to know what you're capable of. We'll make it quick."

Her lips quirked into a grimace. "Was my brutalisation of Freyda's face not enough for you?" She avoided his gaze, looking at a particularly interesting blade of grass.

He sighed. "Josie, look at me."

Reluctantly, she did. His blue eyes were deeper now, reflecting the colour of the sky.

"You were attacked, violently, mere hours ago. You could've died. I'm not surprised you reacted as you did." His blue eyes were reassuring.

"I feel like a monster." The words slipped out before Josephine could reconsider her phrasing.

He huffed. "I happen to know a bit about being a monster. You're not one, Josie, for defending your life. Not even close."

"I know that logically, but I'm feeling torn up about it all. I didn't need to hurt her that much."

Kohlvar sighed and stepped towards her. "And now that you've crossed that boundary, you'll be more aware of it in the future. But, and I cannot stress this enough Josie, you should be prepared to defend yourself at all costs."

Her mouth flooded with the sour taste of bile at the thought. This wasn't at all what she had expected when agreeing to come here.

"Come on, fight me." She could've sworn he winked at her, which was enough to coax a weary half-smile from her.

Internally swearing, Josephine sighed and stepped towards him.

Kohlvar made the same sweeping grab he tried with Seralie. Josephine made the split-second decision to dart forward and swing a knee up into his inner thigh, locking eyes with him.

Kohlvar froze, staring at her with wide eyes as his arms wrapped firmly around her shoulders. She held her knee still, brushing lightly against his inner thigh, allowing herself the tiniest smirk. "Do I need to follow through on that action?" She teased, trying to ignore the pleasing warmth radiating from his embrace.

His head tilted towards her, "Tempting...but no." He smirked at her, seemingly amused by her effort.

"What language were you speaking earlier?" Josephine blurted out as she slowly lowered her leg.

"Dwarvish, Torva taught me. It's been quite useful given that very few people in the Elven Realm speak it."

She tilted her head thoughtfully. "You swear in Dwarvish, don't you?"

He chuffed sheepishly. "How did you know?"

Her foot landed between his. "It just sounded similar to when you've been frustrated."

He chuckled, releasing her and stepping back. "Try attacking me."

Josephine rolled her eyes. "You're impossible to attack. I'm not fast like Persephone, I'm big for a girl but I've got nothing on you. I can barely manage the average human male, let alone a *literal* giant." She considered winking at the play on his heritage but thought better of it.

He shrugged nonchalantly, "Half-giant, and there are ways to bring me down."

She grumbled and scrutinised him for a moment. Eventually, she stepped forward, her arms raised to block and swung her leg up again. This time he caught her around the thigh with one hand, lingering for the briefest second before pushing her away with ease.

Josephine stumbled into a low crouch and swept her leg out towards his ankle. Her shin smashed into his tibia, and she let out a howl of frustration and pain.

Kohlvar struggled to hide his smile as he reached down to offer her a hand. She begrudgingly took it, rubbing her shin furiously as he pulled her up to stand mere centimetres from him.

Josephine threw him a mock glare, before an idea sprouted in her mind. She jabbed her right fist towards his stomach, then threw her opposite heel out to kick the inside of his knee.

He caught her fist, but not her heel. With a grunt he stumbled forward, onto Josephine, toppling them both to the ground. He managed to catch himself and avoid crushing her, however that didn't lessen her impact to the ground.

Josephine was stunned by the pain radiating through her already sore chest. She panted, trying to force air back into her lungs as they looked at each other in shock.

"Huh, that actually worked," she muttered, when she could finally breathe.

Kohlvar's eyes turned from shocked to suspicious. "How did you know to do that?"

Josephine met his steely gaze with a raised eyebrow. "Most of the men I know have started to complain about their knees. Figured yours go through a beating holding your weight up all day."

"Are you calling me *old*?" His tone implied offence, but the smirk pulling at his lips said otherwise.

"It's alright, I'm no spring chicken either." She broke out into a full grin, enjoying his bemused expression far too much.

He scoffed grumpily before pushing himself off her. "Are you hurt?" He asked as he glanced over her ribs.

"Just winded."

Kohlvar carefully stood, his weight noticeably on his uninjured knee. He offered his hand again. "Well, I'm pleasantly surprised. But don't get cocky, you're still at a disadvantage against nearly everyone here."

Josephine grunted as he pulled her upright. "Gee, thanks, you're such a gentleman."

"Just being realistic. I would prefer you to remain alive." His smile slipped away, turning serious again.

"I'm overwhelmed with your concern for me." She replied sarcastically, brushing grass off her pants.

Kohlvar rolled his eyes, a slight flush present in his cheeks. He gestured towards the dining hall. "Come on, I'm starving too."

Chapter Nineteen

Kohlvar

Josephine didn't really take him down with a kick to the knee.

It had been a good move, but Kohlvar had been distracted. The moment her hand was in his, she came flooding into his mind. Her emotions, her warmth, even her gnawing hunger. It had even happened the second time he pulled her up, despite his thorough checks of his mental shield.

Kohlvar reflected on their interactions since meeting. He's felt her emotions when he was trying to calm her down, but they'd *never* broken through his shields previously. Though admittedly, her panic attack this morning had come close to doing so. He'd been innately aware of her from across the room, her fear so palpable it mirrored his own.

He pondered this new conundrum in silence as they trekked up the steep hill. Kohlvar had only experienced such a mental invasion from one person before, and that had been intentional. Josephine didn't seem to notice what she had done. Was this a sign of her magic? He shuddered to think that Josephine could be anything like *her*.

And Souls, when she'd been lying underneath him, sprawled on the grass and panting for breath, it had taken all of his willpower to pull away. She was beautiful, with her warm brown hair splayed, wispy curls floating over the grass. Her hazel eyes shone with a golden centre he hadn't noticed before, the winter sun catching freckles on the bridge of her nose.

She was life in a way he'd never known. Perhaps to be human wasn't such a bad thing. She seemed to radiate warmth even while separated from her family, trapped in a strange foreign world.

Kohlvar glanced at her determinedly trudging up the steep slope. Her brows knitted in concentration, hair escaping her braid as it bounced across her shoulder blades. She caught his gaze and raised her eyebrows, so he looked away, feeling sheepish.

She's your student, you need to protect her. Kohlvar reminded himself, as he pushed away more inappropriate thoughts. He rarely felt this way for anyone, certainly not in a long time. Bad things happened when he got involved with a woman.

Besides, he had failed to protect her once, he would not allow it to happen again.

Chapter Twenty

Josephine

Breakfast was tense, to say the least. Everyone was jumpy, looking over their shoulders at the seething elves. They bore uniform bandages across their palms, wincing as they selected food for breakfast. But they'd only glared when Josephine met their eyes, and any sympathy that had flickered in her chest quickly died.

Kaelith started to make a rude gesture, smirking at the furious elves, but Josephine and Eryndal quickly reached for his hand.

"Don't add more fuel to the fire Kaelith," Josephine murmured as she raised a brow at him.

He shuddered. "It just makes me itch when I can feel them staring! Assholes, they got what was coming to them."

"And so did we, remember?" Josephine stared pointedly, watching his face rapidly morph between furrowed brows, wide eyes and a distinct 'O' for his mouth. She nodded, refraining from tossing an overly dramatic wink his way.

Apparently, Kaelith was not similarly restrained with his intrusive thoughts. He slowly winked, patted her hand knowingly, before turning to Eryndal to wink at him too. Eryndal merely sighed, closing his eyes briefly before devouring his food.

"Rude, you couldn't even wait for me before stuffing your faces?"

Josephine sat bolt upright, tears pricking the back of her eyes. "Persy!" She almost fell trying to extricate herself from the long communal bench. Ignoring her embarrassment, she pulled Persephone into a tight hug, burying her face into the top of her wild curly hair. She was barely taller than her daughters, despite being at least three times their age. Her heart ached for this lost child, who seemed to fight the world at every turn just to keep existing. Who was there to protect her? Because whilst she knew Persephone would loudly declare she didn't need anyone, *everyone* needed someone.

Josephine pulled back far enough to examine the young woman. Her neck was unblemished, skin returned to alabaster, her blood vessels an eerie greenish blue under her near translucent skin. Her blue eyes were duller than usual, reflecting the depth of the sea instead of the sky, but she was alive. She was also staring in shock at Josephine.

"What are you doing?" Her brows rose crookedly, confusion spreading across her features.

After visually confirming that the girl was no longer injured, Josephine pulled her back into a tight hug, feeling her stiffen, before relaxing into her embrace. She felt more arms wrap around them, becoming aware of the others gathering around.

She eventually released Persephone, sighing in relief. "I'm so glad you're okay."

"Well, I only let you hug me because you saved my life. Thanks for that, by the way." She mumbled, averting her eyes as she thanked her.

"You're welcome. Seralie helped too," Josephine nodded across the table at the young woman.

"Not really," her lips twisted wryly at the side. "I tried though." Her doe-brown eyes met Persy's sapphire blues, where they shared a look of mutual respect.

Kaelith, in his never-ending attempts to lighten the mood, stepped towards the young woman with arms spread wide. "Bring it in, Pixie!"

Without even turning to look at him, she extended a hand so swiftly into his chest he nearly fell. "Absolutely not. You weren't even there!"

"Excuse me, I defended your honour yesterday! Come on, you know you want a hug from me."

"Nope." She threw a half-pleading, half-annoyed look at Josephine, who only sighed in response.

"Sure you do. You can't resist my devilish charm." Kaelith grinned at her mockingly, waggling his eyebrows.

Persephone pointedly turned her head towards Eryndal. "And he's related to you?"

Eryndal sighed. "Apparently."

Draka's low growl jolted them out of their banter, his furious glare directed to the back corner of the dining hall. Josephine turned, realising the elves had risen out of their seats, standing mere metres from them. Her brow knitted together as she shot a challenging look at Freyda. Her fists were clenched, eyeing her with the same fury she'd let loose yesterday. Her face looked less swollen than the state Josephine had left her in yesterday, but dark bruises radiated out from her nose across her cheekbones.

Thankfully, the arrival of leadership swiftly shutdown any possible escalation into violence. Silent glares from Galathir at his acolytes had them retreating to their seats. Josephine hooked an arm around Persephone's shoulders, steering her away from them all. "Come on, you should eat some breakfast."

Chapter Twenty-One

Kohlvar

Panic had consumed Kohlvar when he arrived at the infirmary to find Persephone gone. He'd been so close to finding the young man stationed to guard her and threaten to tear him limb from limb, perhaps even making good on that threat if harm had come to her.

Mercifully, the senior physician had taken one look at his face, and told him that Persephone had been discharged, then escorted to breakfast by the soldier.

Relief had flooded through him like cold water thrown over a fire, though the flames had risen again when he saw Galathir's acolytes squaring off. He noticed the matching bandages wrapped around each acolyte's hand, triggering a memory from his initiate days. The sting of Galathir's switch was unique, coated with nettles to cause additional inflammation and pain. He had generally been fair and reserved in regard to corporal punishment, but attacking a fellow student left him little choice. Kohlvar could not even remember why he'd received the punishment, but he suspected he had never repeated the offence. It was concerning to see the acolytes had not learnt the same lesson.

Unease grew in his stomach, though in turn it validated his choice to continue training his students in secret.

"Right, Persy, time to catch up on training." Kohlvar moved into the centre of the dome, arms crossed expectantly. He pulled his mental shields in place, fortifying them to remain distraction free for this fight.

She sighed dramatically and stepped up, hands on her hips. "Give me your worst." Persephone smirked at him, before settling into a defensive position.

Kohlvar chuckled, while the rest of his acolytes shot horrified looks at each other. Persephone was barely a quarter of his size. He could probably toss someone her size into the lake ten metres away without an effort.

Kohlvar lunged at Persephone, lazily sweeping an arm out to grab her. She ducked with incredible speed, pivoting under his arm to face his back. Before he could turn, she leapt onto his back, scaling him like a tree. As her hand reached towards his face, Kohlvar grabbed it and her opposing shoulder to fling Persephone over him.

Persephone curled into a ball and rolled away, rising to a crouch and swiping her legs at Kohlvar's shins. She was realistically too small to connect and stay out of his reach, but the attempt was noted. He would have to teach her a better tactic, one more suited to her size.

Kohlvar watched carefully as she spun so fast that her hair turned into a golden blur. She tapped the back of Kohlvar's knees with her hands, taunting him. Next he knew she'd pivoted to a low lunge in front of him, leaping up and using his thighs as a launching pad for a backflip, forcing him to stagger back to avoid a kick to his chin.

They continue to move around each other, both attacking and defending, whirling in an increasing frenzy. Kohlvar felt himself grinning, enjoying the exertion of a fight worthy of both their skills.

A familiar hum resonated in his ears, increasing as they continued to dance and tag each other. It was an incredibly beautiful, yet terrifying battle of wills, as each tried to gain an advantage over the other.

In his periphery, he noticed Torva stepping closer, clearing her throat loudly. Kohlvar froze, catching Persephone mid-leap and pinning her to his side with an arm around her waist. She flailed petulantly, parallel to the ground, like an upset toddler.

"That's not what we're supposed to be teaching them Kohlvar." Torva glared, pointedly looking towards the terrified team.

Kohlvar scanned his students, "Oh, right, sorry." He set Persephone down on her feet, inclining his head towards her. "I can see how you survived on your own so long."

Persephone smirked back, "Right, I'm good. You're just alright though."

He rolled his eyes. "Go try your luck with Torva." Persephone groaned, turning to face the sturdy woman.

"Hold on, what the *fuck* was that? And why are you both turning blue?" Kaelith exclaimed. A grumble of agreement moved through the team, and he caught Josephine's bewildered expression.

Kohlvar looked down at his exposed forearms, before looking at Persephone. Both of them were emitting a slight blue hue, similar to the light radiating from the glass orb.

Eryndal gasped with understanding. "You both have heritage from the water creatures, don't you?"

"What, you're telling us they're part mermaid?" Kaelith scoffed, before cursing as Eryndal jabbed an elbow into him.

Persephone fixed him with a glare. "If by 'mermaid' you mean sirens, naiads and water sprites, then yes."

Kohlvar cleared his throat pointedly.

"What? They already know I'm part siren. It's hardly a secret." She shrugged, as if she hadn't just revealed the part of his heritage few understood.

"Wait…how?" Kaelith asks hesitantly, looking at Kohlvar. "I thought you were half-giant?"

He nodded, his face turning grim. He hated this conversation.

"But… you know… *how*?" Kaelith's hands start to gesture wildly, as if interpretive dance would make his question any less awkward.

He sighed. "I don't know the *how*, but I presume my mother was a siren or a nymph, and my father a giant."

"Wait, you never asked them?" Kohlvar watched as Josephine shoved an elbow into Kaelith's shoulder. "Why do you all keep hitting me? I'm just asking what we're all thinking!" He spun, scowling at his classmate.

"How many half-giants have you met Kaelith?" Torva called out.

Kaelith gestured at Kohlvar and Torva. "Just yourselves."

"Oh, I'm not part giant." Torva's expression remained neutral, though she shifted on her feet uncomfortably.

"What? But you're huge!" Kaelith looked her up and down in surprise.

"My mother was an elf and my father a dwarf. It appears I inherited my mother's height and my father's build." Torva responded stiffly.

Kohlvar knew she hated talking about her past, so he gave her an appreciative nod.

"The half-giants, why do you think there are so few of them?"

After a silent pause, Torva continued. "Giants favour strength above all else – women will pick the strongest males to reproduce with, which typically would be another giant. However, sometimes the smaller, weaker males will find females to mate with who are not giants."

Josephine murmured, seeming to realise before the others. "Oh no."

Torva nodded. "Those women do not survive childbirth, usually the child perishes with them. The offspring are too large for them to deliver. If the offspring do survive, and are lucky, they wind up in an orphanage."

"Lucky?" Eryndal asked, eyebrows raised.

"The alternative is death, usually by the father or other giants to eliminate the weak."

Murmurs of shock and cursing spread amongst the group. Kohlvar could feel their eyes on him, but particularly Josephine's. Despite his shields he could feel her pity and sorrow radiating towards him. He didn't need pity; his family had perished long before he could remember them. Those who had raised him were the parents he remembered, even if they did not share his blood or heritage.

"Right, this isn't a history lesson. I want you to pair up and practice what we've taught you." Kohlvar declared, nodding towards the red dragonoid to spar. Shame he didn't speak, it was making teaching him rather difficult. Ailish and Quentin, the enlisted dragonoids of the non-magical units, had warned him that this dragonoid was primitive and likely would not produce magic. However, Kohlvar had no intention of giving up hope on him; everyone deserved a chance.

Kohlvar forced himself to focus on the training, rotating through each of the students for practice. Kaelith fought clumsily, throwing wild punches that glanced off him. Eryndal was more focused, precise, yet battled with more hesitancy than Kaelith. Even Seralie, who still trembled at the sight of him, managed to practice blocking his advances and throw a tiny punch in his direction. He smiled at her proudly, hoping somehow, he would look anything but terrifying to her.

Draka nearly eviscerated him though. He shouldn't have been surprised, the young dragonoid had survived in the wild alone for years. His elongated claws had shredded the linen above his abdomen. He'd looked down in surprise as his skin bore the faintest scratches on his now grey torso.

"Shit!" Torva exclaimed, striding over to inspect him. "You good?"

"I'm fine." Kohlvar nodded at Draka. "Impressive, though I'd appreciate it if you didn't try that again during practice. That could've killed someone," he was quite certain Draka knew that already, but it wouldn't hurt to say it.

"Are you hurt?" Seralie's worried voice caught his attention, as he turned to see everyone frozen in horror.

"I'm unharmed," he reassured them, pulling the ruined shirt over his head in a smooth motion. "I didn't intend for today to become show and tell, but if you ever see a giant, or another giant hybrid, this is why you should run instead of fight."

Kohlvar took a deep breath as everyone's eyes closely inspected his mottled grey torso. He felt exposed, more than if he were simply shirtless. He rarely allowed others to see his true skin. He closed his eyes as he encouraged the stone skin to spread up and over his chest, shoulders and down across his back. He felt the familiar itching, like dry skin cracking with movement, as it crawled over his limbs. He left his face clear though, allowing the warmth of the sun to soak into his human skin.

He inhaled deeply and stretched, looking down at the armour that had saved his life on countless occasions.

"Is that stone skin?" Eryndal's voice broke through the silence.

Kohlvar nodded, "Yes, it's a common trait among the mountain giants. It's used for camouflaging, but more importantly, for protection. Like the name suggests, it's hard as stone, though it is not invincible." He looked towards Draka's elongated claws, then down at the faint white scratches over his middle.

"Is it always there?" Persy asked, her brow furrowed in thought. "How the hell do you swim?"

"No," Kohlvar shook his head. "I have to shift into this form, though sometimes it happens instinctively, like just now."

"What would've happened if you hadn't transitioned into this 'stone skin'?" Josephine's smooth voice cut through the whispered chorus of curiosity.

He met her hazel eyes, those familiar specks of gold and green glinting under the winter sun. "I would've been spending some time in the infirmary."

"Your mother must've been a freshwater siren then, right?" Eryndal's scholarly voice drew his attention.

Kohlvar frowned at him, not understanding. Eryndal continued.

"Humanoid hybrids have existed for a couple hundred years between the elves, humans and dwarves, right? But the freshwater sirens have always been able to shift into a human or elf form and walk on land. So surely that explains why you look part elf."

Kohlvar contemplated the thought. "Perhaps. Or perhaps I am part elf too, or part human. I'd never really considered it."

"Well so little is known about the hybrids, that's why I want to research them further." Excitement lit up his amber skin, his warm eyes bright with interest.

His innocent, genuine curiosity surprised Kohlvar, as warmth stirred in his chest. He was so used to others reacting negatively to him, especially when he revealed himself, that he couldn't remember the last time someone had been truly interested without fear or hate.

He exhaled a long, low breath, allowing the stone skin to dry and crack. He pulled the air around him, gently manipulating it into the cracks between the stone and his skin. Then, with a dramatic flourish, he pushed the air outward, just enough for the stone to break free and slough off his body.

Kohlvar had to admit, the sheer amazement on their faces was worth it. He didn't like to show off or draw attention, but it had been a long time since he'd used the skill.

"That's incredible!" Kaelith shouted, rushing forward to look at the discarded pieces. "Can we touch this?"

Kohlvar nodded. "I can reabsorb it, but if it's damaged or I haven't shed it in a while, then it starts to get uncomfortable, so I do that instead."

Kaelith and Eryndal crouched, holding the crumbing stone piece. "Can I keep this?" Eryndal asked. "I want to look at the mineral composition. I wonder if it bears similarities to the mountains and rocks, or perhaps it is composed more like skin. It's so crumbly, I didn't expect that."

Kohlvar hesitated, looking to Torva. She contemplated the question, a guarded look in her eyes.

"Who else would know if you analysed this, Eryn?" She asked, levelling a stern look at him.

He looked up from the grey slate, his smile fading. "Well for my initial tests, no one. I have a lot of the equipment at home, I could go for the weekend and have a closer look. For more advanced testing I would have to talk to the Professors at the Royal College, they have the best geological equipment. Did you know-"

Torva cut him off. "I think it would be best if you kept this information to yourself. Most hybrids are not fond of being researched." Her words were heavy.

His face fell, sending a pang of guilt that twisted Kohlvar's chest. "I don't mind if you do some tests yourself, Eryn. I just...maybe just keep it between us." He gestured around the group, also pointing to the dome above their heads.

"Thank you!" He pulled out a small pouch from his vest, carefully wrapping a piece of the stone skin in its folds.

"Alright, that's enough for today. You are to meet with Professor Fissius in the library after lunch. You will be with Galathir's students. Please," he paused, making sure to look each one of them in the eye, "behave."

"But-"

"Kaelith," several voices grumbled a warning in unison. Kohlvar had to hide his smile. These kids were growing on him, more so than any he'd taught before.

The lanky elf sighed, shoving his haphazard hair out of his face. "Fine, I'll try. I can't promise more than that." He held his hands up at the exasperated looks sent his way.

Kohlvar smiled to himself as he knelt, crumbling the remaining pieces of stone and spreading them across the ground, before he disengaged the dome. He watched as Torva led the acolytes up the hill, feeling that familiar flickering in his chest, the same one he'd felt when he first saw Josephine.

Hope.

Chapter Twenty-Two

Josephine

Josephine was relieved for the break from physical activity, though some of the team did not share her sentiments. Eryndal had been absolutely thrilled, rapidly firing off facts about his favourite written texts.

"Did you know that the King's personal library has several rare books that are the only ones in existence? I've heard he has one of the only written records on the early history of dragons, how they divided into different species and spread across Saltus, before they went into hibernation of course." His warm brown eyes were wide with excitement.

"We don't know if the dragons went into hibernation or died. Besides, we're not going into the King's personal library." Kaelith rebutted ostentatiously.

"I know Kaelith, but imagine! Those books would be incredible to read. What are we going to be studying today?"

"History," Seralie reminded him. Kaelith was fidgeting from side to side, full of frustrated energy. Was he still feeling the effects of adrenaline? Surely not, the fight with Freyda and her friends had been almost 24 hours ago.

"But the history of what? Will it be of the elves? The dragons? The migration of humans?" Eryndal's enthusiasm crept into his voice, his usually serious and somber tone replaced by a youthful joy.

Josephine raised a brow at his last comment but kept quiet. This charade of 'pretending to be from the Human Realm' was going to be difficult. She knew much about her world's extensive history, but little of this one.

"Do they teach Elven history in the Human Realm?" Eryndal's question caught Josephine off guard, she sputtered a response.

"Ah, um, well no, I don't think so. History isn't my strongest subject."

"I'll help you!" The genuine glee in Eryndal's eyes was adorable; Josephine missed feeling that passionately about learning.

"That would be really helpful Eryn, thank you." She gave his back a friendly pat.

"I'm sure you'll be easier to teach than Kaelith. One time, he failed alchemy twice, and Father told me I had to make sure he passed the next time. We spent so much time outdoors, Kaelith climbing up and down trees while he repeated facts with me. I wasn't sure it would work, even Father told me it was a terrible idea. But not only did he complete the course, he got exceptional marks!"

Kaelith grinned at the recount. "What can I say, the professor had the most boring voice. He was excellent at sending me to sleep. And he always made me sit still!"

"I wouldn't trust you to make a wound ointment, much less an advanced potion." Persephone snipped.

He twirled and gave her a dazzling smile. "Oh, Persy darling, how you wound me. If only you could make such an ointment as to ease my sorrows. But alas, I can't imagine you studied Elven alchemy, and thus you would not know the recipe."

Persephone scoffed. "I know how to make a healing ointment you idiot; I just didn't go to a fancy school like yours."

"Of course, so how do you make yours?" He blinked mockingly, with a smile creeping across his face.

The corner of her lip quirked upwards as she delved into a teasing performance. "Ah, but foolish Kaelith, you forget that I am half-siren, and therefore sworn to secrecy on matters of siren medicine. I imagine you'll find it quite different to your perfect little recipes though." A note of bitterness crept into Persephone's voice.

"They use aquatic plants," Eryndal added monotonously.

"Hey! That's a secret!" Persephone's attention had rapidly shifted to Eryndal, fury creasing her brow.

"I didn't say what plants, I just know that whenever one of our villagers goes to the sirens for help, they usually return with a plant." He'd recoiled defensively at her sudden redirection of anger.

Surprise registered across Persephone's face. "And that works?"

Eryndal shrugs. "Sometimes. Going to the sirens is risky, they could take you, they could make your pain worse, or they could help you heal. It's hard to know what happens due to nature taking its course or intervention."

Josephine was surprised by Eryndal's words, showing a glimpse of wisdom beyond his years. "Were there many sick villagers while you were growing up?"

Both Eryndal and Kaelith grew somber. "There was a plague many years ago. We're not sure where it came from, the humans and dwarves hadn't been to trade that year due to a similar sickness. But it was horrible, a lot of people died."

Josephine gave him a sympathetic look. "I'm sorry to hear that Eryn, that would have been difficult to witness."

She could see the raw emotion behind his eyes, unsure what he was feeling.

"Eryndal's mum and dad took in the orphaned kids, that's how I ended up getting to know this one." Kaelith nudged him with a smile.

"I'm so sorry Kaelith, I didn't realise your parents had passed."

"Oh no, they didn't! Our dads are brothers, and when my father heard what my uncle was doing, he sent me over to help. Uncle didn't want me helping though, so I mostly played with the little kids. They were so sad, so I taught them how to climb trees. Uncle wasn't too happy about that one."

"What do the humans use for healing ointments?" Eryndal asked curiously, changing the subject abruptly.

This Josephine could answer, as Susan had produced herbal medicines to help with mild illness or injury. "It depends, often we use honey, lavender, and various herbs. We also have a great plant for burns, it produces a gel that you can rub onto the skin to protect and moisturise."

"Mother taught me that the forest provides all you need, you just have to look in the right place." Seralie piped up. "There were so many varieties of mushrooms, though you had to avoid the poisonous ones. Berries too, and some flowers in the sunnier areas. Also, tree bark can be brewed into a tea, or chewed to draw out sap, but there's only a few of those trees around anymore."

"Is your mum a witch?" Kaelith bounced on the balls of his feet.

Seralie stiffened. "We're Of The Forest."

"Isn't that the same thing?"

"It means they don't like being called witches, which they are." Persephone rolled her eyes.

"Why not?" Kaelith tilted his head inquisitively towards her, eyes bright with curiosity.

Seralie shuffled uncomfortably. "Most people dislike the witches, Kaelith. Sometimes we were welcomed, and other times we were...hunted." Her final word was whispered as their fellow classmates came into view.

Horror registered across his face. "Oh... why though?"

"Because her community failed to fix our magical sources. Yet it was the sirens who were massacred and blamed," Persephone muttered as they crossed the threshold into the library.

Josephine winced as Seralie stiffened, as a low grumble vibrated from Draka. She caught Kaelith's alarmed look, shaking her head slightly to indicate he should drop the topic.

The library was grand, though far from the most impressive Josephine had ever seen. It looked functional, with staggered shelving wrapping around a central auditorium, benches built into the wooden stairs. The echoing nature of this design rendered them all silent, conscious of their voices' ability to travel in this confined space. Josephine spotted pockets of tables and corridors, winding into the shelving, though it seemed the library's primary purpose was that of a war room.

Enormous maps of the Elven Realm and Continent, several with coloured pins, lined the wall behind the epicentre of the auditorium. Professor Fissius was there, talking to Freyda, with a firm scowl of annoyance.

"I don't care that you've been in the infirmary, Miss Freyda. You have been healed, there is no reason for you to miss class."

Josephine winced as Freyda turned around, storming off in a huff and finding a seat halfway up. To the elf's credit, she still looked awful. Similarly to Persephone, she had been healed far quicker than humans or elves could recover naturally. However, it seemed she had not been completely healed. Her face still bore signs of the brutal damage she'd inflicted. Her furious eyes told Josephine that she had not forgotten the incident, and likely never would.

Josephine flexed her stiff hand cautiously. She'd been given a potion to hasten her healing, and it was almost completely healed. Her split knuckles bore soft pink lines, and her joints only offered the mildest of protests.

She didn't particularly want to relive those events, but if Freyda decided to confront her, she may not have a choice.

"Ah, the troublemakers, glad to see you join us. Find a seat on my left please."

Troublemakers?

Josephine was not the only one taken aback. Glances towards her teammates showed similar expressions of shock and offence.

"Who are you calling troublemakers? We didn't start *shit*!" Kaelith hissed, his voice amplifying painfully loud.

Josephine winced as Professor Fissius bellowed with impressive volume. "You dare to use foul language in my library? Watch your mouth Mr Abernathy! And yes, I called you troublemakers, just as I called the rest of your cohort when they arrived. Because you have all brought trouble into my peaceful domain. These fools dare to disturb the peace, MY peace, arrogant, selfish, insolent-" his voice shrunk to mutterings, as he turned away and angrily riffled through pages of work.

Josephine cast a worried glance to Kaelith, who looked surprised, but unruffled. The others were looking around, unsure.

"TAKE YOUR SEATS!" He bellowed, loud enough to make them all jump. A low growl rumbled from behind Josephine; she turned to see the red dragonoid's eyes narrowed to yellow slits, a wisp of smoke escaping his nostrils.

She felt her eyes widen as she ushered the others down the corridor, finally beckoning at the dragonoid to follow. "I don't like being yelled at either," she whispered back to him.

His growl quietened until it faded completely, his yellow eyes fixed on her until she looked away.

Josephine soon found herself seated between Seralie and Persephone, the boys flanking them. She could hear Eryndal quietly scolding Kaelith.

He'd managed to behave for approximately 3 seconds before getting into trouble. She sighed, wondering if he'd ever learn to filter his thoughts before they came out of his mouth.

Professor Fissius brushed a hand over his pale, gold-embroidered tunic, irritation fading from his face. "Given the unique nature of this year's cohort, we will be going over history from an introductory level." He levelled a glare at the groaning elves, who quickly silenced themselves. "Just because you have had prior education does not mean you know everything, so listen carefully."

He turned to a table ladened with books, his wings twitching as they caught the sunlight drifting in from the high windows. Josephine admired the way his wings refracted the sunlight into tiny rainbows, casting colours across the grey stone floor. His ears were pointed, pierced with several small, golden hoops. From one ear a matching chain hung from his point to his lobe. His short white curls ended just above his tunic, giving a strange, juxtaposed appearance. He was both young and old, elven and other.

Josephine heard a soft scratching behind her, as a hand tapped her shoulder. She turned her head just enough to see a scrap of parchment between two fingers. Watching the Professor carefully, she retrieved the note and read it under the table.

He was born an elf, offended the faeries Of The Forest, and they cursed him to look like this.

Josephine raised her brows, allowing Persephone and Seralie to peek at the note. They were both frowning. Josephine grabbed a charcoal pencil, etching two messy words in response.

Faeries, real?

Before she could hand it back, Seralie reached for the pen.

Yes. Only in the forest.

Josephine nodded, tucking the note away as the Professor faced them again. She wanted to ask what other creatures were real, but now was not the time.

"These lands have seen much change in the last two hundred years. We used to be one society, spread across the continent. There are even ancient texts detailing travels to other lands on dragonback, across treacherous waters unable to be traversed otherwise. Then, humans joined us," a sour note entered his voice. "They started appearing and spreading everywhere, claiming they came from another world, called Earth."

Josephine froze, fighting to keep her appearance neutral.

"Soon they were breeding with every race possible, and our species became husks of their former selves. Our magic ability grew weaker, to a critical point, thus our leaders decided actions needed to be taken."

Dread filled Josephine's stomach, her mouth turning bitter at his words.

"All humans and their offspring were restricted to the central region, the desert, where they could be contained. However some groups decided to be lenient on these restrictions, and they spread south, into what we now call the Human Realm. Whilst the rules have somewhat relaxed since," he turned to look directly at Josephine, "humans still are not welcome in the Elven Realm."

Josephine narrowed her eyes involuntarily. *Point fucking taken.*

"Unless they are given express permission to, or are enlisted or employed by Elven nobility." Eryndal's steady voice broke the silence.

Fissius's glare shifted over Josephine's shoulder. "That is correct, Mr Abernathy." A muscle in his face spasmed, causing him to turn and rub at his cheek. Josephine breathed a sigh of relief, making a mental note to thank Eryndal later.

"Then famine hit. The crops were dying, weather events occurred that caused some of the land to become incompatible with life. Years of drought, floods and firestorms took their toll.

"Those that survived then battled with sickness. The professors at the Royal College believe it was due to contaminated water, but some of us disagree. The filth were infiltrating again, bringing their diseases and problems with them."

Draka gave a low growl once again. Fissius didn't even spare him a glance.

"Despite the efforts of our predecessors, magic continued to falter. Our once civilised, enlightened society was reduced to peasantry. We only have the barest semblance of magic left, and we have to use it sparingly. And now, there are barely any new magic users being born. I remember teaching this room overflowing with acolytes every few months. Now there's barely a dozen of you."

Josephine looked around the large auditorium. He had a point, this building was designed to hold hundreds of students.

"And of that dozen a third of you are filthy half-breeds, not even true elves." His sneer turned to them. Now Josephine openly glared, anger coiling in her chest. "The lows we must stoop to," he sneered, shaking his head at their unusual group.

"Dick," Persephone hissed under her breath, her hands clenched into fists. Josephine reached out to cover her hand, squeezing gently. She felt Seralie reach for her other hand, mirroring her action. She squeezed back, thankful for the solidarity.

"Alas, we will only be able to confirm your potential after you complete your elixir ceremony. Then we will get a thorough understanding if the sacrifices made were worth it." He sneered up at them again, his eyes lingering on Josephine. She glared back, keeping her head held high as her mind raced. *What was an elixir ceremony?*

Scoffing, Professor Fissius heaved open an enormous book, dust flying up as its cover thudded to the table. "Today we shall cover an introduction to Elven history, starting with the division of the Elven Realm from the Dwarves and Giants."

Josephine listened intently as Fissius droned on about land negotiations between the different Realms, forcing herself to remain calm every time he released a verbal jab at her humanity. She felt so tense, she absorbed little of the information coming from his mouth. Eryndal frequently muttered, "That's not true," under his breath, telling Josephine everything she needed to know.

Professor Fissius was a bigot, one who particularly did not like humans.

Fantastic.

Chapter Twenty-Three

Josephine

After the demoralising lecture from Professor Fissius, Josephine knew that she needed to vent her frustrations. Nearly everything he'd said about humans had been blatant lies, lies that had reminded her of historic campaigns against particular groups of society in wars past. It was unjust, it was untrue and most of all, it infuriated her that a society of people so determined to be superior to humans, were behaving just like them.

She waved off the others as they left, making a beeline for the lake. The scowl crept onto her face as she stormed down the hill, forcing herself to remain silent while others could overhear her.

Josephine only slowed when her rapid pace threatened to send her tumbling down the steep hill, steadying her breathing and racing heart. She inhaled deeply, the crisp early evening breeze stinging her hot cheeks, as furious tears threatened to spill forth.

No, he does not deserve your tears.

She knew she was in a heightened emotional state with the separation from her daughters, which she was trying to keep hidden, therefore she did not have the reserves to deal with intolerant bullshit.

Her ribs were searing with pain as she reached the edge of the lake, stopping to rest her hands on her knees as she caught her breath. She let the pain distract her from her frustrated emotions as the cold air seared the inside of her lungs.

Josephine straightened, looking over the deep blue lake, reflecting the beginnings of a pastel sunset. The soft hues of lavender and pink were beginning to creep into the sky, soft wisps of clouds drifting through it. Josephine watched as a school of silver fish flitted across her view. She followed them, watching as they twisted suddenly, reacting as if they were one, dodging larger fish and vegetation.

A large dark shape appeared several metres from the edge. Josephine watched it with curiosity. Surely there were no sharks in this freshwater lake?

Her heart raced as she began to worry about crocodiles and other possible predators, as she kept a close eye on the shadow, preparing to run if necessary.

The shadow moved leisurely through the schools of fish, drifting towards the plants on the shallow lakebed near the edge.

Suddenly the shape moved towards the surface, the water exploding violently as the creature erupted from the lake.

Josephine shrieked in surprise and stumbled backwards, tripping on something hard. She felt her backside hit the ground, as she flailed for balance.

Just as she was ready to turn and run from the creature, she froze. It was no creature at all.

It was Kohlvar.

Except, it wasn't Kohlvar as she knew him. His fingers were webbed, a near translucent membrane stretching as his hands flared open in surprise. His skin was shining, covered by some sort of gel-like substance. His skin, normally a tanned almond colour, shimmered blue and green with sporadic scales across his body.

And holy Batman was it a body. He was stunning, with firm chiselled muscles covering every inch of him. He was only wearing a pair of brown boxers, which clung heavily to his sculpted thighs and privates. Josephine realised her mouth was wide open, gaping at the man, which she quickly snapped shut. She looked up at him in awe, completely stunned by his beautiful appearance.

He looked equally as shocked to see her. His hands morphed back into the familiar scarred appendages, his skin looked like it was absorbing the scales and gel lingering on his body. Soon he was back to his more humanoid self, dripping wet with pitch black curls plastered to his face.

Josephine's gaze slowly made its way back to his eyes, seeing a hint of mirth dancing in them. Embarrassed, she blurted out, "Aren't you freezing?"

His lips curled into a smile as looked down at her prone form. "Yes, but it would seem that you are sitting on my clothes."

Josephine looked down in alarm, realising she'd tripped on his boots, and was sitting on a bundle of clothing. She scrambled to her feet, scooping the clothes up to awkwardly hand to him, as she tried not to ogle the incredibly beautiful man in front of her.

"I imagine you have questions for me." His eyes were still laughing at her.

Josephine bit her lip and looked down at his arms, which mere moments ago were covered in scales and fins.

"How?" She raised a hand to touch his arm, pausing, before thinking better of it.

To her surprise, he picked up her free hand, placing it on his chest. She watched as the skin rippled, shifting between scales and skin, the cold slick texture of the scales making her jump.

"This is my siren form; I can shift into it when I'm in the water."

Josephine stared at the skin, which was starting to warm under her touch. "So can Persephone do this too?"

The light in his eyes vanished. "No. She lost her scales as a youngster, and they didn't come back."

Josephine made a sympathetic face. "Do you have gills?"

He shook his head. "Some species of siren do, but many don't. I have exceptional lungs though."

"I doubt there's anything unexceptional about you, Kohlvar," she murmured dryly, blushing as she met his gaze. He looked surprised, as he covered her hand with his.

"You're exceptional too, Josie."

She scoffed, "Not in a good way, but thanks."

He looked at her curiously, his head tilting just enough that his curls flopped free. "Why are you angry?"

Josephine finally withdrew her hand and took a deep breath. "Because Professor Fissius is an ignorant racist bastard?"

Kohlvar's brows shot up. "Walk with me."

The firm command gave her a funny tingling feeling in her stomach. Josephine nodded, attempting to avert her eyes as he dressed, noting that he did not put on his shredded shirt, before they followed the edge of the lake away from the military base.

"What happened?" He finally asked.

She let out a frustrated exhale. "The whole lecture was basically about how elves are superior to all other species, and how humans are the reason everything went to shit. He blames the humans for creating the hybrids, when Eryndal says it was due to magic gone wrong. And whilst I'm sure he's not wrong in claiming that humans screwed every species they could, that trait doesn't seem to be unique to humans, given some of the hybrids here aren't human at all. Yet they call the hybrids 'humanoids' regardless of their heritage, if they're feeling polite. Half-breed if they're not."

Kohlvar drew breath to speak, but now that Josephine had started her rant, she could not easily stop. "And for a group who are so determined to be as different to humans as possible, they are behaving exactly like them. Our world has the same issues with racism, ostracising and murdering people who are different. Don't even get me started on the many issues with religious entities and politics. My world had been slowly collapsing for years, just like your world. But instead of everyone working together to try and fix things, they tear each other apart. It just makes me so frustrated and helpless to see the same issues here. How am I supposed to find a way back home when there is just as much oppression here?"

She looked at Kohlvar questioningly, feeling her hands shake in anger. She couldn't read his emotions, he seemed conflicted. After a long pause, he spoke quietly.

"I understand how you're feeling, and your feelings are valid. You're reminding me of many things Torva has said in recent years, and I was struggling to remain optimistic. At least I was, until an incredible human woman fell through a portal."

That caused Josephine to stop her brisk pacing. "You're optimistic because of me?"

He nodded, holding eye contact with such intensity it made her stomach squirm.

"Then I think you've misplaced your hope, Kohlvar. I can't fix anything here. I could do fuck all in my world to help, it's not going to be any different here." Josephine started forward, emotions building in her chest. She felt a large hand hook under her bicep, gently tugging her to face the giant.

"Why do you say that?"

She reluctantly met his bright blue eyes. "Because the only way to create change is with power. I didn't have it in my world, and I certainly don't have it here."

"You will if you can learn to wield magic."

"Right, so you've said. How's that working out for you?" She crossed her arms defensively.

He looked away at her words. "Progress is slow Josie. 20 years ago there were only elves in the elven army. 50 years ago hybrids, other than elf and dwarf humanoids, started appearing. The reduction of magic has forced a lot of change, both good and bad."

"Well, I don't have time for slow, I need to get back to my daughters. And I certainly don't have space to deal with so many intolerant assholes!" She clenched her fists angrily. "Is it typical for there to be so many attacks and fights between hybrids and elves?"

He shook his head. "No, not at all. Usually, they tolerate each other reluctantly. But Persephone's sentencing was contentious among the Elven Court. Many disagreed with the King and called for her head."

"Why didn't he execute her? Or jail her?"

Kohlvar scratched his afternoon shadow, his fingernails grating across the stubble. "I am still trying to understand that myself. It could be that he senses her power and wishes to use it. It could be due to his fondness for his half-siren niece. Regardless, it unsettled many of his citizens."

"The King has a half-siren niece?" Josephine asked, surprised.

Kohlvar stiffened at the question. "Yes."

Josephine looked at him expectantly, but he said nothing more on the subject. He avoided her gaze as he moved past her, continuing around the lake.

Josephine followed in silence for a moment, though she'd never been good with uncomfortable silences. "Your world isn't at war, right?"

"That's correct."

"Does it feel like it's on the precipice of war to you? Because the tension here is similar to what home felt like before we finally hit World War 3."

Josephine squeaked as she smacked into Kohlvar's back. The scent of fresh water, aloe vera and bitter herbs flooded her senses. She reached out to steady herself, her hands gripping Kohlvar's bare waist. "S-sorry," she muttered, releasing him.

He turned, looking down at her solemnly. "Did it truly feel like this before your world went to war?"

Josephine gave him a sad smile. "Yes."

Kohlvar looked across the lake, sighing. "I hope it doesn't come to that."

Josephine scoffed. "It always does, it's the when that matters. How long are the lifespans for people here?"

He looked at her curiously. "It varies, but up to 200 years for some species. Why?"

"Humans tend to max out at 100 years, and that's rare. People start dying from natural causes from about 50 years old. So, it would take less time for the descendants to forget what the previous generations suffered through, and then they repeat the same mistakes."

"Your point being?"

"It may take longer for war to break out here. When was your last war?"

His eyebrows rose. "Our last war? How many wars has the human world had?"

She sighed. "More than I care to admit. Though it's different when it's a world war or a war between specific countries. We've had three world wars, and several country specific wars in the last 150 years or so?"

Kohlvar looked horrified. "That's terrible Josie, I'm so sorry."

She shrugged. "Like I said, shorter lifespans, more wars. The current one has been brewing for a long time."

Josephine felt uncomfortable with the pitying look Kohlvar was giving her, "What kind of weapons do you use here? I haven't seen any guns or heavy machinery around. Are bombs magical too?"

"The dwarves are experts at weaponry. They're our miners, smiths and masonry. They're stronger than elves, but more civilised than giants."

"Huh, sounds like our ideas of elves and dwarves are fairly accurate." Josephine mused.

"Well yes, where do you think the stories came from?"

Josephine looked at him in surprise. "What do you mean?"

"Historically the portal was able to work both ways. About 100 years ago this seems to have stopped happening. We're not entirely sure why. Humans still came through the portal until 85 years ago."

"So, you're telling me that elves and dwarves live on Earth?"

"Not anymore, but they used to visit. It was strictly regulated according to historic texts, and if they did not return, the keepers of the portal, like Valtherion, would go looking for them to bring them home. We didn't want to meddle with your world."

"Incredible. Wait, including Valtherion? He's over 100 years old?"

Kohlvar shrugged. "Closer to 150 I believe. He only started slowing down recently."

"He doesn't look a day over 50."

"I'll be sure to let him know next time I see him." Kohlvar's eyes crinkled with amusement. "He told me about his time visiting your world, it sounded very different to ours."

Josephine huffed a laugh. "Well, the world has changed significantly in the last 100 years. We don't dress at all like we used to, we have cars, electricity and healthcare. Though it seems like this world has managed to achieve similar progression with magic."

Kohlvar nodded thoughtfully.

"And we have advanced weapons," Josephine muttered bitterly. "The atomic bomb changed the world, and I believe it's part of the reason it took so long to get to World War 3. No one wanted to drop the first bomb. Because then everyone does, and there's no world left to win a war over."

Kohlvar frowned at her. "You speak of these bombs like they are a normal part of life for you."

Josephine flinched, "They are Kohl." She bit her lip and looked at the ground, trying to push away the memory of her last day on Earth.

Kohlvar's hand reached under her chin, pulling her up to face him. "I am so sorry to hear that. You shouldn't have to live through that kind of hell."

His words soothed a wound Josephine had long kept hidden, one that had been suppressed in order to survive. She didn't have the time to break down when every minute was needed to survive and attempt to give her children a vaguely normal childhood.

"Thank you," she whispered, feeling the tears well up. She didn't let them fall, though the words spilled out. "War was declared almost 4 years ago, but the world had been collapsing before that. My daughters have never known peace, and their father never returned home from deployment. He never even knew it was twins." Her voice trailed off as she closed her eyes, leaning into Kohlvar's hand. She drew a deep breath in and slowly exhaled, opening her eyes to find herself reflected in Kohlvar's eyes.

"You're a survivor, Josie."

She shook her head. "Only because I had help. It would've been near impossible to do it truly on my own."

Kohlvar smiled ruefully. "I understand, but you're still an incredible woman."

She gave a small smile in return. Kohlvar glanced overhead and swore.

"It's getting dark, we need to get you back to the dorms."

She raised her brows. "Only me? But who will protect you from the big bad darkness?"

He snorted, placing a large hand on the small of her back, guiding her back towards the steep hill. "Tell me, what are these 'atomic bombs'?"

"Oh, um, well a normal bomb for us has some kind of powder or substance that explodes when set on fire, I think. They can do a bit of damage, like flattening a few buildings if dropped from a plane. But atomic bombs, they're more on the scale of levelling an entire city. If you're lucky, you're close enough to die instantly. Otherwise, you suffer with severe burns and radiation poisoning, and if you are far enough away to avoid that, you can still end up dying from cancer or other radiation diseases. It obliterates everything for kilometres."

"What?" Kohlvar asked in an astonished tone.

Josephine stopped to look at him. "Yeah, it's pretty horrible. They dropped a few in Japan at the end of World War 2, and well, then World War 2 was over."

"When was that?"

"Um, 1945? So, 85 years ago?"

Kohlvar stopped walking again. "You're sure? 85 years ago?"

Josephine nodded, "It's 2030 in the human world, so yes."

"And were nuclear bombs ever detonated after 1945?"

"Not in war, maybe when they were testing them in the middle of nowhere." Josephine started to move, "Oh, but there was Chernobyl."

"What the hell is a Chernobyl?" Kohlvar raised his brows.

"It was a nuclear power plant, which makes nuclear energy, I think? Sorry, I'm not an expert. But they had an accident in the 80's and it completely destroyed the area, it's still radioactive and uninhabitable. Only animals live there now, and they're strange."

"Strange how?" Kohlvar pressed, as he guided her towards the hill overlooking the lake.

"Mutated, sick, though over time I think some of the wildlife is thriving. But exposure to radiation can mutate your genetics, and the water would be contaminated, so anything living in there is affected too."

"My what?"

"Ah, this is all so complicated. The traits you inherit from your parents. They can be affected by radiation from nuclear bombs or medicine. We actually use radiation to treat cancer."

Another bewildered look.

"Oh seriously, this world doesn't have cancer? Abnormal growths in the body? Tumours?"

"Oh, yes, we have something similar. But the healers can treat that with certain plants and poultices."

"Huh. You mean you don't have to almost kill the patient to kill their tumour?"

Kohlvar stopped walking, staring at her in stunned silence. Josephine sighed.

"It's pretty barbaric but we often don't have another option. Plus, a lot of the research into better cancer treatments lost funding when war broke out."

"Souls, that's...strange."

"When did the famine, natural disasters and plagues happen?" Josephine shivered as an evening breeze ruffled her hair.

"Shortly after humans stopped arriving."

"And was it before or after the eviction, and I presume extermination, of humans and their 'half-breed' offspring?"

She felt Kohlvar's hand squeeze into her back as he swore vehemently. "I'm sorry, I didn't know Fissius felt that strongly, or that he would be so..."

"So blatantly obvious in his racism?" She gave a thin smile as she finished his sentence.

"Yeah, that," Kohlvar grumbled, his blue eyes bright against the fading light. "And it happened after, likely because they got rid of the people who tended their crops."

Josephine burst out laughing, trying and failing to stem the noise. She bent over, clutching her knees, as tears poured down her face.

"Josie?" Kohlvar's worried voice only propelled her further into madness. She felt his hands gently pulling at her, bringing her into his arms, as the laughter stopped and the tears continued.

Josephine felt his warm arms wrap around her shoulders as she sobbed into Kohlvar's chest. She clung to him, embarrassment be damned, as her internal cup of emotions flooded over. "I'm sorry."

"Shh, don't be," he crooned, rubbing soothing circles over her spine. "It's fine, I should've realised this would be confronting."

"I'm just angry," she whimpered, feeling utterly pathetic.

"At Fissius? I understand. What he said was unkind. But you're not just angry, are you?"

Josephine sobbed harder in response. "God dammit, Kohl," she muttered as she wiped her face, fighting futilely against the river of tears escaping her. After a moment, she admitted in a trembling voice, "I miss my daughters."

She felt Kohlvar nod, his chin resting on her head. "I'm so sorry, Josie."

She stayed in his quiet embrace, allowing his calm presence to soothe her aching, broken heart.

Chapter Twenty-Four

Josephine

Josephine tossed and turned that evening, unable to drift off into any semblance of sleep. The familiar aches and spasms in her lower abdomen reminded her that she was due for her cycle, and undoubtedly, that was why she could not find any peace.

She threw back her bedding, frustration winning out as she laced her boots and threw a shawl over her nightgown. She tiptoed out of the room of slumbering women, looking over Persephone and Seralie as she left.

The silent moonlit halls were calm, the pale light illuminating the way without the need for a candle. She stopped briefly to look out over the lake, shimmering ethereally under the dark night sky. Josephine tried to let the sight of the deep glimmering lake bring a sense of calm, but it did little to ease her anxiety.

Soon, she was letting herself into the dining hall, sneaking towards the kitchen. It was unlocked, with a soft glow of yellow light spilling out across the dark hall.

Josephine stepped inside cautiously, looking for Hirwen. Instead, she found Kohlvar sitting at the tiny table Hirwen used to prep, chowing down on a large sandwich.

"Oh," Josephine murmured, "what are you doing here?"

Kohlvar raised an eyebrow, bemused. He finished chewing and swallowing his mouthful before answering. "I am a general, who has the authority to go wherever I please throughout this place. You are an acolyte, who does not have such privileges. And yet you ask me, what I am doing here?"

Josephine struggled to avoid rolling her eyes, settling for a simple yes in response.

Kohlvar hummed, taking another enormous bite of his sandwich. "Are you hungry?" He eventually asked.

"No, I came looking for tea, or hot chocolate if this world has it."

He scoffed. "Of course we have hot chocolate, who do you think told your world about it?"

Josephine raised her brows sceptically. "Bullshit, you don't even have coffee."

"Only because it does not grow here." Kohlvar finished his sandwich and rose, reaching into a tall cupboard to withdraw a small bar wrapped in brown paper.

"Thanks," Josephine started, but he shooed her towards the table.

"Sit, Hirwen doesn't like other people in her kitchen. It'd be better if I made it for you." He removed a small pot from a hanging hook, setting it over the stove and adding various ingredients. Josephine recognised the milk, chocolate and a small block of sugar, but she was less familiar with the herbs and spices he began adding.

"Why can't you sleep?" Kohlvar asked as he stirred the pot, which looked comically tiny beneath his hands.

Josephine fidgeted, as a particularly strong cramp made her wince. "Um, womanly issues."

She noticed he paused at that, before reaching for another container and sprinkling another ingredient in. "I see. This herb is used by some of the women to help with that, I'll explain to Hirwen that you needed some."

Relief and gratitude warmed her chest. "Thank you."

Kohlvar turned with a large mug, placing it in her hands. "Did you eat dinner?"

"Not really," she admitted, as she smelt the fragrant beverage warming her hands.

Kohlvar turned away, reaching for an assortment of bread, fruit and cheese, before setting it down in front of her. "Eat."

She picked at a grape, rolling it between her fingers. "You're bossier than normal tonight."

He sighed and rolled his eyes. "I can't have you collapsing from womanly issues or lack of food. And I'm tired," he admitted quietly as he returned to his seat.

Josephine took a moment to take in his appearance, noticing his dishevelled clothing and weary face. "You should go to bed, I won't cause any trouble here."

"Please, Josie, you are all trouble."

She leaned back, clapping a hand over her chest in mock offence. "Excuse you? How am I trouble?" She hid a smirk as she nibbled on the food, draining her hot chocolate quickly.

His bright blue eyes focused on her intently, as though he were assessing her. "Eat faster."

"So bossy," she muttered, sticking her tongue out playfully at him.

He groaned. "Definitely trouble."

Josephine met his gaze, offering him a smile. "Seriously, go, I'll be fine."

"Are you not enjoying my company?"

Hunger gnawed at her as the drink settled in her belly. "You said you're tired," she pointed out.

"I didn't say I'd be able to sleep."

Josephine gave him a sympathetic look. "I see. Man issues?"

He glared at her. "You're more sarcastic than usual."

She shrugged. "Because it's just us, I'm not too worried about being overheard at this hour."

He seemed to ponder that thought, as she finished her food. She rose, moving her items to the sink, before facing Kohlvar. "Do you want to talk about why you can't sleep?"

He had not moved from where he sat while watching over her midnight meal. "I'm worried for our team."

"Why? Persy seems to have stopped letting Kaelith get a reaction out of her. And no one has tried to hurt her, or any of us again." Josephine fidgeted with the shawl wrapped around her.

Kohlvar stared at his empty plate. "Yet something still bothers you."

Tears sprung unexpectedly to her eyes. Stupid hormones. She blinked the tears away, focusing instead on cleaning her plate and mug until they were spotless. She could feel his eyes on her, but mercifully he didn't press further.

"Can I stay with you tonight?" Josephine clutched the edge of the sink, surprised she had spoken the request aloud.

He drew in a surprised breath, hesitating. "We shouldn't."

"I can't sleep in my bed. I won't bother you, I'll take the floor, I just don't feel safe there." She felt Kohlvar's hand on her back as he came to stand by her side.

His face softened when she looked at him, his gaze flicking to her white knuckles as she gripped the bench. "You're not sleeping on the floor, you can have the bed. Come on." He gestured towards the kitchen doorway, following her out.

"I don't want to kick you out of your own bed."

He shrugged. "I wasn't sleeping anyway."

She frowned. "Why not?"

"It doesn't matter." He reached forward, pulling her hands towards him. "You're going to hurt yourself."

Josephine looked down at the large, calloused hand holding hers. He was capable of remarkable gentleness for such a large man. Her own fingers traced over his squared ones, noticing crisscrossed white scars over his knuckles and palm.

"So many scars, from fights?" She could feel callouses beneath her curious fingers as she traced the outline of his hand.

"Not all, but some. Most are just from scuffs and minor accidents."

She smiled. "I thought elves were meant to have impeccable healing."

He scoffed. "They do, but even they scar. Many remove the scars though, there's plenty of magical remedies for their vanity."

"Same in the human world, although not nearly as effective." She felt an overwhelming urge to rest her face in his hand, but she dropped his hand before she could act on the impulse.

"Come on, let's get you to bed."

Chapter Twenty-Five

Josephine

She watched as Kohlvar unlocked the door to his room, casting a quick glance at Torva's door, before ushering Josephine inside. She stepped in, her mouth falling open at the spacious quarters in front of her.

Radiant heat rolled against her exposed skin from a dimly lit fireplace, which Kohlvar immediately moved towards. A simple, yet well-made pair of armchairs sat near the fireplace, a writing desk littered with papers across from it. But the most notable feature was the enormous four-poster bed, with carved wooden frames and headboard. The bedding looked simple enough, a thick doona with a blanket folded down at the foot of the bed. Yet, in her insomniac-fueled haze, it looked like the most comfortable bed Josephine had ever seen.

The fire rumbled and popped as Kohlvar stoked the coals, adding a fresh log. Soon the room was brighter, highlighting the enormous rug covering most of the stone floor, and the dark curtains that hung from the sides of the enormous bed.

"Wow, this room is incredible." Josephine inhaled deeply as she turned, soaking in every detail.

"There are some perks to leadership," Kohlvar murmured wryly.

She felt him move up behind her, his calming presence wrapping around her as she turned to face him. The flickering light danced across his face, highlighting the thick scar wrapping around his jaw. It curled from his left ear, spreading across his cheekbone before dropping down to his neck.

She reached a hand up, tracing the marks left behind by stitches. He flinched before stilling under her touch.

"That must have been incredibly painful."

He grunted. "That's an understatement. My jaw was snapped and had to be put in place before healing started." A shudder ran through his body, as though he was remembering the pain. "Torva saved me that night."

Josephine withdrew her hand slowly. "I'm glad she did, you're lucky to have her. She's an impressive woman."

Her tone felt bitter, and she frowned. "Sorry, that didn't come out how I meant it. I'm glad you had someone by your side when you needed them."

Kohlvar looked at her in confusion, before realisation hit. "Oh, no, Torva and I aren't involved like that. Never have been. I'm not her type. We were just two hybrids who looked out for each other."

"I wasn't trying to pry-"

His hand cupped her face, thumb grazing over her blushing cheeks. "I know, but I figured I should say it." He paused. "Is that why you couldn't sleep?"

A scoff left her. "No! No, gods I wish that was why I couldn't sleep." She squeezed her eyes shut, trying to calm her racing heart with a deep breath. She was acutely aware of the gentle pressure of his fingers, warmth radiating into her sensitive skin.

"When I close my eyes, I keep seeing the night he tried to kill Persephone. I know she's safe behind a locked door, but then I worry that someone is going to try and kill me, and I just can't sleep. I'm so fucking tired but every time I close my eyes..." a hot tear dripped off her face. "I've seen many terrible things, but I can't get rid of the feeling of being covered in his blood while he-" she shuddered a breath out, clawing at her neck.

"Oh, Josie," he murmured. She felt Kohlvar pulling her into his chest. She gratefully wrapped her arms around him, allowing her tears to flow. Kohlvar was the only person she felt safe with in this place. She was so exhausted from constantly watching her back, jumping at shadows and wondering if she'd ever see her children again. How was she supposed to navigate this treacherous world when danger seemed to lurk around every corner?

She felt his hand rubbing soothing circles into her back, his other hand massaging the nape of her neck.

"I didn't realise it had gotten that bad. I'm sorry, I should have helped you sooner."

She shook her head. "You've had enough to deal with." Her voice came out muffled against his linen shirt, the coarse texture scratching her face.

Eventually, her tears dried, and the memory of sticky hot blood coating her skin ebbed away, replaced by the rise and fall of Kohlvar's steady breaths. She listened to his heart, the steady beat pounding beneath her ear. The familiar scent of bitter herbs and soap told her that he'd bathed recently. He didn't have his usual smell of leather and beeswax.

Gods was she scenting him now? Oh no, Josephine, don't do this to yourself. Don't go falling for the one guy that's being kind to you in this bizarre world.

She pulled back, disentangling herself from his warm embrace. "Sorry," she mumbled, wiping her face hastily.

"You don't ever need to apologise to me, Josie."

She looked up to see his pale blue eyes full of concern, and something else she couldn't identify. Looking was a mistake, it reignited the pull she felt between them, tugging on her aching heart.

She winced and rubbed at the spot over her heart. Was she misreading his actions as that of a caring leader? Was she simply trying to fill the void in her own heart?

Stupid, stupid fool, she chastised herself.

"Josie?"

"Mm?"

"Look at me."

With a deep breath, she did. "Yes?"

"What do you need? What can I do?" He looked really worried.

Guilt wracked her. "I'm sorry, I shouldn't have bothered you. You have so much on your plate, I will figure this out. Thank you, for the talk, and the hug, and I, um, I'll leave you to it."

His words came out with a growl as she turned to leave. "Josie. We both know you're not going to sleep if you go back to that dorm. Tell me what I can do to help."

She frowned, trying to think of something to ask that wasn't too much.

"I don't need you collapsing from exhaustion Josie, what will help you sleep?"

She rested her hand on the door. "I think I need someone to hold me. But that is completely unfair of me to ask of you, so I won't. I'll work it out." As her hand started to turn the doorknob, his hand covered hers and pulled her away.

She still had her back to him but couldn't find the words to protest.

"I will gladly hold you, Josie. Truth be told, I think I need it too."

She whirled around at that. "Why?"

His hands cupped her face again. "I've been a stubborn ass. I was trying to protect you, by denying whatever this is between us. But tonight, you've made me realise that we are both so lonely, perhaps we can help each other with that."

She smiled into his hands. "I was beginning to worry I was imagining this."

He sighed. "You didn't. But I still can't act on it. Not fully. Not in the way you deserve. But maybe, just for tonight…" Kohlvar closed his eyes as he sighed deeply.

"Maybe tonight we can make each other feel less lonely," she finished, reaching for his chest. She felt him sigh, as his hand slipped into her hair, cupping the back of her head.

"You're so beautiful, Josie," his lips were so close she could feel his warm breath on her cheek.

Josephine half squeaked in response, caught off guard by the direct compliment. He chuckled, brushing his lips over her forehead.

"Too much?" he murmured.

"Just not used to being told that." Her hands wrapped low around his waist, underneath his thick jacket. She could feel the firm rise of his muscles as she ran her hands over the small of his back. Josephine heard him sigh, as he tucked her under his chin, his stubble scratching her scalp. His free hand moved to her back, massaging his thick fingers into her stiff muscles.

Josephine groaned into his chest as his fingers dug into the stiff muscles of her lower back. She felt herself lean into him as he worked through every tension, every protesting tendon. A whimper escaped her as he moved to her tender hips, where he froze.

"Painful?"

"Just a little," she mumbled against his chest.

He proceeded with broad sweeping motions, pressing on tender spots, as Josephine melted against him. "That's amazing." She reached her hands up his spine, digging her fingers in slightly as he found another sore spot.

"We should get you to bed," she felt his lips brush her forehead again as he pulled away.

Josephine held firm, tilting her head up to look at his lips. She felt her breath catch as she contemplated kissing him, watching as his tongue moistened his lips.

"You're hurting Josie," he looked uncertain, though his eyes were on her lips too.

"It's not too bad," Josephine reassured him. "I would really like to kiss you."

Kohlvar's cheeks darkened, "I know." His eyes glinted in the low light.

Josephine smiled, "Cheeky, reading my mind?"

"Hmm, you are rather difficult to ignore right now." His face drew closer, his nose brushing hers.

She sighed, her heart pounding in her throat. "Then kiss me, Kohl."

His soft lips met hers, brushing lightly at first, his stubble tickling her chin. She smiled into his kiss, pushing herself upwards into him, arms reaching up to his shoulders. She groaned as his arm snaked around her waist, pulling her close, as his tongue ran across her bottom lip. She welcomed the motion, tilting her head back into his palm as they gently explored each other.

Suddenly he withdrew, shucking off his jacket and tossing it over a chair, before reaching for her face again. Her hands found the hem of his shirt, sliding underneath it to caress his bare skin. She felt him moan against her lips as her fingers moved over his stomach, tracing the trail of hair down his waist as he shivered.

"Fuck, Josie," He pulled back, his eyes flaring as they scanned over her nightgown. "I was supposed to help you sleep."

Josephine chuckled. "I think we got a little distracted, I don't mind." She squealed as Kohlvar swept her legs out from beneath her, carrying her towards the bed. She felt him lean down, pushing back bedding while still holding her, before gently depositing her. She laughed, looking up at the towering hunk of a man standing over her.

"It's been a long time since someone picked me up," Josephine remarked, smiling at his bemused expression. She started to shuffle to the far side, when Kohlvar leaned down, boxing her in with his hand. He planted a gentle kiss upon her lips, causing her to melt into the bed, realising just how comfortable it was. As Kohlvar pulled away, he dragged the covers back over her.

"Oh no you don't," Josephine pushed the covers down, reaching for his arm. He didn't budge, hesitation written across his face. "Don't you dare try to spend the night on the floor."

"I'm trying to be a gentleman."

Josephine bit back a laugh. "I'm flattered, but I was hoping to cuddle with you. If you want to, that is." Doubt briefly filled her stomach.

He hesitated, looking back at the rug, then at Josephine. "I do want to. I just don't want to hurt you."

"Why would you be at risk of hurting me?"

"I'm conscious that you're in discomfort, and I wouldn't want to...you know..." He drifted off awkwardly.

Josephine gasped, pretending to clutch her non-existent pearls. "Are you talking about sex, Kohlvar? What could possibly have given you that idea?" She smiled at the bewildered expression that crossed his face.

He looked completely stunned, as if his brain needed a minute to reboot. "Oh, you never fail to surprise me, Josie. So, you're not trying to...?"

"No, I'm not trying to have sex with you. Not tonight at least." She added as an afterthought, one she probably should've kept to herself.

Kohlvar's cheeks flushed pink. "Is this how humans normally talk? So blunt and direct?"

Josephine chuckled nervously, "Sometimes, if we like someone."

"Oh, so you like me now," Kohlvar smiled as he slipped beneath the covers, his warm body pressing up against hers.

"Hmm, maybe, I'm still deciding on that." Josephine grinned as she pressed her lips to his, curling her body about his, relishing the heat radiating from him. "You're so warm," she murmured as his evening stubble brushed over her cheek.

To her surprise, Kohlvar buried his face in her neck, inhaling deeply. He held her tightly, as if afraid to let her go.

"Are you alright Kohl?"

He was silent for a long moment. "I am now."

Chapter Twenty-Six

Josephine

Josephine woke to the first rays of sunshine peaking past the curtains. She peeled her eyes open, squinting until they adjusted to her dim surroundings. Her body felt stiff, though exhaustion no longer completely overwhelmed her. Yet fatigue still lingered, reminding her that a single night could not replenish the weeks of dreadful sleep she'd experienced.

Kohlvar lay beneath her, black curly hairs tickling her fingers where they escaped his linen shirt. She was sprawled across his torso, her legs intertwined with his. She stretched her arm and legs, trying not to disturb him as she sought to relieve the aching tension in her muscles.

Josephine listened to the steady rise and fall of Kohlvar's barrel chest, his heart thudding underneath her. The rhythmic beats soothed her as she drifted in and out of sleep, measuring time by the gradual brightening of the room.

Soon, the familiar cramping in her abdomen reminded her that she needed to leave the warm sanctuary of his bed. As she slowly peeled herself off Kohlvar, his arms stiffened, pulling her back towards his chest.

Josephine sighed as he nuzzled into her hair, his hot breath tickling her scalp. "Kohl, I have to get up," she mumbled against his chest.

He groaned, though his grip didn't loosen. "I don't want you to."

The raw honesty in his voice struck Josephine, her heart aching at his vulnerability. "Oh Kohl," she tilted her head up, pressing a kiss to his cheek. "I don't want to either, but I have to."

He made a noise of discontentment, releasing her reluctantly. "Are you hurting?" His voice came out husky, still laced with sleep.

"Not much, but I need supplies. And I should try to get back before the others wake." Josephine gingerly stood, stretching her body cautiously, bracing for any sudden pain.

Kohlvar rolled out of bed, an audible popping noise echoing as he stood. He grimaced as he shuffled over to her.

"Your knee?"

He nodded begrudgingly. "Don't use it against me today."

She smiled, resting a hand upon his chest. "I'll try not to," she teased, stretching up to brush a kiss over his lips.

He deepened the kiss immediately, his arms wrapping around her firmly. His fingertips dug into her nightgown, bunching the fabric over her hips. Josephine pulled away with a sigh.

"Thank you for last night. I really needed it."

Kohlvar rested his forehead against hers. "So did I."

They remained silently in each other's embrace for a few more moments, before Josephine finally pulled away. "I'll see you at training." She quickly grabbed her shawl and slipped out of his room, taking care to quietly shut the door behind her. As the lock fell into place, she sighed, stepping away into the cold hallway.

"Josephine?"

She froze in horror at the familiar voice, slowly turning to find Torva standing outside her door.

Josephine drew herself to her full height, trying to act nonchalant. "Hey, Torva, early morning for you?" her voice came out higher than usual.

Torva continued to stare at her, her eyes flicking to the door intermittently. She opened her mouth several times, seeming to struggle to find the words.

"Go back to your dorms, cadet. It's not safe to be alone in these halls." Her face was unreadable, her lips pressed into a thin line.

Josephine did not need to be told twice. She turned and almost fled to the dormitory, slipping quickly into the shared room.

Her heart pounded so loudly it was all she could hear, as she leaned against the cool wooden door. Would Torva say something to Kohlvar? Or worse, to anyone else? Would Kohlvar get in trouble, all because she couldn't keep her nightmares in check? She should go back and explain to Torva that he was just helping her, that he wasn't doing anything wrong.

She shook her head, as if that would dispel the persistent anxious thoughts racing through her mind. She just had to get through the morning, one step at a time. First step was the bathroom.

Josephine scanned the room, relieved to see sleeping figures across the dorm. Seralie slumbered soundly under a pile of blankets, her face so young and peaceful at rest. She didn't see the familiar halo of blonde curls, as she tiptoed towards the bathroom at the far end.

A dim light suddenly radiated out from the bathroom as the door swung open, revealing Persephone rubbing the sleep from her eyes. She startled, shifting into a defensive position, as Josephine's shadow fell across her. Then, the largest grin she'd ever seen on her spread across her face.

"Where did you sleep last night?" Her brows raised inquisitively, pointedly scanning her attire.

"What do you mean? I just went for a walk." Josephine met her gaze, her eyes sparkling sapphires in the early light.

Persephone winked suggestively. "Sure, a walk, is that what the old people call it?"

Josephine glared down at her. "Piss off, who are you calling old?"

The shorter woman snorted, her eyebrows wagging sarcastically. "I didn't know you had it in you. Sneaking around is a young person's game."

"If you say so. Wipe that smirk off your face, you're starting to look like Kaelith."

Her face drew to a scowl. "Rude, how about you go to the bathroom before your ancient bladder explodes?"

Josephine flipped her off as she walked past, locking the bathroom door with a quiet thud.

Chapter Twenty-Seven

Josephine

"I need a word."

Those were not the words Josephine was expecting to hear before she'd made it to breakfast. She turned reluctantly, finding an imposing Torva waiting for her.

"What's up, Tor?" Josephine asked as she tried to adopt a casual stance. What did people do with their hands when trying to act normally?

Torva remained silent, nodding to a door leading out of the corridor, away from prying eyes and ears. She took the hint and pushed it open, finding a small deck that overlooked the lake, with a marble railing enclosing it.

The door clicked shut quietly. "Firstly, it's Torva to you. Secondly, we need to talk about Kohlvar."

Josephine sighed as she met her gaze. "Look when you saw me-"

"Please, just listen." Something in her voice surprised her, her usually harsh commanding tone had softened. "I would appreciate it if you didn't tell Kohlvar about this conversation."

Josephine raised her brows in surprise. "And why should I agree to that?"

"Because I'm doing this in his best interest. The last time Kohlvar was involved with someone-"

"We're not involved-"

An exasperated grumble escaped her. "Just listen. The last time he was, it ended badly. Very badly. He doesn't let people in, and it took him a long time to recover from that *bitch*." She spat the final word out, fury flickering across her face.

"She did unforgivable things to him, and no one expected it. So, although I don't think you would ever intentionally do this, I'm asking you not to hurt him."

Josephine stared at her in silent shock.

Torva continued on. "If he reacts strangely, and you don't see a reason why, it's probably because of her. It's not my place to share the details, Souls, I shouldn't be telling you any of this. But I can see that he cares for you."

"He cares for all the acolytes though," Josephine protested.

Torva shook her head. "Not like he does for you. And it's taken him years to rebuild what she broke."

Josephine contemplated her words. "I don't plan to hurt him, Torva."

"I know. But you might anyway." Torva turned without another word, leaving her alone in the morning sun, trying to understand what had just happened.

Chapter Twenty-Eight

Kohlvar

Kohlvar stared at his breakfast with far less enthusiasm than usual. Josephine's angry outburst and eventual breakdown yesterday troubled him. Whilst he was glad she had opened up to him, it made him wonder how Fissius's words were affecting the rest of his team. Would they be similarly discouraged? Angry? Would this incite further violence between the acolytes?

They were barely restraining the two teams, even with Galathir enforcing strict punishments for the recent altercation. He also knew Galathir was receptive to the hybrids; after all, he had trained Torva and himself. Thus, he knew Galathir wasn't secretly encouraging his team's behaviour.

And then there was the other matter plaguing his every waking and sleeping moment, Josephine. He'd grown to enjoy her company, missing the moments they had travelled together, talking about everything and nothing. Sharing meals, working together to set up camp each night, she'd even worn most of his spare clothes. It had been strange, after travelling alone for months, yet Kohlvar had not tired of her company. Nor had he longed to be alone again.

Kohlvar had thought a life of solitude was his only option. Sure, he had Torva, but even they grew frustrated with each other's company during extended journeys.

Being around Josephine felt good, and it completely terrified him.

Last night had been unexpected too. He had been thinking of her when she appeared in the kitchen. He was still riding the confidence boost from her reaction to his half-bare body, especially whilst in his siren form. Most people saw his giant frame and were scared, but combined with his siren abilities in this enormous body? Common folk ran for the hills, screaming that he was a monster.

Some days he believed it too.

Kohlvar continued to mull over his thoughts in quiet contemplation, sipping at the herbal tea Hirwen had provided. He'd long stopped asking what was in the various concoctions she made him, trusting her to know what he needed. He always felt better for it, though sometimes the taste was questionable.

He watched as acolytes and soldiers mingled around the breakfast offerings; elves, dwarven hybrids and dragonoids alike. The soldiers were amiable with each other, respect seemingly earned through the course of duty. Perhaps time would mend the divide between his acolytes and Galathir's, though he doubted it.

As if summoned by the thought, Galathir strode through the door, Alfion by his side. They appeared deep in conversation, walking directly towards Kohlvar's table.

Kohlvar eyed them curiously, nodding curtly at their approach.

"Kohlvar," Galathir greeted him, his mouth set into a firm line. "The King is arriving today."

Kohlvar almost choked on his tea. "Already? I thought we weren't expecting him until the acolytes are due to graduate."

"We weren't."

He pondered the sudden change in plan, until realisation struck him. "He's coming because of Benji, isn't he?"

Galathir's jaw flexed, the only sign of his discomfort on his otherwise neutral face. "I suspect so, it was not explicitly stated though. Everyone needs to be at formation after breakfast."

Kohlvar nodded, pushing away his half-eaten food as he stood. "Thank you, Galathir, I will ensure my acolytes are ready."

He turned without another word, his spine stiff. Alfion gave him a polite nod before turning to follow.

Kohlvar's unease grew as he watched their receding forms. His team wasn't remotely ready to meet the King, or any of his entourage. Was he coming with his family? His full court?

His stomach threatened to regurgitate what little he ate as he rushed to find Torva, his mind racing with the endless disasters today could present.

Chapter Twenty-Nine

Josephine

Josephine had barely touched her breakfast when she and her fellow cadets were urgently ushered into the Great Hall by Torva. She'd overheard mutterings about the King's early arrival, and judging by the looks of the stressed staff running around, they'd had very little time to prepare.

They were dressed in their day wear; their formal uniforms still being made by the tailors. Even Galathir's students looked worried, which did nothing to alleviate the anxiety building in Josephine's chest.

Torva fervently gestured at them, organising them into a close formation. Josephine found herself in the middle with Seralie, Draka and Persephone behind her. Kaelith and Eryndal stood proudly at the front, their backs ramrod straight. Kaelith seemed to be visibly suppressing a stim, squirming like he itched.

Torva stood beside Kaelith, eyeing them warily. Where was Kohlvar? Surely he would be here, Josephine did not want to imagine the consequences for failing to appear.

She caught Galathir's eye as he scanned their entourage, worry creased into his weathered face. Even the elven cadets looked anxious, despite their attempts for neutral expressions.

Seralie held her hand in a death grip, trembling noticeably, so Josephine squeezed back slightly, hoping to reassure her.

Others filed in, she recognised the two dragonoids who had escorted Draka on his first day. Hirwen and a young elf dusted with flour slowly trundled in, standing with the other staff.

The hair on the back of her neck prickled, sending shivers down her spine. Josephine turned, breathing out a sigh of relief as Kohlvar strode through an exterior door. He wore his enormous coat over his linen shirt and tan trousers. His boots echoed loudly, causing several people to jump and turn. His eyes landed on Josephine, relief seeming to flow over his face, before scanning their team. He nodded at Torva as he stood in front of them, turning to face the corridor forming between the groups of soldiers and staff.

Torva turned, leaning down slightly. "Remember, do not speak unless spoken to, do not stare or look directly at the King and above all, do not do anything that could be mistaken for disrespect. You are his soldiers, act like it."

Josephine felt Seralie's grip tighten again. She met Torva's gaze, giving a solemn nod of understanding, before fixing her eyes on the opposite wall.

After what felt like an eternity of painful tension, Josephine heard the giant doors marking the entrance of the hall swing open. She resisted the urge to look as her hand began to ache from Seralie's increasing pressure.

She shifted her gaze across the backs of the four people in front of her. She noticed Torva stood proudly, her chin held high. Kaelith and Eryndal both fidgeted, nervous energy radiating from them. When her eyes moved up to Kohlvar, she almost frowned. He seemed oddly stiff, like he was held upright by a rod in his spine. His hands were clenched together behind his back, his head bowed.

Heavy boots strode across the floor, moving swiftly towards them. Out of the corner of her eye, Josephine could see a cluster of tall slender individuals, dressed in shades of black and brown. The man leading the group strode forward, coming to a stop in front of Galathir. He bowed low at their attention.

"I hear you've been having trouble with your students, Galathir."

"Your Majesty, yes, unfortunately we have." He acknowledged, remaining bent over.

"It was a shame to hear you lost one. What was his name?"

"Benji, sir."

"Ah yes, son of Samuel. Shame. You may rise."

Galathir did, looking up at the tall man. Josephine flicked a glance at Galathir, but still avoided looking directly at the elf she presumed to be the King.

"We were not expecting to be graced with your presence so soon, Your Majesty. Is all well?"

"Of course, we were simply curious to learn why two of my most experienced soldiers could not control a group of teenagers." His voice deepened to a snarl, carrying throughout the room like a cold gust of wind. Josephine tensed, the room so silent you'd hear a pin drop. Her hand was being crushed, so much so it was beginning to turn numb.

Galathir bowed again. "Your Majesty, I must beg for your forgiveness. It was a grave oversight on my behalf, and I can assure you, I have rectified it. The acolytes have been disciplined and will not step out of line again."

Chills shuddered down Josephine's back as the King's voice dropped so low she could barely hear him. "Well should they forget their place, I'm sure my niece will gladly remind them of it."

Heavy footsteps continued towards them, as the group moved forward. Josephine felt her breathing quicken as the King stepped into her line of sight. He was tall, though not significantly more than most of the elves, certainly not anywhere near Kohlvar's height. His raven hair fell in waves to his shoulders, brushing his black jacket. His eyes were a pale green with tanned brown skin. A streak of grey sat just above his pointed ears, which were decorated with small golden hoops. His expression looked like a cross between a scowl and disgust, as he scanned their small cohort. Josephine dropped her gaze as his eyes rolled over her, sending a wave of icy terror through her. She had no idea what this man was capable of, but she had no doubt he was powerful.

"You've hidden away your most interesting acolyte, Kohlvar," he sneered. "Bring her forward."

Josephine frowned, looking towards Torva's back for guidance. She gave a tiny, almost imperceptible shake of her head.

She turned back just in time to see Kohlvar turning, parting Kaelith and Eryndal to step towards her. Nauseating fear lodged in her gut as she locked eyes with Kohl. Worry creased his sun kissed face, as he reached out a hand.

"Persephone, step forward," he murmured, releasing her gaze as his lowered to the young blonde woman.

The split-second of relief was ablated by a new wave of fear. Would she be punished for Benji's death? Surely, they were past this, it had been dealt with already!

Kohlvar led her to the front of their team, his hand resting on her shoulder. "Your Majesty, I-"

He waved Kohlvar off, kneeling to make eye contact with Persephone. His inspection made Josephine squirm, even though she was not the object of it. Yet Persephone, bless her, held still, maintaining direct eye contact with the King.

"Fascinating. Both sired from sirens and elves, yet so different." His gaze turned condescending. "Was it your mother or your father who was the siren?"

Persephone visibly stiffened, remaining silent.

"She does not know, your Majesty." Kohlvar replied, his voice low and calm.

"Hm, of course," the King rose, turning to face his entourage. "Vessara, you must come and see."

Josephine cast her eyes towards the small cluster, noticing a female elf break away and stride towards them. She looked like the physical manifestation of ice, her eyes the palest blue, her skin so pale it was near translucent. White silvery hair pulled back from her face in a single long braid, ending near her hips. Her features were delicate, yet sharp, with a pointed nose and sly pale lips. If it weren't for the malicious sneer on her face, Josephine would've queried if she were dead.

When she locked eyes with Persephone, she laughed. "Seriously?" She looked back at the King for confirmation. "That is what killed Samuel?"

"And his son, Benji."

She tutted. "What a naughty little thing," she crouched down just like the King had, inspecting her closely. She jerked a hand out towards Persephone's face, as chaos erupted.

Kohlvar yanked Persephone back as she *hissed* at the Princess, her needle-like siren teeth projecting from her mouth. The Princess recoiled, furious, her mouth slammed shut. Her jaw twitched, lips spasming as her hands flew to her mouth. Torva stepped in front of Persephone, shielding her from view.

"With all due respect, Your Majesty, there are far too few magic users to risk experimentation before their powers have developed. We could risk damaging their abilities." Torva remained at her full height, looking the King directly in the eye.

Josephine watched as the King laughed humourlessly. "You are lucky I am in a generous mood today, Celindra." Torva stiffened at his response.

"Introduce me to the rest of your acolytes." The King commanded Kohlvar.

Kohlvar nodded stiffly, hand still on Persephone's shoulder. He pulled her aside, introducing Kaelith and Eryndal first. The King looked bored. He moved onto Seralie, stating she was from a remote Elven village in the south. "This is Josephine, she's also from the south. Finally, we have-"

"Where in the south?" Caladorn interrupted. Josephine stared resolutely at Eryndal's back, yet she could feel the King's stare on her.

"I found her in-"

"I did not ask where you found her, I asked where she is from, Kohlvar!" The King snarled, his voice quickly turning to anger again.

"From the Human Realm, your Majesty." Kohlvar relented, stiff as a board.

A prickling sensation ran up her spine again. "As I thought," he sneered with disgust. "Why have you brought such *filth* into my army?"

"An experiment." Kohlvar stated simply. Josephine fought to keep her face neutral, as if she couldn't hear them talking about her.

The King scoffed. "Well, she certainly will be one way or another. How's your dragonoid coming along? I hear he is rather primitive." He made no effort to lower his voice, carrying clearly across the hall.

"Slowly, your Majesty."

A heavy sigh reached Josephine's ears. "I expected so much more from you, Kohlvar."

Josephine winced at the disappointment in the Kings' voice.

"My apologies, your Majesty." Kohlvar inclined his head solemnly.

The King's sharp footsteps continued past, leaving them alone with the deathly pale elf. She stepped closer to Kohlvar, her gaze roaming over his body with an intensity that made Josephine uncomfortable.

"It's been a long time, Kohlvar. Nice to see you again."

Josephine frowned, watching the interaction warily. She noticed Kohlvar's hands, clasped behind his back, squeezing into tight fists. "Your Highness," he responded, keeping his head bowed.

A small smile spread across her pale lips. "Look at me," she commanded, sounding just like King Caladorn.

Josephine watched as Kohlvar slowly tilted his head up to meet her gaze. "Vessara."

Her wicked grin widened as she tilted her head. "Kohlvar."

Torva stepped closer to Kohlvar, blocking Josephine's line of sight. "Hello, Vessara."

The elf scoffed, "I can't believe you're still here. And it's Your Highness, *Celindra.*"

"You know that is not my name."

"It's on your birth record, I was only using your proper name," her voice came out mockingly coy.

"So is Torva, I have every right to go by the name given to me by my father."

The Princess scoffed. "Well, regardless, I'll be seeing you both very soon."

Josephine jumped when Kohlvar quickly stepped back, dodging Vessara's pale outstretched arm. She only laughed, trailing after the King leisurely.

Torva glanced at him, then turned to face the acolytes. "Queen Sylvara is approaching, with Nareth and Eloriel, the King's children."

Josephine turned to the trio approaching ahead of the rest of the entourage. Her jaw immediately dropped as she took in their appearance.

Queen Sylvara was the spitting image of Sienna.

Dizziness hit Josephine so violently she stumbled, reaching for Seralie's shoulder to steady herself. She took a deep gasping breath, trying desperately to regain control. Both Kohlvar and Torva looked back at her in alarm, but she could not tear her eyes away from the Queen.

Her long auburn hair rippled over her back and chest, partially tied back in a soft braid. Her skin was pale, as was common for redheads, with a smattering of brown freckles concentrated over her nose and cheeks. A thin circlet of silver rested atop her head; her body dressed in travelling clothes. Those clothes were far more beautiful than Josephine had ever owned, but clearly not her fanciest attire. Her warm brown eyes roamed the room, a small, elegant smile gracing her lips.

This was cruel. Aside from the pointed ears and elven clothing, this woman could've been Sienna. Those kind brown eyes landed on her, and she couldn't breathe. All she could see was Sienna, her eyes wide open, blood spilling down the stairs, her body broken.

The Queen stopped suddenly, turning her whole body towards Josephine. She trembled, unable to do anything but stare.

"Move," the Queen's quiet voice commanded, causing Torva and Kohlvar to leap apart, pulling Kaelith and Eryndal with them.

Josephine felt herself start to hyperventilate as this version of Sienna walked towards her, arm outstretched. She winced, anticipating pain, but the Queen only rested a hand upon her arm.

The woman gasped, staring in horror at Josephine. "When did you see this?"

Her words broke the trance Josephine had found herself in. For her eerily similar appearance, this woman sounded nothing like Sienna.

"I'm sorry?" Josephine croaked out.

"Your vision. When did you see it?" Her hand gripped her

"It happened over a month ago," Josephine whispered, unsure how to otherwise answer her.

The Queen nodded once. "Thank you," she turned and quickly returned to her two children.

Josephine felt her already broken heart shatter at the sight of her children. The boy, a mirror image of his father, seemed to be a typically sullen and aloof preteen. But the daughter, not only was she a radiant little girl with bright strawberry blonde hair. She was around the same age as Josephine's daughters.

She felt the Queens' gaze on her, yet she could not stop staring at the little girl. Tears welled up in her eyes as they briskly walked through the rest of the hall, Sylvara ushering them urgently away.

She could feel the questioning stares from everyone around her, but she could not bear to look at them. She closed her eyes and focused on breathing, using every iota of willpower and strength to stop herself from collapsing.

Chapter Thirty

Josephine

No one asked what happened with the Queen, and Josephine did not volunteer the information. She just had to get through the day, as was her mantra whenever life decided to throw a new hurdle at her.

They'd all been remarkably silent as they were dismissed, seemingly expected to go about their day as if nothing had changed. Yet all Josephine could feel was anxiety at the dozens of unknown questions occupying her mind.

Josephine circled around Seralie, allowing her to practice the attacks and defenses Torva had instructed them in. She was glad for the physical distraction, while she attempted to shift out of her spiraling mind. It seemed to be similarly cathartic for the entire team, murmured conversations starting up between them after a while. Kohlvar appeared engrossed in training Draka, Eryndal and Kaelith wrestled boyishly, while Torva sparred with Persephone.

"Do you think we'll ever fight like that?" Sera's voice sounded worried.

Josephine turned to the young woman, the sun highlighting amber flecks hidden in her eyes. "Do you want to fight like that?"

She bit her lip contemplatively. "No, I don't think I'm suited to it. But I want to be able to defend myself."

Josephine smiled sadly at her. "I understand, that is a common feeling among many women I know." She exhaled sharply as the image of Sienna jumped to the front of her mind. She staggered backwards, losing her balance on a slick patch of grass.

Josephine felt the world pivot as she hit the ground with a sudden *oof* exhaling from her lungs. She winced, blinking to clear away the shock of hitting the ground, as the sun blinded her now horizontal form.

"I'm so sorry!" came Seralie's cry, "I thought you were ready, did I hurt you?"

Josephine pushed herself to her elbows, her clothes askew. Her necklace had swung wildly, the tags hanging over the back of her shoulder. "I tripped, that wasn't your fault. I'm fine, just give me a second."

She heard Seralie gasp. "Your stomach, did I do that?"

Alarm shot through Josephine's chest, as she looked down at her torso for any signs of injury.

She was unharmed, but embarrassingly, her shirt had ridden up with the fall, exposing her soft stomach, riddled with thick pink stretch marks.

Josephine quickly tugged down her shirt, hiding her ring underneath the collar again. "I'm not hurt, Seralie."

"What were those then? Scars? Did a giant cat attack you?" Her voice was growing shrill, garnering the full attention of their team.

Josephine drew in a breath and rolled to a crouch, straightening to her full height. She ignored the grating pop of her kneecap, as she smoothed her hands over her clothes and body.

"They're stretch marks, Seralie. They're very common for humans."

Surprise crossed her face. "Oh, well, I know what stretch marks are, even elves get them, but they usually magic them away. But I've never seen stretch marks like...that."

The emphasis on her final word drew a hint of annoyance into Josephine's voice. "Thanks, Seralie."

Seralie paled and raised her hands defensively. "Oh, sorry, I didn't mean to be rude, I just had never seen marks that extensive-"

"So you keep saying." She responded dryly, crossing her arms defensively.

"But you must have gone through something crazy for that to happen. Is that something that happens to every human? Is it from your *children*?" She whispered the last word, looking around at their teammates.

Josephine loosened her arms slightly, realising that Seralie was just being curious, and didn't mean to strike her insecurities.

"It was from pregnancy, but not everyone gets them. Come on, put your arms back up." She ignored the stares burning into the back of her head, focusing entirely on blocking Seralie's punches and evading the swing of her leg towards her knees.

Seralie shot at least three more apologetic glances her way throughout the afternoon, even though Josephine had been the one to trip over her own feet. She just needed to keep focused. If she continued to have traumatic memories surface at random, she'd be vulnerable. But even Josephine knew that there would be little she could do to control her response to trauma, especially in this uncertain world.

Eventually, Josephine swapped to spar with Eryndal, bemused at his disgruntlement over the flecks of dirt left on his clothes from Kaelith tackling him. She rotated to Persephone next, who took great pleasure in teasing her with knowing looks, distracting her as she left little bruises and scrapes on her limbs. Her sparring with Kaelith was so awkward they managed to fall in a heap trying to pull off a holding manoeuvre, hysterically laughing as they laid tangled in the dirt.

Torva effortlessly deflected her attacks, sending her scampering backwards on the defensive with alarming ease. Josephine pushed aside the ugly thought that it was intentional, as she rose from the ground again.

Just as Josephine would've rotated to Kohlvar, Torva called their training session to an end for lunch. She couldn't help but feel the sickening sensation of disappointment in her gut.

"You know the drill, you've got history with Professor Fissius this afternoon." Torva reminded them, ignoring the groans and grumbles.

Kohlvar cleared his throat, scanning them thoughtfully. "Tomorrow we're going to test your magical abilities. You're ready."

Josephine absolutely did not feel ready, but there was only so long they could dance around the real reason they were all here. As she turned to walk away, Josephine pondered whether the King's arrival had expedited their magical training.

"Josephine, stay back please."

She cringed, shoulders dropping in defeat. She ignored the sympathetic glances from Seralie and Eryndal, waiting until the others had moved out of earshot to turn and face them.

Kohlvar looked worried, his arms crossed loosely. Conversely, Torva looked furious, heat radiating off her in pulsing waves.

"What did you say to the Queen?"

Josephine winced at her palpable anger. "You were there," she answered warily.

Torva stepped forward, her fists clenched. "Yes, I was there, but I need to know what she meant by your vision. What did you do, Josephine?"

"Bloody hell why are you having a go at me?" Josephine snapped as she stepped back, glaring at the imposing woman.

Kohlvar reached out a hand to the advancing Torva. "She doesn't know, Tor."

"Everyone knows!"

"Not Josie, she's not from here."

Torva scowled, turning away to pace, cursing under her breath.

"What don't I know?" Josephine shifted her attention to Kohlvar, watching as the sunlight glanced off the scar defining his face.

"The Queen was a student from the Order who used to commune with the Eternal Souls, before the King selected her to be his wife."

"Selected her?" Disgust crinkled her nose.

Kohlvar waved her response aside. "The Ascended used to be experts when it came to the Souls. However a sickness afflicted their ranks, and their numbers have significantly reduced since then."

"Okay...so they are a religious organisation? What's that got to do with me?" Josephine's gaze flicked between Kohlvar and Torva.

"The Ascended were said to speak directly of the Souls' desires, see through his eyes and carry out his word."

"Yup, that sounds like religion." Josephine muttered to herself.

"They were revered on a similar level to Kings and placed on their councils to advise on important matters."

"Right..."

Torva snarled, causing both of them to look at her in alarm. "For Soul's sake Josephine! What was the vision? She saw something from you, and we need to know what it was!"

Josephine raised her hands slowly, the cogs in her brain firing rapidly. "She saw my best friend when I found her dead."

Now it was Kohlvar and Torva's turn to look at her in bewilderment. "And?"

"And...she may have looked remarkably similar to the Queen." Josephine's voice trembled as the images flashed across her mind again.

Torva and Kohlvar cursed in unison. "So, the queen saw a vision of her death."

"No," Josephine corrected tentatively. "She saw my memory. It wasn't a psychic vision or anything like that."

"Are you sure?" Torva asked abruptly. "Could this memory have been a vision you've had previously?"

Josephine stared at her in disbelief, answering her coldly. "I think I'd know the difference between a nightmare and watching my best friend bleed out in real life."

Torva's face slackened, her radiant heat dimming as she leaned back in surprise.

Josephine gritted her teeth, fighting the bile that had risen in her throat "Well, if that's all..." she muttered coldly, feeling the familiar ache in her chest that threatened to consume her.

Torva waved dismissively. Kohlvar held her gaze, concern etched across his face. Josephine pressed her lips together, trying to hold herself together under his perceptive eyes, that bore into her back as she walked away.

"Don't tell anyone else what happened, Josephine." Torva called after her, as she walked away.

"Who would I even tell?" She mumbled, staring forlornly at the ground beneath her feet as she left them behind.

Chapter Thirty-One

Josephine

"Magic is a fickle beast, and today we're going to see if any of you can connect with it." Kohlvar boomed as he paced in front of his squad.

"Several of you can perform tricks from the residual magic that is all around us, but the goal of today is to connect with the source directly, rather than pulling a piece of it to play with."

How the hell was she supposed to do that? She couldn't feel or use magic at all.

"Everyone connects with magic differently. Some of us need an environmental connection: the lake, or the forest, and the sky are available to you. Others can feel the pulse of magic as if it is a part of themselves, only needing to open up to connect."

Josephine looked around quickly, half-expecting the cadets to start laughing. Instead, they were all very seriously focused on Kohlvar, taking in every word.

"I want you to pair up, for safety, and one at a time," he strongly emphasised those words, "try to feel the magic. You don't have to reach out, don't force the connection. But if it feels right, you can open yourself up to it. Just please be careful."

He made it sound so damn simple.

Josephine looked at Seralie, who nodded, and together they moved towards a grassy spot, overlooking the lake.

"So, any idea what we're supposed to do? Can you perform those tricks?"

Seralie shrugged. "Kind of? It mostly happens by accident. But my mother has told me a lot about feeling the magic." She elegantly descended into a cross-legged position, closing her eyes as she inhaled deeply.

"She said magic was part of the earth; that its vibrations were essential to all of nature. That without magic, nature would fail."

"Interesting. I'm pretty sure we don't have magic in the human Realm." Josephine knew it was a stretch to speak of the Realm she did not come from, but given Fissius's repeated sentiments on the talentless humans, she felt it was a safe gamble.

"Really? And nature is not suffering?"

Josephine winced. "Well...that's a more complicated issue. Humans might have contributed to natures' suffering, and now everything is unbalanced."

Seralie contemplated her words for a moment, before gently placing her hands on the ground. Josephine watched intently as she murmured a low foreign chant, her long black hair fluttering in the gentle breeze.

A strange hum reverberated from the ground, as if the earth was responding. Blades of green grass rose and twisted around her slender fingers, embracing her.

Josephine felt her mouth fall open. "That's incredible!"

Seralie smiled warmly. "I've always felt a strong connection to the earth, and this source is strong. You should try it!"

"You know humans rarely have a connection to magic, Sera." Josephine murmured.

Regardless of her doubts, she placed her own hand on the ground, trying to make the same connection. She felt absolutely nothing, and her anxiety immediately started to spike. She closed her eyes and drew in a deep breath, listening to the chirping of distant birds, feeling the rustle of the breeze tickling her face.

At first, it didn't feel like anything out of the ordinary. A pleasant, soothing vibration resonated through her, subtle enough she almost missed it. She felt a warm sensation spreading up her arms and through her chest. But just as quickly, the sensation left her, leaving her alone in a cold darkness.

Josephine had never been one to fear the dark, ordinarily she found it peaceful. She breathed deeply, willing her eyes to adjust to any minutiae of light, or detail, in this seemingly endless night within her mind.

Was this what people saw when they died? Josephine only remembered darkness from her brushes with death, no glowing entity or friendly animal to guide her to the afterlife.

She wouldn't mind a friend though. It felt lonely here, though she was no stranger to the feeling.

A wisp of cloudy smoke trailed into her vision. She followed it with her eyes, watching it rise and fall, like a ribbon in the wind. Just as she reached up to brush it, a voice echoed inside her head.

"What are you?"

Josephine frowned. The voice was strange, like an amalgamation of many voices, all echoing over each other. The sound bounced painfully in her head.

Unsure how to respond, she reflected on her life back home. Her daughters, her aunt, her little house just outside the city. Her late husband, her friends and family who had perished. She remembered the sunny days walking along the esplanade, before the bombs fell and turned the world grey.

She was too many things to describe with words, so she tried to show this being with her memories.

Grief and loneliness weighed heavily on her, as she pictured her daughters. All she wanted was for them to be safe and happy, for the damned war to end. She didn't want to fight, but she had to, for everyone's sake.

She returned her gaze to the wisps, willing the voice she'd heard to understand. The movement slowed, reaching down to swirl around her arms, her torso and legs. It felt like it was examining her. Was it looking for flaws, cracks? It would find plenty, as the elves loved to remind her.

The smoky tendrils withdrew, spiralling into a large humanoid figure, with vacant space where their eyes should be.

"You are human." The ricocheting voices boomed through her head. "You are from her."

"Her?"

"Where is she?" The voices ricocheted painfully around her skull. Josephine clapped her hands over her ears instinctively. But it did nothing to lessen the deafening roar of his question.

"I...don't...know," Josephine gasped, trying to fight the agony in her mind.

His scream echoed so violently that Josephine felt herself screaming too. Pain, endless pain surrounded him in the darkness. She could feel his heart breaking, just like hers had when her husband died. Just like when she realised she might never see her daughters again. She could drown in this much agony, never finding peace or light ever again. Everything good in the world was being destroyed, was there even any point in continuing?

It just hurt too much to keep on living. She felt herself begin to fall, as the darkness closed in on her, swallowing her whole.

A hand on her shoulder startled her out of the trance, and Josephine opened her eyes to find the grass under her knees now brown and curled.

She looked around to see she sat in a circle of dead or dying vegetation, with Seralie, Torva and Kohlvar standing at the edge of it. Kohlvar's heavy hand rested on her, shaking gently.

"What happened?" Josephine asked, bewildered.

Kohlvar and Torva exchanged glances. "I have absolutely no idea," she murmured, leaning down to touch the ground.

"Josephine, don't attempt that again. Not until we can figure out why that happened." Kohlvar paced around the circle, examining it thoroughly.

"He's in pain," she whispered, staring at the brown stalks beneath her fingers. "He's angry, sad, and so incredibly lonely."

Kohlvar knelt, meeting her lowered gaze with difficulty. "Who, Josie?"

She sighed, shaking her head, unsure how to explain.

"She connected with an Eternal Soul." Seralie gasped behind her. "She connected with *him*."

Josephine stared into Kohlvar's face, noticing the concern in his gaze. His mouth opened to respond, a frown creasing his weathered face.

"Kohl, we've got company." Torva interjected.

Kohlvar reached for Josephine, swiftly pulling her out of the brown sphere with his arm wrapped tightly around her waist. "Burn it, Tor."

"What, why-" Josephine flinched as heat singed her ears and neck. She turned to look as Kohlvar pushed her behind him, shielding her from the flames.

With a loud hiss, the heat died as quickly as it rose. Josephine peaked around his massive frame to see Kohlvar extinguishing the flames with a stream of water from his hand.

"What seems to be happening here?" Galathir swiftly moved into the once grassy grove, stopping to frown at the scene before him. "I heard screaming."

Kohlvar straightened as the water ceased. "Just an overly enthusiastic response to earth wielding. Nothing Torva and I can't handle."

Galathir eyed him warily. "Right. Well, I hope you two know what you're doing." His gaze met Josephine's, scanning her face suspiciously. Josephine glared defiantly back, feeling Kohlvar stiffen.

"Thank you, Galathir, we do." Kohlvar clipped, his dismissal unmistakable.

He looked between the four of them sternly for a beat, turning on his heel and vanishing into the trees.

Kohlvar turned to face her, his hands firmly gripping her elbows. "We will discuss this later, in the library. Do not try that again." His voice was quiet, gravely serious.

Josephine stared blankly at him, shaken to her core. The visceral pain she'd felt, pain she knew was not her own, had rattled her.

"Josie." The sound of her own name brought her out of her reverie, making her aware of her rapid breathing. "Josie, hey, look at me."

His crystal blue eyes anchored her, his giant hands braced lightly on her shoulders. She focused on the pressure, on the calming influence resonating from him, allowing her breathing to deepen.

"I'm okay," she murmured, her eyes drooping as exhaustion slammed into her.

Kohlvar appeared unconvinced, his mouth tight with worry. "Seralie, could you take Josephine to the dining hall and ask Hirwen to make her a cup of tea. She'll understand."

Seralie wrapped an arm around her, her floral scent washing over her. "I can do that. When should we meet you in the library?"

Kohlvar raised a brow. "We?"

"Yes, we. I'm more useful than you know." She straightened slightly, her head held high.

Josephine half-smiled, enjoying seeing Seralie develop a stronger spine. Kohlvar seemed to share the sentiment, judging by the way his lip quirked.

"Very well. After dinner, the four of us will talk."

Chapter Thirty-Two

Kohlvar

Kohlvar watched as Seralie escorted Josephine away, arm in arm. "We need to check how the others are doing," he murmured in Dwarvish.

"Hang on, Kohl," Torva held up a hand to stop him. "What the fuck just happened?"

Kohlvar sighed. "I truly don't know, Tor."

She frowned at the burnt ground. "I thought you were mad for bringing a human woman here."

Kohlvar stiffened, frowning at his second in charge.

"But maybe you were right, perhaps there is more to her than meets the eye. The Queen seems to think so, and once they learn about this-" Torva gestured over the ground, "it'll be out of our hands."

"No." Kohlvar barked, surprised by the ferocity in his voice. "Not yet, we're getting ahead of ourselves. We don't know if she connected with an Eternal Soul, maybe it was something else."

"The Queen saw a vision from her."

"She said it was a memory, not a vision." His hands were clenching as this conversation progressed.

His second sighed, her hands resting on her hips. "Kohl, we have to be realistic. We know what happens to those who connect with them."

"No one has been able to communicate with the Souls in decades, why would she be able to?" He felt his arm fly out, hand gesturing wildly. Josie couldn't be one of them. Anyone but her.

Torva stared at him pityingly. "You really care about her, don't you?"

Kohlvar looked at her in alarm. "What?"

She sighed. "Look, I'll help her as much as I can, but neither of us are experts on the Souls. There will come a time where we have to send her elsewhere for help."

Kohlvar nodded reluctantly, still feeling guarded from her question.

"Come on, we need to make sure the others are alright. I can only imagine the trouble Kaelith is getting into," Torva grumbled, moving towards the clearing they'd left him in.

He scoffed. "We have a dragonoid with unknown abilities, and you're worried about Kaelith's magic?"

"Absolutely, have you seen him? He's pure chaos. Imagine how that'll manifest through magic."

Kohlvar had to admit, she had a point. He could probably set half the forest on fire by accident if his boundless energy translated to magical potential.

Chapter Thirty-Three

Josephine

Hirwen had taken one look at Josephine, before immediately disappearing into the kitchen and rummaging about. Seralie didn't even need to ask for tea, yet she soon returned with a steaming pot of fragrant amber liquid and insisted they drink it all.

Three cups of tea later, Josephine felt like she'd been roused from a deep sleep. She was still tired and numb, but the bone aching sadness no longer plagued her.

"Are you alright?" Seralie's deep brown eyes were worried, hands cupped around her own mug of tea.

"I don't know," Josephine admitted. "I feel strange, I probably just need some sleep."

Seralie reached out and squeezed her hand comfortingly.

"Where the blazes have you two been?!" Kaelith's voice roared through the dining hall, causing them to jolt back in alarm.

Josephine turned, ready to scold Kaelith, only she froze in astonishment at the sight of him. The right side of his face was covered in ash, hair singed at the ends, the shoulder of his shirt burnt clean off him. She leapt from the table, knocking over her nearly empty cup.

"What the fuck? Are you hurt? What happened?" She gingerly peeled the shirt away from his shoulder, revealing reddened skin.

Kaelith grinned. "Guess who's got fire?" He pointed his thumb behind him, where his three companions stood equally shocked.

Seralie frowned. "Um, who?"

Kaelith rolled his eyes. "Draka of course! He blasted a fireball at me when I was egging him on, it nearly destroyed this beautiful face. That would've been a shame, but lucky I can move wicked fast. Where did you guys go? Did you manage to pull on magic? Torva said something about a plant."

The girls looked at each other, sharing a look of mutual alarm. "It was me," Seralie blurted out. "But I already knew that, I've always been good with the earth."

"How about you, Josie?"

She just shook her head, still trying to ascertain the severity of Kaelith's injuries. He gently batted her worrying hands away.

"Don't worry, it was only the first session! I couldn't do much either, nor could Eryn or Persy."

Josephine looked up in surprise. "Really?"

Eryndal came to stand beside his cousin, his normally neat attire rumpled. "Yes, it was the vein of magic we were over. It's best for earth wielders, though when we get stronger, we theoretically should be able to pull from any natural source."

Seralie frowned, looking towards Draka. "But then, how did Draka wield fire?"

"He didn't." Kaelith leaned onto the table with a shit-eating grin. "He *breathed* fire. He's like... a proper dragon."

Josephine raised her brows in surprise. "Is that common for dragonoids?"

"Nope!" Kaelith's grin grew wider as he turned and clapped a hand on Draka's shoulder. Draka's eyes narrowed menacingly, but Kaelith didn't seem to care.

"He says that's the first time he's ever done that," Seralie translated, her eyes vacant as she spoke with the dragonoid. "He didn't mean to hurt you Kaelith, and he..." she trailed off. "He's commending you on your air magic."

"Air magic? Nah, I was just fast. But thanks bud, I'm glad you don't actually want to kill me."

"He's alone in that sentiment," Persephone grumbled as she plopped down next to Josephine. "Kaelith did not stop speaking the entire time we were practicing, even *after* Draka nearly vaporised him. Do you think someone can be rendered deaf from annoyance?"

Josephine chuckled. "Judging by the fact children continuously yap at their parents all hours of the day, I'd say no."

Persephone sighed. "A shame, it'd be better to be deaf. Silence is so peaceful." She rested her arms and head on the table, her small frame limp with exhaustion. "I'm definitely not an earth wielder," she grumbled, eyeing Josephine's pot of tea.

She filled a small cup and handed it to her. "Hirwen made it for me, my attempts were taxing too."

"Looks like Galathir's students had a rough time too." Eryndal chimed in, nodded towards the opposite corner. The elven acolytes slumped over the table and each other, their food sitting untouched.

Kaelith chortled. "Well, at least we're not the only ones."

"Why do we even have to test all the elements when we already know what we can do?" Persephone sighed.

"Your full potential needs to be unlocked before they administer the elixir, otherwise your advanced powers may not come through properly.

Therefore we must test all elements and any capabilities prior, as the elixir can only be given once." Eryndal recited patiently.

Josephine turned to him, surprised. "Hang on, what elixir?"

"You don't know about the elixir?" Kaelith asked, incredulously. "Ow!" He yelped as Persephone kicked him under the table.

"She's from the Human Realm, idiot, of course she doesn't know. I barely know about them, how would she?" Persephone glowered fiercely at him.

"When magic stopped flowing naturally, there were many investigations and experiments to attempt to bolster it. Those well versed in alchemy turned to potions, using a mixture of-"

"For Souls sake don't recite the damn recipe Eryn," Persephone groaned, her head flopping back down onto the table with a dull *thunk*.

"Right, sorry," he gave a sheepish grin. "They created an elixir that helped the newer generation transition from their minor abilities: wielding the elements and minor tricks, to their unique powers. Metallurgy was a common one among the dwarves, regardless of which element they were strongest to begin with. Conversely shape-shifting was almost always found in strong air wielders, which is interesting, given its the manipulation of one's appearance. The worshipers of the Souls often received heightened communicative abilities, though they consume a different version of the elixir. This elixir has helped society continue to function as normal, relatively."

Josephine took a moment to process this information. "So, elves and dwarves take this elixir?"

"Yes, dwarves receive it upon becoming of age, and elves used to do the same, but now it's only administered to select individuals."

"Why?"

Eryndal blinked rapidly, like he'd never considered the question. "I...I don't know. I would presume it's a supply issue, it's not easy to make."

"And has it ever been administered to a human before?"

He tilted his head thoughtfully. "Definitely to humanoids, I cannot say for certain regarding humans though. I'll have to research it. Speaking of, anyone want to go to the library tonight?"

Kaelith and Persephone groaned.

"Shouldn't we all be resting after today's exertions?" Seralie fiddled with her empty cup as she asked.

"I suppose you're right, another night then. It *was* a tiring day," Eryndal nodded agreeably, watching as Hirwen started to bring out the evening food.

Josephine shot a look of relief and thanks to Seralie, her cheeks flushed slightly. She gave a shaky smile back, glancing tentatively at Draka.

"Come on, we all should eat." Eryndal clapped Kaelith on the back, his head moving up to glance at the kitchen.

"Food? Food." He agreed, scurrying off the bench and half-running to Hirwen, who tutted at his impolite haste.

"As much as I hate to admit it," Persephone yawned, cutting her off mid-sentence. "He's right, we should eat."

Josephine nodded, begrudgingly rising from the bench to follow them.

Chapter Thirty-Four

Josephine

All Josephine wanted to do was crawl into bed, yet she trudged to the library with an impressively alert Seralie as requested. She listened as Seralie babbled, trying to focus, but ultimately nodding along to her happy conversation.

"I've never been able to use my magic in this way before, the sources feel different here."

Josephine eyed her curiously, "What exactly does it feel like, when you touch the source?"

Seralie hummed contemplatively. "Well, back home it was difficult, the forest would only listen to you occasionally, like it was an animal caught in a trap. You would really have to wrangle it some days, and usually it wasn't worth it. It worked better when it agreed to it. But here it's just...there. You can pull on it so easily, at all times it seems."

Her answer intrigued Josephine, though it hardly helped her find the sensation she was missing. "Interesting. I wonder why it's so different."

She looked around the auditorium, noticing several people spread amongst the shelves and tables.

"There you are," Torva's deep voice startled them as she emerged from the shelves. She gestured for them to follow as she weaved through the corridors of books with impressive grace.

Josephine felt a flutter of relief seeing Kohlvar, though it was quickly dispelled by his stiff posture and incessant pacing. He locked eyes with her immediately, the smallest smile brushing his lips.

"Come in," Kohlvar gestured to the seats behind him, neatly placed around a dark wooden table.

Josephine watched as he braced his hands on the door frame, his brow knitting in concentration. She took the briefest moment to admire the way it accentuated his broad muscular frame, watching as his hands slowly slid over the wooden slats.

"There," he breathed, stepping back into the small room. "No one will hear us now."

Josephine frowned at the doorway, unable to see any difference. She moved to his side, hesitantly raising a finger and poking the air.

At first, she felt nothing, just as she expected. But as her hand moved through the frame, her finger met a surprising resistance, pushing her hand back into the room.

"It's a sound barrier," Kohlvar explained, his head angled towards her. "We can leave, though it would be easier if we jumped through it. But it redirects sounds and air back in, so others are less likely to hear."

Josephine poked it again, marvelling at the way the air eddied under her finger, tickling her. Seralie mirrored her actions, giggling as her hand bounced off the invisible shield.

"Can you stop playing with the sound barrier?" Torva grumbled, irritation lacing her voice.

Josephine bit back a retort and took her seat, noting Kohlvar's bemused expression beside Torva's grumpy one.

"So, did I see an Eternal Soul? Whatever that actually is."

Kohlvar anxiously ran a hand through his hair. "We're not sure. Very few people can anymore, the skill seems to have died out with time. Have you ever experienced anything like this before?"

"No, I don't normally see shadowy demon things in my dreams," Josephine deadpanned.

Torva scoffed. "An Eternal Soul isn't a demon. They are the guardians of our world."

"Hm. And how's that working out for you?"

Torva scowled deeply as heat radiated off her with renewed energy. Kohlvar looked between them and sighed, shaking his head.

"The Eternal Souls keep the balance, both in our world and between others." Seralie chimed in, fidgeting nervously as she looked at Torva. "The Ascended used to commune with them to learn how to maintain balance, and they'd carry out their orders. Villages would celebrate and make offerings at the change of the season for good health and crops."

Josephine looked at her thoughtfully. "Did it work?"

She shrugged. "Well, people say it did, until we lost the ability to speak with the Souls.

"But Fissius blames the humans for that."

Kohlvar grumbled discontentedly, "No one truly knows what triggered this. Some blame the witches, the humans or the elves. Many blame the hybrids."

"Right, because blaming the result of unions between races will clearly solve the problem." Josephine replied sarcastically. Kohlvar and Torva both looked at her in surprise. She frowned back at them.

"What? I was clearly being sarcastic; it's been an issue with humans for centuries. Kids of mixed heritage get picked on by either side for being different. Just typical that elves would perpetuate this same shit."

"What do you mean for centuries?

Josephine froze under Torva's furrowed gaze. "Um..."

"Humans have only been here for maybe a couple hundred years. And hybrids only started appearing in the last 50 years. So, what do you mean by mixed heritage?"

Josephine winced, trying to figure out a way to roll back her slip of the tongue. "I mean between humans of different skin colours."

Torva's frown deepened. "Which village did you say you were from?"

"A coastal one," Josephine fought the urge to look at Kohlvar. Why didn't they figure out a village for her to claim to be from before she arrived?

Torva's radiant heat blasted her, causing her to recoil in surprise. "You *fucking* idiot," she hissed, glaring vehemently at Kohlvar. "What did you do? She's from the human world, isn't she?"

Kohlvar sighed, seeming resigned to his fate. "You two should go to bed." Josephine caught his eye, trying to silently communicate her apology, but he looked away before she could read his expression.

"Oh, she can join us, seeing as she's a part of this." Torva gestured angrily towards her. Josephine jumped at her increasing volume, her anxiety skyrocketing.

Josephine felt Seralie's hand grip hers tightly, pulling her with surprising strength through the sound barrier. They were met with a startling coolness, as they both hastened to put as much distance as possible between them and the furious Torva.

Chapter Thirty-Five

Kohlvar

Torva was fuming.

Even with his mental shields raised, he could feel the physical rage pouring off her. The radiant heat of her barely restrained fire magic threatened to singe his eyebrows. Kohlvar didn't like the way Josephine had flinched away from her, nor did he like the apparent volatility of Torva's emotions lately.

Her dark eyes narrowed accusingly. "What did you and Valtherion do? Messing with the portals will get you, and all of us killed Kohl!"

"Can I say one thing before you yell at me for the next hour?"

He could hear Torva's teeth grinding. "Fine," she growled.

"Your magic seems particularly unstable right now, and although you're angry, I suspect you're not intentionally radiating enough heat to burn me."

Torva recoiled, appearing offended by his suggestion. Then she looked down at herself, at the shimmering heat distorting the air around her, and groaned.

"What did you do, Kohlvar? You fucking fool." She ran her hands down her arms and body, providing immediate relief from the thermal radiation.

"Do you need ice?"

"No, Kohlvar, I don't need ice, I need a god damned explanation. What the fuck?"

Kohlvar drew breath to respond, but Torva wasn't finished.

"First, you show up with a human woman, who despite your claims, clearly has no elven heritage or magical abilities. I thought perhaps you'd just gotten yourself a girlfriend and recruited her as a cover, which was a little weird, but whatever it's your love life. Then she forms what might be the first connection with an Eternal Soul in over a century, only she's never even heard of the Souls. Really, I should've known then."

She paced frantically, waving her hands energetically as she shot fuming glares at him.

"I've had your back for 15 years! Since when do we keep secrets from each other? I've seen you almost die, from your own stupidity and others. I've pulled you back from the brink countless times, when no one else looked after us. And for 10 years we've tried to build a place for hybrids like us here. When did that stop mattering to you?"

"Torva-"

"And to top it all off, you risk the agreement we've fought tooth and nail to make to follow an impossible dream. Are you trying to *fix* the bond with the human world? They're the reason everything is broken! The last reports we had from the portal were of bombs, Kohlvar. We should be grateful that they broke the connection instead of obliterating our world!" Torva was rapidly pacing, gesturing wildly as she spoke.

"Where is Josephine really from?"

"She's from the human world. She came through Val's portal when I was visiting him." Kohlvar answered, keeping his tone calm and level.

Torva stopped, staring at him in shock. "But that hasn't happened in decades."

"Correct."

The tall woman resumed her pacing, "Then what happened?"

"She wanted to go back to the human world, she has children there." A pang of guilt hit Kohlvar at the reminder.

She whirled to gape at him. "What? She's separated from her family?"

"Yes, that's why she's struggled so much with being here." His chest sunk with the reminder, the sympathetic pain he felt for her every time he could feel her grief.

"Souls, Kohlvar, you should've at least told me that! I've been an arsehole to her, all because I didn't know." Regret flashed across Torva's face, her radiant heat dimming with shame.

He shrugged, "It made it too difficult to explain why she was here, we agreed to keep it quiet. But she decided to come here and try to find a way to return home."

"So, you and Val were working together to try and send her back through the portal?"

"Yes, he thought that she might be able to help mend the connection, because she was from the human world."

"And she could?"

"We haven't tried. It's too unstable."

"Right. And what were you planning to do when the King realises you've failed to report a functioning portal?" Her fists were clenched with barely concealed frustration.

Kohlvar winced. "We don't know if it functions, Valtherion had to seal it up to stop it from forming a permanent rift. To reopen that would be extremely dangerous."

Torva took a deep breath, finally ceasing her pacing. "Kohl, what if the King kills you for this? What if he kills the recruits?"

Guilt sunk in Kohlvar's stomach as he saw the genuine fear in her eyes. "No, he can't, he needs us. He needs our magical abilities."

"The last time someone tried to fix the flow of magic, they were exiled to the opposite side of the country! The only reason they weren't killed was because they had *permission*." She raked her hands through her short hair, heat still rolling off her.

"The witches were exiled because their magic didn't work correctly, hybrids were created. Something has changed, can't you feel it?"

Torva's lips shifted into a thin line. "Look, if it has, then you've upset the balance of magic. That's going to piss the King off."

"Well, it was only a theory that the problems with magic were related to the portals and the lost connection between our worlds. But this could prove it, which means we can fix things." Kohlvar implored her to listen, to see the hope he desperately clung to.

"The King doesn't want to fix things Kohl! Don't you get it?" Torva's hands flew up in frustration. "He is in power, and no one can challenge him. But if you upset the balance that he has carefully curated over the last half-century, he could be usurped."

Kohlvar frowned. "Are there people who want to overthrow him?"

"Yes!" Torva sighed. "I forget you've rarely left the Elven Realm these past few years. He really does like to keep you on a close leash."

"What are you saying? The dwarves?"

"It's not just the dwarves, Kohl. It's most of the communities outside the Elven Realm. They've been in a state of unrest for years, but the fact that elven crops flourish every year and never face the same environmental problems as them is really starting to cause resentment. Some of them are starving for Souls sake. And even you know better than most how the sirens feel about him."

Kohlvar frowned. He'd known that trade relations between the King and the neighbouring regions had been tense, but he had not been a part of those. He was rarely involved unless the King wished to intimidate those he was negotiating with. Even then, it rarely came to violence. The sirens however, were not inclined to forgive the King for his brutal decimation of their species after his sister's death.

Torva remained silent for several moments. She looked as though she was working through complex mathematics.

"Tor?"

"Not yet," she held up a finger as she started to pace again. Kohlvar obliged, waiting for her to work through it.

Finally, she spoke. "I don't see a solution that doesn't get everyone killed. What's your plan?"

"Wait for Valtherion's next letter, try to get everyone through this damned training and figure out if Josephine is a new Ascended."

Torva sighed. "I don't like that plan."

"I don't see another option. We need to know if Josephine connected with the Eternal Souls." If she had, it would change everything. Kohlvar had brought her along to help her, to try and find a way for her to go home. But perhaps she was meant to forge a different path.

"And if she did commune with them?"

"Then I need you to make me a promise."

Chapter Thirty-Six

Josephine

Seralie didn't ask Josephine about Torva's revelation, and she didn't tell. She suspected that Seralie didn't need to ask, that she inherently knew it was true. Still, she appreciated the silent solidarity the young woman shared with her.

Soon, the days blurred together in a haze of monotony. Breakfast with the team, dodging the glares and snide comments from the elven acolytes when their supervisors weren't looking. A morning walk around the lake, where Kohlvar and Torva drilled them with questions, testing if they felt anything new at the sites of magical significance. The acolytes would practice their physical training, before their elemental magic, with Torva diligently recording the results.

Josephine was enjoying the familiar routine, despite her inability to do anything with magic. Kohlvar had firmly advised her not to initiate a connection again, and she hadn't. However, when she tried to sense the magical sources that everyone else could access, she felt nothing. Honestly, she shouldn't be surprised, she was only human after all. But a part of her was disappointed every day at her continued failure.

In the afternoons they endured Professor Fissius, as he taught them about the history of the elves and magic, with a handful of snarky comments directed at their unit. The sting of his words had eased for Josephine, though they continued to irritate the others. Kaelith and Eryndal were particularly frustrated, not having experienced this type of prejudice previously.

After dinner, they would congregate in the library for additional study. Most nights it was Eryndal, Seralie and Josephine huddled around a table piled high with books. After realising the majority of the books were not written in English, she had decided to include the young scholar in their research. She told him it was due to the Queen's comments about her visions, which she'd felt a little guilty about. But given the seriousness with which Kohlvar had reacted, she decided on taking the precaution.

By the time night came, she was exhausted. Yet sleep eluded her, as the silent bedchamber allowed her mind to roam, frantically stressing over her children. Were they safe? Hungry? What were they studying in school? Had they outgrown their shoes again? Was Aunt Susan crumbling under the sole responsibility of raising two rambunctious little girls?

And when she finally drifted off, she was haunted by nightmares. The bombing, the day she found out her husband would never come home, or the night she'd almost been strangled to death. She'd wake, drenched in sweat, biting back screams as she thrashed in her bedding.

Yet she continued, for what other option did she have? She could not give in to despair.

They'd made very little progress on learning about the Order of the Ascended. There seemed to be few books in the elven library with the information they sought, and those that might be applicable, were written in an ancient language none of them could decipher.

At least other members of their team had made progress. Seralie could pull from the earth sources with ease, each attempt eliciting a stronger response from the plant matter. Persephone drew on water and air equally, though she could only manipulate water from the lake. Torva had encouraged her to focus on pulling from alternative sources, learning to draw water up from deep reservoirs to extend her ability beyond lakeside.

Kaelith was still playing with simple tricks, and Eryndal was struggling to find the connection to the sources. He'd read dozens of books in Josephine's company, yet all the knowledge in those books didn't seem to be translating to success for him. Josephine could see the toll it was taking on the young man, the enthusiastic spark in his eyes dimming every day.

Then there was the enigma that was Draka. Seralie had taken to spending time with him, trying to help him connect with the sources and learn about him. Yet, aside from the singular incident of *fire breathing*, Draka had not shown any proclivity towards wielding.

Josephine sat, watching Seralie encourage a section of grass to grow, as her eyes drifted back to Kohlvar. They'd barely spoken since the royals had arrived, both kept so busy with studies or duties they'd hadn't had a chance to be alone. He'd been away more, often leaving Torva in charge of their training.

She missed him, and that realisation startled her. She missed his calm, protective presence that always put her at ease. She missed conversations with him, talking about the idiosyncrasies of both their worlds. He'd taught her more about the different creatures of this world in a day than Professor Fissius had during her entire time here. She'd told him about electricity, modern medicine, the war and what a world with only humans as the dominant species was like.

Josephine wanted to wake up next to him again. She wanted to share kisses by the firelight, gently exploring each other and taking comfort in each other's arms. She hadn't had someone like that in years, and now that she'd had a taste of such affection, she craved it like a drug.

She watched as a royal messenger came down from the fortress, strutting directly to him and issuing a tightly bound scroll. His face fell as he read the scroll, nodding to the messenger as he walked towards Torva. He interrupted her supervision of Kaelith's manipulation of air, murmuring a few words, before leaving them.

Josephine felt a pang of sadness, wishing he'd said goodbye. But she knew it was foolish to feel that way. He had said it was just for that night, that he couldn't be with her the way she wanted.

Nonetheless, she wanted what she could not have.

Chapter Thirty-Seven

Josephine

Josephine sighed into the dusty tome spread open before her. She had always struggled to read cursive handwriting, and this text was proving particularly difficult to decipher. Which, given it was written in a language she could read, was not inspiring any confidence in her ability to decipher an Elven text.

She squinted, tilting her head until she recognised the slanting swirls, pulling out letters as she adapted to the delicate handwriting.

A Royal History, written by Professor Elwin Fissius

Princess Liora of Saltus was said to be the most beautiful woman in the Elven Realm, though those rumours grossly underestimated her fairness. She shone with radiant light, her hair so pale it looked like moonlight, her presence bringing peace and comfort to those around her.

She was doted upon by her parents, the King and Queen, and her elder brother Prince Caladorn was fiercely protective of her. She was rarely seen outside the palace grounds, though every day she would go to the nearby river and swim under the watchful eye of her maid. Servants said she longed for the open ocean with a fierce desire considered unusual for most elves.

It was quite the surprise when she became with child, at the tender age of 16. Elves do not typically procreate until late in their 30's at the earliest, unlike humans and dwarves, who seem content to reproduce like animals.

She claimed she did not know how she came to be with child, causing great alarm to many. Legends had begun to whisper about strange hybrid children, but this would be the first born to the royal family.

When she laboured, she struggled for many hours with a precarious birth, her child arriving feet first. The child bore her mother's likeness, with pale features and fine hair. Unlike her mother though, the child was covered with scales over her legs and back, likely contributing to the difficult birth.

The Princess would never fully recover from this ordeal. For weeks she remained in a stupor, barely interacting with her child or eating and drinking. One night she snuck out, leaving the baby with her nursemaid, and swam from the river into the Great Lake beyond the palace grounds.

Liora never returned.

Some say her love for the water was too strong, others say the sirens were jealous and took her for their own.

Soon the Sirens were banished from the elven Realms, their lakes encroached upon. This hatred only continued when the King died, leaving the young Caladorn to rule while the Queen Mother succumbed to her grief.

The orphaned infant was raised by her servants, kept away from the public eye. The child lost her scales by the age of two, baring no resemblance to her presumed non-elven heritage. The royal family initially denied the rumours of her scales, claiming they were lies spread by those who did not support them. The King threatened those who made such claims with imprisonment and death, for beseeching the late Princess's memory.

However, when the young hybrid came into womanhood, her immense siren abilities confirmed every whispered suspicion. She was sent away for training, after several unfortunate incidents with the Royal staff, returning as an unrecognisable adult.

King Caladorn named her his heir apparent upon her return, presumably only intended whilst his children were so young. She has since remained by his side, assisting with military and magical matters as a close adviser.

Josephine rubbed her eyes, the words blurring beneath her. This wasn't the book she needed, nor had the previous dozen led her to any useful information. With a sigh, she looked down at the sheet of parchment Eryndal had given her, setting out into the endless shelves to search once again.

Chapter Thirty-Eight

Kohlvar

Kohlvar ruffled his damp hair, finally feeling clean after spending the day scouting for the culprits of the raids on the nearby village. He had his suspicions, based on the descriptions in the incident reports, but he needed to confirm them before presenting a plan for approval.

He just needed to verify which subset of creatures he'd seen, and if they had caused similar troubles previously. That answer would drastically impact the King's direction.

If they were from the community that he suspected they were...well, Kohlvar's job would not be pleasant.

He strode into the library, his steps echoing despite his attempts to tread quietly. He glanced around, not seeing another soul. Not surprising, given it was almost the weekend. Most residents would be enjoying their time off down at the village tavern or visiting other questionable establishments.

Still, he did not dare reach out to sense for others. He'd kept himself fully guarded at all times since the monarch's had arrived, to the point he was experiencing headaches most evenings.

It was exhausting being on edge constantly.

Kohlvar padded towards the history section, his eyes scanning every corridor for danger. He sighed, rubbing the bridge of his nose. He was in the library, what danger did he expect to find?

His boots met the padded carpet of the outer corridors, leading into study nooks and quiet reading corners. He scanned over his shoulder one last time as he moved onto his intended destination, coming to an abrupt halt as he collided with something solid.

Her scent struck him first. It was always a subtle scent, soap and earthy freshness, with hints of the tea she drank in the morning. She must have bathed recently, for her hair smelt of lavender as it brushed against his face.

"Josie," he breathed, the words coming out as a sigh of relief. His hands gripped her shoulders, holding her steady among the scattered books on the floor.

"Kohlvar," she smiled, her eyes dark in the low lighting. "Where have you been?" Concern echoed in her words, her eyes flicking over him as if looking for injuries.

He returned her assessment with one of his own. She looked well, no visible injuries or bruises to remark. In fact, she looked beautiful. She was wearing his spare shirt, tucked into a long flowing skirt, the hem brushing over her ankles. The skirt fit firmly on her waist, falling over her hips and thighs close enough he could see their faint outline. A small slit from below her knee exposed her calf, bare skin catching the light between the dark fabric folds.

"Fuck," he murmured, forgetting himself. "Where did you get this?" He dropped a hand to her waist, trailing the seam down to her hip.

She shivered under his touch. "Torva gave it to me."

His brows rose questioningly at that. "Torva would never have worn this." His voice came out surprisingly husky.

Josephine looked down at the skirt, smoothing it down with a hand. "That explains why most of her hand-me-downs were in such good condition."

"You have more clothes like this?" Kohlvar's imagination started to run wild, wondering how her perfect body would look in a fitted dress.

Josephine smirked at him, clearly amused by his reaction. "If only I'd known sooner, I would've worn a dress to summon you."

Kohlvar sighed, brushing his nose over her unbound hair. "Is there anyone else around?"

She shook her head underneath him. "I haven't seen anyone for a while."

"Where are the others?"

"At the pub, or tavern as they call it." Her arms encircled his chest as she buried her face into him. "I've missed you."

Kohlvar melted into her embrace, holding her firmly. Her scented hair soothed the ache in his chest, the one he hadn't been able to shift lately. "I've missed you, too."

Unwillingly, he pulled back, glancing around just to make sure they really were alone. His eyes drifted to the books and papers scattered across the carpet, frowning as he read the titles. "Those books are in Elvish. Did you learn to read another language overnight?"

Josephine scoffed, bending to collect the fallen items. "No, Eryndal wrote down words in Elvish I should look for in my research of the Eternal Souls."

Kohlvar crouched to assist her, scanning the paper with neat cursive handwriting. The Elvish symbols for Eternal Souls and Order of the Ascended caught his eye, the translations written in Common beside them. He nodded thoughtfully, looking over the books they held.

"Do any of these look like the right thing?" Josephine asked as she walked them back to her study nook, piled high with dozens of books.

Kohlvar deposited the tomes, flicking through them thoughtfully. "I struggle with Elvish, so it's hard to say. Though this one," he held up a small red book, "probably won't be useful."

She took the book from him, flipping through it. "Why would you say...*oh*." She tilted her head, a curious look on her face. "That does not look comfortable."

Kohlvar felt his cheeks turning red, as he backed into the door frame of her study nook. "I, uh, I need to find something."

She looked at him in alarm. "Are you coming back?"

He nodded, turning towards the silent library. After a short search through the familiar shelves, Kohlvar returned with half a dozen tomes, setting them down across Josephine. She was still flicking through that little red book, chuckling at the diagrams.

"Here," Kohlvar handed her an enormous textbook. She took it, frowning. "It's a translation text, it'll help with your research. It's more extensive than the one you're using."

"Oh, thank you." Her fingers brushed his, surprisingly chilly.

Kohlvar frowned at her. "You're cold. Where's your coat?"

"It was warmer when I got here, I didn't bring one. I'm fine-" She fell silent as he wordlessly slipped out of his overcoat, rising to drape it around her shoulders. He watched as her eyes lingered on his torso, his linen shirt loosely tied over his chest. Her hand rose, fingers lingering above the strip of skin visible over his sternum. Her eyes met Kohlvar's, her breathing noticeably faster than before.

He froze under her gaze, staring at her hand. He could feel Josephine's emotions stirring distantly, outside his barriers, but it was enough to drive him to distraction.

"I can't," he breathed, regretting the words immediately. He wanted her to put those soft hands on his bare skin, to kiss her like he had that night. But he felt too exposed, too on edge, to allow himself to accept her affection.

Josephine gave a quick smile, pulling away to stare at her books. "Of course, I understand." She flipped open the translation text, fingers trailing down the index thoughtfully.

Kohlvar clenched his jaw, steeling himself with a deep breath as he settled into the small seat opposite her.

"What are you reading?" Josephine murmured, still staring intently at her text.

Kohlvar partially closed the tome to check the title. "Classification of water creatures."

She threw him a quizzical expression. "Sounds riveting."

The corner of his mouth quirked. "I think Eryndal would find it interesting."

Josephine rolled her eyes. "Eryndal would find this entire library interesting, that's hardly a fair metric."

Kohlvar's gaze lingered on the red book. "There are drawings."

A noise that sounded like a cough combined with a splutter escaped her. "What are you trying to imply, Kohl?" Her voice was mockingly accusatory, amusement dancing in her eyes.

He just shrugged, opening the book again. He looked over a handful of classifications he did not suspect, just to rule them out. When he finally landed on the correct section, his frown deepened as he read, his worst fears confirmed.

"What's wrong?"

"Dammit," he breathed, looking over the subclasses and specific variations between the different clans. There was no mistaking it. It was them.

"I have to go." Kohlvar stood, snapping the book shut with more force than intended.

"Kohl, wait-"

The frantic, panicking voice in his head drowned out Josephine's words as he nearly sprinted from her sight.

***

Kohlvar kept his shields high, still not allowing himself to scan for people ahead. He just had to get behind his bedroom door, then he'd be safe for the night. Then he could find a way to avoid the King inciting another war.

He'd been short with Josephine too, guilt gnawed at him. He would apologise later, and hope she understood.

Kohlvar scanned the doors to the men and women's dormitories, confirming nothing seemed out of the ordinary. As he rounded the final corner he came to an abrupt stop, watching in frozen shock as a tall slim woman pushed off his door.

"There you are. I've been looking for you." She smiled, her serrated teeth peeking out between her pale lips.

"Princess." Kohlvar inclined his head, feeling his heartbeat rapidly increase.

"You've been avoiding me." She stalked towards him, slowly, like she was a predator toying with her prey.

"I've been occupied with my acolytes and my duty." His tone was even, voice steady.

"Yes, I hear they're a challenging group. Are you sure you can handle them?" She smirked, scanning him up and down. "You've gained weight."

"If you say so Princess," he stared at the roof above her head. "If you'll excuse me-"

"Look at me, Kohlvar. That's an order."

Dread filled his stomach as he met the blue eyes that matched his own. He fought to keep his shields in place, refusing to bend to the overwhelming presence before him.

"Hmm, I've missed you." Amusement laced her words.

Kohlvar gritted his teeth. "What do you want, Vessara?"

"Oh, don't be like that. We used to have such fun together. Don't you miss it?" She stepped closer, brushing a hand over his arm.

"Don't touch me." Kohlvar growled, pushing the fear aside in favour of his anger.

She tutted, "Are you still upset over that little misunderstanding? Come on Kohl, that was years ago."

"I said, don't touch me." He stepped back, careful not to touch the King's niece.

Her face turned into an angry snarl. "Souls, I didn't realise you were so sensitive. Get over it, I'm tired of you being hurt about it."

"You almost killed me. If it wasn't for Torva, I'd be dead."

"Ah yes, that brute. How is she, still skulking about like the miserable cretin she is?"

Kohlvar knew an answer would only fuel her on. "I'm going to bed, goodnight, Princess." He tried to move past her again, but she stepped into his path. He knew, the second he laid a hand on her, she'd have his neck offered to the King.

"You miss it, just like I do, Kohl. You're just as sick and twisted as I am. You're the abomination of two foul creatures; how could you not be? Just embrace it already, I'm sick of you acting like you're superior because you don't give into those urges. It'd feel so good if you did." She placed her hand on his chest, grabbing his shirt roughly.

His shirt. Shit. Where was his jacket?

"Let go of me!" he cried, panic lacing his voice.

"Kohlvar?"

He turned to see the last person he wanted to be there, Josephine.

Chapter Thirty-Nine

Josephine

As the dormitory doors came into view, Josephine heard two voices speaking tensely from the corridor. She slowed, straining to eavesdrop.

"Hmm, I've missed you." The voice was unmistakably female, elven by the lilting tone.

"What do you want, Vessara?" Definitely, Kohlvar, his growling voice had a sharpness to it she hadn't heard before.

Josephine crept closer as silently as she could, watching with intense focus at the scene before her. Princess Vessara stood unbearably close to Kohlvar, his posture rigid beside the wall.

Her fingers suddenly grabbed his chest, digging into his exposed flesh. Kohlvar stiffened, closing his eyes and clenching his fists. His neck muscles bulged as he seemed to fight an invisible war against this elf.

"Let go of me!" The alarm in Kohlvar's tone shocked Josephine. She'd never seen him rattled, let alone whatever this was. She surged forward as Kohlvar's back pressed against his bedroom door, the tall elven woman leaning into him.

"Kohlvar?" His name spilled from her mouth unbidden. His azure eyes met her, pure fear radiating from him. Josephine didn't fully understand what was happening, but she would not stand for it. She felt the familiar stirring of anger in her chest, just like when Robert had grabbed Sienna that way. Right before his actions got her killed.

Rage flooded her system, pouring down her outstretched arms, as a loud *bang* echoed through the corridor. Doors rattled as an invisible force blasted out from her, right into the elven woman.

She flew sideways, landing with a satisfying thud onto the floor. Kohlvar remained standing, looking as though he was being pressed into his door, his fists still clenched rigidly by his side.

Josephine stumbled forward as the force left her, rolling through the corridor a final time, before evaporating. She rested a hand on the wall, panting, as she looked back to a stunned Kohlvar.

He stumbled free from the door first, immediately rushing over to her. "You need to go." His arms reached for her, just as a screech rose from behind him.

"How *dare* you!" Vessara screamed, her words growing rapidly closer.

Before she could react, Kohlvar had spun, pinning her to the wall behind his back. "I must apologise," he declared, his body shaking despite the firm tone.

"What the hell was that?" she demanded. Josephine could see a flurry of silver-blonde hair as the woman tried to look around Kohlvar's body at her.

"My students are only just learning to control their magic, sometimes accidents happen." His attempts to deescalate the situation were ignored, as the woman grabbed his wrist again.

"Move out of the way." She demanded coldly.

Kohlvar stiffened again, just like he had before. Haltingly, he stumbled to the side, until the woman released him. He sagged against the opposite wall, drawing in deep breaths.

Josephine locked eyes on the woman in front of her. Tall, similar height to her, with long pale hair, but the most astonishing part of her was her eyes. They were such a pale colour, they almost looked white. Perhaps they were a light shade of grey, or were they blue? Very unusual, even compared to the dozens of elves she'd met.

The woman noticed her stare, her lips curled into a cruel sneer. "What are you staring at? Did no one tell you it's rude to look at the Crown Princess without invitation?"

Josephine ignored her, turning to Kohlvar instead, and held up the jacket. "You forgot your jacket." He looked frozen in terror. She forced her features to remain neutral, but a person that could terrify him was clearly someone she should be worried about.

"I was talking to you, you ungrateful brat." She felt a slim hand grab her wrist, nails digging into the sensitive underside. "Who are you? What magic did you cast?"

Fear and panic mingled in Josephine's chest, emotions she saw reflected in Kohlvar's face. Yet she felt nothing, no calmness or rage like she'd expected. Perhaps this woman's magic was different to Kohlvar's?

Josephine turned back to her haunting eyes, as the words from her earlier reading came to mind. Tilting her chin up in defiance, she asked, "Didn't your mother ever teach you not to touch what isn't yours?"

Shock rippled across her face, before pure fury contorted her ethereal beauty. "You insolent bitch," she hissed as she released her, drawing back a hand as if to slap her.

Josephine braced for the impact, shielding behind her arm and averting her eyes. Only, instead of magic or a fist striking her, she felt a weight lift from her and a distant thud echo down the hallway.

Josephine opened her arms to darkness. Frowning, she reached her hand out to feel a material surrounding her, completely encasing her in darkness. Her hands brushed a fleece-like material, warm, smelling like bitter herbs and soap.

Kohlvar's coat. It was Kohlvar's winter coat encasing her.

Bewildered, she felt along the fleece, until she reached the leather collar, and pulled it down from over her head. She gaped at the scene before her.

The Princess was sprawled on the floor at the far end of the hallway, her ghostly hair fanning out around her. She appeared conscious, albeit stunned, as she worked her jaw open and closed a few times. Siren teeth jutted from her mouth, transforming her delicate features into a grotesque mask.

Josephine cast a quick glance to Kohlvar, who still stood leaning against the wall, hand raised towards her. A sigh of relief crossed his face, as he turned back to the fallen woman.

Vessara scoffed indignantly, rising with a surprising grace, patting down her rumpled tunic.

"So, this is what you prefer. Human filth." She spat the words out with disgust, eyeing Josephine up and down. The Princess turned back to Kohlvar, shaking her head mockingly. "Come find me when you break this one. She's no match for you." She stalked off, throwing an icy glare over her shoulder at Josephine.

Break her? What the hell did she mean by that?

Josephine watched her until she was out of sight, before turning back to Kohlvar. He was running a hand down his face, chest heaving with deep shaking breaths. She wanted to ask a million questions, but only one felt of any real importance.

"Are you okay?"

He looked at her in surprise, scoffing with half-hearted laughter, "No, not at all." The crack in his voice nearly broke her heart. What the hell did this woman do to him?

Josephine fussed with his jacket, folding it over her arm. "Do you want to talk about it?" She asked tentatively, like she was approaching a cornered animal.

He shook his head. "I'm just tired, I'll be fine."

"Kohl-"

"It shouldn't be your concern. Although, you could've said I left the jacket in the library. Now she thinks there's something between us."

Josephine shrugged and smiled. "She was always going to think that. Besides, I have seen far too many cadets sneaking off in the shelves, the library wouldn't have convinced her."

Kohl frowned at her. "What, really? Oh, for fucks sake..." He ran his hand through his hair again, pulling at the top.

"Hey," Josephine reached for his forearm, gently making contact. "Not your concern."

He groaned, head in his hands. She gently rubbed a thumb over his arm, hoping he would find it comforting. Kohlvar eventually dropped his hands, finally looking at her.

"So, can I ask what the hell just happened? Was it the jacket? Was it you?"

Kohlvar looked down at the coat, mildly bemused. "I suppose that's a fair question. The jacket is resistant to magic, depending on what is cast. If someone were to attack me, especially from behind, it would reflect the spell."

Josephine looked down at the jacket, running an admiring hand over the warm brown leather. "Good jacket." She patted it for a job well done.

That managed to prompt a small laugh from him. "The jacket is not sentient, Josie."

She shrugged, "You never know in this world." She swore she could feel a hint of warmth radiating back from the jacket. "So, was the cow magical?"

"What?"

"The cow, or sheep maybe, that this jacket was made from. Was it magical, and that's why it's resistant?" She flipped the jacket inside out. "Hm, definitely sheepskin. This fleece is nice, made for a colder climate than here though."

Kohlvar looked like he was barely containing laughter. "No, Josie, it was just a sheep. It was imbued with a protection spell."

"Obviously, not protected well enough, they're a jacket now." She deadpanned.

He stuttered, "No, the-oh you're messing with me now." He huffed a laugh, rubbing his hand over his evening stubble. His face soon grew solemn though.

"How did you resist her?"

Josephine frowned at him. "Uh...creepy elven princesses aren't really my type."

"What?"

"What?" Josephine countered.

He sighed, though his eyes showed a twinkle of mirth, to her relief. "Her *magic*. How did you resist her magic?"

Josephine quirked a smile. "You really need to be more specific with your questions."

"Josie," he sounded so tired, she just wanted to give him a hug.

She shrugged with a sigh. "Sorry, I don't know. I don't even know what happened when I found you two. I was just..."

His eyebrows shot up. "Just what?"

She closed her eyes, willing away the painful memories. "It reminded me of a similar situation...one that cost my best friend her life. I was so angry, it was like all that anger for my friend, for you, poured out of my arms." She opened her eyes to look down at her forearms, unblemished despite the heat she'd felt.

"It might mean you can wield air, impressively well." Kohlvar's fingers grazed her forearms, tracing over the three small welts rising on her wrist. His brows furrowed.

"I'm sor-"

"You have nothing to apologise for," Josephine almost smiled, remembering the last time she'd been the apologetic one. After a brief pause, she pushed forward with the thought burning in her mind. "I take it that's not the first time that's happened."

He shut his eyes tightly, before reaching out for his jacket. "Thank you for bringing me this. Goodnight, Josephine."

She winced at the use of her full name and sudden coldness in his tone. She'd pushed too far. But she quickly schooled her features into a neutral expression. Kohlvar moved away to unlock his door, his forehead brushing against the coarse wood.

"Kohl?"

His head angled towards her, just making eye contact. His eyes looked dull, exhausted, like he'd just fought some kind of battle. To see him look so defeated spurred on her courage.

"I don't care that she's a bloody princess. If she hurts you, or any of our team, I will make her pay." Josephine felt her hands clench into tight fists.

His eyes widened slightly. "Don't say things like that."

"I mean it."

"I know you do. But I'm not worth it."

Josephine softened, surprised by his response. "Yes, you are. Besides, what happens if she targets someone who can't stand up to her?"

They stared at each other silently, as Kohlvar seemed to consider her words. She quickly looked him over, looking for any sign of injury. He appeared unharmed physically, although she noticed his shirt had been tugged to the side, exposing a strip of his dark chest hair.

Without thinking, she stepped forward, pulling the shirt closed and patting him gently as she smoothed his clothing back into place. His look of utter bewilderment made her freeze.

"Oh shit, sorry." She stepped back, wincing at her instinctual actions. Six years of straightening up children really had left the habit ingrained. "Uh, well, you should get some sleep, Kohl."

What a great way to sound even more like his mother, she mentally chastised, as she scratched the back of her neck awkwardly.

A smile twitched at his lips, like he was holding back a laugh. "Thank you, Josie."

Once she saw him safely behind his door, Josephine let out the tension she'd been holding. She walked back to her dormitory quickly, looking around to ensure this so-called Princess did not attempt to harm her again.

Once Josephine was safely behind her door, she took a deep stabilising breath. Only then did the realisation hit. Could she channel magic? Holy mackerel. She could channel magic!

Chapter Forty

Kohlvar

"We have not received the last two shipments from the dwarves, Your Majesty." Fissius peered over his spectacles at the King, fiddling with the numerous scrolls half-rolled beneath his fingers. "There have been additional conflicts at the border, we've received reports that sirens have attacked several elven residents and drowned one."

The cold churning pit that had loitered in Kohlvar's stomach all weekend suddenly plummeted. He had been charged with maintaining the precarious relationship between the elves and sirens, but with his acolytes taking up most of his time, his absence from his duties had been noticed. He felt the King's searing gaze, though he kept his attention respectfully focused on Fissius.

"Are the missing shipments due to crop failures?" Galathir asked as Alfion dutifully scrawled notes.

The door behind Kohlvar banged open, a cold feeling of dread sinking into him. He looked to Torva, her paling face confirming his suspicions.

"My apologies, Uncle," Vessara's lilting voice radiating throughout the room. "May I join you?"

"Of course, my dear, come and sit beside me." Caladorn nodded at the empty seat to his right. Kohlvar shifted his gaze to the Queen, noticing the thin line of her lips.

"Thank you," she bowed to place a kiss on his cheek, before taking her position. "Has Kohlvar told you yet of the progress his human made?"

This time he could not avoid the King's painfully sharp gaze. "Oh?"

Kohlvar inclined his head. "I'm not sure what her Highness is referring to, Your Majesty."

Vessara tutted disapprovingly. "Come now, Kohlvar, she wielded air last week, did she not?" Her pale eyes glinted, her lip quirked at the corner.

"I'm not so sure she did, and I would need to see her repeat it before confirming any abilities." Kohlvar responded neutrally, trying to keep a respectful expression. What was she playing at? The Vessara he knew would rather die than admit a human sent her flying across a hallway.

"Oh, well, I would be happy to assist if you do not possess the skills to coax her ability out."

Silence fell across the room as Kohlvar levelled a glare at the Princess. "She is my acolyte; I will train her as I see fit." His voice was quiet, barely restraining the burning anger rising in his throat.

"That is no way to speak to the Princess." Caladorn admonished, his face unreadable as he looked between them.

Kohlvar nodded to him. "Of course, my apologies, Your Majesty." He shifted his gaze back to Vessara, his stomach sinking at the coy smile on her face. "Torva and I will train her, your Highness."

She rolled her eyes, her silvery hair shifting over her shoulder as she leaned towards the King. "But I could grant you quicker results, Your Majesty. And we do need more magic users, urgently."

"Respectfully, Your Highness, your methods carry too much risk of destroying a magic user." Galathir's deep calming voice soothed Kohlvar's racing heart, as panic threatened to take over. "We need them alive."

She scoffed, not even sparing a glance at him. "I only mean to bring out her true power, then she can better serve the Kingdom." Nausea struck Kohlvar suddenly as his fists clenched beneath the table.

"No."

Every head turned towards the Queen, her quiet power thrumming through the air with one single word.

"My love?" The King arched a brow at her.

She turned to him slowly, locking her doe-brown eyes with his green ones. "I could feel her power when we arrived. She is not like the other acolytes, and it would be a disservice to the Souls to force her ability."

Quiet fell as the couple stared at each other intently. Kohlvar chanced a look at Torva, who remained pale and stony-faced. Galathir bore a deep frown, Alfion looked confused and Fissius was surprisingly angry. Kohlvar met Galathir's questioning gaze, to which he gave a small head shake. He didn't know what power the Queen was referring to either.

"Are you suggesting that *woman* is one of your associates, Your Majesty?" Fissius's voice struggled to control his disgust, a sneer curled across his face.

Sylvara did not honour him with a response, continuing to silently stare at her husband.

"Bring her to me." Caladorn ordered.

Chapter Forty-One

Josephine

When Torva had interrupted their breakfast with a stormy expression, Josephine felt the stone of dread drop through her stomach. She'd expected a scolding, trying to remember what she'd done wrong, only to be given a blunt instruction to follow her.

"I don't suppose you can tell me what's going on?" Josephine murmured, scanning around them cautiously.

"Hard to do when I don't know. The King demanded your presence."

"Oh...so what do I do?"

"Don't lie, he will know. And follow any instructions he gives you." Torva stops suddenly, spinning to face Josephine. "Do you have power?"

"What? No, I told you-"

"The Queen says you do."

"Torva, I really don't. This is just a stupid misunderstanding, I can explain-"

"Don't, it's better if you just say as little as possible. Don't need you to dig your own grave."

"Bloody hell, Torva, don't overwhelm me with optimism."

She scoffed. "The only reason you're not the new plaything of the Princess is because the Queen thinks you're special. I honestly don't know which is worse."

Dread flooded Josephine's chest, as Torva shoved open the tall wooden doors to the battle room, the sound bouncing throughout the chamber.

A dozen men and women sat at a rounded table, King Caladorn on the far side. To his left, Queen Sylvara sat with a poised elegance, her back straight. On his right, Princess Vessara stood, her frosty glare sending daggers through Josephine's stomach.

Josephine quickly skimmed the familiar faces around the table, noticing that Kohlvar and Galathir had risen from their chairs, inclining their heads respectfully towards her.

"So, you are the human. Look at me child."

Josephine turned her body towards the ruler of the Elven Realm, clasping her hands together in front of her. "Your Majesty."

He scoffed, sitting forward from his relaxed position. "How old are you?"

"32."

His brows raised. "A little old for a typical acolyte. Why are you here?"

Josephine ignored the temptation to shoot back a sarcastic remark. "Kohlvar found me and recruited me."

"Yes, I know that. But why?"

Josephine flicked her gaze to Kohlvar. "Honestly, I-"

"DO NOT look at him." Caladorn thundered, rising from his chair with a murderous glare.

Josephine scrambled backwards in alarm, trying to work out what she had done wrong. "I'm sorry?" The apology came out sounding painfully like a question, which only furthered the King's anger.

"When the King of the Elven Realm gives you permission to look upon him, you do not look at another unless he has dismissed you."

"Oh," Josephine exclaimed, feeling her hands tremble. "My apologies, I did not know."

His pale eyes, two orbs of jade, bore into her curiously. "No, I can see that you did not. For only a fool would dare to behave like that in front of me."

Josephine held his gaze silently, as the pause grew painfully long between them. She heard nervous fidgeting from her right, but she did not dare do anything but focus on the terrifying man in front of her. Her head throbbed painfully, directly above her right eye, as if the King were drilling a hole into her skull.

"What is your power?" He barked, cutting the silence so sharply that Josephine felt as if air had finally been allowed back into her lungs.

"I do not have power, sir."

His gaze darkened. "Are you lying to me?" His voice was so quiet she nearly missed his question.

"No sir. I am unremarkable. I do not know of any power that I possess."

"Then why are you here?"

"I...I don't know, sir." She winced at the answer; she was not trying to be intentionally vague or frustrating. But it was the truth, she didn't know what Kohlvar saw in her to recruit her.

His nostrils flared. "Why were you in my lands? Humans are forbidden."

"I was lost." Also true, but this was about to get hard to explain.

He took a deep breath, fury radiating off him. Yet unlike Torva, his anger was cold, not unlike his niece's presence. "How did you come to be lost?"

"There was an incident that killed many people." A lump formed in her throat at the memory. "Things have not been easy for humans in recent years. I was lucky to survive, and in my confusion, I ended up here."

His brows drew together. "The Human Realm is on the opposite side of the continent. Do you truly expect me to believe that you wandered through the desert, through siren territory, or past the witches, and ended up here?"

"I do not remember the journey. I was injured, and my memory after the incident is patchy, at best."

"Show me your injuries."

Josephine looked down, tensing as she anticipated an outburst, but it did not come. She knelt, dutifully rolling up her pant leg of her injured right leg. A thick pink scar marked where concrete had burst open her skin, starting halfway up her shin and curling diagonally around the outside edge of her calf, ending behind her knee. Smaller marks and thin scars adorned her shin around the scar, from previous injuries and lesser wounds from the bombing. She was certain her tibia bone had been fractured, potentially her fibula too.

She rose, leaving her leg exposed, as she unbuttoned the cuffs of her oversized shirt, exposing the faint lines scattered across her forearms from debris and shattered glass.

Finally, she reached for her long braid, unravelling it to reveal the rigid bump that seemed to have taken up permanent residence behind her temple. She did not expose her chest, for her rib injuries had been internal, and left no visible scars now she was healed.

Josephine turned her gaze back to the King, standing tall with her scars on display. She was unprepared for the sheer level of disgust etched into King Caladorn's face.

Low murmurs were exchanged around the table as heat rose in Josephine's cheeks. She'd always been quite practical about her appearance, but to be exposed to these critical people was stirring a long-buried insecurity inside her chest.

"Well, clearly my people did not help you. Our healers would never leave scars like that. And I presume you will tell me you don't know who healed you."

Josephine ignored the ire in his voice, allowing her hair to fall down her back once again. "I do not remember being healed, only waking and being far further from imminent death than I was."

He scoffed. "Cover yourself up, before I lose my breakfast."

Josephine recoiled, though she tried to keep the movement subtle. She certainly did not want the attention of the King, but there was only so much one's ego could take.

The King turned away from her, looking towards his wife. "Well, my dear?"

Josephine glanced towards Queen Sylvara, her breath hitching at her incandescent beauty. Her red hair shone with the morning light, loosely tumbling over her back and shoulders. Her liquid brown eyes were locked on Josephine, framed with delicate blonde lashes that gave her an other-worldly aesthetic.

"I believe she was brought to us for a reason, my love. She holds a great power unlike any I've ever seen."

Her words both soothed her wounded ego and resonated like a slap. Was this a good thing? Or would this declaration of her nonexistent ability bring about her demise?

She felt the King's gaze fall upon her again, so she quickly returned her attention to him.

"Be that as it may, it is one thing to have great power. It is another thing to wield it and not be consumed by it." His eyes flicked over her body again. "Leave us, human."

Josephine bowed her head respectfully, keeping her head lowered as she made her swift departure.

Chapter Forty-Two

Kohlvar

"There's another report of siren attacks on the far side of the village, and it's affecting our travel routes. Kohlvar, Torva, you will remedy the issue."

Kohlvar forced his features to remain neutral, still reeling from the King's interrogation of Josephine. "How large was the attack? It must be significant if it is bothering the main roads."

Caladorn shrugged, his eyes on the scroll held flat between his palms. "I'm sure a soldier of your calibre can handle it." His words were cold, dismissing his concerns. "If not, you can always take your recruits with you. It will be a good experience for them."

Kohlvar bristled, pressing on precariously. "I appreciate the offer, your Highness, but I'll handle it."

His eyebrows raised at the response. "Do you think your recruits so incompetent, Kohlvar?" Colour started to rise to his cheeks as he heard Vessara chuckle quietly.

Torva interjected, "I think the healers would be quite unhappy if we filled the infirmary with students suffering from siren envenomation."

A murmur of agreement rose from around the room.

"I do not care how you deal with it, as long as it is done," Caladorn's pale eyes landed on him, his authority unmistakable.

"I understand, your Highness."

He waved his hand, dismissing them. Kohlvar swiftly moved to the exit, feeling Torva's seething presence behind him.

"Is he trying to kill them?" Torva muttered under her breath.

Kohlvar didn't acknowledge her frustration. "I'll deal with it. I'll be back before dinner."

"Don't be ridiculous, I'm coming with you."

He whirled around, shaking his head fiercely. "I need you here to watch over them."

She sighed. "But you need someone to watch your back. Why not take one of the recruits? Persephone can fight-"

"Persephone almost died a couple weeks ago, I'm not endangering her life again."

"Fine, then take another one."

"Who?" he challenged, crossing his arms as he leaned back against the stone walls. "Seralie is terrified of fighting, Draka doesn't communicate, Kaelith would probably insult the sirens as a joke, so who is truly capable of helping?"

"You need someone to watch your back, you get into trouble when you're alone." Torva grumbled, crossing her arms to mirror his defensive stance.

He scowled at her. "That was a long time ago, we're not kids anymore."

After a long moment of determined glares, Torva relented with a huff. "Fine. But if you're not back this evening, I'm bringing *all* the students with me to find you."

His brows furrowed even deeper. "That would be ridiculous-"

"So is facing an unknown number of sirens by yourself, but today seems to be the day for idiotic decisions." She cast a quick glance back towards the King's war room, rolling her eyes.

"Careful," Kohlvar murmured.

"You too, I have no interest in wrangling your recruits for you." She frowned, looking back at the door. "Are we going to talk about the other thing that happened in there?"

Kohlvar did not respond, instead he pushed himself off the wall, briskly striding towards the dining hall.

"Kohl?" Torva's voice echoed across the quiet halls.

He pushed on, ignoring the barrage of questions he was sure she was prepared to unleash.

"Kohl!"

"I don't know, Tor. I need to find her. Where is she?" Kohlvar exclaimed in dwarvish as he scanned the near empty breakfast hall.

"Probably outside with the others waiting for us."

Kohlvar shook his head. "No, she wouldn't have gone to them. Not yet."

"What are you talking about? What's going on?" Torva hissed as they encountered acolytes and soldiers enroute to morning classes.

Kohlvar paused, assessing his statement. "I don't think she would want to rejoin the group so soon after that interrogation. She would've needed a moment to breathe, right? Where would she go?"

Torva contemplated his words, scanning the dozens of elves migrating to the open courtyard. "I'll check the bathrooms, you check the library."

Kohlvar stormed into the library seconds later, his heavy footsteps alarming the handful of patrons studying at this hour. He'd arrived before Fissius, thank the Souls, and wasted no time methodically searching the library. For a uniform, circular design there were a surprising number of alcoves and hidden rooms one could vanish in. He disturbed two couples in the middle of interesting conversations and was just beginning to give up when he heard a low voice murmuring.

"The Order of the Ascended are devoted to the Souls, intended to deliver the word of Orias to his subjects. They reigned supreme in all matters regarding the Eternal Souls, until a sickness struck their ranks 80 years ago."

Kohlvar approached the room cautiously, shifting to get a better angle into the tiny room. Josephine stood over a small table, several books flipped open, spread in a haphazard fashion. She held one book in each hand, looking between the passages, her brows furrowed just enough to crease her brow.

Kohlvar's breath hitched at her appearance. She was still wearing her hair down, loose and long, the sleeves from his shirt rolled up to her elbows.

She looked like she'd just rolled out of bed, having enjoyed a splendid night's rest. To see her like this was intoxicating, making Kohlvar want to see her in this state at all times.

"Josie," he hummed, keeping his voice low.

She jumped, her hazel green eyes jumping to his as she snapped shut the books. "Bloody hell, you scared me."

"Sorry love, I tend to have that effect on people." He winced at the casual term of affection. He hadn't intended to say it.

She smiled weakly at him, unease evident in her stiff posture. "So...what was that about?" Her hands trembled as she set the books down.

Kohlvar nodded, stepping into the crammed space and altering the air around them to buffer sound. "That was unexpected. The Princess showed up, I worried she was going to inform the King of our altercation last week. But I should've known her pride would be too great for that. Instead, she tried to convince King Caladorn to allow her to experiment on your abilities."

"Experiment?" She regarded him suspiciously. Smart woman.

Kohlvar scratched the back of his head. "Vessara likes to push people to their absolute limit, and sometimes that produces interesting magical responses."

"Push? As in tease? Or are we talking about something like torture?" He saw her nose wrinkle in disdain, hiding the worry in her eyes.

"The latter, I'm afraid." He closed his eyes, pushing away the memories surging forth from his training.

"Oh," she said shakily, looking down at her trembling hands. "Did he agree?"

"No."

"Why not?"

"Because the Queen objected on account of your abilities."

Josephine's brows shot up. "You mean the abilities I don't have? You do realise she's wrong, right?"

Kohlvar eyed her carefully, watching for any sign she was deceiving him. "Is she?" He finally asked, his voice a low grumble.

"YES!" Josephine shouted, loud enough that Kohlvar stepped back in surprise. "For *fucks sake*, Kohlvar! I've told you a dozen times, I'm not special. I don't have any special powers, she just saw a memory of mine and assumed it meant something. All it meant is that my home, my people are dying, and somehow that's important for her symbolically." She scoffed derisively, pulling her hair back from her face.

"Have you considered that you may have a power you don't know about?"

Josie rolled her eyes as her hands dropped. "I think we'd know by now!"

"You connected with an Eternal Soul," he countered.

"Once."

"And you wielded against the Princess that night."

"Again, I'm not so sure that's actually what happened-"

"And you're the first human to survive travelling through a portal in over 80 years."

"Barely! I was on death's doorstep, I only survived because you two were right there."

"Josie."

"Kohlvar." She levelled a glare at him.

"There might just be more to you than either of us realise."

"Look, I know most girls want to hear that they're special and different from everyone else, but I truly am not!" Her eyes were red-rimmed, hair askew from her anxious hands.

Kohlvar sighed, rubbing the sharp headache brewing behind his temples. "Josie-"

"And what the *hell* am I supposed to do when I fail to produce these abilities like a monkey on display for the King and Queen? They'll realise soon enough that I am nothing special, and then I'll be thrown to the evil incarnation of Frozen for her to torture me. I'm fucked, Kohl." Despair overtook her features, striking Kohlvar with guilt.

"Hey," he rumbled, reaching for her wrist. "Look at me."

He watched as she drew a steadying breath, eyeing him warily. "I won't let that happen," he murmured, his thumb rubbing the back of her hand.

She laughed, unkindly. "Really? What would you have done if the King said yes today? If the Queen hadn't interfered?"

Kohlvar fell silent. Because she was correct. He protested, and he would've continued to, vehemently. However, if the King had agreed, the only actions he could take would immediately break the vows he'd made to the Elven Realm, jeopardising the safety of all hybrids in his army.

"That's what I thought," she whispered, pulling herself out of his grasp. Josephine brushed her fingers over the open books. "No matter how much reading I do, I cannot find anything to explain what happened in that grove, Kohlvar. I cannot explain anything that's happened since the bombing."

He moved to stand beside her, gently wrapping an arm around her shoulders. "Then it's time for a new plan." His stomach fluttered as she looked up at him, the freckles scattered across her face easily visible at this proximity.

"What do you propose?" Her eyes scanned his face, looking down at his lips for the barest moment.

"It's time for you to reach out again."

"When?"

"Soon, but today I must deal with other matters." He tried to keep his voice level as a heavy sense of dread settled in his stomach. He turned away, avoiding her gaze.

"Kohl?"

He paused, half turning his head to look over his shoulder in her direction.

"Be safe." Her eyes held a surprising amount of concern, her lip quivering slightly as she clutched her hands tightly.

He simply nodded, not trusting himself to leave her if he spoke. She looked scared, and he hated it.

Chapter Forty-Three

Kohlvar

Kohlvar walked the perimeter of the lake, glancing back towards the military fortress stationed high on the opposite bank. He should be training his acolytes right now, not going on a fool's errand. He should be preparing them mentally, as well as physically, in case Vessara came after them.

Instead, he shucked off his boots, goosebumps prickling over his torso as his shirt came off. His toes brushed the water's edge as he called upon his siren form. He shivered as water flowed over his skin, submerging himself until he was covered in slick blue-green scales, dark fins sprouting from his limbs and spine. A membranous webbing appeared between his fingers, allowing him to push through the water with ease despite his size.

He waded out, relishing the sensation of the lake rippling around him, the vibrational sounds of the vast ecosystem beneath him calling out. This was one of the only places he felt peaceful, for he could not intercept the emotional discord of the thousands of creatures beneath the water. Even the sirens were difficult to read, preferring to communicate through song beneath the surface. Their danger significantly increased when they rose to the surface, not that they made the fact well known. Their notoriety played a significant role in deterring unwelcome guests.

Kohlvar hovered in the centre of the lake, taking a deep breath before diving, propelling himself into the darkness. Fish surrounded him, their cool bodies darting erratically past him, as he moved towards the familiar song that guided him home.

A curious trilling echoed towards him, questioning his approach. However, at the sight of him, several of the smaller sirens scattered, shrieking obscenities as they dived into the tangled reeds surrounding their nest.

"You dare to come into our home?" The song echoed from a young female, her scales a deep blue, nearly invisible at this depth.

Kohlvar dug his toes into the lakebed, anchoring himself in the sand. "I do. I wish to discuss peace."

The female drifted towards him, baring her serrated shark-like teeth. "Peace? You wish to discuss peace? Tell that to that bastard boy the elves call King. He murdered our elders, sirens, who had nothing to do with Liora's death. We do not harm innocents."

He listened intently, despite having heard these arguments countless times. "Why are you targeting the villagers? Our roads? What has changed?"

She hissed vehemently, her maw extending wide in a blatant threat. "We grow tired of our confinement and will no longer endure it. Our offspring are innocent, yet they are paying for events that occurred before their time."

Kohlvar frowned, keeping his arms spread in a wide, calm stance. "Do you speak of the hybrids?"

She scowled, "Persephone belongs with us!"

"She will die with you!" He roared back. "I am keeping her safe, she cannot survive here."

"Lies, all you do is lie! You are a traitor, you are not welcome here anymore," the female shot forward, her venomous talons extending towards his throat.

Kohlvar pushed off from the lakebed, floundering beneath the all-consuming darkness, fighting the song luring him to return.

Agonising pain shot through his leg, lightning flashing white hot across his vision. He howled, losing what precious air remained in his mammalian lungs. He kicked out, his uninjured leg slamming into the siren as her claws scraped at his chest. Her screams threatened to deafen him, his senses altered by the venom pounding through his bloodstream.

The faintest sphere of light trickled down to him with his heightened vision as he continued to push himself skyward. Fire burned through his lungs, his body threatening to succumb to the incessant pain. He just had to reach the surface, and he could escape.

A strange vibration resonated through him, the only flicker of warning before he collided with something solid, his vision turning black.

Chapter Forty-Four

Josephine

Josephine was itching to try her hand at magic again, but Torva had drilled magical theory into them instead. She hadn't seen Kohlvar all day, which wasn't exactly unusual, but she felt wrecked with worry. He'd been out of sorts ever since she'd seen him in the library, since the Princess had harassed him.

She felt distracted too, as Persephone, Kaelith and Seralie argued over dinner. Eryndal watched with muted frustration, Draka tearing into his food as though he couldn't hear them.

Josephine gazed out the enormous windows that overlooked the shimmering lake, wondering what her daughters were doing. Were they enjoying the last few rays of sunshine before winding down for bed? How cold was it back home? She hoped they were only experiencing a mild winter, rather than Susan struggling to keep the house, or themselves, warm.

"Jo? Are you with us?" Seralie's question disrupted her rambling thoughts. "We were just discussing who would win in a fight; Kohlvar or Torva?"

Josephine contemplated the question, "Hmm, that's a good one. I imagine it'd be a pretty close match."

"Kohlvar is huge though!" Kaelith exclaimed, his hands gesturing broadly.

"But she wields fire magic, surely that's a better offensive weapon than water and air." Josephine countered.

Four sets of eyes suddenly landed on her. "What?" Josephine leaned back at their shocked stares.

"She wields fire?" Persephone leaned forward, her voice suddenly low and quiet.

Dread lurched in her stomach. She hadn't realised that wasn't common knowledge. "Uhhh..."

"Torva had to take out a plant that got a little too excited when I tried to wield my earth magic." Seralie whispered back. "And yes, she does. We saw it."

"Why didn't you tell us?" Kaelith exclaimed loudly, earning a shushing from Eryndal. Even Draka was fixated on the two of them, pausing his relentless devouring of food.

"I didn't realise it was a big deal." Josephine admitted.

"Fire wielders are very rare, mostly found in the dwarven populations. They usually work in the mines, predominantly forging weaponry." Eryndal recited academically.

"Well, Torva is part dwarf, it would make sense she's a fire wielder," Persephone mused.

"I guess that's why she radiates heat when she's angry," Seralie glanced at Draka, questioningly.

Kaelith frowned. "I thought that was just because she's a big person. I'm not being rude!" He narrowed his eyes as Eryndal looked at him accusingly. "But she is very tall with large muscles."

"But Kohlvar doesn't radiate heat like that, and he's even bigger. Perhaps it's related to her fire wielding, not her size," Josephine countered.

"You should investigate more thoroughly, to confirm how big and warm Kohlvar is," Persephone muttered slyly, an innocent expression on her face.

Josephine glared at her, ignoring the confused looks from their companions. "What about dragons?" She deflected.

"Well, dragons themselves aren't considered wielders; they breathe fire. But dragonoids..." Eryndal trailed off as one by one they turned to Draka.

"He says he doesn't produce heat like Torva does," Seralie translated, a small smile gracing her face as she looked at him.

Draka didn't say or indicate any further information. With a huff he turned back to his meal, shredding another rare steak with his carnivorous teeth.

Josephine listened as the conversation continued on, wondering how Torva ended up here with Kohlvar. She had dwarven heritage, why didn't she join the Dwarven Army? Did being half-elf give her other abilities as well? What had the elixir done to her and Kohlvar, presuming they had taken it.

So many questions she wished to ask him, if only he were here.

****

"Are you coming up to bed Jo?" Seralie's soft voice floated through the chatter of their friends.

Josephine looked outside at the last few wisps of sunlight. "I think I'm going to get some fresh air first. Go fight the others for a hot shower, I'll be up soon."

The young woman nodded, leaving Josephine to her thoughts. She trailed away from the receding voices, wandering through the hallway until the front courtyard came into view. Her mind was a jumbled mess today. She was still trying to process the possibility she could connect with the Eternal Souls. The implications set her mind ablaze with endless questions she could not find the answer for.

She reached for the cool sandstones lining the courtyard, allowing the coarse cold rock to graze her fingertips. When Josephine felt lost in her mind, she needed physical touch to bring her back into the present. When the days were truly dark, that physical connection often became painful, just to make her feel something.

Josephine closed her eyes as she gripped the side of the stone bench, allowing the grooves and ridges to dig painfully into her sensitive palm. Breathing deeply, she focused on the scratching pain to drown out her mind.

It was a habit she'd picked up as a child, after her brother died. She knew it wasn't a good one, but it seemed better than turning to drugs or alcohol.

Besides, she rarely broke the skin, so it wasn't really that bad, right?

Josephine scoffed, annoyed that in the absence of endless questions her mind had turned to justifying her self-harm tendencies. And whilst she could argue the point for days, she didn't want to. She just wanted her mind to *shut up* and let her sleep. She was barely functioning with the insomnia and raging anxiety. Maybe she'd just drop dead of exhaustion, then she'd get some decent rest.

With a defeated sigh, Josephine pulled her hand away from the sandstone. She rubbed her thumb into the dented pads of her palm, as if she could erase the marks. They wouldn't last long, wouldn't even bruise, but the guilt and shame that came after the act would plague her in the morning.

Josephine was just turning to return inside when she heard an odd grunting noise. She frowned, tentatively looking around.

If that was someone's efforts at lovemaking, she felt sorry for the recipient.

She rolled her eyes and turned away, only to hear a pained gasp from down the hill. Alarm shot through her, causing her to rush to the top of the stairs leading down from the courtyard.

Half-collapsed against the stairs was Kohlvar, clutching his side. He was covered in strange luminescent stains, but more concernedly, were the dark red stains seeping down his leg.

Blood.

"Kohl!" Josephine yelled as she raced down the stairs. "What the fuck happened to you?" She slipped down to his side, hooking an arm under his shoulder.

"Need...to get...inside." He pushed against the steps with his free hand, staggering to his feet. A black backpack shifted across his back, causing him to stagger.

"Give me that," Josephine ordered, yanking at the leather strap unsuccessfully. Kohlvar shifted the bag off his shoulder with ease, allowing her to grab it from him. It was heavier than she had expected, similarly covered in glowing blue slime.

She ignored the unpleasant squelch against her hip, wrapping her arm around Kohlvar's waist. He really was enormous, but thankfully he seemed to mostly need stabilisation, which she could provide.

"Okay, just take one step at a time, Kohl. We are not falling down these bloody stairs."

Kohlvar grunted in response, his arm weighing heavily across her shoulders. Dutifully, he took each step carefully, his gasping breaths rattling her.

As they slowly made their way into the courtyard, quickly approaching steps sent a bolt of panic through Josephine's chest. She looked up to find Torva thundering towards them, fury marring her strong features.

"You took the *human*?" She hissed, her rage sizzled the air, striking Josephine with blistering heat. Josephine flinched at the burning pain.

"No," Kohlvar gasped. "She...found me."

Her fury shifted to Kohlvar. "You *idiot*, I told you not to go alone." She yanked his other arm up, throwing it over her shoulder despite his moan of pain. "Jo, go ahead to the infirmary and let them know we're coming."

"No!" Kohlvar gasped, doubling over to cough. Dark fluid splattered on the pale stones.

"Shit, Kohl, what happened?" Torva pressed, urging him inside the doors.

"Sirens," he muttered, his lips stained with blood.

"Why did they attack you though?" Torva's brow creased with worry. Her radiant anger had simmered down, mercifully allowing the cool night air to soothe Josephine's irritated skin.

"My room," Kohlvar grunted as they reached the hallway that led to the infirmary.

Josephine looked to Torva for guidance. She appeared to be debating the two options, before sighing. "Fine, Kohlvar. Jo, can you take that pack to the infirmary? They need to make the antidote."

She nodded and went to pull away, but Kohlvar's grip on her tightened.

"No, I don't need it," he growled.

Torva threw her hand up in exasperation. "Why not Kohl? It will help you recover more quickly."

"She's not meant to be involved. You take it." Kohlvar's breathing had improved, marginally.

"She became involved when you got injured and she found you, Kohl. She can take the damned siren venom to the healers!" Torva argued.

Josephine screwed up her face, eyeing the sticky pack at her side suspiciously.

"That's...an order, Tor." He grunted out.

Torva stiffened. "Fine," she spat icily. She released Kohlvar suddenly, allowing him to sag against the wall, before snatching the backpack from Josephine.

Josephine watched her receding figure, once again filled with questions and no answers. She turned to Kohlvar, wanting to unleash the buzzing queries, but one look at his ashen face silenced them all.

"Come on, let's get you to bed."

***

They made it to his chambers without crossing paths with another person, which was a minor miracle. Kohlvar had opened his door with a flourish of his hand, slamming it closed with another.

The room was still as impressive as she remembered. His enormous bed was covered in knitted throws and blankets. The desk was covered in papers across from an unlit fireplace. The woven rug started to absorb drops of blood and siren venom by the hearth, startling Josephine out of her thoughts.

"Now what?"

Instead of replying, Kohlvar shuffled towards his desk, yanking open drawers. He grabbed a handful of jars and tubes out of it, ripping corks out with his teeth. He drank from two tubes, breathing deeply, before limping over to a seat near the fireplace. A paste filled jar rested in his hand, but he seemed in no hurry to use it.

"Fire," he grunted.

Josephine crouched by the fireplace, poking the coals with a stick. A few dying red embers flared. She quickly set about placing kindling, blowing air to encourage it to light. After several tedious moments, she managed to keep a stable fire going, with a central log finally catching alight.

She looked to Kohlvar for further instruction, surprised to find him relaxed with his eyes closed. Josephine nudged his foot with hers, his eyes flew open.

"Don't you go passing out on me, or worse. What needs to be done with that paste? Where are your wounds?" She eyed the dark stains, which seemed to have stopped progressing.

"I should bathe," he gestured at the glowing slime, "This is not good for infection, but I don't know if I can. I'll just sit for a minute." His eyes started to drift closed again.

"Oh no you don't, you're going to pass out on me. Get up, we'll get you bathed." Josephine commanded.

She pulled at his arm, unable to budge him. But he humoured her and stood, groaning in pain. They slowly walked into the bathroom. His gait more unsteady than before.

"Are you sure we shouldn't be at the infirmary?"

"No!" He barked, coughing from the harsh sound. "They can't know."

"But will you heal? I would prefer it if you didn't die." Josephine tried to keep her tone mild.

He huffed, "Would that inconvenience you, Jo?"

"Just a little. Sit, can you undress?"

Kohlvar tried, but judging by the way he clutched his ribs, every movement hurt him. Josephine went searching for scissors, hoping he would not fall in her brief absence. When she returned, he'd managed to unbutton his jacket and half-unlace his shirt.

He spotted the scissors, his eyes widening. "Not the jacket!"

"Alright, don't panic." Josephine put the scissors down, helping Kohlvar out of his jacket, vest, belt and boots. Once he was down to his pants and linen shirt, she grabbed the scissors again. She quickly snipped away the shirt, frowning at the green plant wrapped around Kohlvar's torso. The same slimy plant was wrapped around his right thigh, above his clothing. His hand slowly peeled the vine away from his thigh, allowing her to access his clothing.

The pants were more difficult to remove than his shirt. They fit him snugly, clinging to his muscular thighs and calves. If he wasn't in such a dire state, she would've admired the way the fit accentuated his toned muscles.

Under the plant, his pant leg was shredded, falling away with a few snips. The material was uncomfortably sticky, clinging to the skin between four weeping slash marks.

Josephine inhaled sharply looking at the wounds. The bleeding seemed to have slowed, despite the wounds still being open. She looked curiously at the plant on the floor.

"It's from the lake, it clots bleeding. Good for when you're caught off guard," he gasped, his hands shaking.

"What's wrong?" Josephine asked as she continued cutting away the pants.

"Nothing," he said, too quickly.

"It's clearly not nothing, so tell me."

He coughed, leaning his head back against the wall. "When did you get so bossy?"

"When I found you bleeding out on the fucking stairs, Kohlvar, that's when!" Josephine winced. "Sorry, that was harsher than I meant. It's just that I can't read your mind, I don't know if you're shaking because you've lost blood, or you need pain medicine, or if this glowing blue shit is affecting you. So, I need you to tell me what is wrong, and how to fix it. If you pass out the best I can do is to clean your wounds and throw a blanket on you."

She focused on snipping away the rest of his pants, leaving him only in his underwear. She averted her eyes respectfully, but noticed that he was clutching his shaking hands in his lap. He flinched as she stood, pausing her movement towards his ribs.

"Kohl?"

His eyes were closed tightly, his hands clenched into fists. His breathing was rapid, his entire body shaking.

"Kohlvar, I need you to talk to me." Josephine crouched back down, hoping that making herself smaller would help.

A loud knock at the door caused both of them to startle, Josephine losing her balance and slowly falling onto her backside, the cold tile seeping through her pants. She scoffed, brushing herself off as she rose.

"I presume that's Torva, I'll let her in." Josephine looked him over to make sure he wasn't about to fall off his chair, before quickly moving to the door. She reached for the handle, only it wouldn't budge.

She frowned, twisting it in different directions and wiggling it.

"Kohl? Is that you?" Torva's familiar voice echoed through the wooden door.

"It's Jo, he's cleaning up. I can't seem to open the door?"

She heard the jiggling of a handle from the other side, followed by cursing in an unfamiliar language. "Did he lock it with magic?"

"Um...I think so? He did something with his hand." Josephine recalled.

More swearing followed. "Only he can unlock it then, he has very strict wards on his private chambers. Go get him, I brought food and medicine."

"I can try, but he doesn't seem right."

Alarm entered Torva's voice. "What do you mean by that?"

"He said he needed to bathe, and he couldn't undress himself, but he's...he...he's acting strangely, I don't think it's from his injuries." Josephine glanced back at the ensuite, feeling like she was betraying Kohlvar. But Torva had been the one to warn her about this, it seemed fair to relay this information back to her.

Silence echoed from the hallway. "I understand. He...Can he clean his wounds himself?"

"No, it's a fight to keep him conscious. What should I do?" She asked, feeling helpless.

"Get him cleaned up and bandage his wounds. If he has a jar that smells like cloves, or garlic, apply that to any wounds. He usually keeps some in his room, probably in his desk."

"And then?"

A deep sigh rumbled through the door. "Then settle in for a long night, he'll need monitoring, and you can't leave until he unlocks the door."

She would've loved to point out that having a door unable to be opened from the inside was a huge safety issue but now was not the time.

Josephine walked back into the bathroom, relieved to find Kohlvar where she left him. He'd peeled away the plant wrapped around his chest, revealing a large purple bruise radiating from a puncture wound on his lower ribs.

"Bloody hell, what caused that?" Josephine whispered.

He jumped, startled by her return. "A rock. I fell when I ran from the sirens, tumbled down a hill and smashed into a sharp rock. Bad luck really."

"Are your ribs broken?"

"Oh definitely, at least cracked."

"Shit. I can't help much with broken ribs. Can I look at the wound?" she waited for his hesitant nod of approval before approaching.

She slowly placed her hands on either side of the wound, watching his reaction for any signs of distress. He met her gaze, his blue eyes cautious and guarded.

"I want to see how bad the puncture wound is, and check to see if you have a collapsed lung."

She looked back at the wound, which seemed to have mostly hit two of his ribs and not penetrated too deeply. There was no whistling, or complaints of inability to breathe from Kohlvar. Still, she should bandage it in a way that allowed any trapped air to escape.

"Were you a healer in the human world?" Kohlvar murmured, his voice faint.

"No, but my aunt was a nurse. I learnt a lot from her, and the girls had their fair share of injuries and illnesses over the years."

She noticed he'd draped a towel over his lap while she'd been gone. It really wasn't the time to be worried about modesty, but she understood why he might be struggling to appear vulnerable in front of her.

Josephine pushed aside the sharp flare of anger that rose in her chest, focusing on the injured man in front of her.

"Do you think you can stand for a shower, or should I fill a bucket?" Josephine met his eyes again, noticing the bloodshot whites. He looked utterly exhausted.

Kohlvar looked at the shower, then shook his head. "I don't have a bucket, but if you fill the sink I can wet some towels."

Josephine noticed him taking ownership of bathing himself. "Do you want my help with that?"

He hesitated. "Preferably not, but if I cannot do it, then yes."

She nodded, moving to the sink.

"S-sorry," Kohlvar stuttered out.

"Why are you sorry? You don't need to be." The water turned warm quickly.

"I shouldn't have put you in this position."

"I'm happy to help, Kohl. Besides, you did the same for me when I came through the portal." She hasn't forgotten the genuine care she'd received from both men during her recovery.

"This isn't...easy for me," he hesitantly confessed.

Tenderness blossomed slowly in her chest. The last time they had gotten remotely close to this conversation, he had shut down. "Why not?" She dunked a small towel into the warm water, wringing it out before handing it to Kohlvar.

He took the cloth and began wiping his torso clean. "I've had to be quite suspicious of those who offer help. Safer to do it yourself." He winced as he moved over his thighs, refreshing his towel in the sink for his wounds. The water turned pink.

"I'm sorry you've not been able to trust people." Josephine murmured as she prepared another towel.

Kohlvar paused, breathing deeply as he ran the towel over each slashing wound. "Thank you." He murmured, and Josephine wasn't sure what for.

He finished bathing, slumping against the back of his chair. "The medicine I took...it's wearing off. Need to dress these wounds...and...sleep."

Josephine nodded, leaving him to search for supplies. Once she found the jar he'd held earlier, which smelt strongly of cloves, bandages and fresh clothing, she returned. He was half asleep leaning against the wall.

"Wake up, Kohl, we're nearly there. Can I put this on your wounds?"

He eyed the jar and groaned. "Yes, I'll hate it but do it."

She slathered it on his thigh wound first, noticing the way Kohlvar tensed and grabbed at the sink when she did. She quickly wrapped his thigh in a thick bandage, before repeating the same on his ribs. She couldn't find the same equipment as they'd had in the human world, so she settled for wrapping his ribs. Kohlvar insisted on binding them tightly, despite the pain it appeared to cause.

She helped him into a long shirt, supporting him to stand. He seemed to breathe a little easier, but his face was alarmingly pale, almost grey.

"Do you need another of those tubes? The ones I saw you drink?"

"No, just sleep." He was grunting with every step on his injured leg, but soon he was at his enormous bed. Josephine pulled back the covers, watching him gingerly shuffle under the covers.

When she tried to ask him about the locked door, he was already asleep.

Chapter Forty-Five

Josephine

Josephine spent the evening pacing, checking Kohlvar's breathing and generally feeling useless. Whilst curiosity to explore plagued her, she knew that Kohlvar had invested a great deal of trust in her, and she didn't want to lose it.

She avoided the desk littered with handwritten letters, skimmed the bookshelf with unfamiliar languages, and mostly kept herself warm by the fire.

Her anxiety always spiked in the evening, when she was trying to wind down for sleep. Except tonight it was worse, striking while she had another person to worry over.

Why was Kohlvar out by the lake so late? Why did he go alone? Was it usually this dangerous? Why were there sirens? Were they the same kind of sirens that Kohlvar, or Persephone were descended from? It was becoming difficult to know which creatures of lore were real or purely fantastical.

She tried to soothe her racing heart, intentionally slowing her breathing and trying to distract herself with the physical sensation of radiant heat on her bare skin.

She was filthy, covered in siren venom and Kohlvar's blood. Normally she'd hesitate to shower and borrow clothing in someone's home without permission, however the longer she wore Kohlvar's blood, the more she fretted.

She quickly bathed, setting aside the ruined clothing and cleaned up the bathroom. She found another linen shirt, which was nearly a dress on her, along with a pair of black pants with a tie at the waist. It seemed the best option she would find here, did Kohlvar never wear pyjamas?

There was a thought she shouldn't pursue. Typical bloke though, if he was the kind to sleep naked. It seemed impractical for him though.

She brushed aside the nonsensical thoughts, and she checked Kohlvar once more. His breathing and heart rate had remained stable, which seemed to be a good sign. Josephine felt her shoulders sag a tiny bit, as her clean body started to relax. She spotted a thick blanket draped over one of the armchairs, and the sight of it seemed to break the mental barrier holding back her exhaustion.

***

"You're still here."

Josephine startled awake, almost rolling off the chair, still wrapping in the borrowed blanket.

"Bloody hell, you scared me!" Josephine clutched at her heart, the sudden acceleration of its beat leaving her breathless.

She looked up to see Kohlvar standing, favouring his uninjured leg.

"Should you be standing?" She looked pointed to his injured thigh, noticing the muscles tensing and relaxing tentatively.

"Didn't you once tell me it's better to move after an injury?" A glint of humour sparkled in his eyes, causing relief to flow through Josephine.

She scoffed, "True, I did say that."

"So why are you still here?" His head tilted slightly, as if she were a puzzle he was struggling to solve.

"Well, there were two reasons why. Firstly, because Torva told me to, and I'm not one to defy her without a very good reason. And secondly," she gestured towards the door, "I couldn't open the door."

Kohlvar frowned, looking from her to the door, until understanding clicked. "Ohhh... Oh."

"Yes, you locked us both in here. You know that's really not a good idea safety wise. How would a guest escape if there was a fire? I don't fancy my chances of climbing out the window."

"I don't normally invite guests back to my private rooms." Kohlvar shrugged.

Josephine raised her eyebrows. "Oh?"

He looked away, scratching his ribs through the bandages. "Torva has been in for quick chats, but never with the door locked."

"What about when you have romantic company?" The question blurted out before she could stop herself.

Kohlvar shot her a startled look. "My earlier statement still applies. Do you have any other topics you'd like to discuss?"

Point taken. "Yes, how are your wounds?" She stood, looking pointedly at his leg.

"Good, they're healing. The paste you applied has kept infection away." Kohlvar was running a hand through his hair. Josephine wondered if he always made that movement when he was anxious, or if it was just a coincidence.

"Can I have a look? It's okay if not, I just want to make sure." Josephine searched his eyes, trying to gauge his reaction.

He hesitated for a split second, before rolling up his long shirt to reveal his thigh. He deftly unwrapped the bandages, revealing four closed slash marks.

Josephine hadn't stitched the wounds, yet they were knitting back together perfectly without them. She gasped at the progress.

"That's how fast you heal?" Her tone was incredulous.

"It was accelerated by the tonics I drank and the paste you applied, but yes, I heal quickly." He gave a pleased smile.

"You lucky, lucky bastard." Josephine swore, thinking of how long it had taken her to heal after the bombing.

An unexpected laugh broke out of Kohlvar, before he gasped and clutched at his ribs.

"Hmm, I'm guessing bone still takes some time?" Josephine grimaced sympathetically.

He nodded, taking short staggering breaths against the pain.

"Can I ask what happened?"

The question hung in the air for a moment, long enough Josephine didn't think he would answer.

"There were reports of sirens attacking the villagers." His words came out halting, as he shuffled towards the dying fire. "I went out a few days ago to confirm the reports. They were sirens, which isn't unheard of and something we've dealt with before. They usually only attack if directly harmed or starving." He leaned against the top of the fireplace, stretching his leg out.

"However, these sirens were from the clan that were blamed for the demise of the late Princess, King Caladorn's sister."

Josephine frowned, a memory niggling at the back of her mind. "I think I read about that. She was Vessara's mother, wasn't she?"

Kohlvar flinched at her name. "Yeah," he mumbled hoarsely. "When Caladorn became king, he ordered to have them slaughtered. They were supposed to be extinct."

"How exactly do you eliminate an entire clan of sirens? Surely that would be rather difficult."

Kohlvar drew a deep breath. "He used an exceptional amount of magic to drain their lake, leaving them to suffocate. They can breathe out of water for a short while but...I've heard it was a truly horrific scene. Then he let the water return, washing their bodies downstream, as a message to the other siren clans."

Josephine stood next to him, horror written across her face. "That's barbaric."

"He is one of the strongest wielders alive, but he drew too much magic from the sources. It had severe consequences, for the environment, for the other wielders, for everyone. I suspect it is part of the reason we are getting less recruits every year."

Josephine watched a coal flare, flickering between red and orange. "So, what happened last night?"

"I tried to talk to them," Kohlvar sighed, resting his head against the warmed stone. "It was a terrible idea. Torva even said so. But I figured, being half siren, maybe they'd listen to me. I didn't want another massacre to happen, especially not if I could prevent it." His blue eyes found her, burning coals reflecting in them.

"They called me a traitor for serving the King. They attacked me, but they didn't intend to kill me."

Josephine's heart fluttered in alarm. "How do you know that?"

"Because I'd be dead now if they had." His lips were pulled into a grim line. "And they used siren venom, instead of a blade."

"I don't understand."

Kohlvar reached a hand out, pulling Josephine to his side. "Siren venom isn't fatal for me. It will make me sick, but it's not a death sentence. However, in my siren form, my flesh is easy to pierce. Even though they were angry, I think they knew that killing me would shatter any remaining truce between the sirens and the elves."

Josephine looked at him in surprise. "Why would killing you start a war, but not the villagers?"

"Because I'm the only one fighting to keep the peace." His forehead rested on hers, clammy against her warm skin. "I've been fighting for it for years, and I'm so fucking tired, Josie."

She embraced him, conscious of his wounds, and nuzzled her face into his shoulder. "I understand." Josephine knew what it felt like to fight for a cause that felt pointless, like at any point everything could come crumbling down despite your best efforts. Hell, that was the story of her life.

"I know you do." His rough cheek grazed over her scalp as he planted a kiss on her head. "I'm sorry things haven't been going smoothly for you."

Josephine scoffed. "When does life go smoothly for anyone?"

"Fair point," he pulled back just enough to find her eyes again. "But nonetheless, I am sorry. I still intend to help you find a way home."

"When can we try reaching out again?"

"Soon. I just need to figure out the siren situation, then we can try again. One crisis at a time, please."

Josephine looked into his eyes, a myriad of emotions swimming through them. She raised a hand tentatively towards his face, pausing before she made contact. His eyes fluttered closed as he rested his cheek in her hand, humming as her thumb brushed over the jagged scar splitting his face.

"Can I kiss you?" Josephine murmured, surprising herself. She hadn't entirely intended to ask, knowing he had struggled being vulnerable with her last night.

For a moment she was convinced he would say no. Instead, he surprised her by whispering, "Please."

She slowly reached up, stretching onto her toes, as she gently brushed her lips against his, drawing away to check his expression. His eyes were still firmly closed, but his hands pressed into her back, pulling her to his lips again.

She kissed him gently, letting him set the pace. She didn't want to push him too far, but she also wanted to show him how grateful she was that he'd let her in. That he'd let her care for him, the way he did for her every day.

Kohlvar broke away with a hiss. "Bloody ribs," he gasped. "I can't breathe when I'm kissing you."

Josephine carefully brushed her lips over his cheek. "So tell me, how long will it take for your ribs to heal?"

He chuckled. "A few more days."

"Is that really all?" Josephine looked at him in astonishment, her arms still looped around his neck.

He nodded. "Giants heal quickly, and the potions I drank helped too."

"Good to know," she murmured, pulling back from his firm embrace. "We have to go."

He sighed, "Yeah, I have a leadership meeting."

Her eyes widened at the thought. "Will you be okay? Do you need help dressing?"

Kohlvar shook his head, "No, I'll be alright."

"Alright then, mind unlocking the door then?"

Kohlvar's face paled. "Oh, shit, I'd already forgotten about that." He made the same hand gesture he'd made last night, the soft click echoing.

"Josie," his voice was low, like rocks grinding together. She turned to face him, one hand on the doorknob.

"Thank you, for last night." Gratitude and affection warmed his voice. Josephine smiled back, before slipping into the hallway.

Chapter Forty-Six

Josephine

"What do you *mean* we're taking the elixir this week?" Eryndal's panicked voice rose about the others. "I haven't honed my magic yet, I am not prepared. What if it rejects me? What if I am not good enough?" His voice trembled, causing Josephine to step forward and place a hand on his shoulder.

"Hey, it's not a reflection on you. Your skills just might not lie in water and earth like the girls do." It seemed to do little to calm his fears, his eyes watery.

Even Kaelith was subdued, staring intently at the ground. Seralie seemed on the verge of tears, trying to explain to Draka what was happening. Persephone looked uneasy, pacing back and forth.

"Why is he doing this?" Persephone shouted as she hit the edge of the lake. "You were all trained for *months* before you took the elixir. We've barely had weeks!"

"I don't know," Kohlvar answered calmly. "Both Galathir and Torva protested, and even Professor Fissius argued against it. But he was insistent."

Seralie hiccuped, her eyes red. "C-can you tell us what might happen? Especially if it goes bad?"

Torva nodded. "We don't know why the elixir reacts poorly sometimes. But if it does, sometimes it causes immense pain, other times your magic can turn inward and hurt you. It usually causes your abilities to weaken, rather than develop into your full powers."

"Is that the worst it can do?" Seralie squeaked.

Torva hesitated. "No. Depending on what magic you draw on after taking the elixir, it could kill you if it backfires."

"We could DIE?" Seralie shrieked, promptly bursting into tears. Draka growled, his golden eyes narrowed at Torva.

"It's very unlikely-" Kohlvar started to say, but it was too late. Hysteria had struck the group, creating a chorus of angry shouting, screaming, crying and staring off into the distance. Josephine felt surprisingly calm, having long resigned to the worst happening. But these acolytes were barely of age, no wonder they were terrified.

Judging by the cacophony echoing from the courtyard, Josephine suspected Galathir and Alfion were dealing with the same response from their own students.

She looked at Kohlvar and Torva, who both looked stunned, clearly unsure how to manage the situation.

Josephine assessed the crowd, trying to determine who was the most volatile. Persephone was screaming and shouting, Eryndal was sitting defeated, swaying as he murmured to himself. Kaelith looked lost seeing his cousin so altered, kicking the ground pointedly as if that would fix anything. Seralie had collapsed into a sobbing heap, and Draka stood by her side, glaring furious golden daggers at Kohlvar and Torva.

"Right," Josephine breathed, pushing up her sleeves determinedly. "Sera," she cooed, kneeling down to unfurl the young woman. "Look at me. It's going to be okay, we will get through this together. I know you're scared, but I need you to breathe."

Seralie spluttered, "But we could *die-*"

"Yes, but it's still unlikely. You can wield, quite well, I doubt you'll be at risk of dying. But I need you to calm down, because I think it's scaring Draka."

Seralie looked up, recoiling at the simmering gaze Draka was sending towards the fortress. "I'm sorry."

"You don't need to be sorry, but do you think you can breathe and settle yourself?" Josephine squeezed her shoulder gently.

She hiccuped as she wiped her face clean. "I think so."

"Good, it's going to be okay." She rose, turning to intercept Draka's line of sight. She watched as his eyes slowly dropped to her, anger still simmering, but less lethal than before.

"Good," Josephine nodded to him, moving to Persephone. "Persy-"

"FUCK OFF," she roared, her Siren teeth jutting out of her mouth, hands balled into clenched fists by her side. Josephine took an alarmed step back, jumping as she collided with something solid.

Kohlvar moved past her, picking Persephone up with ease, while she flailed and cursed him, walking swiftly towards the lake.

"What the-" Josephine gasped as he hurled Persephone into the water, sending her deep into the lake.

"What the hell?" Kaelith and Torva exclaimed, both stepping towards him.

Kohlvar held out a hand, signalling for them to stay put. "Just trust me, it'll help."

They stared at the spot where Persephone disappeared, worry churning Josephine's stomach. Finally, she surfaced, her curls dark with water, pressing against her face.

"I *just* washed my hair Kohlvar," she said grumpily, but she waded towards the shore calmly. Kohlvar reached out a hand, which she ignored.

"Better?" He asked, voice calm as always.

She grumbled begrudgingly. "Yeah. Sorry."

"That *worked*?" Kaelith asked incredulously. "So next time Persy is angry with me I should just throw her in the lake?"

"Absolutely not," Kohlvar responded, just as Persephone levelled him a glare.

"If you *ever* try to throw me in the lake, I'll drown you." For Persephone, it was a mild threat, but one Josephine had no doubt she'd follow through on.

Kaelith winked at her. "So, it's a siren thing, I get it, okay." He raised his hands in mock surrender. They all stared at each other, hysteria now abated.

"So...what do we do now?"

Torva cleared her throat. "Now, we teach you everything you need to know about taking the elixir in two days."

Kaelith raised his hand eagerly. Torva rolled her eyes but nodded.

"Does that mean we get to skip history with Fissius?"

Josephine noticed the smirk on Kohlvar's face. "Absolutely."

Chapter Forty-Seven

Josephine

The door opened before she could knock, with Kohlvar quickly pulling her inside.

"Hello to you too," she teased, deflecting from the worry crushing her chest.

"Hello," he murmured, pausing just long enough to look her over. "We don't have much time."

"I know," Josephine nodded, tearing her eyes away from his lips. "So, tell me how this works."

Kohlvar turned away from her, grabbing items from his desk and setting them out on the floor. His armchairs had been pushed aside, leaving the rug in front of the fireplace completely exposed.

"As you know, elemental magic runs across the continent, with different streams offering a stronger connection to certain elements. But according to the Order of the Ascended, a connection with the Eternal Souls can be made anywhere. It's the items that are of importance, at least according to this account." Kohlvar held up a small leather-bound journal that Josephine recognised from her fruitless attempts at research. "It suggested that holding items that represent your past, present and future, as well as an offering to Orias, will improve the chances of communing."

"Orias?" The name rang a bell for Josephine.

"He's believed to be the Soul responsible for our world, though there are other Souls too."

Josephine raised a brow, feeling dubious. "I connected last when I touched grass over a source, wouldn't it have made more sense to go back there?"

He shook his head. "You didn't see the Soul in the form of a person, right? You only saw them as a shadowy figure. If you wish to truly speak with them, it'd be wise to follow the advice of those who have done it before. The Ascended who wrote this said that Orias appeared like a human to them. What they looked like seems to differ, but ultimately they were a person."

Josephine watched carefully as he laid out an assortment of items, ranging from pieces of rock to coloured pendants to leaves and flowers.

"These are items I thought could represent your future or present. They're from across the continent. I presume you still have your necklace?"

Josephine reached up and pulled out the chain with her rings, fingering the familiar pattern. She'd yelled furiously at Valtherion when he'd tried to take it away for destruction. "What will happen to it?"

"Nothing, I believe. It's more about using it to initiate the connection. Do any of these items speak to you?" Kohlvar gestured broadly.

Josephine looked warily at the items. "Speak to me?"

Kohlvar shrugged. "I guess just imagine what your future will be like and pick something that represents that. Same for your present."

Josephine lightly touched each item, watching as the flickering light danced across stones and small gems. A milky white gem on set into an oval brooch glinted brightly, flickering red in the firelight.

"Is that.. an opal?" She held the brooch up, twisting it as blues and greens reflected, before reverting to its cloudy appearance.

"It's from the dwarves, they mine precious gems and metals. Do you feel a connection with it?"

Josephine shrugged. "It's my daughters' birthstone, so yes." She set the carved brooch down in front of her, along with her chain and wedding band.

She scanned the items again, selecting a light blue river stone that reminded her of the lake for her present. She looked away from the rocks and coloured gems, pondering the meaning of an offering. Her eyes caught on a pale flower, lying alone next to small bundles of herbs. She plucked it, held it for close inspection, before placing it in the middle of her selection.

Kohlvar nodded, looking over a passage in the leather journal, before setting a small bowl of fragrant water in front of her. "Submerge your hands, relax your mind. Having each of the elements present is supposed to help, but apparently not essential. Regardless, you'll need to be open to the connection and trust that he will come to you."

Josephine gave him a nervous look, before shutting her eyes. She focused on the water surrounding her fingers, the radiant heat from the fire warming her cheeks. She could feel Kohlvar's calming presence all around her, easing her anxious heart.

Was she supposed to reach out through the water? Was it like a source? She didn't know how she'd achieved it last time.

Would the Soul understand her items? The opal brooch was obvious, but the flower had been instinctual. Sure, she could come up with an explanation, as once drilled into her in English class, but would it be worthy of Orias?

You're getting distracted Josephine, focus.

She reminded herself of her purpose, trying to focus on the heat of the fire, the lapping of water over her hands. A salty breeze tickled her nose as her toes dug into the floor, trying to ground herself in this moment.

What would her daughters think of this world? She was sure they'd be amazed by it. Were they safe? What if more bombs had landed? What if something happened to Aunt Susan? Did they have enough to eat?

"Is it always so noisy inside your head?"

Josephine let out a startled shriek at the voice booming through her mind.

"Gah! I haven't spoken to another in over half a century, and you scream in my ear?"

Josephine forced her eyes open, realising immediately that she was no longer in Kohlvar's bedroom.

She was on a beach, kneeling in the sand, her hands elbow deep in the lulling waves. She didn't recognise the beach, though it looked similar enough to the ones back home. Pale creamy sand for as far as she could see, curving around the deep blue ocean. Salty air infiltrated her eyes, nose and mouth, her eyes watering as she scanned for the source of the voice.

"What the fuck!" She gasped, jumping to her feet, her eyes falling on the dark figure backlit by the sun.

"Usually, those who commune with me are a bit happier to see me." Irritation crept into his voice.

"I'm sorry! I just didn't think it'd work. Where the hell are we?" Josephine stared at the cloaked figure, his features obscured in a swirling dark mist. "Why can't I see you?"

"Is this form not enough for you?"

"I...uh...I don't know? Should it be?" She squinted as she tried to focus on him, the sun conveniently situated just behind his head.

A scoffing noise echoed from him. "This is actually rather impressive for your second attempt. Though I shouldn't be surprised, you commune with Rhea easily enough."

Josephine's brows shot up. "What?"

"Rhea, you spoke with her when you arrived, in your dream state."

Josephine frowned, trying to recall the hazy memories of her arrival in Saltus. "Do you mean Death?"

The man recoiled from her. "*Death?* How *dare* you call her that!"

Josephine flinched as his fury collided with her, her feet splashing into the ocean. She wobbled, nearly losing her footing and careening into the ocean. "I didn't know her name! She appeared most vividly when someone died, I guess I just associated her with death." A wave of grief struck her, as memory after memory arose of the times she'd lost loved ones. Josephine's lip trembled, her eyes squeezing shut and she tried to regain her focus. "I'm sorry that I offended you, it wasn't my intention."

Silence resonated for so long, Josephine opened her eyes in a panic looking for him. He was still there, unmoving, except for his glittering navy-blue cloak.

"You have seen a lot of death, haven't you?"

The question struck her already vulnerable heart. "More than most, I hope."

"How is she?" The quiet question surprised her.

"Weary," Josephine answered honestly. "My world is...going through a lot. And she was tired when I last spoke with her." She frowned, considering. "You know what's strange? I haven't spoken with her since that dream. And there has...there has been death." She squeezed her eyes shut again, the memory of Benji's life blood splashing over her choking face leaving her shaking.

The man stepped forward, a shrouded arm extending. "Take my hand, Josephine."

Josephine considered it for the briefest moment, throwing a mental *fuck it* to the wind, and grabbed his hand. She yelped as she felt herself being thrown into a memory, into the backseat of an old Ford wagon, listening as her parents bickered over the directions.

"No, please," Josephine whispered. "I don't need to see this again."

Orias did not respond, as the scene played out. Josephine fought his grip, yanking her hand away, but he held steadfast. Soon, the car turned onto the highway, hurtling towards the dance recital she'd never make it to.

"Please," she begged, tears threatening to spill.

"Mum, why do I have to go? I don't even like dancing." John, Josephine's brother, whined, fidgeting with his bright red firetruck.

"Because Jojo is dancing, we have to go and support her." The dark-haired woman in the passenger seat responded, with a slight hint of annoyance. Josephine knew the tone well, both as a mother and her daughter.

"Besides, champ, she goes to your soccer games. Those are the rules, quit complaining." Josephine locked eyes with her father in the rear viewed mirror, her heart twisting as his eyes crinkled in a smile.

She knew what came next. She knew the truck with the unconscious driver would come hurtling across the highway, wiping out three cars and killing four people in a matter of moments. She knew because she'd relived this moment a thousand times in her dreams. She still bore the scars from her injuries that day.

She closed her eyes as the moment happened, though she could not block out the screams of her mother and the agonised cries of her father. She heard her 11-year-old self whimper, as she reached across for her brother.

This was where she saw Death, Rhea, for the first time, as she reached into the crushed car and scooped her brother up, his truck carefully tucked against his chest. She'd watched as Death had carried his sleeping soul away, leaving behind his tiny broken body.

He was only 8.

Nausea flooded her as she was thrown into another memory, hurling her dinner into the toilet in the middle of the night. The intensity of first trimester sickness made her mouth water uncomfortably, as she breathed heavily over the bowl. She felt a blissful cooling sensation across the back of her neck, finding a damp cloth she didn't remember putting there. She pulled it across her face, clammy from the exertion.

When she finally found her feet, swaying slightly, she looked at her ghastly reflection in the mirror. She splashed water over her face, breathing deeply through the rolling nausea.

Unease prickled at her, the kind that never fully dissipated when one was home alone. She glanced into the mirror, only to scream at Death's image reflected there. She whirled around, sending the room spinning as she staggered to the door, clutching at the frame. "What are you doing here?" Josephine yelled, clutching at her stomach. "You can't have my baby."

Death said nothing, her expression unreadable as she shook her head. Josephine rubbed her eyes, convinced she was still half asleep, as she stumbled past the ghostly woman and climbed back into bed.

The next morning she'd receive the call that her husband was lost at sea, never to return.

They flicked through half a dozen similar moments together, where Josephine had seen Death. At the hospital, when she'd drop lunch off to Susan, only to find pandemonium as a patient passed over. Or when her train was delayed due to another suicide, and Death would be standing on the platform, blending in with the other passengers like she was meant to be there.

Eventually, they arrived at the bombing. By now she was sobbing, her heart breaking from being forced to watch the worst moments of her life over and over again. She watched herself burst into the emergency stairwell,

Sienna in her grasp. She saw Death in the corner as she ran for her life, the bomb hitting like it was yesterday, as she felt the building collapse onto them. Her world faded to black, the only sound her gut wrenching sobs as tears dripped off her face.

"Josie?" A familiar voice echoed in the darkness, calling her to the surface of the ocean she was drowning in.

"Sweetheart, come back to me. I'm so sorry, Josie, please wake up."

With great effort, Josephine peeled open her puffy eyelids, finding Kohlvar's worried face hovering over her.

"Thank the Souls," he gasped, his great hand brushing back her hair. "I thought I'd lost you for a moment."

"Don't thank the Soul," she murmured. "He's an asshole."

Kohlvar sucked in a sharp breath. "What did he do?"

More tears leaked out of her eyes. "Went through my worst memories, looking for Death."

She briefly registered confusion on Kohlvar's face, as she faded into unconsciousness.

Chapter Forty-Eight

Kohlvar

Kohlvar rose carefully, cradling Josephine in his arms, ignoring the sharp pain stabbing his injured side. He moved her to his bed, ensuring her airway was clear and the blankets were tucked in around her.

Then he paced.

He paced his room for hours, pondering over Josephine's words and the guilt eating him alive. He'd suggested that she should try and commune with Orias, and as soon as she'd slipped into the dream state, he knew he'd made a grave error. The emotions resonating from her were incredibly distressing to experience, especially given he could do nothing but hold her as she sobbed. It had made him feel weak and helpless, both emotions he struggled to tolerate at the best of times.

Kohlvar read over the passages in the journal a dozen times, trying to find new meaning. He looked at the items, scattered alongside the overturned bowl. Josephine's necklace, the opal, the river rock and twin flowers on a single stem.

He frowned at the items, picking the stem up as gently as his mammoth hands could manage. He'd never been particularly good at the art of divination, writing it off as an old wives tale. Hirwen could probably help him, only after she finished giving him an absolute hiding for risking Josephine's life. He tossed the flower back down, continuing to pace.

Would the Queen know what they'd done? There were so few left from the old religion that he truly didn't know the extent of their abilities, especially the Queen's. He'd erected every ancient ward possible to protect them in his room, in addition to his usual security. Hirwen had been suspicious when he asked for the old protections she'd taught him, but she'd given them to him anyway.

He really wished he had more to go off than an old journal from a long dead Ascended, whose post-vision ramblings made him question the mental acuity of the writer.

By the time the sky was starting to lighten, and the fire had reduced to coals, exhaustion finally overwhelmed Kohlvar. He crawled into bed beside Josephine, pulling her close to his chest. His guilt flared as she snuggled into him, fitting underneath his chin, as if she felt secure in his arms.

She was safe, he reminded himself. At least until tomorrow.

Chapter Forty-Nine

Kohlvar

"There are two important moments when taking the elixir. The immediate reaction, which involves a sudden burst of magic which you must dispel completely. Then there is the delayed one, which is when your evolved abilities will come through." Torva slowly walked back and forth, projecting her words across the group.

Kohlvar looked over his acolytes, noting the anxious glances and fidgeting. They were still terrified but seemed to be handling it better today.

"Your abilities can appear days, weeks or even months after taking the elixir. So don't be disheartened when nothing changes for you tomorrow. We will be focusing on how to manage the immediate reaction; what it feels like, how to control it, and how to avoid getting hurt. Any questions?"

Kaelith's hand shot into the air. "What does it taste like?"

Torva shot him a bewildered look, frowning. "Herbal, and kind of bitter. It wasn't the best. That's really not the priority here though."

He gave her a big thumbs up and mouthed 'thanks'. Kohlvar felt irritation from Torva, but he could see what Kaelith was doing. He was trying to break the tension, something he clearly was uncomfortable with.

To his credit, it seemed to be working. The acolytes were murmuring to each other, Eryndal looked exasperated, and Persephone was teasingly jabbing Kaelith's ribs.

Kohlvar cleared his throat. "Let's divide into groups, and we'll practice together. Draka, Sera and Josie, start with Torva, then we'll swap."

The elven cousins flanked Persephone, Kaelith throwing an arm over her head. Her elbow collided with his stomach, his breath coming out as a *whoosh* as he doubled over.

"You know the hair is off limits Kae" Persephone snipped, grinning at his contorted features.

It warmed Kohlvar's heart to see her making friends. She was a far cry from the terrified, violent child he'd met in the King's prison. He just hoped that they would be able to continue providing this safe space for her and other hybrids to exist in.

He guided the trio through practicing a fast expulsion of magic. For Persephone and Kaelith, this was relatively simple; they'd become proficient with their elemental abilities. However, Eryndal was more of a concern, still struggling to connect reliably.

Kohlvar watched as the young scholar grew more frustrated. He motioned to Persephone and Kaelith to take a break, pulling him aside. "How are you?"

Eryndal looked up at him with tear filled brown eyes. "I'm going to die tomorrow, aren't I? I won't be able to expel this magic and it'll consume me."

"Hey," he placed a hand on his shoulder, dwarfing his slimmer frame. "Don't think like that. You have power, I know it. We just aren't using it correctly."

"I've read so many books! You'd think I'd know what needs to happen, or things I could try. But maybe something is wrong with me."

Kohlvar shook his head. "I don't believe that. I think there's something unique about your power that we don't understand, and hopefully after tomorrow, we'll be able to learn about it. Together."

The young man looked up at him thoughtfully. "It would be kind of cool if I had a rare ability. Then I could write the literature on it."

Kohlvar smiled. Of course that's what would excite Eryndal about an unusual ability. "Did you find out anything interesting from the stone skin?"

His face lit up immediately. "Oh yes! I only had time for a brief look, especially with this new development. But it was very interesting. There were several metals and salts present, which was expected, but a lot of calcium and potassium too. I imagine the shedding of your stone skin would make quite a good fertiliser for crops once it breaks down. I wonder if you have to absorb those nutrients in your diet to be able to produce this, and if you weren't eating enough, if the stone skin would weaken."

Eryndal continued animatedly, sufficiently distracted from his immediate worries. Kohlvar listened as he watched Torva with her trio. Seralie was good with her earth wielding, Draka would likely breathe fire again. It was Josephine he worried for. He clung to the hope that whatever had affected her that night in the hallway with Vessara would happen again and allow her to survive the transition.

He breathed deeply, feeling that tiny flicker of hope in his chest. Maybe it would be alright. Maybe they'd all still be here, part of this unusual team, by sundown tomorrow.

Chapter Fifty

Josephine

Sleep didn't come easily for any of the girls in her dormitory, and Josephine imagined the boys were similarly anxious. Some cried, a couple argued with each other for making noise despite the fact they could hear a pin drop. Ultimately, it was incredibly tense in their dormitory.

Her mind drifted to Kohlvar, one of the only places in her head she'd happily go. She worried what he was doing, if he was also awake and stressed. He'd been exhausted today, pushing himself to make sure he prepared every one of his acolytes as best he could. She'd seen him covering a yawn, then cheering on every success they'd had today. He'd even been excited when Draka had breathed fire at him, leaving him with a mild burn to his arm. But he'd been ecstatic, his smile so large he looked genuinely happy.

Josephine smiled fondly at this image of Kohlvar. Her thoughts gradually shifted to the memory of their last kiss. She could still feel his gentle lips on hers, the way he'd caressed her body with his huge hands, the heat from the fire warming them both. When she closed her eyes, she saw his; burning with lust and desire as he looked at her. He really looked at her, and saw all of her, and despite that, he'd wanted her. He'd kissed her on multiple occasions, despite his initial decision that they couldn't be together.

Whatever this was between them, she knew it affected them both. The dull ache of desire was stirring in her belly, something she could hardly resolve here.

With a frustrated sigh, she threw back her bedding and slipped on her shoes. Persephone's curls rustled, their eyes locking. She expected her to make a snarky comment, but to her surprise, she didn't.

"I'll keep an eye on her," she nodded towards Seralie, curled into a ball under her numerous blankets.

Josephine nodded gratefully, leaving the painfully quiet dormitory behind.

***

She knocked quietly on his door, unsure if he'd be awake at this hour. A sane person wouldn't be. Doubt crept into her as she waited, perhaps she'd misread his emotions, overestimating his feelings for her.

She pushed aside the spiralling anxiety as the door slowly creaked open.

"Josie?" He was mostly hidden behind the door, although his bare chest peeked out.

"Hi," she breathed. Anxiety flooded in, and she gripped her fingers tightly to suppress it. "May I come in?"

He slowly opened the door, shutting it quietly behind her. "Are you alright?" She cut him off by stepping into him, placing one hand on his chest and the other on his cheek.

His eyes slid closed as his arms wrapped around her. "Fuck," he breathed, "we shouldn't."

"Do you want to?" Josephine asked, watching his eyes flash open and meet hers.

"I...I think it's pretty obvious."

"Say it," Josephine commanded, her hand kneading into his chest.

He chuckled. "Why? Does that turn you on?"

She rolled her eyes. "I just want to make sure you want this." The unsaid implication caused him to frown slightly.

"Souls, yes Josie, this is… this isn't like that. I know you're not… using me." His eyes closed with a wince.

She tilted her head forward until her forehead brushed his chin and chest. "I love it when you call me Josie. Everyone else calls me Jo, but I like that you're the only one here that calls me that."

He groaned, the vibration stoking the embers of heat nestled in her groin. "Fuck, Josie, I don't want to hurt you."

She massaged her hand into his bare chest, feeling his dark hair curl around her fingers. "You won't," she looked up to see his eyes still firmly closed. "But if you're worried, we'll just take it slow." She stroked his cheekbone with her thumb.

His breathing deepened, like he was trying to control himself.

"How are you doing this to me? It feels like witchcraft." His eyes finally opened to meet hers. The vulnerability in them made her blush, like they were fully exposed to one another.

She smiled and shook her head. "I wouldn't know how to put a spell on you, Kohl."

"But that's the problem. You already have." She felt his arms tighten around her as she rose up to kiss him, moving slowly to give him time to change his mind.

He didn't.

As soon as their lips touched, fireworks exploded in her chest, as every nerve in her body fired off. She moaned into his mouth, feeling the tension of the last few days ebb away as she wrapped both arms around his neck. She needed to be closer, have more of him. Every touch simply wasn't enough.

His hands splayed across her back, one between her shoulder blades, the other sweeping lower. He growled as he dug his fingertips into her hips, pulling her closer against him.

"Fuck," he whispered against her lips, as he walked her back until she was leaning on his door. She gasped as his erection pressed into her, rocking into her with a teasingly slow pressure.

He smiled at her reaction, then groaned when she tugged his head back and nipped at his neck, teasing his Adam's apple with her tongue. She nibbled and sucked her way to his jaw, where his afternoon stubble grazed her cheek. She finally reached his ear, taking the sensitive lobe between her teeth and grazing it.

He slammed a hand into the door, letting out a yelp and a string of curses.

Josephine leaned back, a teasing smile spreading across her face. "Was that a good reaction or bad?"

He looked down at her, panting. "You are dangerous."

Josephine giggled, biting her lower lip. "Good then."

"Put your legs around me." He growled, staring intensely at her lips.

"Gladly," Josephine nipped at his earlobe again as she hooked a leg around Kohlvar. He grabbed her other leg and pulled it around him, leaning into her again. They both sighed as his stiff erection pushed into her groin, her back against the door providing the perfect resistance.

"You are irresistible." He murmured against her neck. "Everything from the way you smell, the way you fight, the way you care for everyone. You are the most incredible woman I've ever met."

Josephine pulled back, trying to look at him. "Kohl..."

"I just wanted you to know that; that I'm not just interested in your body." His eyes finally met hers. "I mean, I like that too, I-"

"I understand." Josephine caressed his face. "The feeling is mutual. You're not like anyone I've ever met, and that's not because you're half-giant. You're amazing, Kohl."

She wanted to say more but his mouth covered hers, causing the fire in her belly to roar as he pulled her off the door. She squeezed her legs tightly around him, running her fingers through his hair as she kissed him back, wanting every part of him touching her.

She felt Kohlvar squeeze her backside and caress her spine through the pyjamas covering her.

Josephine didn't realise they were moving until gravity shifted, and she felt her back meet his familiar bedding. Kohlvar leaned over her, looking up and down her body hungrily, before leaning down and flicking open a button on her shirt. He looked to her, checking for her approval, before continuing to slowly unbutton her.

Impatience overwhelmed her, and she tried to use her legs to pull him closer, but to no avail.

He placed a large hand on her equally large breast, gently massaging it through the fabric. He moved to her other breast, giving equal attention as she sighed at the physical contact.

"More," she begged, arching into his hand as she gripped his shoulders.

He removed his hand, staring at her raised nipples before sweeping back the fabric and lowering his mouth to her left breast, sucking her into his mouth.

She gasped at the hot, wet contact, pressing her legs tightly around his waist as his tongue swirled and sucked on her stiff nipple. He groaned, the vibration sending a shock through her, as he rocked against her again.

"So impatient," he muttered as he released her breast, moving to the other one and repeating the tantalising motion.

"Fuck," she breathed, her nails starting to dig into his shoulders. She tried to roll her hips up into his stiff cock, but he pinned her down with his hand.

"What happened to taking it slow?" He asked as he released her again.

"That just feels too good." And it had been far too long since someone had made her feel that way.

Kohlvar lowered his lips to her sternum, tracing teasing kisses down her abdomen. He swirled his tongue around her belly button, locking eyes with her as he descended to her waistband, kneeling at the foot of his bed.

"Oh yes," she murmured, running a hand through his hair to grip his black curls.

She could feel his smile against her as he hooked a finger into her pants and teased them down. She had to release her tight grip on him, and by the time her pyjamas had hit the floor, she could feel his warm breath against her inner thigh.

"Fuck, you smell perfect." That was all the warning he gave before he devoured her. For all his earlier gentleness, he was unleashing himself on her. His tongue lapped and swirled, teasing her entrance and clit. He sucked and flicked, eating her like he was a starving man, and she was everything he needed. She yelped as lightning jolted through her, gripping the sheets beneath her as her body spasmed.

He moved her legs over his shoulders, giving her a mischievous look. She closed her thighs around his head, hiding him from view as he buried his face into her.

His groan as she squeezed him sent her arching off the bed in shock. She looked down, surprised, catching his eyes as he did it again. She moaned loudly, the vibrations from his mouth so intense that she suddenly found herself close to orgasm.

"Yes!" Was all she could splutter out, as he groaned again and again, building her pleasure until finally she exploded.

With her legs trapped in Kohlvar's strong embrace, all she could do was arch her back and scream as the violent orgasm crashed through her, sending shocks throughout every limb and fibre of her body. She clung to Kohlvar's hair fiercely as he soothed her through her release, sucking and lapping up the growing wetness between her legs.

She lay trembling as she tried to catch her breath, shaking too hard to push herself up.

Kohlvar released her, carefully setting her legs down on the edge of the bed.

His face was glistening, and Josephine couldn't help but laugh. If that was just what he could do with his tongue, what else should she expect?

Kohlvar crawled up the bed, hovering over her limp body. "Are you alright?" He asked, brushing her hair back from her sticky forehead.

"Just...need a moment." She gasped, reaching up to brush his chest as it hovered over her.

Kohlvar smiled and rolled to the side, scooping her into his embrace as she recovered. He kissed her gently, the taste of her still on his lips. It was divine, tasting yourself on the man who made you explode. Josephine reached down to grip him through his pants, surprised by the considerable girth of him.

Kohlvar groaned into her mouth, his cock twitching as she rubbed him up and down through the soft material.

He pulled back from her. "As lovely as that is, I won't last long with you touching me like that. Is that what you want?"

"No, I want it all," she emphasised her sentence with a tight squeeze, relishing in the way it made him jump.

"Fucking hell, Josie." His eyes had fluttered closed. He took a deep breath as he reached for her hand. "Climb up the bed." He commanded, and Josephine was more than happy to comply.

Kohlvar stood from the bed and stretched, allowing her to admire the way his grey pants clung to his thick thighs and buttocks. He moved to the bedside table, retrieving a jar from the drawer.

"What's that?"

Kohlvar dipped a finger in, retrieving a small amount of clear gel on his finger. "It's lubricant and protection." He reached for her arm and rubbed it on the inside of her wrist.

Josephine raised an eyebrow. "I hope that's not where you think it's going."

Kohlvar scoffed. "Just making sure it's alright on you. Does it itch?"

Josephine shook her head. "What is it made of? How does it work for protection?"

Kohlvar gave her a bemused look. "The gel is made from some sort of plant. The protection is magically added."

"Magical lube, huh, never thought I'd see that."

He examined her wrist, rubbing his thumb over the sensitive skin. "Also works in a pinch for wounds."

"I hope we're not going to need it for that." Josephine felt a little queasy at the thought of that feature being intentionally added.

"Hey," Kohlvar murmured, hooking his finger under her chin until she met his gaze. "If it's too much, or you want to stop, then we will. At any time. I do not want to hurt you."

She smiled, relaxing into him. "I know, I trust you."

He leaned down to kiss her again. "Lie back," he murmured against her lips, and she shivered with anticipation. He moved between her legs, removing a liberal amount of lube and gently applying it to her entrance.

She gasped at the cold gel, but it soon warmed, as he worked a finger inside her, moving back and forth to spread the gel inside her.

Fuck, who knew being lubed up could feel so damn good.

She started to squirm as he curled his thick finger inside her, teasing the spot that made her shudder, before he was gone, leaving her wanting.

Kohlvar rolled to lie beside her, shucking off his pants with ease, as his rock-hard manhood sprung free.

Damn. She knew he'd probably be large, and whilst she wasn't unfamiliar with well-endowed men... this was on another level. Now she understood why he was worried about hurting her.

Not impossible but pushing new boundaries for her.

She closed her mouth, which had fallen open, before reaching for the jar. She scooped a similar amount of lubrication out and spread it down the underside of his cock. A low moan echoed from Kohlvar as she spread the gel on his erection, enjoying the feel of his long smooth shaft and sensitive tip. She pumped once, twice to check the distribution. Josephine looked to Kohlvar to find his eyes closed, and hands fisted in the sheets. She smiled, pleased he was similarly affected, and threw a leg over his hips.

His eyes flew open in surprise, his hands moving to her hips. The head of his cock nestled against her clit, sending pleasing sensations through her. She reached down and adjusted him before settling herself on the tip.

Kohlvar's breathing quickened as she slowly lowered herself, centimetre by centimetre. She slid onto him just a little, pausing to allow herself to stretch, before moving up and back down on his thick cock. She felt herself spasm around him as he hit that spot deep inside her, and judging by Kohlvar's increasing groans, he could feel it too.

She steadied herself with a deep breath as she felt stretched to capacity, a delicious humming ache filling her. She allowed herself to relax as she continued down, enjoying every part of him.

Finally, she felt herself brush his thighs, and she was able to seat herself fully on his giant cock.

His hands were shaking on her hips, as he kept himself perfectly still, allowing her all the time she needed to feel comfortable.

She tested herself, moving up and down with increasing speed. She shifted forward, placing her hands on Kohlvar's chest, leaning on him as she slid up and down, gasping as his thick girth stretched her.

Kohlvar broke his silence with a string of muttered curses. "Souls Josie, that feels amazing."

"It does," Josephine groaned, digging her fingertips into his strong chest. "I think I've adjusted," she ground her hips down for emphasis, smiling as a guttural moan escaped Kohlvar.

His thumbs rubbed circles into her hips as he held her steady, slowly rolling his hips into her. "Does this feel good?"

Josephine leaned forward onto his chest, resting her head against him. "Yes."

"No pain?" He panted, his tense shoulders catching the evening light.

"No, I just feel very, very full," she breathed out, feeling his thudding heart racing beneath her hands.

Kohlvar increased his pace, slowly, teasingly, while watching her closely for any signs of discomfort. She smiled reassuringly, rocking her hips for that sweet angle that sent shivers through her body.

His grunts and groans of restraint made Josephine want him to unleash himself with her fully. She reached up to cup his face, drawing his gaze to her.

"I want more, Kohl. I'm ready." She pressed a kiss to his lips, melting into him. His arms wrapped around her, holding her tightly as he deepened their kiss. His body hummed underneath her, radiating warmth and protection as he caressed her, exploring all of her.

With quick confidence, he rolled them over without breaking their contact, thrusting into her. She gasped against him, relishing the friction and the weight of him above her.

Josephine tangled her fingers in his hair as his pace quickened, driving her deeper into the mattress with every carefully calibrated thrust.

His breathing grew ragged, catching on his inhale as Josephine felt herself squeezing around him. Her thighs shuddered as she felt her orgasm nearing, letting out a shocked cry as pleasure rolled through her, building in waves until she was screaming Kohlvar's name. Her elation continued as Kohlvar kept his rigorous pace, angling his hips so his cock stroked the sensitive spot inside her.

His fingers on her spine suddenly tightened, and with a strangled yell he buried into her neck, thrusted hard once, twice, burying himself inside her as he reached his completion. She relished in the feeling of every twitch and spasm of him, as warmth flooded within her quivering channel.

They lay panting and trembling for many moments, attempting to recover the strength needed to disengage. Eventually, Kohlvar pushed himself off her, groaning as he released her.

"Josie, are you okay?" He asked, still hovering over her.

Josephine smiled, reaching up to push back the curls sticking to his forehead. "Yes, I'm fine. More than fine, I'm rather satisfied," she offered with a grin.

She was surprised by the amount of relief that crossed his face. "I didn't hurt you?" The vulnerability and concern in his eyes sent a fluttering sensation through her chest. She reached up and gently ran her fingers over his cheek.

"No, not at all. I mean, sure, you're large, but we took it slowly and the magic lube helped." She gestured with amusement to the jar by the bed.

"Thank the Souls," Kohlvar murmured. He leaned down to kiss her, gently, before he pulled away, breathing deeply as he sat upright.

"Are you worried about tomorrow?" Josephine asked, watching the tension gather in his shoulders once again.

"Yes," he sighed. "Aren't you?"

"Not for myself, I'm already prepared for the worst, so no, not really. I'm concerned for the others though. They were really scared when you told them." She pushed herself up, nestling her head into the back of his shoulder.

"Yeah, they were." His voice trembled. "Thank you for stepping in, by the way. I was...I was overwhelmed."

She placed a kiss on his bare skin. "What do you mean?"

"When they all panicked, I could feel it. I couldn't think about anything except their terror and fear that they were going to die. And Draka, his emotions are strange, they're more primal than the others. So, I was trying to work out what he was about to do, and it wasn't until you got Sera to calm down that I could actually think."

Josephine hummed thoughtfully. "About that...why did you throw Persy into the lake?"

A grumbling chuckle vibrated through him. "Sirens can get cranky when they're out of water too long. Technically we're only half-siren, but I figured it might calm her down."

"That still sounds like it was a risky move. I was honestly waiting for her to murder you when she came back up."

"I was too, or I was going to dive in to make sure she hadn't somehow drowned. She can't hold her breath for long." Kohlvar sighed, twisting to plant a kiss on her scalp. "Come on, let's bathe and sleep, before the night is over."

Josephine nodded, apprehension for the morning seizing her again. She pushed it aside, trying to focus on the present moment instead.

Chapter Fifty-One

Josephine

Josephine woke up feeling comfortable and well rested, two things that rarely happened for her overnight. She peeked at the early morning light filtering in between the long curtains, trying to gauge what time it was. Still early it seemed, the light had not gained its full strength yet.

Josephine looked down at Kohlvar's arm wrapped around her belly, the veins on his hand catching her attention. She traced them with her fingers, brushing the dark hair on his muscular forearm. She snuggled into him, her back to his chest, as she tangled her legs through his. His arm snaked around her tightly, his face burying into her neck. She really had missed waking up like this, in the arms of someone she loved.

Josephine froze as the thought crossed her mind. Shit, how well could he read her mind? And was she really at that stage already? Judging by the warmth spreading across her chest, she was.

She felt Kohlvar pull away from her. "What's wrong?"

Josephine let out a shaky breath, "Nothing, just my mind getting away from me." She shivered as Kohlvar placed a lingering kiss on her shoulder. "How well can you read my mind?" Her attempt at a nonchalant voice was suspiciously high pitched, especially to her own ears.

His head shook, feeling more like a nuzzle with his proximity. "It's not mind reading, it's just emotions. Sometimes it's clear what someone is feeling, other times it's complicated."

"It's almost like people are complicated creatures." Josephine rolled to face him, smiling at his handsome face. She reached up to caress his jaw, over the scar that split his cheek. "Morning," she murmured as she pressed her lips to his, enjoying the low moan that vibrated from his chest.

"Morning," he murmured between kisses. "Why were you asking about the mind reading?"

Josephine blushed as she smirked at him. "Just curious how well you can hear the dirty thoughts that may be running around in my brain." Not entirely the truth, but also, not entirely a lie.

Kohlvar pressed his lips together. "I can tell when you're...aroused." His blue eyes sparkled with mischief.

"Gosh, I wish I could read you like that."

He froze, hesitation washing over him. "Do you truly mean that?"

Josephine frowned. "Yes, why wouldn't I?"

Kohlvar seemed to consider her words. "It can be overwhelming, and it's hard to distinguish what emotions are your own. I wouldn't want to confuse you."

"Why would I be confused?"

He stroked her hair as he answered. "If I was really angry, and you weren't, I could manipulate your behaviour. If I shared my emotions with you, then you acted out in anger, it'd be my fault."

Josephine nodded thoughtfully. "Okay, I understand the concern. But I don't think either of us are angry at the moment." She gave him a flirtatious look that made him groan.

"No, no you definitely are not angry." He muttered as he shifted his body over hers, pinning her to the mattress. "You sure about trying this?"

Josephine nodded, excitement pulsing through her.

Kohlvar closed his beautiful eyes, framing her head with both of his hands. His forehead lowered until it rested on hers, their breathing moving in sync with each other.

Josephine felt a trickle of emotions that felt similar to her own. Sleepiness, warmth and contentment. Other emotions that didn't quite register.

The connection opened slowly as Kohlvar gradually poured more into her. She felt warmth flooding across her chest as his emotions turned into a tidal wave, causing her to gasp in surprise when the full depth of his feelings hit.

She could feel his protective instincts, lingering grief and insecurity alongside his more immediate emotions from their union. Satisfaction, calm and happiness. She felt an emotion she could only describe as horny, which caused a pleased blush to spread across her cheeks. And there was that lingering warmth, connected to the unmistakable feeling of *love*.

Josephine opened her eyes, unaware she'd closed them, in shock. She registered Kohlvar's bright blue eyes watching her carefully, as he took in ragged, shaky breaths. He looked unsure, so young and vulnerable in this moment.

"Oh, Kohl," she whispered, reaching up to brush back his black curls. She felt a tear slip out the corner of her eye. "I feel it too."

A shaky laugh escaped him, as relief flooded the emotional connection. He pulled away, both physically and mentally, rising up on his arms over her. "I've never felt it before," he admitted in a rush. "Not truly, not in the way I've sensed it in others. I didn't understand why people did foolish things for it, but now…" He reached down and kissed her, harder than their earlier sleepy kisses.

"But now you understand." She whispered against his lips, wrapping her arms around his neck. She felt his knee push apart her legs as he settled between them, slowly caressing her body and kissing her senseless.

A knock sounded at the door, causing both of them to freeze. Kohlvar turned his head towards the door, frowning.

"It's Torva," he murmured, pulling away from her.

After donning pants, Kohlvar opened the door. "Is everything alright?"

"The King wants the elixir ceremony to occur immediately after breakfast. He seems impatient to leave." Torva's voice dropped lower, beyond the reach of Josephine's ears.

Kohlvar nodded, listening intently. "We'll be down soon."

There was a pause at the door, before Kohlvar closed it. He looked to Josephine, his weary eyes lighting up slightly as he saw her.

"It's time."

Chapter Fifty-Two

Josephine

Josephine breathed deeply as she stood beside Seralie and Draka, watching Galathir's acolytes move into position. Both teams stood in parallel lines to each other, leading up to a slightly raised wooden platform beside a small table with scholars clustered around. She felt Seralie's hand brush hers, shaking. She grabbed it, squeezing tightly.

"It's going to be okay," Josephine whispered, her eyes never leaving the entourage moving steadily down the hill.

"I'm so scared," she admitted. "I just want this to be over."

"Would you like to know what I do when I have to do something I'm afraid of?" She saw Seralie nod jerkily out of the corner of her eye. "I volunteer to do it first. Then I can relax once it's over."

"Huh," she mused. "That's an interesting idea."

Josephine gave her hand one final squeeze, before releasing her, as King Caladorn approached. She hadn't realised he would be here to bear witness to this, nor had she expected Queen Sylvara and Princess Vessara to be present. The Queen's red hair shone in the morning light, as she moved with a proud elegance down the steep hill, her eyes briefly meeting hers.

Josephine tore her gaze away from them, focusing on Kohlvar instead. He was engaged in conversation with Galathir, both wearing frowns and speaking quietly. Torva wore a stoic expression, though Josephine felt it was a mask for her true feelings. Even the easy-going Alfion looked unsure. Clearly, the proceedings were being conducted in a way that made everyone uneasy.

Professor Fissius cleared his throat as he unfurled a large scroll. "Good morning acolytes," he smiled warmly at Galathir's students, giving the rest the barest glance as he continued. "We are joined by his Royal Highness, King Caladorn, and his entourage, Queen Sylvara and Princess Vessara, to witness the elixir ceremony." He rambled on about the elixir, its purpose and how the day would proceed. Fortunately, it was information Kohlvar and Torva had already explained, for Josephine was struggling to remain attentive.

"Before we begin, do we have any volunteers to go first?" He looked up expectantly, only to be met with silence. "Very well." He motioned to the two scholars standing by a small table with a dozen vials neatly set upon it. "Haemish, please step forward."

A tall, lanky elf stepped forward from Galathir's team. He walked to the small podium overlooking the lake, turning to the scholar holding out a single vial.

"May the Eternal Souls watch over you," Fissius declared, others murmuring alongside him. Haemish nodded, downing the vial immediately. He looked back at Freyda and his teammates, hesitancy in his eyes.

For a moment, nothing happened. It was long enough that some started whispering to each other. He let out a sudden cry, clutching his stomach as he lurched forward.

"Haemish," Galathir's cool voice cut through the chatter. "You need to dispel the magic. Draw upon it and release it."

The elf cringed, taking sharp breaths in, as he focused over the lake and raised his hands. With a yell, he released a blast of air magic that flew through the forest, pushing trees back and sending several birds flying from their roosts. Haemish knelt, breathing deeply as he clutched the edge of the raised platform.

"Very good," Fissius declared, quickly scrawling a line on his scroll. "Next we'll have-"

"I'll go!" Seralie's voice squeaked as her hand shot up. Fissius turned and scowled, waving her towards the podium.

"Fine. May the Eternal Souls be with you," he muttered unceremoniously.

Seralie's hand shook as she took the vial, sniffing it curiously, before she drank it. She made a face as she turned away from them. She stepped down from the podium, crouching out of sight.

"What are you-" Fissius's words died in his mouth as a deep rumbling shook under their feet. Josephine tried to move to see Seralie, but her eyes caught movement near the forest. At the periphery, several young saplings were rapidly rising, reaching taller by the second. They were unusually pale, with silvery green foliage, contrasting sharply with the rest of the evergreen forest. As they reached a similar height to the forest, their growth slowed, spreading outwards, white flowers budded and bloomed, falling to the ground in a snowy show.

Josephine heard a small whimper from Seralie as the trees stopped changing. She started to move until she saw Kohlvar striding towards her, reaching out a hand. Seralie's tiny hand found his, covered in dirt, as he pulled her to her feet. She was ghostly pale, shaking, with the biggest smile on her face, as Kohlvar led her to sit next to Haemish, behind the remaining acolytes.

Josephine smiled back, clapping her hands together loudly. "Go, Sera!"

"Yeah, go Sera!" Kaelith whooped gleefully, fist punching into the air.

"Silence!" Caladorn barked, his eyes flicking to Draka's as he growled deeply. His dark eyes narrowed, as if challenging the dragonoid.

Thankfully, Fissius broke the tension by selecting another acolyte from Galathir's team. The young woman screamed as the elixir took effect, but she also managed to dispel the magical build up with a small earthquake. Josephine started to wonder how this much magic being released would affect the ecosystems surrounding Balidran, though she suspected it would do little harm compared to natural disasters.

Persephone was selected next. Josephine couldn't help but notice Vessara and Caladorn's keen eyes on her, as she drained the vial. Kohlvar lingered closer to the platform than he had for Seralie, his hands raised. She groaned, swearing vehemently under her breath. She started to pant, as sweat beaded on her forehead, her pain written across her face.

"Persy," Kohlvar grumbled. "Remember."

She raised a hand shakily, dispelling a burst of air that rattled the small table beside her. Yet she still groaned. "It burns," she whimpered, clutching at her ribs, her face bright red.

"Get in the water!" Kohlvar suddenly yelled, moving towards her. She tumbled off the platform, limping towards the lake.

"You must not intervene Kohlvar!" Fissius called after him, as he followed Persephone down to the lake. Kohlvar didn't acknowledge him as Persephone stumbled into the water, crawling over the river stones until she dove beneath the surface.

Steam rose from the spot where she had vanished. Josephine watched with bated breath, trying to discern any movement or sign of life from the water's depth.

Kaelith swore behind her. "Is she okay?" He whispered, his voice heavy with worry.

Josephine didn't answer, only looking at Torva, whose worried expression did nothing to reassure her. She turned to the lake again, remembering Kohlvar's words from last night.

She can't hold her breath for long.

Fear clutched at her chest, as they watched the lake ripple innocuously. Suddenly the water rose up forming a wall around the lake's perimeter several metres high. Through the translucent shields Josephine could make out a small humanoid shape, hovering in the air.

Kohlvar stepped back from the lake, just as the walls came crashing down, drenching him and the surrounding vegetation. Persephone floated to shore, her body limp in the eddying waves.

"Persy!" Kaelith and Sera screamed, starting to move towards her. Torva blocked their path, shaking her head.

A violent coughing noise echoed towards them, and Josephine breathed a sigh of relief. She watched as Kohlvar scooped up her tiny frame, carrying her up the hill.

She was soaked, her long hair hanging over her face as she coughed up water, but she was alive.

"Thank the Souls," Eryndal breathed, his face deathly pale.

"Impressive," Caladorn murmured, looking at Vessara. She seemed displeased with the results, though Josephine couldn't fathom why.

As Kohlvar set Persephone down next to Sera, Fissius called Freyda to the podium. Josephine stiffened slightly, remembering their altercation from what felt like an eternity ago. She threw a smug glare in Josephine's direction, before mounting the platform and throwing back the drink.

Freyda's screams were different from the rest. Hers began immediately, the high-pitched shrieks piercing through Josephine's ears. Galathir moved towards her, calling her name, but she gave no response.

She fell to her knees, vomiting so violently, Josephine winced in sympathy. She continued to retch and gag long after her stomach had been completely emptied.

An annoyed sigh reached Josephine's ears. She turned to see Caladorn brushing something off his arm, as if Freyda's ordeal was nothing more than an inconvenience for him. "That's a shame, next!" He called.

"No!" Freyda wailing, trembling violently on all fours. "I can do it! I just need to try again!"

Galathir crouched beside her, murmuring to her. She recoiled, screaming at him.

"No, it's not fair! Why would it reject *me*? I'm an elf, I have power, I can prove it-"

"Take her away," Caladorn ordered coldly. Galathir pulled her to her feet, handing her to Alfion. He gave her a sad smile as she burst into tears, leading her behind the others.

"Eryndal! Your turn."

Josephine jumped at Fissius's sudden order. Eryndal shot her a look of panic, his skin-tinged green.

"I'll go!" Kaelith volunteered, clapping Eryndal on the back. "Breathe, it'll be fine Eryn." He quickly hugged his cousin, before bouncing over to the podium. Fissius scowled, muttering about order and manners, but Kaelith ignored him as he jumped on the platform.

He winked at his teammates, holding his nose closed as he chugged the vial dramatically. He spun towards the lake, opening his arms wide, and screamed "I believe I can fly!" As he jumped off the platform.

Unsurprisingly, Kaelith did not fly. However, he *did* send a wave of air out from himself that not only sent him tumbling down the incline towards the lake, also knocking into Fissius, the scholars and his table of vials clean over.

Kaelith jumped to his feet, looking back up at them. "Did I do it?" He called eagerly.

Torva looked aghast, her gaze flicking between the scattered scholars, the furious nobility and Kaelith's grinning face. "Get back up here," she growled, pointing to where Seralie and Persephone sat.

"It was worth a try," he shrugged, winking at Eryndal as he walked past.

Josephine bit her lip to keep from laughing, only to catch sight of Kohlvar's bewildered expression. She bit down harder, avoiding his questioning gaze as she fought for neutrality.

Mercifully, another of Galathir's acolytes was called next. He swaggered to the podium, cocked his hips and threw back his vial. He held his hands out expectantly, breathing deeply, seeming only mildly affected by the pain others had experienced. A small flame flickered in his hand, causing a murmur of surprise from the scholars. He grinned at them, winking, as the flame grew.

"Dispel it, Jaxon." Galathir commanded, stepping closer as he watched his acolyte intensely.

The young man smiled, rolling the flame over his hand. "Why would I dispel it? This feels amazing."

"Jaxon," Galathir warned, "It will consume you. Let it go!"

Josephine sucked in a breath as Jaxon's sleeve suddenly caught alight, spreading rapidly up his arm. His cocky grin slipped, as he opened his hands to release the flame. Instead, the fire channelled over his body, wrapping around his torso and limbs as Jaxon started to scream.

"Oh god," Josephine gasped, as the burning scent of linen gave way to the familiar scent of burnt flesh, one she hadn't even realised was familiar. Her mind threw her back to the day of the bombing, fire and death surrounding her.

As the visceral flashback threatened to blind her, she saw Galathir and Kohlvar running towards Jaxon. She buckled over, closing her eyes as she tried to push the memory out of her mind. But the scent was too strong, too similar, and all she could do was fight the overwhelming nausea that threatened her. She was lost in her memory, reliving it over and over again.

"Jo," a woman's voice echoed, as something heavy rested on her shoulders. Josephine followed the voice, focusing on the pressure as she tried to push the memory back into the tiny box of terrible things that she never wished to open again.

She gasped deeply as her sight returned, finding herself kneeling in the grass. Eryndal was vomiting on all fours beside her. Torva was crouched in front of them, one hand resting on Josephine's shoulder as the other patted Eryndal's back.

"Breathe, Jo, it's over."

Chapter Fifty-Three

Josephine

Josephine looked towards the podium, despite her better judgement. It was blackened, collapsed in the centre where Jaxon had stood.

"Is he...?" She let the question linger, looking at Torva questioningly.

"No," she murmured. "They took him to the healers."

Josephine knew burns were tremendously difficult to recover from. Even here it seemed to be the case, Kohlvar's minor burn from Draka had been more difficult to heal than his cuts and fractured ribs.

"Should we reschedule, your Highness?" Professor Fissius, his usually white robe stained with grass and dirt, ash trailing along the hem.

"No," Caladorn declared. "Continue."

Fissius looked horrified, for once showing a sentiment that Josephine related to. Regardless, he stiffly turned and called Eryndal's name again. He'd stopped vomiting, looking in horror at the former elf, as if he'd asked for the sun and the moon on a platter.

"Come on," Torva muttered, pulling Eryndal to his feet.

"He's joking right?" He whimpered, clutching at her thick forearms for stability.

Torva grimaced. "No, take a breath, you can do this."

Eryndal looked to Josephine pleadingly. Her heart ached for him, so she stepped forward and pulled him into a hug. "I believe in you Eryn, you're the cleverest person I know. If anyone can do this, it's you."

"For Souls sake, how much coddling do your acolytes need Kohlvar?" Vessara spat out vehemently.

Josephine threw her a stern glare as she released Eryndal. "You've got this."

He didn't seem to believe her, but he walked in a daze towards the platform anyway. He considered it momentarily, before moving to stand beside it. Kohlvar was next to him, his clothes damp and covered in soot.

The young man took his vial, drinking it slowly, briefly coughing at the end. He sat down, legs crossed in a meditative position, his hands loosely curling into the grass by his side.

Josephine felt Kaelith move to her side, his hands clenching tightly. "He'll be okay, right?" He whispered, his fear shining through unabashedly.

Josephine took his hand wordlessly, squeezing tightly as they watched Eryndal sit in silence.

Minutes passed, with Eryndal twirling his fingers lightly through the long blades of grass. It was like he was searching for something, drifting with the breeze. Josephine's fingers were tingling from how hard Kaelith squeezed them, but they continued to quietly watch Eryndal.

He did not seem to be in pain, judging by his silence, but also the lack of tension or guarding of his muscles. He seemed surprisingly at ease.

A thunderous *crack* jolted them out of their reverie, surprised shouts echoing across the group. Josephine jumped violently, her hand slipping from Kaelith's, as they turned to look up at the fortress.

The sandstone courtyard had been split in two, one side sagging slightly. Two chunks of stone had been cleaved off the corners, rolling down the hill with alarming speed towards them.

"Shit," Kaelith muttered as he ran for Eryndal. Josephine ran to the girls, jolting them out of their shock and frantically ushering them out of the path of the slabs of stone tearing up the hillside.

She turned back to watch as Galathir and Kohlvar ran towards the stones, seeming to use air magic to try and slow the stones down. It wasn't working.

Alfion and Torva frantically moved the scholars and nobility out of the way, though the King refused to move.

As the stones rapidly approached, soaring past Kohlvar and Galathir, Caladorn raised his hands. The stones stopped rotating, slamming into the ground and sliding to a stop, mere metres from the Elven King. The ground was ruined, deep ruts and tracks where the grass and topsoil were gouged out.

Josephine looked between Kohlvar, his breathing fast and laboured, to the King, wearing a bemused smirk, to Eryndal, who was staring in complete shock at the mess he'd made.

"You really do seem to have an interesting group of trainees this time, Kohlvar," Caladorn mused as he ran his hands over the pale-yellow stones.

"Did I do that?" Eryndal whispered, looking at Kaelith in shock. He nodded, seemingly lost for words.

"Who remains to be tested?" Caladorn called to Fissius, whose attire was still becoming progressively dirtier and crumpled with each acolyte.

"One more from Galathir, then the dragonoid and human."

The King nodded. "Then let's finish this, I do have other matters to attend to."

Galathir's last acolyte mercifully drank his elixir and discharged it without incident. Draka was summoned next, with everyone eyeing him cautiously as he belched loudly, flailing with discomfort. After a tense few moments of people dodging his potential line of fire, Draka finally breathed fire into the sky, scorching the air over everyone's heads.

Josephine let out a sigh of relief at that. They'd made it. Her fellow acolytes, who'd been absolutely terrified of today, had all successfully survived the elixir. They would be alright.

Out of nowhere, her anxiety struck like an all-consuming rage. Her own fears and concerns, which she'd hidden behind concern for others, were brought to the surface, raging in her mind uncontrollably. She buckled over as wave after wave of nausea rolled through her, saliva pooling in her mouth.

"Josie? What's wrong?" She could feel Kohlvar's hand land on her shoulder, before releasing her with a surprised grunt.

She couldn't answer, she couldn't do anything. All she could do was fight to keep the contents of her stomach down, fight to breathe.

"Vessara," Caladorn's low lilting voice cut through the noise. "Don't play with the human."

Chapter Fifty-Four

Josephine

Just as quickly as it began, the anxiety and nausea dissipated, reducing down to a mild hum. Josephine took in a gasp of air, looking up into Kohlvar's eyes. They were soft, concerned and caring, though the rest of his body was formed of rigid lines.

"You cannot interfere," Kohlvar grumbled, his teeth gritted, his eyes never leaving her.

"Sorry Uncle," Vessara sighed coyly.

Josephine refused to look at them, to give them any satisfaction from affecting her. "It's time," she murmured.

The corner of Kohlvar's mouth quirked, but he stepped back and nodded to Fissius. Josephine took the offered vial, swirling the clear contents once before tipping it into her mouth.

Surprisingly, the taste reminded her of soap. Specifically, the one they used here, with its herbs and bitter notes. Suffice to say, it was not pleasant.

Josephine copied Eryndal's actions, sitting down in the grass. She stared out to the lake as she waited for the pain or discomfort the others seemed to feel. She felt Kohlvar's looming presence behind her, but she did not turn to look at any of the people there. She just watched the lake, allowing herself to take inventory of the sensations moving through her body.

"We meet again, Josephine."

She jumped, startled by the echoing voice. She turned, not seeing Kohlvar or her friends, but an unfamiliar man.

"Do you prefer seeing me like this?"

She frowned, as it clicked. This was Orias. Was it a dream? A vision? Some sort of trance brought on by the elixir?

"What do you want?" She asked coldly, turning away from him.

The man sighed and came to sit beside her. "I see you are angry."

"Of course, I'm fucking angry. You had no right."

"I had to know if she was safe." His voice held a surprisingly pleading tone.

"You could've asked." She glared ahead, not wanting to look at his infuriating face.

He was silent for a beat. "You're right, I should've. I was afraid you'd say no."

Josephine scowled. "Why would I have said yes? It would've been one thing if you'd just looked at those memories. But making me relive them again? My own brain does that to me, I don't need anyone else to torture me with it."

The anxious nausea started to build, as those memories flashed before her eyes.

"We don't have much time. I need you to do something."

She scoffed. "I'm a little busy trying not to die from this elixir, thank you very much."

"Luckily for you, what I need involves helping you dispel that energy."

She finally turned to look at him. He was tall, with golden blonde hair and skin that shone like he lived under the sun. His eyes were an other-worldly turquoise, his teeth a little too canine to be human. He wore the same cloak as before, though his hood laid flat across his shoulders this time.

"And why should I agree to this?"

He tilted his head, seemingly amused by the question. "Because to dispel it would be a waste of what little magic you can access. I'd rather see it used to reopen the portal and help you return home."

Josephine stared at him in shock, her mouth falling open. The nausea in her belly was turning into a strange discomfort, like she was inflating from the inside.

Orias rose smoothly, extending a hand down to her. "Make your choice Josephine. We don't have much time."

Josephine glared at the offering, before reluctantly taking his hand.

The pressure within her continued to build, pushing into her chest. She struggled to draw breath, as she felt the Eternal Soul's presence wrap around her. She focused on her breathing as the lake vanished from view, sending her into a momentary panic.

"Think of the portal, Josephine. You need to hold onto this magic until we can reach it."

She was already struggling with the overwhelming pressure inside her torso. She groaned, clutching at her stomach, buckling over. She tried to release it, to dissipate some of the pain, but Orias's presence was so tightly wrapped around her, weighing her down, she couldn't.

"I need to release it," she whispered desperately, as her ability to think coherently started to fade.

"Just a moment longer, keep thinking of your children."

Her children. She could do anything for them, including suffer through this pain. But gods, it burned. It was burning through her veins, through her body and limbs. Her eyes were on fire as the world shifted rapidly around them.

"Why is this taking...so...long?" She gasped, feeling arms wrap around her.

"It's difficult to channel this much magic," Orias murmured. Josephine didn't understand, couldn't understand. The pain was unbearable, the pressure building in her head until she was sure it would explode.

"I'm dying," she squeaked, her shallow breaths turning rapid. She tried to push this force away from her, but she could feel him restricting her, containing it. "You'll kill me," she whispered as black spots appeared in her vision.

"Now, Josephine, release it," Orias commanded calmly, the pressure around her vanishing. She wanted to, but she was too far gone. The pain consumed her, she felt hands gripping her shoulders, shaking her.

"Release it, Josie! Release it!"

With a guttural scream Josephine pushed at the pressure ripping her apart. She was blinded by pain, unable to see or try to use the magic in any specific way. She just needed to get it out before it killed her. She screamed until she was hoarse, unable to speak, see or hear anything. Every sense was shutting down, leaving her alone in the echoes of her agony.

When the pressure finally lifted, she felt herself collapse into a heap, finally allowing herself to submit to the all-consuming darkness.

Chapter Fifty-Five

Kohlvar

Kohlvar anxiously paced outside the infirmary doors, his gaze flicking to the row of beds every time he passed by. It was pandemonium in there, given each acolyte needed to be thoroughly checked over after the elixir, and Jaxon's significant burns were stretching the healers to their limits. Kohlvar knew his presence often unintentionally frightened the staff, which was the only reason he was not amongst the chaos.

Nonetheless, he couldn't bring himself to leave the entryway. He needed to know they were alright, that *she* was fine. He couldn't stop hearing her screams, feeling the way she'd clawed at him as the agony of the elixir threatened to destroy her. The violent assault of her terror on his mental shields had almost broken him.

He'd brought her straight here, ignoring Vessara's furious glare and the King's questions. She must have dispelled the magic, but they didn't know how. They hadn't seen or felt anything to indicate it. There were questions he could not avoid forever, but ones he had no interest in until he knew she was safe.

A polite cough caught his attention from the doorway. "She's awake," a young healer murmured, her tired eyes going wide at the sight of him.

"Thank you," he murmured as he followed her, walking past Jaxon groaning in his bed, past Kaelith and Eryndal chatting animatedly.

The healer pulled back a curtain at the far end, and there she was. Sitting in bed, her hair a mess of frizzy curls, her skin pale, but she was alive.

Kohlvar felt relief radiate through him. "Josie," he knelt beside her, taking her hand in his. "How do you feel?"

She gave him a small smile, leaning into him. "So very tired. But I'm fine, good even."

Kohlvar kissed her forehead, not caring that others might see. He pulled her into his chest, wrapping his arms around her tightly. "I thought I was going to lose you," he admitted, burying his face in her hair.

Her fingers dug lightly into his chest, rubbing slow circles over his pounding heart. "I'm not that easy to kill, remember?"

He chuckled, breathing in her scent. "Thank the Souls for that."

Josephine stiffened in his grasp; he pulled back and gave her a questioning look. "He was there," she whispered.

Kohlvar's eyes widened. "What? How?"

She opened her mouth to say more, before her eyes darted behind him. Kohlvar turned to find Kaelith and Persephone approaching.

"You're alive!" Kaelith whooped with glee, earning him a firm shushing from a flustered healer. He grinned sheepishly, plonking down on Josephine's other side. "So, you scared us the most, I think. Or maybe Draka, I thought he was going to burn us alive. Luckily, he didn't."

Persephone moved beside Kohlvar; he gave her a warm smile. To have her listen to his instructions when she was in pain, to trust his actions in a crisis, meant the world to him. He truly was proud of her, of all his acolytes, and how far they had come.

Her eyes flicked between Josephine and Kohlvar, a small smirk ghosting over her face. Kohlvar felt his cheeks heating, turning away from her questioning expression.

"Did they clear you yet? Sera's almost done too." Kaelith's leg bounced rapidly, his movement shaking Josephine's bed slightly.

"I think so, I feel fine, though I might sleep for a week," she admitted wearily.

Kaelith tutted jokingly. "Absolutely not! We're going to the tavern."

Josephine rolled her eyes. "I think we should rest, we all had an exhausting day."

"Yeah, we all could've died, but we didn't! We didn't even set ourselves on fire." He mumbled the last sentence, his eyes glancing to Jaxon's bed. His lighthearted mask slipped for the briefest moment, pain flashing across his face. "We have to celebrate."

"I don't think that's the best idea," Kohlvar grumbled, trying his best to give a stern look. Kaelith ignored it, unsurprisingly.

"Well, I'll be down at the tavern, Eryn's coming, so Sera, and I guess Persy can come."

"Hey!" She snapped, crossing her arms as she narrowed her eyes. "What does that mean?"

He grinned cheekily at her. "Fine, if you insist Persy. I just know how much you want to join, and out of the goodness of my heart, I'll invite you."

Persephone gestured rudely to him.

"Just don't go crazy, your abilities could come in any time now." Torva's voice joined them, suddenly enough that Persephone jumped. Kohlvar looked up at her, noting her impassive expression. "The King wishes to discuss these results tomorrow," she explained. "So don't show up hungover, or worse, still drunk."

Kohlvar frowned at her revelation. The royalty was usually only involved in the ceremony, and tomorrow was far too soon to determine everyone's abilities.

Kaelith saluted her with a wink. "As you wish, boss. So, Jo, you in?"

She sighed, "Fine, but only after a shower. And I'm only doing it to keep you from doing something stupid."

"I appreciate your sacrifice," the lanky elf slid off her bed, throwing an arm around Persephone's shoulders. She stomped on his foot, snickering as he yelped.

Torva sighed, smacking a hand to her forehead at their antics. Kohlvar tried to hide his smile, sharing a quick glance with Josephine. His heart fluttered again, something it had taken to doing in her presence lately. He liked the feeling, even though he found it unsettling.

Above all, he liked that she felt the same way.

Chapter Fifty-Six

Josephine

Josephine rifled through the handful of outfits from Torva, her standard issue clothing filthy after today's events. She pulled a grey smock from her wardrobe, considering it thoughtfully.

"Pick the green one," Persephone chimed in. "That one is just depressing."

Josephine huffed a laugh. She wasn't wrong, it was a bit of a drab colour for her. She pulled out a green sleeveless dress with a square neckline, slits below the knee on either side. She layered it with thick leggings and a navy woollen jacket. It was too big, slipping off her shoulders, having been designed for Torva's broader torso. But it was warm, effectively shrouding her from the outside world.

She straightened her necklace, the gold ring nestled between her breasts. She looked at it thoughtfully for a moment. It seemed foolish to feel guilty about loving another person, yet she couldn't fully eradicate the feeling. Her husband had died over 6 years ago, surely that was enough time to have moved on?

She tucked the ring and tags beneath her shirt, smoothing the forest green fabric over her stomach.

"You look beautiful," Seralie murmured as she joined her. Josephine smiled warmly at her, wrapping an arm around her shoulders.

"So do you, I think red is your colour." The deep maroon pinafore fell just below her knees, swishing as she moved.

"Really? My mother made it for me, but I haven't worn it before." Her thin fingers trailed along a tiny, embroidered flower on the hem.

"It does," Josephine reassured. She turned to find Persephone staring at them, dressed in her uniform. She gave her a questioning look.

"I don't have anything else to wear," she mumbled glumly.

Josephine hummed thoughtfully. Anything she had would be far too big on the four-foot-tall woman. Seralie moved to her trunk, rifling through them.

"It's fine, you're much taller than me anyway." Persephone said dismissively, fidgeting with the sleeve of her dark grey shirt.

Seralie pulled two blouses from her trunk, one white with short flowing sleeves, the other a sleeveless mossy green tunic. Persephone scrunched her nose up at the tunic.

"Try it on," Seralie held out the shirt. Persephone begrudgingly did, looking at them expectantly.

"That actually looks lovely on you," Josephine offered. The shirt was a little long and wide on her torso, but not in a way that made it obvious that it was too big for her.

"I have this jacket too," Seralie held out a short navy jacket. "I'll wear the cloak tonight, you can borrow this."

Persephone shrugged it on, the hem of the jacket falling to her mid-thigh. "Thanks," she murmured quietly.

They found the boys waiting impatiently by the courtyard, which had been declared off limits since Eryndal destroyed it. They could still access the stairs descending to the village thankfully.

Kaelith whistled as they walked into the afternoon sunlight. "Looking fine ladies!"

Seralie blushed, Persephone scowled, and Josephine chuckled. "Thanks Kaelith, you're not looking too bad yourself."

He grinned, his loose white shirt billowing over his dark trousers in the fresh air. Eryndal wore a brown vest over his shirt, his hair neatly combed and face clean shaven. Draka wore the standard uniform of grey shirt and dark pants, his scaled taloned feet bare unlike the rest of them. Josephine imagined finding boots for him would've been an impossible task.

A squeak rose out of Seralie, causing everyone to look at her. She was blushing furiously, staring at Draka in wide-eyed shock.

Josephine turned to Draka, noticing his mouth agape, eyes narrowed at Seralie. She frowned, trying to discern his expression beneath the scales encroaching on his face. His golden eyes were dilated, roaming up and down Seralie's clothing.

"What did he say, Sera?" Eryndal asked, looking mildly concerned.

She shook her head furiously, "N-nothing."

Kaelith barked out a laugh, hooking an arm through Draka's and leading him towards the stairs. "Look, Draka, we need to have a chat about how to politely tell a lady she looks pretty. Whatever you said, probably wasn't it."

***

After a mug of ale, Kaelith's jovial spirit had become contagious, even Josephine found herself relaxing. They laughed at the endless stories he told, his animated movements increasing with every emptied drink. His tale about a drunken dwarf attempting to serenade a wild bear left everyone crying with laughter. If Kaelith ever pursued his desire to travel the continent, he'd be able to make an excellent living as a bard.

Josephine looked around the table. Seralie was tickled pink, sipping from a lemonade and swinging her legs off a bar stool. Persephone was exchanging razor sharp barbs with Eryndal and Kaelith, alternating with whom she bantered. Draka stood close to Seralie, smiling occasionally at her laughter and Kaelith's stories.

Everyone was happy, even Josephine. She still missed her children dreadfully, and thought about them constantly, but she allowed herself to enjoy this moment. They'd all made it. They had all survived the elixir ceremony, and now they'd continue to train together until their abilities revealed themselves.

Eventually, Josephine excused herself for the bathroom between wildly recounted tales. She didn't exactly have the best bladder on a good day, and alcohol only accelerated that particular human need.

After relieving herself, Josephine washed her hands and took note of her appearance. There was a happy flush in her cheeks, an easy smile and the green of her hazel eyes was shining particularly brightly. Her hair floated around her face, curling lazily around her shoulders and arms. She never wore her hair down; it was too much hassle. But tonight, she had embraced it, feeling truly relaxed for the second time since arriving in Balidran. The first had been last night.

Josephine noticed in her periphery as the door to the bathroom opened, a young elven woman stepping inside. Freyda. Her face was pale, with blotchy pink spots over her cheeks. Her usually neat attire was askew, she seemed to still be wearing her clothes from earlier in the day.

She nodded politely at her, before looking back in the mirror to attempt to smooth down her hair.

"Having a nice night?" Freyda's high voice cracked. Her jaw held stiffly as she stared her reflection down.

Josephine sighed, turning to face her. "Freyda, I-"

"Don't," she spat, stepping towards her. "Don't you dare. Don't tell me how sorry you are, how you pity me. Because you probably think I deserve this, huh?" She jabbed a finger into her face.

Josephine stood silently, watching as the young woman's face crumpled.

"I don't need your disgustingly human *pity*. So stop looking at me like that!" Her hands shook as she clenched them into fists, rage contorting her delicate features.

Josephine took a small step back. "Listen-"

"And to think I was not found worthy, but you were. *You!*" She hissed vehemently. "What's so special about you?"

"Nothing." Josephine interjected firmly. "I don't understand what happened today either. But we'll figure it out tomorrow, okay?"

Freyda scoffed, wiping her face angrily. "Oh yes, I hear the Queen took a particular interest in your abilities."

Josephine frowned. How did Freyda know that? When did her connection with the Eternal Souls become common knowledge?

The young woman continued talking. "Although, really everyone seems to be interested in you. The poor lost human, so far from home. You've caught the eye of the royals, you're in Kohlvar's bed. You shouldn't even be here!"

Unease sunk in Josephine's stomach. "No, I shouldn't."

She let out an angry yell. "Stop agreeing with me!"

"What do you want then, Freyda?" Josephine snapped, surprising herself. "I don't want to be here either, but I am, and I am doing the best I can. You are the one who has it out for us since the very beginning."

Freyda fell quiet, her eyes staring daggers into hers. "I think I'm going to enjoy this."

Josephine frowned at her, taking an uneasy step back. "What are you talking about? You know what, never mind, I don't have the patience-"

The scent hit her first. It smelt sickly sweet and floral, making her gasp for fresh air. She felt a fine powder brush over her mouth and nose, as she gagged and retched, clutching at the sink for air as her knees gave way.

There was nothing but endless darkness, with no one to pull her out.

Chapter Fifty-Seven

Josephine

Josephine woke to darkness, a raging headache the only sign this was not a continuation of the empty abyss she'd been sent to. She was prone, on a hard flat surface, which swayed rhythmically with a faint clunking sound. Urgent nausea rose in her throat as she pushed herself onto her side, heaving until her stomach was empty. The nausea still struck her, but she had nothing left to expel.

She found her hands were bound with a thick rope, wrapped too tightly to pull free of. She wiped the back of her hand over her mouth, the remnants of that sickly sweet powder brushing over her nose again. She retched again, her stomach cramping painfully, as she carefully wiped her face clean of the strange substance.

She was still wearing her clothing, even the small coin pouch she had been given was still in a hidden pocket. It didn't seem like she'd been robbed, though she didn't realistically expect Freyda had been trying to rob her. She'd expected to wake up bloodied and bruised, but surprisingly she was unharmed, just uncomfortable from lying on this unforgiving surface.

Breathing deeply, Josephine examined her surroundings. She could feel coarse wooden slats underneath her, the tiniest slivers of light trickling in between gaps in the walls. She reached up, running her fingers over the taut thick fabric blocking out any light. She pushed at it tentatively, but it did not give.

Josephine fought against the rising panic of being stuck in this enclosed space, which seemed to be moving swiftly. A wagon? Was that clipping noise the sound of hooves? Trying to focus on the cacophony of sounds echoing around her only made her head pulse painfully.

There wasn't enough room to sit up, but she could shuffle into a slight leaning position propped against the corner. She took another deep breath, trying to reach out to the Eternal Souls, Orias or any of them would do. If she couldn't escape, maybe she could ask for their help.

Did her friends know she was missing yet? How long was she gone before they realised? Would they even know where to look?

She ignored the throbbing headache squeezing her skull, clutching her necklace as she tried to seek out the strange presence that was Orias. Her eyes squeezed shut, she tried to find any sign of him in the swirling darkness. A wisp of smoke, a pinprick of light, the static stuttering behind her eyelids.

"Come on," she whispered, even though she was sure the Soul was silent. Why did he only come to her some of the time? What was she doing wrong?

The wagon veered sideways, Josephine bracing to avoid sliding across the wooden boards. They seemed to be slowing down, on a bumpier section of road than before.

Just as she had begun gnawing at the rope with her teeth, trying to loosen it, the wagon pulled to a halt. She froze, curling her knees towards her, ready to fend off whoever might open the wagon.

"Do you think she's awake?" A low voice spoke quietly, Josephine struggling to hear them over her pounding heartbeat.

"Didn't you hear her vomiting? Pathetic. She's awake." This voice was higher, potentially female, equally as soft spoken.

Suddenly Josephine could see stars, glittering brightly overhead. They were encroached by a ring of trees, framing the midnight sky where the moon sat high. Josephine blinked to adjust to the sudden light, casting her eyes around to determine who had spoken.

Her blood ran cold as Princess Vessara smiled down at her, her siren teeth hidden, but her viciousness evident, nonetheless. "Hello, Josephine."

Josephine recoiled from her, trying to shuffle to a far corner in the wagon. She shrieked as arms grabbed her, hauling her out. She was dumped unceremoniously to the ground, coughing as dirt dusted up into her aching sinuses.

"What have you done?" A familiar voice called, strangely thick.

Josephine saw Vessara's legs appear in front of her, clad in black leathers and boots. "I thought you'd like to be reunited." Long fingernails gripped the underside of her jaw, digging in painfully. Josephine yelped, trying to free herself, to no avail.

"Stand up," Vessara commanded.

Icy pain shot through her spine and down her legs, as Josephine felt her body respond to the command. Her legs wobbled, threatening to give out, when she felt a hand grab her elbow.

"Let go of me!" She yanked backyards, flailing until she fell to the ground again.

She heard Vessara swear, her boots crunching on gravel as she approached. Josephine rolled, trying to stand and run, as she grabbed a fistful of her hair and yanked her head upright.

"I said stand!" She thundered, dragging her to her feet as that same icy pain shot through her body. Josephine tried not to whimper, not to let the

Princess know how much pain that had caused her. But judging by the smug huff resonating behind her, she suspected she knew.

"I had wondered how you resisted me that first night," Vessara's words whispered into her ear, the breath sending shivers through her. "I'd forgotten about that fucking coat. Turns out you're just as vulnerable as the rest of them. So easy to bend to my will, it's not even a challenge anymore."

Josephine gasped as her eyes landed on a hunched figure, blood dripping slowly from his nose. "Val!"

He looked up, his face a bruised mess, the blood trickling from a wound over his brow. "Jo," he breathed. "I'm so sorry."

Josephine noticed two unfamiliar elves standing behind Valtherion, bearing similar uniforms to Vessara. Soldiers? "What happened, Val?"

"What's happening," Vessara interjected, tauntingly, "Is that Val told me all your little secrets."

Josephine flinched as the ghostly woman walked her long fingernails up her shoulder towards her face.

"He told me that you're really from the human world." Her nail curved up her neck and over her ear. "That you fell through the portal by accident. And that you just want to go home to your darling children."

Unadulterated fear lurched in Josephine's chest, as she remained frozen under Vessara's cruel touch.

"He did try not to tell me," she soothed. "But all men succumb in the end to me. They just can't take the pain." She tutted, her hand burying into Josephine's hair as she exposed her neck.

She felt her eyes fall shut as Vessara ran a nail over her exposed throat. "I could send you home," she whispered, her lips brushing her lobe. "Or, I could slit your throat just to see the look on Kohlvar's face when he sees you, bleeding out like the pig you are."

Josephine dropped to her knees as Vessara shoved her forward, her eyes flying open as she inhaled. She hadn't realised she'd been holding her breath.

"What makes you think he'll find me?" Josephine murmured, her mouth uncomfortably dry.

Vessara shrugged nonchalantly. "Maybe he will, maybe he won't. Matters not to me." Her eyes flashed for the barest moment, before turning away.

Josephine looked past Valtherion, past the guards, to the field they had come to. It looked vaguely familiar, though it was difficult to see much besides trees in the dark. A pair of yellow eyes blinked at her, vanishing into darkness. To her distant right, faint lights flickered through the softly swaying foliage.

"What does matter to me though," Vessara continued, apparently still talking. "Is where you dispelled your magic yesterday."

Josephine looked at her in surprise, remaining silent.

"I thought it would've been here," she gestured behind her, at the dimly lit field. "Given this is the portal you arrived through."

She looked around, realising why the field looked familiar. She'd never seen it at night, she'd only visited during the day when she and Valtherion had walked together.

"But apparently not," Vessara's voice had turned bitter, clearly frustrated. "So, I will ask you once, politely. Where did you dispel the magic?"

She stared up at the Princess, her white hair shining ethereally in the moonlight. Her glacial eyes bore into her, any emotion hidden behind a thick wall of ice.

"Does the Queen know you're doing this?"

Vessara recoiled as if she'd been struck. "That's not what I asked you."

"No, but I suspect given her interest in my abilities," the words felt like lies in her mouth, but she continued, "she would not appreciate you damaging me."

She'd chosen the word carefully, not wanting to acknowledge Vessara's potential to obliterate her. She was grasping at straws, and if she grabbed the wrong one, it would end very badly for her.

"No," Vessara admitted, to her surprise. "But the King does."

Dread coiled in her stomach, remembering the way the King had looked at her with total disgust. *Cover yourself up, before I lose my breakfast.*

"Do you know why we have to be present for the elixir ceremony?"

Josephine shook her head.

"Of course you don't," she spat with vitriol. "It's because there is so little magic left in the sources. Ever since we lost contact with your world, the King has enhanced them so there is enough for acolytes to develop their true powers. It is why elves can no longer achieve that by themselves. All the magic that the acolytes used is returned to the sources once it is dispelled, to continue fuelling our world. But you," a finger hooked under her chin, "did not return your magic, did you?"

Icy numbness crept through her jaw, shooting painfully into her molars. "I don't understand."

Vessara huffed in irritation. "You *stole* the King's magic; it belongs to the elves and our lands. I want to know where it is."

Josephine frowned, genuinely baffled. "Oh."

"Oh? *OH!* Is that all you have to say for yourself?" Rage burned in her eyes, her hand dropping. "Where did you put it?"

"I'm afraid I have absolutely no idea." Josephine responded earnestly.

For a moment, she expected the princess to raise a hand to her, judging by the pure fury contorting her face.

"We'll soon see about that." Freezing hands grabbed her face, pinching unkindly. "Where is the magic?"

Icy agony burned through her, shooting through her jaw into her skull. Her brain was on fire, shrinking away from her skull with enough force she screamed.

Then it vanished, so quickly it felt as if it were never there. Josephine reeled forward, her bound hands falling into the dirt, gasping for breath.

She felt Vessara kneel beside her, her fingernails tracing down her arm. "That is just a taste of what I can do. It would really be in your best interest if you just told me."

Josephine coughed, spitting a wad of phlegm to the ground. She pushed off the ground, resting back on the heels of her boots as she looked into the Princess's eyes. She didn't have the information Vessara wanted, and even if she did, she did not want to give it up.

"I already told you, I don't know."

The Princess seemed to enjoy this response, a slow smile crawling over her face. "What a shame, it won't be Kohlvar who breaks you. It'll be me. I can promise you won't enjoy this, but I will."

Chapter Fifty-Eight

Josephine

Vessara had been right about one thing; Josephine did not enjoy being tortured.

Physical pain was a sensation Josephine was familiar with. From childbirth, to broken bones, to the monthly monstrosity that was her period, she was well acquainted. This pain was unlike anything she had experienced previously, causing her body to seize up, her breathing turned shallow, as she wordlessly endured. She counted the seconds, focusing on the stars above and the earth below as she waited for the agony to end.

Initially, the Princess seemed to be enjoying her pain. Perhaps that was her thing, Josephine wondered absentmindedly through another round of frozen torture. Did that make her a sadist? Was it different in this world? Could she feel her pain, like Kohlvar could feel her emotions?

Thank goodness Kohlvar wasn't here. The thought of him experiencing this pain through her was too much to bear.

After a while however, Vessara grew visibly frustrated. It brought a small spark of satisfaction to Josephine, watching the blood vessel at her temple pulse rapidly, her jaw clenched as her lips twitched, struggling to contain her siren teeth. Every time she had given the same answer, which was easy when she had no other to give.

She'd been surprised when Vessara struck her, her fist connecting with her cheek with enough force she almost fell over. Almost.

"Vessara," Valtherion's voice croaked out. "Please, stop this. She doesn't know."

She did not. Her fists pummelled her face, her bound hands doing little to deflect her blows. A swift kick knocked her back, scrambling to protect her stomach from several kicks aimed there.

"Vessara! Stop this!"

She let out an irritated scream, her voice echoing across the clearing. Josephine remained curled into a tight ball, her breathing painful against her bruised ribs.

"You don't even realise what you've done," she hissed, crouching down to meet her wide eyes.

Josephine flinched, holding her protective position, anticipating her assault.

Instead, the elven Princess stood, turning towards Valtherion, where he sat flanked by her two guards. Josephine felt her stomach drop, watching with wide eyes as she towered over him.

"Open it," she commanded.

Valtherion frowned up at her. "Vess-"

"It's Your Highness to you, and I demand you open the portal!" Her hands clenched into fists by her side.

Valtherion seemed to consider his words carefully. "This portal has been incredibly unstable for the last 50 years. If I open it, I risk ripping a permanent rift between our worlds. You already know this, Vessara, because I taught you about this when you were a child. Please, reconsider your actions."

Vessara was quiet, rigidly staring down at him. She drew herself to her full height, reaching for his throat. "I command you to open the portal."

Josephine watched in horror as Valtherion's spine stiffened, haltingly rising to his feet as he walked to the centre of the clearing. Vessara followed him, keeping a hand on the back of his neck as he raised his hands. He began to chant, murmuring strange unfamiliar words, gesturing into the air.

A spark appeared beneath his fingers, fizzling out. Several sparks sprung to life, eradicating an invisible sheet piece by piece, before vanishing. Josephine watched in awe as Valtherion slowly carved open a window, no bigger than a dinner plate, with a clear view into a dilapidated building, crumpled concrete piled high by splintered wooden beams and a bright red emergency door.

Josephine felt the air rush out of her body. It was her office, or rather what was left of it. She felt herself moving, pushing to her feet as she walked soundlessly to the portal. She felt driven by a deep urge, her emotions compounding into a single train of thought: *go home.*

"That's it?" Vessara scoffed, releasing Valtherion with a flick of her hand.

Valtherion stumbled backwards, leaning on his knees as he drew in heaving breaths. "It's highly unstable, it could unravel further if we leave-"

Vessara shot him a withering look, silencing him. Her cold eyes flicked to Josephine, surprise briefly registering, before she gestured to the guards.

Josephine found her path blocked, twin swords barring her way. She frowned at the Princess, "I thought you wanted to get rid of me."

She huffed a laugh, "I did, but you have yet to tell me where the missing power is. I suppose I will have to resort to other methods."

Vessara raised her hands to either side of the portal, just as quickly she yanked away. The smell of burning flesh reached Josephine, her knees buckling as nausea struck her. The Princess swore, looking down at her hands, then to Valtherion. He merely shrugged.

"Fine," she hissed, storming over to Josephine, reaching past the guards to grab at her loose hair. Josephine scowled, trying to pull free of her vicious grasp. "Seeing as the portal brought you here, maybe it will listen to you!"

"Take your hands off her."

They froze as a deep growling voice projected into the clearing, loud enough to rattle Josephine's bones. A smile curled over Vessara's lips, the tips of her siren teeth exposed.

"Finally," she breathed, yanking Josephine forward as the guards moved past her. Josephine fought the movement, swinging at Vessara's face, clawing at her eyes. As she made contact, the same icy pain burned down her fingers, flaring through her nerves and muscles. She let out a frustrated yell, clutching at her arms as Vessara slowly dragged her towards the portal, as the clanging of swords reached her ears.

Josephine tried to turn to look, but the Princess had ensnared her tightly. Vessara tried to shove her face first into the portal, just as Josephine threw her hands out. Her hands bounced, meeting a strange resistance, similar to the sound shield Kohlvar used in the library.

Kohlvar!

The voice had been strange, eerily deep and menacing, unlike anything she'd heard before. It didn't sound like Kohlvar, but could it be him? She wanted to believe he'd come after her, though how would he know where to find her?

"Josephine."

She frowned, a new voice whispering beside her. She darted her eyes as far to either side as she could but couldn't identify it.

"Let me help you."

Orias.

"Nice of you to finally show up," she muttered, ignoring Vessara's frown. She closed her eyes, fighting to ignore the clash of swords, the painful hold on her hair, the heat from the portal's burning edges.

"You need to-"

"Don't *fucking* tell me what to do. I've just been tortured because of something you did. I'm in no mood to be bossed around." Josephine snapped, her anger radiating from her.

The Soul was silent for a moment. "I understand," he finally murmured. "I am sorry for that."

She drew a deep breath. "How do I fix the portal?" She could feel smooth hands covering hers, pressing her into the force beneath her fingers. She tensed, remembering the last time he touched her.

"Imagine where you want to go, picture yourself opening the portal and stepping through. I will do the rest."

Josephine opened her eyes, her hands pressed into the centre of the portal. She did not feel or smell burnt flesh, nor any discomfort anymore. The distant grunts and shouts threatened to pull her attention away, but Josephine fought to block them out.

She felt her anger throbbing in her chest, heat radiating from her. She felt it move up into her throat, threatening her ability to breathe, until it shifted, moving down her arms and out her palms. She felt it pouring into the portal as the ring of embers flared to life, spreading and growing as the window before her expanded.

She closed her eyes, not wanting to see the place Sienna died, not wanting to see the evidence of others demise. She thought of her children, what they would be doing, if they were having dinner, or playing, or reading a book before bed. Was Aunt Susan working or home with them? Were they safe?

She felt the resistance beneath her fingers flutter, as her eyes opened. She gasped, watching as her daughters chased each other around the backyard, giggling and squealing. They'd grown taller, their clothes were beginning to get too small, and Isabelle's shoes had seen better days, but they were alive. They were together, as Aunt Susan watched them from the kitchen.

If she could just push her fingers a little farther, perhaps she could break through and be with them. She felt the pressure swell around her fingers, up to the first knuckle, as she dug them in, fighting to break through.

An agonised scream broke her concentration, the sudden flash of pain in her hands enough to send her staggering back. She turned to see the source, her mouth falling open in horror.

Kohlvar stood there, his skin grey with giant skin, chunks flaked off and littering the ground around him. The two guards lay motionless by his side, their bodies arranged at strange angles. Valtherion crouched behind him, his fingers reaching towards a fallen sword.

Vessara held a long knife, its blade curled upwards, glistening with a dark substance. The blade glowed with a strange blue hue beneath the liquid dripping off it, shimmering as Vessara raised it towards Kohlvar.

Josephine took in his frozen form, the way he clutched at his shoulder, the despair in his bright blue eyes.

"No!" She shrieked, holding her hands in front of her, her blistered palms searing with pain. She felt the same blast of energy rush from her, knocking both Vessara and Kohlvar to the ground. She focused her rage on Vessara as she screamed, clutching at her skull. Her high keening only irritated Josephine further, after being kidnapped and tortured over something she didn't do. She pressed on, almost relishing her suffering as her screams turned into whimpers, her words of resistance nothing more than a stutter.

"Josie, stop." The words were barely audible, but Kohlvar saying her name felt like a bucket of ice-cold water. Her hands dropped, exhaustion shrouding her, as she swayed on the spot. She turned, looking back at the portal, hesitating as her daughters circled each other, dancing under the starlight.

"Help him!" Valtherion shook her from her reverie.

"What?"

"Go, help him, while I keep working on the portal. Put this on the wound." He shoved a jar into her hands, pushing her towards the prone figures.

She blinked in confusion, before moving to the crumpled heap that was Kohlvar. She pushed him onto his back, watching as blood seeped from his shoulder, spreading quickly over his torso. "Shit," she swore, pulling at his shirt to find the source.

The wound was small, the blade leaving a slit between his top two ribs, just above his heart. She quickly scooped the entire contents of the jar, slapping it down and pressing on the wound with her full weight. Kohlvar groaned, his eyes flicking to her briefly, before looking past her. His mouth opened to speak as his face became illuminated with a strange light, but a terrifying gurgle projected instead.

Josephine grimaced at the unhealthy sound, swivelling her head to see what he'd noticed. She'd expected to see Vessara standing over them, knife raised for the killing blow.

Instead she watched as Valtherion's dark figure was back lit by the brightening light of the portal. His cat, Ginger, stood by his side, fur standing on end.

"Val? Is the portal working?" She called, applying more pressure to Kohlvar's chest as blood continued to flow under her palms.

He didn't answer, kneeling down to stroke Ginger's fur, murmuring gently to the creature. The cat leaped into the blinding light, vanishing from sight.

She gasped. Did it work? She looked down, noticing the light in Kohlvar's eyes dimming. Her hands squelched as she squeezed his wounded chest. "Kohl?"

His hand grazed her arm, moving to her cheek as he brushed back errant strands of hair. "Josie," he murmured, his voice still strange. "It's okay."

"Are you going to die?" Her voice cracked with the final word, her lower lip trembling.

He smiled, a dark liquid trickling from the side of his mouth. "Go," he breathed.

Hot tears fell from her as she shook her head. She closed her eyes, reaching out to Orias. *Help him,* she begged.

He was silent, that strange warm sensation nowhere to be found.

She screwed up her face as sobs escaped her. Why did everyone she loved die? Why did the Souls always vanish when she needed them? Kohlvar's giant hand shook as he tried to stroke her face, his eyes drooping lower with each blink.

"Josephine?"

She turned, squinting through her watery eyes at Valtherion.

"I'm so sorry." His face was impossible to read, though his tone caused dread to sink in her stomach.

She set Kohlvar's hand over his chest and rose to her feet, tears dripping off her chin. "It doesn't work? Don't say that was all for nothing."

Valtherion shook his head. "It does, but I can't let you through."

Josephine's jaw fell open as Valtherion stepped through the blinding light of the portal. She sprinted from Kohlvar's side, jumping over Vessara's prone form, as she bolted for the portal.

She watched as he reappeared in the window, his hands raised with palms faced towards her, his mouth moving.

"No!" She screamed, willing her legs to move faster. She reached out a hand, the radiant heat from the portal brushing her fingertips.

Just as she thought she could make it, the portal's edges spun, sending out violent pulses of air, knocking her to the ground. She rolled, pushing herself to her knees, but the wild energy sent her skidding backwards.

Josephine tilted her head back and screamed. She let out all the pent-up anger, rage, hurt and denial. She screamed until her voice was hoarse, as she clawed towards the rapidly shrinking portal.

The heat was unbearable, singing her eyelashes, burning her lungs, as she crawled inch by inch. Despair filled her heart as the portal shrunk to the size of a fist, the flames receding to a dull ebb, before winking out of existence.

Josephine fell through the space the portal had just been, the sudden absence of resistance sending her flying. She felt her body strike the ground, earthen debris digging into her skin, as her sight started to blur.

She forced her exhausted, screaming body to roll over, determined to gaze upon the stars one last time. She watched as leaves shook themselves free of the ancient trees surrounding them, floating down as an ethereal frame for the midnight sky.

She'd never make it home again.

It was over.

Epilogue

"Is that a cat?" Danielle stopped running around her sister, turning to point to a bristly orange creature at the base of their mulberry tree.

Isabelle squealed with glee. "Here kitty!" She knelt down, holding out an open palm towards the beast. He sniffed it cautiously, letting out a low grumble.

"I don't think it likes you," Danielle stated pointedly, stepping back.

"It's scared! Let's get some food for it," as Isabelle stood, a gust of wind struck them, sending them stumbling onto the grass.

"Oh no!" "Uh-oh!" they declared simultaneously, looking at each other before brushing themselves off.

"Girls, are you alright? What-" The words fell from Susan's mouth as she stepped out to the verandah. "Get inside, quickly!"

The panic in her voice sent the girls running inside. Susan grabbed a nearby broom, brandishing it in front of her.

"Whoever the hell you are, I suggest you get out of my backyard right now!" Susan watched as the dark figure turned towards her, an orange cat moving between his legs. "Move it!"

The man crumpled, dropping to his knees, vomiting violently onto the grass. Susan rolled her eyes, cautiously stepping towards him.

"Had too much to drink, have we? Go sleep it off somewhere else!"

He raised a hand, meeting the bristled end of her broom. "Are you Susan?"

Susan's eyes grew wide. "What? How do you know my name?"

"I am a friend of Josephine."

About the author

C K Scott is an Australian indie author with a loving husband, twin toddler daughters, two cheeky dogs (a beagle and a miniature foxie) and a sassy tabby cat. She writes predominantly between 8pm to midnight, after the children have finally fallen asleep, and is a self declared night owl. Her other hobbies include growing vegetables, crocheting, reading (mostly audio-books and the occasional paperback) and cooking like a medieval witch throwing ingredients willy nilly into a pot.

You can follow her social media (linktr.ee/authorckscott) for updates on her daily coffees, cooking adventures and writing journey. Her plan is to release the prequel, *Fire of the Forgotten*, before starting on the second book in The Eternal Souls Trilogy.

She hopes you have enjoyed this book, and would love to see your feedback through reviews or direct messages.

Thank you.